Atonement
The BloodStone Legacy Book 2
V.E. Huntley

Published in the United States by V.E. Huntley

The Cataloging-in-Publication Data is on file at the Library of Congress

Paperback ISBN 979-8-9907982-5-0

Hardcover ISBN 979-8-9907982-6-7

Ebook ISBN 979-8-9907982-2-9

Book Design by V.E. Huntley

Book Cover Design by 100 Covers

First Edition 2025

Acknowledgements

I have so many people I want to thank; I don't know where to begin.

First—Hubby Chris. I couldn't do this without your love, support, and belief that my writing will one day get us to our Mediterranean retirement beach house. Thanks for letting me ignore you when I'm under a deadline or so deep inside my head that I don't even know my own name anymore.

Elle, you always catch my mistakes—plot holes, when I don't get inside my characters' heads and bodies enough, or when I fall back on my writing crutches. As always, this book wouldn't be what it is without you.

My ARC Ladies—thank you so much for reading and reviewing. Your support and sharing and shout-outs make my heart happy. You ladies are awesome!

My Parents—I know you're looking down on me and saying, "Why can't you just write good, clean fiction?" Nope, Nan, this book isn't for your innocent Catholic eyes. And yes, Gramps, this is a real job! I love and miss you both something fierce.

Finally, My Readers—thank you for the love you've given me, Ellie and Aden. I know he's a hot mess, but Ellie and I are working on him.

To all the ladies out there who like a little biting during sex

Content Warning

This book contains dark themes and scenes that start on page one. If any of the themes below bother you, please don't read this book.

- Biting

- Blood

- Graphic Violence

- Explicit Sexual Situations

- Non-consent

- Blood Play

- Knife Play

- Rape

- Adult language – the word "fuck" is used a lot

- Scenes and references of physical and/or sexual abuse/assault that some readers may find uncomfortable and/or triggering.

Prologue

Her entire existence could be summed up in just six words.

"I like to hear you cry."

Tears streamed down her face, leaving scorching wet trails on her skin, burning her cheeks as he thrust between her thighs. His harsh breath mingled with the muffled words against her skin as his fangs burrowed deep into her neck.

Each agonizing thrust was a white-hot knife stabbing into her abdomen, scraping against her raw insides, leaving a trail of fire in its wake. Her body convulsed with sobs, each one stealing the air from her lungs, leaving her shuddering and gasping for breath. Every inhale was a painful, desperate gulp of air, and each exhale was a harsh, ragged sigh, heavy and hopeless, like a deflating balloon.

He retracted his fangs from her neck, and her head lolled forward, her muscles spasming from the venom coursing through her veins. He stilled his hips, pausing his assault momentarily to reach for something on the table nearby.

Her high-pitched shriek, raw with agony, pierced the air as the razor-sharp edge of his knife sliced through her skin.

The warmth of her blood, hot and slick, coating her chest, made her whimper in pseudo-relief, a relief that was interrupted by the next scrape of the knife over her breasts. Its coppery scent filled her nostrils as she flailed against the unforgiving metal chains binding her wrists, securing her to the ceiling above. Her feet kicked the air, the rough stone floor too far below to provide any leverage.

"Your screams are music to my ears," he murmured, the sensual rasp of his voice a stark contrast to her shrill cries.

Another scream tore from her lips as the blade sliced through her nipple. She convulsed, sweat slicking her skin, each muscle screaming in protest as she thrashed, the searing pain a vise-like grip of agony she desperately fought to escape.

More blood poured from the fresh wound, flowing down her body, across the raw, open, crisscross cuts on her stomach, painting her flesh crimson. It soaked them both, running in rivulets onto the stone floor beneath them.

His low groan vibrated through her, the obvious thrill of his pleasure rattling her battered body against her bonds, the slick evidence of his climax leaving its repulsive mark inside her. Hot, salty tears continued to stream down her face. He pulled out and stepped back. She struggled to focus her eyes, but the sight of blood coating his abdomen and cock was unmistakable.

Her body sagged, a wave of relief washing over her, but it was short-lived. More agony exploded, igniting every nerve ending in her body as he trailed his tongue over the fresh cuts, sending a sharp surge of pain rippling through her. His come seeped out of her, trailing down her thighs and mingling with the blood to form a slick layer on her skin, causing her to shudder.

Memories of her previous life faded, leaving behind only the harsh, gray reality of her present, a world of constant agonizing pain that felt like icy claws tearing at her and fear so profound it choked her.

"Your blood is so much sweeter when I cut you."

He stepped away, leaving her suspended in mid-air, her weight pressing down on her aching, burning shoulders, making her arms tremble. Her head hung low, long strands of sweaty blonde hair obscuring her face. A prickling sensation crawled across her skin like the chilling slither of snakes. He was watching again.

Master Matthais.

He enjoyed watching her master torture and rape her whenever they visited the capital. She rarely pleaded or begged. Master despised it. But the pain, a sharp, persistent throb deep in her bones, felt like a second heartbeat, and she wasn't sure how much more she could endure tonight.

"Please, master. No more." Her voice was so faint, she could barely hear it herself.

He approached her, syringe in hand, shushing her in an equally quiet voice. "Now, now, my pet. We're only getting started."

He plunged a needle into her neck, a sharp prick accompanied by a sudden, searing pain that made her gasp. Her body jerked, a strangled cry escaping her lips before dissolving into a whimper when the BloodStone hit her bloodstream.

"That should help. Once the cuts close, we'll start over."

He hiked her thighs over his forearms, spreading her wide as he stepped between her legs.

"Please," she begged, her sobs growing louder as the BloodStone coursed through her veins, reviving her weakened body. The tears in her flesh knitted shut, leaving a throbbing ache behind.

Her pleas fell on deaf ears as he grabbed his knife again, running the cold, unforgiving steel along her cheek, leaving a burning trail.

"That's it, my pet, cry for me."

Ellie

The grip on Ellie's wrists tightened, the pressure cutting off her circulation, making her arms ache as she fought against her captor. A metallic taste of blood filled her mouth as the tip of her tongue brushed the corner of her split lip.

The bruises blooming beneath the skin of her jaw, collarbone, and side only intensified the aching in her shoulders, serving as a cruel reminder of her helplessness. Aden's voice, sharp and angry, echoed in her mind. He was going to be furious at her for getting herself in this situation.

"You don't stand a chance, little girl," a deep voice taunted close to her ear. "Humans are no match for us."

She scowled at the soft sound of a snicker nearby, struggling harder, twisting and thrashing as her boots fought for traction in the deep snow. Her groans echoed in the otherwise silent night, her warm breath mixing with the frigid air to form a misty cloud around her head.

Hot breath grazed her ear. "Are you actually trying to get away, or are you just having another seizure?"

Ellie swung her leg back, a growl escaping her lips as her kick collided with her captor's shin. She let out a gasp, a sharp pain shooting up her calf as if she kicked solid rock.

"You'll have to try harder than that."

"This was too easy," his cohort said from a few feet away. "What do you think? Should we give her a fighting chance?"

She felt the hot breath against her ear again. "I'll give you a twenty-second head start. But you better hope those short legs can run fast."

Ellie's body jolted with a mixture of relief and adrenaline as the grip around her wrists eased. She dashed forward, sprinting across the field, her boots sinking into the deep snow with each step. The sound of chuckles followed her as she broke through the line of trees at the edge, weaving through the labyrinth of large, twisted trunks. She moved faster in the shallower snow, but the dense foliage conspired against her, blocking her path at every turn.

Shards of silvery moonlight pierced through the mostly bare branches, lighting a spotty trail through the maze. Sharp pine needles on low-hanging limbs slapped against her body and face as she wound under and around them.

Escape was impossible.

It was only a matter of time before they caught her. She leaned against a tree trunk, taking a second to catch her breath, her nose filling with the scent of pine, dirt, and snow as she reminded herself why she was doing this. Master Matthais stole her and her father once from the Westcotts. She knew it was futile. She was powerless against him, or any other vampire, but she refused to be that vulnerable again.

A twig snapped, the sharp, brittle sound making her heart leap, sending her fleeing once more. Weaving through the trees, Ellie broke through to the other side and found herself in the meadow Aden took her to the previous winter—the one where he proposed to Aly. Ellie came to an abrupt stop, assaulted by the memory of the bloodstained snow and littered body parts juxtaposed with the tender one of him kneeling, a diamond ring gleaming between his fingers.

She was still grappling with the memories when two massive hands clamped onto each of her arms from behind, trapping her in the clutches of her relentless pursuers.

"Never stop running. It signifies unconditional surrender."

She let out a frustrated screech that echoed through the air, struggling against her restraints, but she refused to give up, despite the throbbing aches in every part of her body.

"She's like a wet cat squirming in a bag."

"When the world finds out who you are to him, there's nowhere you'll be safe. I bet Matthais would pay a hefty bounty for you."

At the sound of a dark chuckle beside her, Ellie whipped her head to glare at one of the few people she trusted. She trusted both men, but now she was starting to think it was misplaced.

"He'll kill both of you without a second thought," she growled.

"Maybe so. But it'll be worth the money. Your arm's gonna snap if you keep flailing like that."

A bone-chilling, inhuman roar reverberated through the meadow. Ellie's heart pounded, the sound all too familiar. The rough hands released their grip, and she braced herself against what was coming. In a blur of movement, she was airborne and propelled across the field.

Her world spun, and she found herself standing fifty feet away from her previous spot, caged between Aden's powerful arms. She stumbled and grabbed for him as he let her go, turning to stalk toward the two men.

"Aden, no!"

Her feet slid through the snow as she clung to his arm, her boots carving a wide path as he dragged her toward Kane and Drake.

Both guards held up their hands.

"Hey, boss, it's not what it looks like," Kane said.

"I will peel the skin from your bones." Aden's snarl cut through the stillness of the night.

"Aden!" Ellie yelled again to get his attention, but he shook her off as he reached the two half-breeds.

He lifted them by their throats, their weight insignificant in his fierce grip. Because of their impressive height, their toes never left the ground. Yet, they didn't try to escape his hold.

"You have exactly ten seconds to tell me what the fuck you were doing to her before I snap your necks."

Ellie ducked under Aden's arms, jumping to grab his forearms. She had to get him to listen before he did something he'd regret.

"Aden, listen to me," she pleaded, tearing her gloves from her hands and reaching up to his face, hoping her voice and touch would get through to him. "They weren't hurting me. I asked them to do this."

His eyes snapped to hers, the angry crimson orbs flashing with a rage that frightened her. Not for what he'd do to her, but for what he'd do to Kane and Drake.

"What the fuck did you just say to me?"

"Aden, let them go," Ellie said, her panic subsiding. "I'll tell you, but you have to let them go."

The red in his eyes faded, but the fire still burned. He released Kane's neck, dropping his guard to his feet, but he tightened his grip around Drake's, cutting off his air supply. Ellie heard him choke, and she whipped around as Aden tossed him to the ground.

"What did you do?" She gasped, watching her guard wheeze as he clawed at his throat.

"Remind him he solely exists to protect you."

She rushed over to Drake and dropped to her knees in the snow. His face was turning blue.

"Don't worry, Ellie. He'll be fine," Kane said as he kneeled beside her. "It's just a crushed windpipe. I brought provisions because I figured something like this might happen when Aden found out."

Kane reached into his pocket and took out a sharp knife and a small, round plastic tube. With a tight grip on Drake's hair, he pulled his head back and inserted the knife into his trachea. A gush of blood erupted from the wound, splashing Ellie's jacket as Drake inhaled. The pinched look on his face eased, and his complexion returned to its normal color.

Ellie stood and turned to Aden, glaring at him as she brushed the snow from her jeans.

"I can't believe you did that. Are you out of your mind?"

He grasped her arm and drew her closer. "Tell me why they were hunting you?"

"They weren't." She rested her hands on his chest. "Well, yes, they were, but I asked them to."

"You what?" His eyes flashed crimson again.

"I asked them to teach me self-defense."

"Why the fuck would you do that?"

His snarling tone and constant cursing no longer fazed her. She was immune to it. It was his usual way of expressing anger, though it was rarely directed towards her.

"In case anyone tried to take me."

He looked at her like she'd grown three heads. "Ellie, there's no need for you to learn self-defense. You have a guard who will die for you." He shot Drake a venomous look before returning his gaze to her. "And he might tonight, depending on how I feel in a few minutes."

She glanced over her shoulder to see Kane handing Drake a vial of BloodStone. She turned back to Aden.

"But what if something happens to him?"

"It won't."

"But what if it does?"

"Then you're already dead," Kane said from a few feet away. "We told you. You don't have a fighting chance against a vampire or half-breed, no matter how well you know how to fight."

Ellie shot him a glare. He wasn't helping.

When her eyes returned to Aden, his gaze had zeroed in on the unmistakable bruise on her jaw. He reached for her face and tilted it to the side. His touch was gentle, a contrast to the ferocity in his eyes. He wiped the blood from the corner of her mouth with his thumb before lifting it to his lips. Ellie both heard and felt the low rumble in his chest as his eyes flared.

"Which one did this to you?"

The deadly tone of his voice sent a shiver up her spine. She pushed his hand away. "It doesn't matter."

"I did it," Kane said at the same time.

Turning her head, she shot him a scathing look. "Shut up, Kane. You're going to get us all killed."

"It was an accidental slip of my wrist when I reached out to grab her. She caught me off guard with how fast she was on those short legs."

Ellie scowled. She wasn't that short.

"Give me your fucking hand," Aden demanded, and Kane walked over, extending his arm.

He seized Kane's wrist, twisting it until the bone gave way with a sharp crack. The sickening snap echoed in the night's stillness, amplified by the surrounding darkness. Then the bones in his hand and fingers collapsed with a series of wet, popping sounds, like knuckles cracking but infinitely more disturbing, sending a shudder down Ellie's spine.

A single, sharp grunt, quickly stifled, escaped Kane's lips.

"Aden," Ellie gasped, horrified. She expected him to be upset that she'd asked for their help, but she never expected him to hurt his own guard.

"He's lucky that's all I'm doing to him. Now, what else do I need to break on you?" He snarled at Drake.

Ellie tugged him aside. "Aden, stop it. I'm fine. You need to calm down."

From the corner of her eye, she saw Kane use his unbroken hand to retrieve another small vial of BloodStone from his pocket. He tore the top off with his teeth and gulped it down.

"This is fucking ridiculous, Ellie. You don't need to know how to defend yourself."

"I want to."

Suspicion flickered in his eyes as he crossed his arms over his chest. "Did you deliberately ask them to do this while I was sparring with Aurick?"

"Yes."

"Why?"

"Because I knew you'd react this way." Ellie bent to pick up her gloves.

"Is that why you're doing it out here? So I wouldn't hear?"

"Yes."

Aden scoffed, but his anger seemed to dissipate. "At least you're honest."

"I always tell you the truth."

"Why didn't you ask me to teach you?"

Surprised by the question and his wounded tone, she shoved her gloves in her pockets and closed the distance between them.

"Because you would've said no."

"You're fucking right I'd say no."

"Aden, I know I don't stand a chance against a vampire or half-breed, but I still want to know how to defend myself."

Beside them, Kane removed his jacket, lifting his shirt so Drake could plunge a syringe into his side. Since the release of AEON, a drug that halted the aging process for half-breeds, Kane no longer needed a daily dose of Aden's blood. But he must have still had some on hand for emergencies because vampire blood healed injuries almost instantly.

"I'll never let anyone hurt you, Ellie."

"I know," she murmured, Aden's unwavering conviction softening her heart. "But I'm tired of just letting things happen to me. I want some control over my life."

"Then I'll train you," he replied, his tone firm. "Now, this ludicrous exercise is over. Come on."

He grabbed her hand and tugged her toward the trees. A sharp pain shot through Ellie's wrist and up her arm, making her flinch. She hoped he wouldn't notice, but he did, stopping and pinning her with a glare before turning it on Kane and Drake.

"This will not go unpunished," he growled, his voice a low, dangerous rumble. Ellie pulled her hand away. "No."

Aden spun to look at her, his body again vibrating with anger. "Ellie," he seethed through clenched teeth, but she stood her ground.

"You won't do anything to them, and they're still going to teach me."

"I said I'll train you."

She crossed her arms over her chest. "No, Aden. This isn't up to you."

"Yes, it fucking is!" The sound of his roar filled the meadow, bouncing off the trees and startling a group of night birds into flight.

"No, it isn't," Ellie said, her own frustration bubbling up. "I want them to do it. They won't treat me like a fragile human. And I trust them."

"Where is this coming from?" He narrowed his eyes. "Has one of the thralls threatened you?"

"What? No." She shook her head. "I just want to know this when we go to the capital for the council gathering."

"You're not going to the capital."

"Yes, I am."

Aden averted his gaze, signaling he was aware she wouldn't be happy with what he was about to say. "No, you're not. You're staying back with Keeley. It's already been decided."

Anger flooded Ellie's body in a rush, and her fists clenched. "Why wasn't I part of this decision?"

"Because you didn't need to be."

She closed her eyes and took a deep breath. Fighting with him about this right now, and in front of their guards, would just make him more obstinate and get her nowhere. "I want to see my dad and Carrie, Aden."

"Ellie, I'm not arguing with you out here. Your body temperature is dropping. We'll talk about this back home."

He grabbed her forearm this time and started tugging her across the meadow. She felt Kane and Drake's curious eyes on them and yanked out of his grasp again.

"Stop pulling me. I'm fine. I'm not cold, and I'm not done here yet. Go back to the city, and I'll see you there in a little while."

He inhaled deeply, then slowly exhaled, a sign that his anger bubbled just below the surface.

Ellie stepped closer and wrapped her arms around his waist. She tilted her face up to look at him, lowering her voice, though Kane and Drake, with their exceptional half-breed hearing, would hear anyway.

"Aden, let me finish my lesson, and then we'll take a bath when I get back."

Aden's reaction was instant. He softened against her, his eyes darkening. She smiled, having learned in the last few weeks that Aden Westcott loved taking baths with her. The water not only synchronized their body temperatures, but it also meant they could spend uninterrupted time naked. It was a favorite pastime for both of them.

The first time she suggested taking a bath together, he laughed at her, not having taken one since he was a child. But after some teasing and cajoling and a striptease, she lured him in. Now she was hard-pressed to get him out of the tub.

Aden gripped her hips and tugged her against him. "Why do we have to wait?"

"Because my lesson isn't over."

A flicker of reluctant agreement shone in his piercing blue eyes, easing the effect of his scowl. Without taking his eyes off her, he called out to the two guards.

"You have a half hour. Then bring her back to me unharmed."

Ellie looked up at him tenderly, rising onto her toes and tilting her face to kiss the cool skin under his chin.

Aden turned his head to glare at Kane and Drake. "Every bruise I find on her body will be another broken bone."

"No, it won't," she said, and he pinned her with his fierce gaze again. "I mean it, Aden. They can't train me if they're worried about you punishing them every time I get bruised."

"Don't worry, Ellie. We're not afraid of him," Kane called over as he shrugged back into his coat.

"Thirty minutes," Aden said, kissing her swiftly and releasing her.

She watched him stride into the trees before turning back to Kane and Drake, a triumphant smirk spreading across her lips.

"Well, that went better than I thought it would."

Ellie

E llie made her way down the hallway towards their suite. It felt odd to consider it both hers and Aden's. She'd never had something of her own before. But her life had changed in the past eleven months. She went from being one of Master Matthais' thralls to Aden Westcott's girlfriend. His dead girlfriend reincarnated.

The door slid open as she approached, and Mina walked out.

"Oh, I was going to call you."

Mina's eyes swept over her, then narrowed. "No wonder Aden wanted a vial of laced BloodStone. Why are you covered in blood? What happened to you?"

Ellie looked down at herself, having forgotten about Drake's blood on her.

"Kane and Drake are teaching me self-defense. Aden wasn't happy when he found out. And what are you talking about, laced BloodStone?" She asked as she tugged off her wet gloves.

"Aden asked me to bring him a vial laced with his blood. Has he seen your bruises?"

"Just on my face."

"But you've got more?"

"A couple, I think."

Ellie didn't need to see the bruises to know they were there. Her body ached everywhere. When she told Kane and Drake not to go easy on her, she meant it. And they took it as a challenge, even after Aden found them, though they didn't truly hurt her.

"I guess I should get some supplies together for the next time he sees those two idiots. What the hell were they thinking?"

"I asked them to train me. And Aden promised me he wouldn't hurt them."

"Uh-huh. Sure he did." Mina looked skeptical. "Are you sure you aren't hurt other than the bruises? Do you want me to check for broken bones? It'll set Aden off in a rage if anything is broken."

"They didn't break anything."

"Then why are you cradling your wrist?"

"I think it's sprained. That's all. That's why I was going to call you."

Ellie hissed as Mina took her wrist between her fingers and rotated it.

"Yeah, just a sprain." She leaned toward Ellie and lowered her voice. "Take that BloodStone right away, and you should be able to hide most of it from him."

Ellie arched her eyebrow. There was no way she could hide any of it. He'd see her naked in a matter of minutes.

"I'll deny saying that." Mina stepped back and gave her a pointed look. "Have a good night."

"Night, Mina," Ellie replied as she entered the newly renovated suite.

Though she helped design it with Aden's mother and sister, the finished renovation still surprised her, even after two weeks. There was no longer a hallway leading to the living area. Now the suite opened up to a large living room, filled with plush furniture and soft, ambient lighting.

Aden's chunky, masculine furniture dominated the center, but it was now accented with feminine touches, accent pillows, and lamps on the side tables. The beige, brown, and green color scheme was gone. Ellie's love for the beach house decor, with its soothing blues, subtle grays, and warm tans, now beautifully decorated the space. Aden gave her free rein to decorate as she pleased but sulked about the loss of the green shade that matched Ellie's eyes. So they compromised and moved the color to the bathroom.

His studio remained unchanged, accessible through an arched alcove on the left, while a small dining area now sat off to the right of the entry door, giving Ellie a place to eat.

Pushing back the wall opposite the entrance expanded the suite to include previously unused storage areas and the hallway that she once used to access the concubine suite. A newly constructed room to the left provided her with a small library, fulfilling her one condition of having her own private space before agreeing to Aden's demand to move into his room.

The entire right side of the suite had been extended and transformed into an oversized bedroom, complete with double, joined walk-in closets. Ellie now had more clothes than she thought she'd ever wear, thanks to Keeley's crazy shopping sprees. Two large double doors stood open, offering a view of the king-sized bed against the opposite wall.

She limped through the living room and into the bedroom. "Aden?"

"In here. And you better be naked by the time you cross this threshold."

His voice floated from the bathroom, and she smiled. Of course, he was already in the tub.

Ellie threw her heavy coat onto a lounge chair in the corner, then took off her boots and socks before heading to the bathroom. It was almost as spacious as the bedroom, boasting a wet room complete with a jetted tub, large enough for five people. She and Aden spent a lot of time in it, relaxing, talking, and exploring each other's bodies.

With dual showerheads on either end and spray jets on the ceiling and walls, it was impossible to stand anywhere in the wet room without getting soaked. The white, dark green, and brown tiles had been replaced with ivory and pale coral, accented by a shade of emerald green that shimmered like her eyes. The two neutral colors balanced and softened the intensity and vibrancy of the jeweled tone, creating a tranquil, spa-like atmosphere.

A private toilet, dual sinks, and a vanity with a chair completed the bathroom. Although Ellie seldom wore makeup, Keeley insisted that no woman's bathroom would be complete without it.

She leaned against the door frame, taking in the sight of Aden propped against one side of the tub, covered up to his chin with bubbles, smirking sexily at her, a glass of blood in his hand.

He loathed drinking from anything but a vein but sometimes drank from custom heated glasses Sophie gave him for his birthday the previous month. Though he didn't care for them, he occasionally used them during shared mealtimes with her.

"You look comfy." She pushed off the doorjamb and walked further into the bathroom.

Aden's smirk faded. "And you look dressed."

Ellie lifted her wool sweater over her head, her movement slow and deliberate, dropping each additional article of wet clothing on the floor as she approached the tub. Aden's eyes darkened with desire as he watched her with rapt attention. But his expression hardened as she revealed her body, the deepening purple bruises stark against her pale skin—on her ribs, collarbone, and around her wrists.

A chilling silence filled the air as Aden gulped the last of his blood. "I'm going to flay them alive."

"No, you're not. You're going to give me the BloodStone Mina left, and they'll be gone in a few minutes," she said as she gestured toward the bottle on the rim of the tub.

He held out his hand to steady her as she lifted her leg over the side, trying to mask her discomfort. As she slipped into the warm water, the tension in Ellie's body melted away. She closed her eyes and leaned back against the side of the tub, a contented sigh escaping her lips.

"You're making it a habit of telling me I can't do things lately."

"How does it feel?" she asked, her eyes shut, a subtle smirk playing on her lips.

"Come over here and find out for yourself?"

Ellie laughed as she lifted her head and opened her eyes. "I'm serious. How does it feel to always hear no to everything you want?"

"I don't say no to everything you want."

"Not anymore," she conceded. "But it's still your automatic go-to response."

"Only when you want to do something stupid."

Ellie's eyebrow arched as she tried to kick him, but he was out of reach. Aden's hand closed around her ankle.

"I mean it, come here."

Ellie looked at him, and the look in his eye dared her to defy him. She held out her hand. "Can I have the BloodStone?"

"When you get over here, yes."

Refusing him was tempting, but she wanted the BloodStone, so she floated across the large tub. Aden grasped her waist and pulled her onto his lap, wrapping his arms around her. She reached for the vial, but a syringe lay next to it.

"Why is there a needle?"

Aden snatched the bottle from her fingers. "Because this isn't an oral dose. It's a shot."

Ellie leaned back to look at his face, tightening her thighs around his to keep from floating away. "Why?"

"Because I wasn't sure how much you'd need, and by the look of you, it's good I did. Hold out your arm."

She eyed him skeptically as he filled the syringe with the entire bottle of liquid.

"Don't look at me like that. Hold out your arm."

Ellie leaned forward and held it above the water. Aden reached for an alcohol wipe and swabbed the inside of her elbow. She braced herself for the pinch and cringed when he slid the needle into her vein. But her body relaxed as soon as the BloodStone hit her bloodstream, her aches easing.

"That stuff is a miracle," she murmured, and Aden snorted out a laugh as he tossed the needle into a trash can across the room.

"That's because it has my blood in it. And that isn't what you called it before."

Ellie twisted and sat with her back against him, pulling his arms around her waist.

"I have conflicting feelings about it. Especially now that I know some of the history."

"How so?"

"Your mom told me it saved your grandmother's life and cured all human diseases. Plus, it heals injuries fast." She held her hand out of the water, the bruises on her wrists already fading. "That's miraculous. But it also replenishes blood quickly so vampires can feed on humans more often. And that's the opposite of miraculous."

"Vampires would still feed on humans repeatedly without BloodStone, so isn't it better that it exists?"

"That's debatable."

Aden pulled her closer and bent his face to her neck. "You've been talking to Aurick, haven't you?"

"Your dad told me about the woman he loved who died. She was his inspiration for creating it. But he also said it gave vampires too much leverage over humans."

"It seems the Gerent is flapping his gums quite a bit lately. What else did he say?"

Aden's hands explored higher, cupping the bottom of her breasts. Ellie pulled them back to her waist, threading her fingers through his.

"Not much. He said there was more that he wanted to show and tell me, but he wants me to read an entire list of books before he does. He said I should learn human history before I learn vampire history." Aden's lips, warm and insistent, grazed her neck, his tongue tracing the faint scar left by his fangs, making her tremble. "My tablet is loaded up with books, and he also said I can visit his private library any time I want to."

"He doesn't even let me in his private library any time I want."

The corners of Ellie's mouth turned up in response to the jealous tone in his voice. "I guess he likes me better than you."

"I know I do." His teeth gently nipped at her shoulder.

The tub's heater kicked on as the water temperature dropped below its setting. The jets also started, and the water swirled around them. Ellie leaned her head back against his chest.

"We need to talk about earlier."

Aden's hands started exploring her body again. "Why? Talking is overrated."

She saw right through his ploy but held firm, tugging them back to her stomach.

"I want you to let Kane and Drake train me."

His fingers flexed against her abdomen, pressing into her skin, a clear sign of his disapproval. "I don't like the idea of them manhandling you."

"They need to, so I can learn. They taunted me to get me to struggle, but they were careful. You saw how they were with me."

"No, I didn't. It wasn't until I was done with Aurick that I realized you weren't in the compound. When I tracked you and saw you running frantically through the woods, I nearly lost my mind."

She turned her face and brushed her nose against his cheek.

"That's not what I'm talking about. You continued to watch us after you left the meadow."

"Hmm?" he murmured as he tugged his hands out of hers and slid his fingers lower, dipping them between her thighs.

"I know you didn't leave." Ellie's breath hitched as his fingertips swept over her rapidly swelling clit. "You were lurking in the woods watching us."

"I don't know what you're talking about."

Aden lifted his head, his eyes wide in an attempt at innocence that made her laugh as her hips started rocking. Aden's finger slid inside her.

"Uh-huh." Her head fell forward, a low moan escaping her lips.

"So what if I was?" he said, his voice defiant. "I had to make sure they didn't hurt you."

How could he possibly focus on speaking right now?

It took all her strength to reach down and pull his hand away. It was the last thing she wanted to do, but they needed to talk about this.

"Aden, you know they'd never harm me."

"When did you start trusting half-breeds more than I do? And tell that to your bruises." He lifted her wrist to his lips, brushing them over the bruises that were almost gone.

"Human flesh is fragile. Bruises are inevitable."

He froze behind her, releasing her wrist. She glanced back at him to see him scowling.

"What? What did I say?"

"Nothing."

"Aden?"

"Nothing. I just said something like that to Keeley once, and hearing you say it makes me realize how fucking terrible it sounds."

Ellie snuggled back against him, offering her comfort. Aden's recent self-reflection on his three centuries of attitudes and actions proved heavier on his conscience than expected.

"This is important to me, Aden."

Those words usually persuaded him, and despite his doubts, he agreed again. But only after a dramatic sigh.

"I still think it's a waste of your time and theirs, but if you're determined to do it, I won't stop you."

She lifted their combined hands and kissed his fingers. "Thank you."

"But if you don't want to end up battered and bruised, which, fair warning, will drive me to break more bones, you need to work on developing your muscles so you can fight back."

"Are you implying I'm out of shape?" Ellie asked, half insulted, as she ignored his passing threats to Kane and Drake.

"To me, you're perfect, but you lack physical strength. You need to build up your muscles so you have a fighting chance against them. If you're serious about this, use the equipment in my workout room and learn boxing and kickboxing."

"Will you teach me?"

He stilled behind her again before slowly nodding. His silence spoke volumes, a confirmation that his earlier hurt was real and not a ploy to manipulate her into feeling guilty.

"Thank you," she said again, sincerely.

"We'll start tomorrow." He squeezed her gently. "Now, can we stop talking? I thought bath time was for relaxing?"

"And talking."

"And fucking."

Ellie chuckled, expecting his response, and turned on his lap to face him. She wrapped her arms around him, relishing in the sensation of his body's warmth against her own. She shifted closer, and the hair on his thighs grazed the sensitive flesh between hers, eliciting a soft moan.

They needed to discuss his earlier comment about her not going to the capital, but that was a topic that needed delicate handling. Fortunately, the council gathering was still almost a month away, so it could wait until the trip got closer, and he had less time to be stubborn about it.

It should also wait until after she told him of her other decision. While that conversation required more immediate attention, the feeling of his hands caressing her smooth, bare skin was undeniably distracting.

Yes, telling him could wait a little longer.

Leaning forward, Ellie kissed the base of his throat. With a soft groan, he pulled her closer.

"I guess talking can be overrated sometimes," she whispered against his skin, her lips trailing along his jawline.

The moment their lips touched, she felt the familiar tingling sensation of his venom, which always made her shudder. Grinding against him, she rolled her hips over his hard erection, trapped and twitching between their bodies.

Aden let out a low growl that reverberated throughout the bathroom.

"Bath time is the best."

Ellie laughed into his mouth as he lifted her. It quickly morphed into a groan as he pulled her down onto him, pushing his cock deep inside her. While she was incredibly aroused, the sensation was always a little shocking, the stretch a delicious burn that stole her breath.

"Fuck," Aden choked as he gripped her ass in his large palms. "You feel so fucking good."

"Shut up and fuck me already," she blurted out, surprising them both with the rare curse.

"With pleasure, goddess." He grinned against her lips as he moved beneath her, lifting and lowering her as he plunged into her tight body.

Ellie tightened her thighs around his hips, rocking with him until everything else but the feel and taste of him faded away.

Ellie

Ellie's back hit the mattress with a bounce as Aden tossed her onto it.

"Aden, we're gonna get the bed wet."

She inched her way up the mattress, her wet skin sticking to the duvet. Pushing the wet hair out of her face, she flung her arms above her head.

Aden chuckled as he crawled between her thighs, settling on top of her. "Yes, you will, but not because of our bath."

She shifted with a groan, their damp skin clinging.

"We're sticking together. Get up," she urged. He grunted but did as she asked, his face contorting as they untangled. He sat back on his calves, grinning down at her.

"You look thoroughly fucked."

"That's one word for it." She smiled, letting her thighs fall open.

His heated eyes traveled down her body, and Ellie's breath caught. When he looked at her like that, she could almost feel his intense gaze searing her skin, the heat of it like a silent promise, making her tingle with anticipation. With her bruises mostly gone, she stretched her aching muscles, the lingering soreness more from their escapades in the tub than from her earlier lessons with Kane and Drake.

The gentle teasing brush of Aden's fingertips against her inner thighs made her pulse quicken.

"You're so fucking soft."

His words sent a tremor through Ellie's body, each syllable resonating in her core. How could she possibly still be aroused after he made her come three times in the bath? But her body couldn't help but respond to him, always craving his touch.

She tilted her head as Aden licked his lips, his eyes on the swollen flesh between her thighs. He'd yet to go down on her, something she remembered he loved to do. They'd both loved it, but he'd always had a particular obsession with performing oral sex on her.

Well, Alysia.

Memories of her past life still felt incredibly strange to her. Usually, something specific triggered one of her memories, something someone said or something new she encountered. Or it would happen in her dreams. She slept more now, which was also odd. After a lifetime of insomnia, sleeping barely three to four hours a night, she now slept between six and seven, depending on how long Aden kept her awake and how many orgasms he wrenched from her body first.

Not that she minded.

Though less frequent now, they continued to resurface. As her memories of Aly's life emerged and intertwined with her own, the distinction between the two became increasingly blurred. It often felt like she was two distinct people living inside one body. But as more of Aly's life came back to her, the more Ellie began to understand herself better.

Despite the oddity of having another woman's memories, it was comforting to know that their personalities aligned so closely as if they were two halves of a whole. They shared an innately kind, empathetic nature, the same unwavering stubbornness, softened by a sense of humor, the same inner resilience, identical core values, and a spirited, almost mischievous nature Aden affectionately dubbed her wiseass side. Years of living in fear in Matthais' house suppressed that part of her personality. But it blossomed now, in a place where she felt safe.

Her newfound sensuality was also a surprise, emerging only after she and Aden became intimate. She never knew this side of her existed, having spent her life simply trying to survive in a world ruled by vampires. Sex was the last thing on her mind when living under Matthais' rule. But the more of Aly and Aden's sex life

Ellie remembered, the more her own sensuality awakened, stirring her untapped inner desires.

Aly and Aden may have been young, but they shared a love that was all-consuming, a connection that seemed to transcend time because Ellie felt it bleeding into this life. Even though he'd killed her.

There was that.

Her feelings for him had been growing before she remembered him. She'd been falling for him, despite her best efforts to resist. But when her memories resurfaced, the floodgates opened.

That she and Aden were soulmates, unable to exist or even breathe without each other, was undeniable, and she was eternally grateful that they found one another again. He'd been alone for so long, suffering in his grief and guilt, living a life of darkness and torment, doling out pain to deal with his own, and leaving destruction in his wake. Ellie still had yet to ask him about what happened in those almost three hundred years. She knew it was horrific and twisted. And although she loved him despite his past and his flaws, it still left her nauseous to think about all he'd done to his thralls. All of whom bore a resemblance to Aly with their pale skin and shades of red hair.

But now was not the time to think about that. Not when he was looking at her like he wanted to devour her whole.

Aden licked his lips again, the gesture sending a wave of heat through her, and Ellie couldn't stop the moan that escaped. He looked like a starving man. Starving for a taste of her.

His desire was obvious. So why wasn't he taking the initiative when he so clearly wanted it? Had he done it with his thralls?

Nope. Not going there either.

"Why do you look like you just tasted something sour?"

Tilting her head, Ellie chuckled before she met his eyes. "You haven't put your mouth on me."

He flashed her his most charming smirk, the one that once made her scowl but now made her panties wet.

"I have my mouth on you all the time."

"No, you don't," she countered, reaching down and brushing her fingers against her swollen sex. Though still tender, the sensation made her tremble, igniting a fresh wave of desire for him. "You used to love that as much as I did."

"Fuck, Ellie." He gulped, and his eyes darkened as they followed the movements of her fingers.

"Is there a reason you don't want to?"

Disbelief flickered across his face as he met her eyes again. "You think I don't want to?"

"Then why haven't you?"

His mouth twisted into a snarl. "Because if I get my mouth that close to your femoral artery, I might fucking lose it."

She sat up, ignoring his snarling, and caressed his cheek. "I don't know why you don't trust yourself, Aden. I do."

His gaze held hers, his eyes revealing a storm of heartbreaking emotions.

Love. Longing. Uncertainty.

Ellie leaned forward, brushing her lips against his in a gentle kiss. "You won't hurt me." Her words were soft as she kissed him between each one. "I. Trust. You."

"You shouldn't."

His reply was so matter-of-fact. If it had been anyone else, she would have heeded the warning, but she had absolute faith in him.

She grasped his hand and brought it to her sex, stroking his fingers over her, sweeping them through her wet flesh, and coating them with her arousal.

"You have no problem touching me." She lifted them to her mouth. "Why won't you taste me?" She wrapped her lips around his fingers, swirling her tongue, moaning as she tasted herself and the residual remnants of him.

A choked sound escaped him, and Aden's eyes flashed crimson before a low growl rumbled in his chest. Her lips curved as she pulled his hand away. Then she cupped his face in both her hands and brought his mouth to hers.

He groaned, capturing her lips, his hand reaching between them to touch her again. Ellie gasped as he pressed his other hand between her breasts and urged her onto her back with a gentle push, following her with his body.

Aden trailed his lips down the length of her throat. He stopped and buried his face in her neck, inhaling deeply. She smiled and slid her fingers through the soft strands of his short hair. He always told her how incredible she smelled everywhere, but he was obsessed with the scent just beneath and to the right of her chin, the exact location of her jugular vein.

"I want your mouth on me," Ellie breathed against the side of his face. Her body arched beneath him, grinding against his fingers as they teased and taunted her, gliding over her slick flesh. A rippling sensation began in her clit, radiating outward until her entire body trembled, her thighs shaking and eyelids fluttering.

He kissed his way down her chest, his lips lingering on her breasts before closing around her right nipple. His warm, wet mouth and the teasing flick of his tongue over the tip ignited a fire inside her that made her toes curl. A fiery heat, tingling and pulsing, engulfed her nipple as his venom intensified the feeling.

Ellie moaned, flexing her fingernails on his scalp. He lavished her breast with slow, tantalizing sweeps of his tongue, completely unfazed by her sharp nails. She arched her back, pressing more of her breast into his mouth, begging him for more.

He tugged on her nipple with his teeth, eliciting a delicious sting that blossomed in her chest and spread out and down, straight between her thighs, where his fingers were still teasing her. He'd only recently begun using his teeth on her after she assured him she enjoyed the feeling. But he was careful to keep his fangs retracted.

"God, Aden, yes," she hissed, a breathless plea.

He released her nipple with a soft pop and then followed the delicate curve of one breast over to the other with his nose before capturing her other one. He bit down a little harder, and her breath hitched, a rush of arousal coating his hand. His skilled fingers danced across her quivering flesh, creating tantalizing patterns along her swollen, pulsing clit, before slipping a finger inside her.

The sensation became too intense, and she pulled his mouth away from her. The exquisite pleasure, coupled with his teasing fingers, was too much. Too pleasurable and overwhelming.

Especially when she wanted his mouth elsewhere.

"Aden, please."

He chuckled against her skin and continued to explore her body with his mouth, tracing a path down her abdomen, dipping his tongue into her belly button, making her giggle. She felt his lips curl before he shifted his body down the bed to lie between her thighs.

He pushed them wider, hiking her legs over his shoulders, showering the inside of her thighs with wet kisses. His nose grazed over the spot where her femoral artery pulsed, and he froze. The deep growl that escaped him seemed to reverberate through the mattress. Ellie's breath hitched, and a brief flicker of fear coursed through her before it vanished just as quickly.

He raised his head, pinning her with his intense, dark gaze, flashes of crimson appearing around his irises. His throat rippled as he swallowed his venom, and then his eyes slowly cleared, filling with a mix of desire and mischief. The hunger swirling in them made her heart race.

Ellie caressed his cheek. "I trust you," she said, and he turned his face, pressing a gentle kiss to her palm before looking back at her. He held her gaze as he slid his hands beneath her ass and tilted her hips up, lowering his mouth to her.

The first sweep of his tongue over her swollen clit was an exquisite agony, pleasure so intense it was almost painful, leaving her breathless. With a long, low moan, Ellie's head dropped back to the pillow, her eyes closing.

"Fuck! You taste so good." The wet, muffled sound of his groan filled the air as he devoured her.

She reached down and tangled her fingers in his hair, tugging hard as his tongue lashed against her. He wrapped his lips around her clit, taking it between his teeth, the delicate pressure and rhythmic motion sending waves of pleasure through her as she spiraled into oblivion.

Memories flooded her mind, a kaleidoscope of images flickering and flashing like a movie reel. Images of him consuming her like this, using his lips, tongue, teeth, and fingers to wrench unfathomable pleasure from her body. The memories slammed into her, then vanished as quickly as they came, and she was back with Aden.

Ellie cried out, shock filling her as her orgasm crashed into her, coming on so fast and forcefully that she swore her heart stopped. Her back arched, but he kept her hips pinned to the mattress as he continued to consume her.

"Aden," she moaned his name over and over until it became breathy whimpers as he wrenched one orgasm after another from her helpless body until she begged him to stop.

As she drifted off into an exhausted sleep several hours later, a sated smile curving her lips, Ellie couldn't help but wonder if she'd just unleashed a monster.

Aden

Aurick's office door slid open as Aden approached. He found his parents seated on the sofa, deep in conversation.

"You wanted to see me?" he asked, not in the mood for another argument with either of them.

"I spoke to Matthais today," Aurick said as Aden sat in the chair opposite them.

"And?"

"Well, first, I didn't address the Ellie situation with him."

Aden bristled, tired of his father's delay tactics. It had been two months since they discovered Matthais' abduction of Ellie and her father from the Westcott's region eighteen years prior. She'd recognized her childhood home in a southern village when she accompanied Aden on an eval trip. He wanted to confront Matthais right away, but Aurick insisted on waiting. He had yet to offer a satisfactory explanation for the delay.

"And when do you plan to do it?"

"Soon. I had other matters to discuss with him today. But that's not why I called you here."

"Then why did you?" Aden stood and walked over to the bar. His desire to drink while in Aurick's presence was stronger recently. "I have work to do, and you're keeping me from it."

"The annual council gathering is in less than a month. Matthais said he's looking forward to seeing you at the HEW games. He's still bothered by your failure to take part in the summer games."

Aden scoffed as he turned, sipping his whiskey. "I don't think it's in anyone's best interest if I attend this year. I'm thinking maybe I should skip it altogether."

It would be the first time in almost two and a half centuries that he would be absent. But the thought of seeing Matthais after their discovery just reignited his fury.

Yeah, it would be best for everyone if he stayed home. His absence would also keep Ellie from going as well.

"You will attend." Aurick's voice hardened. "And you need to hold your tongue, be social, and act like all is well."

"I'm not a fucking puppet you can parade out in front of everyone any time you feel like it."

"No, but you're my son and my Commander General, and you will do what is in the best interest and safety of this family and this region, whether or not it is best for you."

Sophie remained quiet, which was unusual for her.

"What is going on? The two of you have something you're not telling me. Why haven't you confronted Matthais about Ellie and demanded restitution? What's the fucking hold-up?"

"Aden, we want to get restitution for Ellie, too," Sophie said.

"And we will," Aurick added. "I give you my word. But timing is everything when dealing with Matthais."

Irritated, Aden sat back down, swirling the ice in his glass. "Ellie is insisting on going. She wants to see her father."

"That's understandable," his mother said. "She hasn't seen him in a year."

"I don't want her anywhere near Matthais, but she's going to put up a hell of a fight."

Aurick stood and walked to the bar, letting Sophie lead the conversation now because she could always more easily reason with Aden. Their strategy was so predictable, he would have laughed if he weren't so irritated.

"You'd keep her in your suite's concubine room, right?"

"Yes. If she was going. But she's not."

"Then he won't have access to her," she continued as if he hadn't spoken. "Drake will guard her, and there's no reason for Matthais to see her."

Aurick returned to the sofa and handed Sophie a drink.

"This is Ellie we're talking about. You know that, right? She wants to see her friend, too. There's going to be no keeping her in that room. And Drake will have to follow her, and someone is bound to notice that."

"I can have Georgina track her friend down so she can visit Ellie in your room," Sophie said.

"You're not making it easy for me to refuse her."

She smirked like she knew refusing Ellie wasn't an option.

"You'll have to get Matthais' permission for her to see her father," Aurick said.

Fucking hell!

"Now you've just made it very easy to refuse her."

"Uh-huh," Sophie murmured before taking a sip of her drink, and Aden snarled under his breath.

"Oh, by the way, Keeley, Ellie, and I are leaving on Friday for Bíonn súil le muir. Are you going to come with your father on Christmas Eve or beforehand?"

"Excuse me?" Aden asked, his gut tightening. "What the fuck are you talking about?"

"Didn't Ellie tell you?"

"No, she fucking didn't. We're not going anywhere near that house."

"But it's Iain's first Christmas," Sophie said, her smile a permanent fixture since Keeley and Ryan's baby boy joined the family.

"I don't give a fuck."

"Aden, the family is spending the holiday there."

He set his glass on the coffee table, the urge to hurl it at the wall too strong to resist.

"Have fun then, because Ellie and I won't be there."

"Aden, she's excited about going." Sophie paused and glanced at Aurick before looking back at him. "I've had your entire wing rebuilt. Nothing about it is the same."

Aden stood, his fists clenching at his sides. "I said no, Sophie! Why the fuck would you even suggest this?"

"We always spent Christmas at that house."

"We haven't in almost three hundred years."

"And we stopped out of respect for you," she said. "But there's a new child in our family now. And there's no reason to stay away anymore."

"You're out of your fucking mind."

"Watch it, Aden," Aurick growled.

"I said no!" Aden turned and stormed toward the door. "I can't believe you'd fucking do this to me."

"Aden," Sophie called after him, but the blood pounding in his ears drowned her out.

By the time he reached their suite, Aden was ready to breathe fire.

"Ellie!" He thundered as he strode into the living room, his heavy footsteps echoing like a stampede on the tile floor.

Ellie's head snapped up in surprise. Tucked against her side, his mother's cat, Vlad, hissed in protest. "What the fuck is this about going to Bíonn súil le muir with Sophie and Keeley?"

Eyes wide, she set her tablet aside and stood up from the sofa. He strode over, towering over her, his muscles tense, the air crackling with the barely contained fury radiating from him.

She didn't even flinch.

"And why the fuck didn't you tell me about this?"

Ellie let out a quiet sigh, her eyes softening. "I was planning to tell you later when I saw you for my kickboxing lesson. Your mom only told me about it a couple of days ago?"

"A couple of days? You've known for a couple of days?" The pulsing in his temple was so intense that spots danced in front of his eyes. "What the fuck, Ellie?"

Frowning, she folded her arms across her chest. "Can you dial back the fucks a little? It's overkill, even for you."

Aden's lips twitched despite his anger. He loved the way she stood her ground now, unafraid to stand up to him. And the "fuck." She'd only ever used the word once to his knowledge—in the tub the other night when she told him to shut up and fuck her. A fraction of his fury dissipated, and his cock hardened at the memory. The view of her cleavage pushing above her crossed arms further fueled his arousal, quelling his rage.

He took several deep breaths, trying to "dial back the fucks" as she requested.

"Why didn't you say anything when Sophie first mentioned it?"

She bit her lip, betraying her anxiety. "I didn't know how to bring it up."

And just like that, Aden's anger flared to life again.

"Oh, I don't know. How about you say, 'Hey Aden. Wanna burn your world to the ground? Let's go back to the scene of the crime.'"

"Aden—"

"No. Fuck, Ellie." Seizing the nearest object, he hurled the lamp across the room, shattering it against the wall. "You're one of the most kind-hearted and considerate people I've ever known. But when you decide to be insensitive, you go all the fuck out! What the fuck were you thinking?"

Let her tell him to dial back his "fucks" again.

"Are you done?" she asked, tightening her crossed arms, her own anger flaring now. "Are you going to stop yelling at me and listen, or are you just going to stomp around here like an angry elephant for the rest of the day?"

Did she just sass him?

It made him want to toss her over his shoulder, take her to bed, and fuck her until her head popped off. Well, not really. But at least until she screamed herself hoarse.

Instead, Aden walked over to the bar and poured a glass of Jameson. Ellie detested the taste of whiskey and refused to kiss him when he drank it, so he rarely did. And that thought just inflamed his anger again.

He turned to face her, and his eyes dared her to say something as he gulped it down. But she was crouched on the floor, picking up the pieces of the broken lamp.

She stood, and even though her eyes held a vulnerability that reached straight into his chest and ripped his beating heart out, he couldn't keep the snarl out of his voice. "Do you have any idea what you're asking of me?"

A hesitant, regretful sigh escaped her lips. "I'm asking you to come with me back to the room I died in."

Every ounce of breath Aden had in his body whooshed out in a long exhale. Fuck!

Her ability to halt one of his tantrums with a single sentence was nothing short of stellar. He turned back to the bar and poured another drink.

"I really fucking hate how blasé you are about all of it, now that you've regained your memories."

He gulped his whiskey before turning back to her. "And Sophie sure knows how to get what she wants. Prey on the girl whose innate curiosity and need to learn everything is a morbid fucking character flaw."

Though he meant his words when they left his lips, a wave of regret washed over him, bitter and immediate. If anyone had character flaws, it was him. Not her.

Ellie tilted her head, a curious expression on her face. "I've been meaning to ask you, when did you start calling your mom and dad by their first names?"

"When I turned into an asshole. And don't change the subject. Why didn't you say anything when Sophie first mentioned it?" She bit her lower lip, and he narrowed his eyes at her. "Ellie?"

"I was waiting for the right time. I knew you'd be upset—"

"Never would be the right time, because we're not going."

She rubbed her temples. "Why not? Your mom wants Iain's first Christmas to be there. Your family always celebrated Christmas at that villa. It's so beautiful there."

Aden poured another drink and gulped it down. "You're all fucking out of your minds if you think I'm stepping foot in that house again."

Ellie dropped her arms with a gentle sigh and walked over to him. She took his hand and tugged him toward the sofa.

"Go away, Vlady." She shooed the cat before pushing Aden down and straddling his thighs, pressing her forehead against his.

His anger melted away. But not the knot in his chest, the tight, suffocating feeling brought on by the mere thought of that place. The knot pulsed with agonizing pressure, a sensation he imagined was similar to a heart attack.

He wrapped his arms around her, pulling her closer, burying his face in her neck. She slipped her fingers into his hair and dragged her nails over his scalp gently. A low rumble reverberated in his chest.

"It's just a house, Aden."

He stiffened, his anger returning. He lifted his head, unable to contain the snarl. "It's not just a fucking house!"

"Aden—"

"No! We're not going."

"Because that's where you killed me?"

The audacity of her question, so blunt and unexpected, caused him to choke. He pushed her off his lap, tossing her to the cushion beside him, and stood.

"You asked me once if I could possibly fathom what it was like to relive your death. Well, I fucking have, Ellie." He yanked on the short strands of his hair. "I've relived killing you over and over for almost three hundred years."

She stood. "You'll never get past it if you don't confront it."

"I don't want to confront it." His roar reverberated through the room. She didn't flinch, despite the earsplitting volume. "Or get past it. It's the most horrific thing I've done in my life, and I don't deserve to get past it."

"Aden, I'll be right there with you, sweetheart."

Her endearment flooded his body with warmth, down to his bones. He loved it when she called him that. But that didn't mean he was going to change his mind.

"I said no, Ellie."

"You need to go back there and get closure. We both do. It's been hanging over you for too long."

"Do you need to look up the definition of the word 'no' in your dictionary?"

"Don't be a jerk, Aden. That's the room I died in. Do you think this is going to be easy for me, either?"

"Then why fucking do it?"

"Because I don't want to live in the past. I want to live in this life. Not that one."

"No!" he snarled. Looking around for something else to throw, Aden grabbed a sculpture from the coffee table and threw it against the wall.

Sighing, Ellie shook her head and closed her eyes.

Perhaps throwing the sculpture was a little much.

He sighed and shook his head, mirroring her movements. "I can't do it. Not even for you. I'll never step foot in that house ever again."

Without another word, Aden spun on his heel and walked out of the suite as abruptly as he stormed into it.

Aden

A den heard her heartbeat before his office door slid open. Of course, she found him.

The room had been turned upside down. His desk was in splinters on the floor, and the rest of the furniture was flipped over and in pieces, except for one chair. The one he was sitting in, drinking a glass of whiskey laced with blood.

This was the third time in less than a year that his office and all its furniture had been destroyed. Maybe he needed to think about some anger management intervention.

She'd left him alone for a few hours, and for that, Aden was grateful. He regretted blowing up at her, but didn't she realize that what she was asking would destroy him?

"Did you feed?"

He nodded as he held up his glass and took the last gulp. "Just having dessert now."

He couldn't suppress the snark in his tone, but it pissed him the fuck off that blood was the only thing that calmed him. Other than Ellie. But he had nowhere else to turn when she was the reason for his distress.

She took the glass out of his hand and set it on the floor before climbing onto his lap. He grasped her hips and pulled her into his arms. "I'm sorry," he murmured against her throat, and it was for a whole myriad of things.

For a man who never apologized, he was saying those two words to her a lot.

"I shouldn't have pushed you like that." She nuzzled his cheek, brushing her lips over him. Just the feel of her and her lips caressing him comforted him. "I'm the one who usually runs when we fight."

"How quickly the tables have turned."

"I'm sorry, sweetheart." She tightened her arms around him. "I knew how much this was going to upset you, but I was a coward. I should've told you as soon as your mom brought it up."

"Yes, you fucking should have."

She leaned back and looked into his face. "How did you find out?"

"I saw Aurick and Sophie earlier, and she mentioned that you're leaving Friday. Like it was no big deal that she wants me to go back to my hell on earth."

Ellie tangled her fingers in his hair, gently massaging his head, and a low rumble, almost a purr, vibrated in his chest. Every time she did that, it made him shudder, especially when she scratched right above his ear.

"I'm sorry you felt blindsided. I should've told you sooner, but I wanted to find the right time. I was planning to talk to you about it yesterday after our bath, but you ambushed me with your tongue."

An unrepentant grin spread across his face. "I think it was you ambushing me when you sucked my fingers into your mouth. Not that I'm complaining. You can ambush me with sex anytime."

Ellie laughed against his lips as she kissed him. "It was completely worth delaying this conversation." Her expression sobered as she leaned back again, meeting his eyes. "And I understand why you don't want to go back there. I do. But can you understand why I need to? Why I have to?"

A long, weary sigh escaped Aden's lips. He was about to give in. The weight of it all pressing down on him was too much to fight. The slight tremor in her voice made it impossible for him to deny her.

"Can't we just go to the villa? Do we have to go into that room? We can sleep somewhere else."

"That kind of defeats the purpose of the exercise."

He'd been sitting here for hours, fuming and sulking. Once his furniture had succumbed to his aggression, he tried to see it from her point of view. Considering or prioritizing anyone else's needs was new to him.

He swallowed. "I haven't stepped foot in that villa since that night. I would have burned the entire thing down if Aurick hadn't chained me up."

"What?" Ellie's eyes widened. "What do you mean, your dad chained you up?"

His frown at the memory of his captivity turned into a grimace. "Are you sure you want to hear this? Because once you do, there's no going back."

He didn't want to tell her, wasn't sure he could even get the words out. But he owed it to her. He owed her everything, and he'd never deny her anything important to her. Even if it tore him apart.

She nodded, the trepidation in her eyes in perfect harmony with his hesitation. "I don't know if I want to hear it, but I need to. I need to know what you went through." A soft brush of her fingers against his lips made his eyes drift shut, a warmth spreading through him. "Please tell me."

Aden took a deep breath, his hands tightening around her hips. He needed to touch her, feel her real and alive beneath his fingers, to relive this.

"To say I lost it when I came back from the brink and realized Aly was dead doesn't even begin to cover it. I was catatonic. I don't know for how long, but when I came out of it, I couldn't breathe or speak. It felt like my heart had been ripped out of my chest."

Ellie's eyes welled with tears as she listened. He averted his gaze—had to if he was going to do this.

"My mom removed Aly's body while I was—" Aden swallowed over the words. Seeing her again was something he could never bring himself to do. "I tore the entire room apart. I was unstoppable." Ellie trembled beneath his fingers, and he looked at her. "I'd barely come into my vampire strength yet, but it took Aurick, Kane, Horatio, Roderick, and a half dozen other guards to take me down. I killed two of them. They had to put me in chains in the vaults."

Confusion clouded her features as she blinked rapidly through a veil of tears. "What are the vaults?"

"Vampire prison cells. They have UV chains and lights to keep vampires weak so they can be contained."

"Oh my God," Ellie choked. "Aden, I'm so sorry."

"Don't fucking pity me!" He snarled. It didn't deter her from wrapping her arms around his neck and burying her face in his throat, pressing her lips against him. Her breath, warm and soft, grazed his skin. It calmed and comforted him, as did the feeling of her in his arms.

"No pity," she whispered. "Just love. And heartbreak for what you went through."

He clutched her closer, dropping his head on her shoulder. They were silent for several minutes.

"How long did they keep you in the vaults?"

"A decade."

Ellie's head snapped back, her eyes wide in shock. "What? Ten years? How could they do that to you?"

"They should have kept me there longer."

He'd gone on a destructive rampage after his release that his father spent years cleaning up.

"When they let me out, I still wasn't in my right mind. Any other vampire would have been executed for the devastation and death I caused. If I hadn't been Aurick's son, I would have been. It took almost a century before I didn't see Aly's broken body every time I closed my eyes."

Warm tears coursed down Ellie's cheeks, and he cupped them in his hands. "Please don't cry, mo ghrá."

She swiped her tears with her fingers. "We don't have to go. We'll stay here for Christmas."

Aden's laugh was humorless, a dry, rasping sound that seemed to match the gravity of their conversation. "Fat chance of that happening when my mother gets something in her head."

"It's not up to her. I'll ask to go sometime when you're away."

"I'm not letting you go there alone. Either we both do it or neither one does."

Ellie shook her head as she looked at his chest. She reached out, and her fingers toyed with the top button of his shirt. "I can't ask you to go through that."

He lifted his hand to cover hers, holding them against his heart. "I know you have to do it. It's the only way you'll get closure."

Her eyes met his. "It's not worth it. Not at the expense of your sanity."

A sardonic smirk, barely concealing the depth of his regret, tugged at the corners of his lips. "No one has ever accused me of being sane. I'll be fine, Ellie."

She shook her head. "No."

"Seriously, I'll be okay."

Doubt clouded her expression. "Are you sure?"

He nodded and pulled her closer. "There's nothing I won't do for you."

"And there's nothing I won't do for you." Her fingers tangled in his hair, and she pressed her forehead to his. "You know that, right?"

Aden closed his eyes and breathed her in, letting her soft jasmine and honeysuckle scent surround him. He knew she would. The unwavering honesty and warmth in her voice left no doubt in his mind.

Ellie kissed him, her breath mingling with his. "I'll be right by your side. We'll confront those demons together. Then they'll never overshadow us again."

He wasn't sure he believed that, but he'd try for her.

He tilted his head back. "Why are you going so soon? Christmas is still two weeks away."

"We have to decorate."

He scowled. Christmas was always a big deal for his mother. It was her second favorite holiday, Halloween being the first. They stopped celebrating it a long time ago because Bíonn súil le muir was specifically built for that purpose. Eventually, his mother started celebrating it again at the compound, but it wasn't the same. And now that Keeley and Ryan had a baby, she had an excuse to make it a big deal again.

That's why he didn't want kids.

"I can't go on Friday. I have to go to Sever Seb-Ir at the beginning of the week to handle a couple of things."

"Can't you go before you leave?"

"I'm not doing this and then leaving you alone there."

Ellie shifted on his lap. "Your mom said your dad wouldn't be able to go until Christmas Eve, either. We're just going early to decorate."

"I don't know how long I'll be gone."

He hated being away from her for extended periods, especially now that they were together. But he couldn't avoid this trip. He needed to get some intel on why Sever Sib-Irian rogues were sneaking into Réimse Shíochánta without registering.

"Then just meet us there when you're done."

"Are you sure you want to go alone? You don't have to help Sophie decorate. You can wait for me if you don't want to be there by yourself."

"I'll be okay," she said. "Are you sure about this, Aden?"

No, he wasn't.

"Yes."

She nodded, pecked him on the mouth, and used his shoulders as leverage to stand.

"Where are you going?" He hadn't meant to pout, but he needed to be close to her right now.

"I thought we were going to start my kickboxing lessons tonight?"

"Do you still want to do that?"

"If you do, yes."

He gave her a long, lingering look. "I think kickboxing is a great idea. Just what we both need to get out a little of our anger and aggression."

Ellie glanced around the room and arched her eyebrow at him. "You didn't do that already?"

"Not even close."

She shrugged. "Okay. But you promised you wouldn't go easy on me. If you do, I'm going to ask Drake and Kane to teach me."

"No, you fucking won't," he snarled, but with very little heat as he stood. "I don't have any desire to kill our guards, so you're going to work with me."

She stepped closer, wrapping her arms around his waist.

"Normally, I wouldn't tell you this because it would go to your head, but you're kinda sexy when you're bossy and snarly."

A self-satisfied grin stretched his lips. "Is that so?"

"Yes. But don't ruin it by getting cocky. And you have to trust me to know what I can handle and what I can't."

"Fine." He released her and slapped her on the ass. "Go change and meet me back here. I need to feed one more time before we do this."

Ellie

"Oomph."

The air rushed from Ellie's lungs as she landed on her back on the mat for what felt like the hundredth time.

"You're just doing this to retaliate, aren't you?"

Aden smirked at her. "You told me not to go easy on you."

"I didn't tell you to break me." She grinned up at him, though she felt more like grimacing. He wasn't being overly brutal with her, but he wasn't being as careful as she expected. She should have given him more credit.

After their fight, all she wanted to do was curl up in bed with him, soothe his tortured memories with her lips and body, but he needed a different kind of distraction after the weight of their conversation. So, she let her body be used as a punching bag. She now questioned the wisdom of her decision.

"It's unfair how biologically superior vampires are to humans. You're barely even winded, and I'm ready to crawl into bed for a week. Considering you're supposedly undead, you have a lot of physical advantages."

"You've been reading too many of Sophie's vampire books." Aden snorted. "It's ironic that's what they used to call vampires because our bodies are as alive as humans. They just work a little differently."

"How are they different, really?" She asked, glad to distract him from beating her up for a few minutes.

"Every biological system inside a vampire works slower than a human. Our heartbeats are slower. We breathe but only need ten percent of the oxygen humans do. The flow of blood in our veins is slower. The only exception is our rapid healing. But major wounds with significant blood loss prolong recovery, even with the help of human blood."

She pushed up on her elbows. "When you fed me your blood, I was completely healed in only a few hours."

"Yes, vampire blood is more potent than human blood. But if I were seriously injured, I'd require a significant amount of blood to heal, and the recovery period would be longer, anywhere from a few hours to a few days. A severed arm, for instance, could be reattached, though regaining full use would take several days."

Ellie's jaw dropped. "You can reattach limbs?"

He nodded. "But quick reattachment is crucial to regaining the use of a severed limb. Otherwise, the damage is permanent. But decapitation is different. Once a head is gone, it's gone."

That mental image made Ellie wince. "That's wild. So vampires' bodies are slower than humans internally, but externally, you're stronger and faster."

"Yes."

"That doesn't make sense."

"I didn't make the rules." He held out his hand. "Come on. Quit stalling. Let's do it again."

With a sigh, she let him pull her to her feet.

"I want you to start working with my weights. It will build your muscle strength."

"Will you work with me? I like doing this with you, even when you beat me up."

"When I can," he said. "But you need to, even when I can't be here. I'll tell Drake to work with you when I'm not available."

"So, what's next, teach?" Ellie bounced on her toes, the padded floor springy beneath her feet.

"Raise your hands in a guard stance again."

She lifted her hands to protect her face and staggered her feet, shoulder-width apart, one foot slightly forward.

"Now block me."

Aden turned and executed what he'd taught her was a roundhouse kick. His move was deliberate and slow, allowing her time to dodge and block, but she felt the vibration in her forearm when it connected. A proud grin spread across Aden's face, his eyes shining as he pulled her into his arms.

"You're doing great. Is there anything you're slow to pick up?"

She pressed against him. "I don't know. Tell me, did I catch on to sex quickly?"

The playful glint in his eyes intensified, setting her heart racing with a mixture of excitement and a nervous flutter of desire.

"Fucking yes, you did."

Aden swept his leg behind hers, knocking her off balance, and they tumbled to the floor in a tangle of limbs and muffled laughter. He broke her fall with his arms before pinning her to the mat. Ellie couldn't hold back her moan as his hard body pushed into hers. He buried his face in her neck as one hand slid up the front of her tank top.

"Are you two having sex again? Jeez, Aden, will you give the girl a break already?"

Keeley's voice startled Ellie, but not enough to get her to move.

"Go the fuck away, Keeley." Aden didn't move either, his voice muffled against Ellie's skin.

"No."

Disappointed, Ellie pushed on his chest and slid out from beneath him, pulling her shirt down as she stood up.

"What do you want?" His snarl was halfhearted at best as he flopped onto his back.

Keeley stopped a few feet away. "I'm here to talk to Ellie, not you, so mind your own business and go away."

"This is my office."

"What happened in there?" She gestured towards the disaster in the next room.

"Your mom told him about the Christmas plans," Ellie answered before Aden could.

"Oh, shit. Is that why you're beating up your girlfriend?"

He pushed to his feet. "I'm not beating her up!"

Keeley gave Ellie a once-over. "Blink three times if you need help."

"Don't be an instigator," Ellie said, flipping her hands back and forth. "How do I get these wraps off?"

Keeley snorted as she crossed her arms. "You're no fun."

But Ellie saw the concern in her eyes as the brunette looked at her brother. Aden pulled Ellie toward him. His face twisted into a frown, his fingers tracing a path down her arm, towards her wrist.

"What the fuck are you doing here, Keeley?"

She ignored him and turned to Ellie. "I talked to my mom, and she said she can free you up on Wednesday."

Ellie's eyes lit up. "Really?"

"Yeah, so are we on, then?"

"Yes!"

"What are you two talking about?" Aden removed the last of the wrapping from Ellie's hands. She flexed her fingers and sighed softly when he massaged them.

"Ellie's coming to BloodStone with me."

"Why?"

He tossed the wraps in the trash as Ellie sat on the weight bench and pulled off her sneakers. Her feet were killing her.

"What should I wear? My pet uniform or a regular thrall one?"

"No teal. Just your thrall uniform. If you decide to work with me, we can figure out how you can wear regular clothes so you blend in with the other lab techs," Keeley replied, before turning to Aden. "Because unlike you, she's interested in what we do at BloodStone?"

"Why would she be interested in that?"

"She's right here, you know. You could ask her yourself." Ellie wiggled her toes and stood.

"Is this some kind of take-your-kid-to-work day thing?"

"Don't be sarcastic and condescending," Ellie said with a frown. His usual lack of filter was even more pronounced when he was brooding.

"You're pissed she has interests beyond just letting you defile her constantly," Keeley said.

With a gentle hand, Ellie stepped closer, her fingers lightly brushing his arm, attempting to soothe his obvious irritation. "Aden, I'm interested in learning more about BloodStone. Keeley and your dad agreed to let me. I'm extremely grateful."

"But what about working with Sophie?" He asked, his face still creased in a frown.

"If I like it, she's willing to let me go work at BloodStone."

"You're going to love it. I just know it," Keeley said with a smile. "Did you read the rest of those books I gave you?"

Ellie nodded. "I finished the last one yesterday."

"Good. You'll be all set. Hannah can't wait to meet you."

"Oh, hell no. Keep Hannah away from her."

"Why?" Ellie asked as she looked at Aden.

"Because she's evil."

Keeley let out a chuckle. "He just doesn't like that Hannah's the only one who's ever slapped his ass and got away with it."

"Huh?"

"She delivered him when he was born."

"Oh, that's who Hannah is," Ellie said. "I kinda remember her. She used to tease you a lot."

Aden grunted, and she wrapped her arms around his waist, tilting her face up to look him in the eyes. "No one could turn me against you."

Aden's posture was stiff again. The tension in his body returned now that they were done with her lesson. Gently, he loosened her arms and stepped back.

"I have to check on training before I call it a day. I'll see you back in the suite."

He kissed the side of her head and walked out, leaving the two of them gaping at his abrupt exit.

"I know he usually just bolts like that when he's pissed, but that was weird, right?" Keeley said, wrinkling her nose.

"He's still really upset about Christmas."

Keeley sighed. "I hope you and my mom know what you're doing. As much as I want to celebrate Iain's first Christmas at that house, I'm on record saying I think it might be too soon. Especially making him go back into that room."

"It's been almost three hundred years, Keeley. This is something he and I both need to do. I just hope…" Ellie trailed off, not willing to share her other plans with anyone just yet. Not until she spoke to Aden, and after his reaction tonight she was even more nervous about asking him.

"Just hope what?" Keeley asked, eyes fixed on her. She was too observant for her own good.

Ellie shook her head. "Nothing."

"You're a terrible liar. I guess that's a good thing though, isn't it?"

"I just never want to hurt him, and I'm afraid I might."

"How?"

"By asking him for too much." A prickling unease spread through her, raising goosebumps on her arms.

Keeley grasped her hand and gave it a quick, reassuring squeeze. "For you, there's nothing that's too much for Aden. There's nothing he won't give you."

"I know. That's what worries me the most."

"What else are you planning?"

Ellie shook her head.

"Okay. I won't pry even though I want to." Keeley looked at her, her expression serious. "But you know you can talk to me about anything, right?"

Ellie gave her a grateful smile. "Yeah. But this is between him and me. I'll never deliberately hurt him. His heart is the most precious thing in my life."

"I know it is. Look, I've got to go. I haven't seen my baby all night, and I need some cuddles before bed. I'll come by and get you at six on Wednesday." She rubbed Ellie's arm. "Don't look so worried. Aden will be fine."

She walked out, and Ellie looked around, her eyes sweeping over the chaos in Aden's office through the glass doors.

She hoped Keeley was right.

Keeley

Aden entered the courtyard, a scowl twisting his lips.

"Hello, baby brother," Keeley said softly from her spot on a chaise lounge in the shadows.

He stopped mid-stride and turned to her, his perpetual scowl morphing into a smirk. "Well, that wasn't creepy at all."

"Keep your voice down," she shushed, gently bouncing Iain in her arms.

He strolled over to her. "Why isn't your spawn in bed?"

"He just finished his feeding with the wet nurse. I wanted some baby-mommy alone time with him before he goes back to sleep."

"Aren't rug rats supposed to sleep all the time?"

Sighing, Keeley shook her head. "Why can't you just use the word 'baby'? Why do you have to use every derogatory name that comes into your mind to describe my son?"

With an indifferent shrug, Aden ignored her reprimand and turned to walk away. "Well, I'll leave you to it then."

"No, stay and sit with me. I was waiting for you."

He turned back, hesitation clear on his face. "I thought you wanted alone time."

"We've been having it. But I want to talk to you."

His eyes flashed with annoyance. "Keeley, I don't want to talk about Christmas. I've already agreed to go against my better judgment. I don't need it battered into my brain that I need to face my demons. Ellie's made it clear I have no choice."

"Just sit your ass down already." She pointed to the seat beside her. "I've been sitting here thinking about it. And I originally thought it was a terrible idea. But the more I think about it, Ellie's right. This is something you both need to do."

Aden dropped into the chair dramatically, and Keeley smiled. Even when he was being a dick, he still let her boss him around. Well, only when he was out of sorts, which he clearly was now.

"I blame Sophie for this," he said.

"Having Christmas as Bíonn súil le muir was her idea, but she didn't expect you and Ellie to come with us."

"Sure she didn't," Aden scoffed.

"She didn't. She hoped, but wasn't optimistic."

Keeley nuzzled Iain's head, reveling in his clean baby scent, the soft tufts of his hair tickling her nose. Born with a head full of light brown hair like Ryan's, Keeley was secretly relieved that the baby favored him over the surrogate.

"In what universe did she think Ellie or I would want to go back there?"

"Ellie does. Don't you remember how much Aly loved Christmas there?"

Aden grunted, and Keeley expected no less—or more—from him. Even with Ellie in his life, he still grieved for Aly, but the pervasive darkness that consumed him for centuries had finally lifted.

"Mom just wanted to spend Christmas there. She even renovated a suite in the guest quarters, so you didn't have to go anywhere near your old wing. The whole 'let's tackle the room' thing came from the love of your life. Take it up with her. Mom's not trying to torture you."

"I know." Agreeing with her appeared painful for him. "But why can't she just leave things the hell alone?"

"Because your mother loves you. Probably more than anyone else. Except Ellie. And Ellie isn't trying to torture you either. This is going to be excruciating for her, too."

"I fucking know that!" His snarl was swift and loud.

It wouldn't normally bother her, but it startled Iain, who jumped in her arms.

"Shh!" Keeley shot Aden a glare as the baby stirred and woke up.

He lowered his voice. "Why do you think I don't want to do it? Facing that room changes nothing, Keeley. Nothing. It doesn't change what happened."

Keeley cradled Iain against her chest, trying to calm his fussing. "But maybe it will eliminate the perpetual black cloud that's hung over you since that night."

"I'll never be free of that night."

"Neither will she if you don't do this."

A long sigh escaped Aden's lips, a rare nonverbal sign of surrender.

"I know Ellie is Aly's soul, but she's even more fucking stubborn than Aly was."

Keeley couldn't stop herself from laughing. "You're not kidding. I've never met anyone so freaking stubborn. Except, maybe, you. But she's stronger than you give her credit for. Trust her to protect your heart, Aden. She'd never ask you to do anything she didn't think you could handle."

Keeley believed that. There was no one she trusted with Aden's heart more, even before Ellie's comments earlier.

"I do trust her, but this isn't some off-the-cuff, whim idea we're talking about here. We're opening Pandora's box with this."

"Now you're just being a drama queen." Keeley laid Iain on the lounge between her legs and leaned down to blow on his belly. He let out a giggle, blowing bubbles through his lips. Keeley's lips curved as she sat up. "You know, in some ways, I think I like Ellie better than Aly. I know that sounds weird, and don't lose your shit when I say that," Keeley said when Aden leaned forward, his eyes flashing with anger. "Part of me feels like I'm betraying her memory because I loved Aly like a sister. But I love Ellie, too. And maybe it's because she's the same soul that I feel that connection to her."

He sat back. "I know what you mean. It's fucking weird because sometimes I feel like I'm betraying Aly by loving Ellie. Other times I feel like I'm betraying Ellie for still grieving for Aly."

"But she's the same soul. You can't betray her... with her. Shit! Does that even make sense?"

"No. But none of this fucking makes sense. And I don't care. I love Ellie, whether she's Aly or not." He let out another heavy sigh. "And so I'll go to that fucking villa even though I suspect it might just kill me." Aden pointed at her. "And no, I'm not being a drama queen, so fuck off."

Keeley snorted, on the verge of calling him that again, but then she bit her lip and turned serious. "I want to say something else, but I don't want your head to explode."

He waved his hand dismissively. "Just say it."

A worried frown creased her brow, knowing this wouldn't go over well. At all.

"I think everything that happened was supposed to."

"What the fuck, Keeley!"

Aden's snarl caused Iain to jump and cry.

Keeley picked him up and cradled him to her chest again. "Thanks a lot, asshole."

"Why am I the asshole? You're the one who just said I was supposed to have killed my wife on my wedding night. What the fuck, Keeley?"

"I know how that sounds," she said, gently rocking Iain and kissing his forehead. "But something in my heart tells me Ellie is supposed to be here with us. Who she is. Right here. Right now, like this. Like she was fated to come to us exactly in the way she did to heal you. Maybe all of us."

"I wouldn't need fucking healing if I hadn't killed my wife." Running his fingers through his hair, Aden tugged at the strands. "Jesus Keeley, you sound more like Sophie every damn day."

"Thank you. I take that as a compliment."

"I didn't mean it as one."

Aden eyed Iain warily as Keeley's gentle bouncing quieted him.

"So, you're really going to try to steal Ellie from Sophie?" He asked once Iain settled down.

"Yup. And I feel no remorse about it. Ellie is gifted. Mom knows it too. How could I not steal her for BloodStone?"

"How is that supposed to work? The board is bound to hear about it eventually."

"No idea, but I'll figure it out."

"Don't put her in harm's way, Keeley."

Aden's warning was threatening and ominous, but Keeley wasn't surprised by his tone. Any perceived threat to Ellie's safety triggered that response in him.

"I'll protect her with my life, Aden."

He nodded, but his eyes still showed his hesitation.

"Thank you for not making her wear teal."

"If she wants to come work with me, I'll figure out how she can wear regular clothes. It's a shame, though, because teal really complements her skin tone. It's a beautiful color on her."

"She's beautiful in everything she wears."

A smile touched Keeley's lips. She missed this side of Aden, had for centuries, and it made her heart swell with love for him.

"I told her about the vaults," Aden said quietly.

Keeley's eyes went wide. "Oh, shit. How did she take it?"

"I made her cry."

Keeley expected that. Ellie rarely cried, but she had a tender heart, especially for Aden.

"I also told her she isn't going to the capital. She wasn't happy."

Iain's slow, soft breath tickled her neck. He was asleep again.

"Why don't you want her to go?"

"I don't want her anywhere near Matthais ever again."

"Forever is a long time to keep them from crossing paths."

A flash of anger crossed Aden's face. "He took her once. I don't trust him not to do it again. He's too fucking creepy about her."

"He'd never dare take her." Keeley shifted Iain to her other shoulder.

"He did once."

"But she wasn't yours then."

"She was always ours. He stole her and her father right out from under our noses. That's an act of treason."

"So what are you going to do?" Keeley swung her legs to one side of the chaise lounge. It was time to put Iain down for a few hours before his next feeding. "How are you going to be around him without—"

"Tearing his fucking head off?" Aden finished for her.

"Yeah, that. Diplomacy isn't exactly your strong suit."

"Fuck diplomacy. Let Aurick do that. But I'm losing my patience. I want restitution, and he's dragging his feet. And I have no idea why."

"I'm sure he has his reasons."

"Well, he better fucking hurry up, or I'll do it myself."

"Don't do anything rash, Aden. You can't protect Ellie if you get your ass thrown in the vaults again. Or worse, executed."

"Now, who's being the drama queen?"

She looked at him with a resigned shake of her head. Her brother was his own worst enemy sometimes.

"I have to get this little guy to bed." Shifting Iain to one arm, she offered her other hand to Aden for support as she stood. "Thanks for sitting with me. I miss spending time with my grouchy brother."

"I miss you too. When you're not being a pain in my ass."

Keeley sighed as she looked down into Iain's sleeping face. "He looks so much like Ryan. I can't help but fall in love every time I look at him."

"Have you ditched the incubator yet?"

His habit of using derogatory nicknames was getting old.

"Yes. She was his wet nurse for the first six weeks, but she's gone back to her village, and we have a new one."

"And how do you feel about that?"

"More determined than ever to find a way for female vampires to conceive."

"That's not what I meant, but okay."

Keeley knew what he meant, but she wasn't about to admit to her relief that the surrogate was gone.

"If we can make vampire sperm viable, then enabling female vampires to carry and give birth should also be possible."

"If anyone can do it, it's you, Keel."

"And maybe Ellie too." Keeley walked closer to him. "Can you just imagine a baby girl with Ellie's eyes?"

"Put your spawn to bed, Keeley. And fuck the hell off."

She leaned down, grinning, and kissed the top of his head. He jerked away but remained seated.

"Night, baby brother."

Ellie

"A den!"

Ellie's vision blurred, her back arching off the bed as her orgasm slammed into her. Her thighs clenched around his head, fingers tangling in his hair, as she yanked on the short strands. But that didn't deter him. He kept lapping at her, relentlessly teasing her sensitive, throbbing clit.

Her grip on Aden's hair loosened, and she rubbed her fingertips over his scalp in apology. Not that her tugging hurt him, but she still felt bad for almost tearing his hair out.

Ellie's hips bucked as her thighs relaxed, quivering around his head. Aden continued to lap at her with a hunger that never seemed to abate until she couldn't take any more and pushed his head away.

The man's tongue should be illegal.

"Aden, I can't," she panted and felt him smile against her, pressing one last kiss to the tender flesh of her inner thigh before lifting his head. His smug smirk, slick with her arousal, stretched so wide his eyes crinkled at the corners.

"That was six." Resting his chin on her pelvic bone, he took one more shot at her by brushing his fingers over her, causing her hips to jerk again. "A personal best, I think. In this body, at least."

Ellie chuckled at his reference to her past life and the time he'd spent with his head buried between Aly's thighs when they were teenagers, relieved he could now speak about it without it tearing him apart.

"And just think, a few days ago, you were afraid of being that close to my femoral artery."

Aden lowered his head and pressed a kiss over the spot where the life-sustaining blood vessel lay beneath her skin.

"It's not without its temptations, Ellie. Don't take it for granted because my self-control only goes so far."

She caressed his damp cheek and bit her lip. He was offering her the perfect opening.

"Aden, I need to tell you something."

He pushed himself to his knees in the space between her thighs. His erection stood tall and proud, almost as if reaching out to her. Unable to resist, she licked her lips, a faint taste of anticipation on her tongue.

"Right now? Really?" He asked with a scowl, pulling her attention back to his face. "I hate when you say shit like that after I've made you come, but I haven't yet."

"Why?" she laughed.

"Because it usually means whatever you have to say is going to make me lose my hard-on."

"How often do you ever lose your erection?"

"Every time you say something like that to me."

She looked down between them. He was already deflating. "Well, maybe we should let you finish before we talk."

He moved away from her and dropped his feet over the side of the bed, reaching down to grab his boxer briefs and sliding them up his legs.

"Do I need a glass of whiskey for this?"

She pushed on her hands to sit up. "Not if you want to kiss me when we're done."

"We have to find something you can stand the taste of because you make me want to drink too fucking often." He took a deep breath and exhaled slowly. "Alright, let's do this. But if this isn't worth losing my hard-on for, I'm gonna be pissed."

He sat on the edge of the bed and looked over at her.

"Do you want me to put on my robe?"

His scowl twisted into a smirk, the corners of his mouth twitching upwards, but his eyes remained guarded. "No. I can at least enjoy the view while you're tormenting me."

He was acting like a sulky child, and Ellie worried he was going to get much worse before they were through. She scooted closer to him.

His curious gaze held hers. Though annoyed, he gave her his undivided attention. She brushed her fingers against his cheek.

"I love you, Aden."

"Oh, fuck, this is going to be bad, isn't it?"

She dropped her hand. "Stop being so dramatic."

"Then just spit it out, Ellie."

She braced herself for his reaction, closing her eyes as she blurted out the words.

"While we're out west for Christmas, I want you to bite me."

"What?" He surged to his feet, his eyes filling with shock. "Are you out of your fucking mind?"

"Just hear me out."

He paced next to the bed, tugging at his already messy hair.

"Are you fucking kidding me, Ellie? You're throwing a lot of shit at me in one go here. First, you want me to face my biggest fucking regret, and now you want to tempt me into a repeat performance in the same place I killed you?"

"Aden."

He turned to her. Despite the harsh tone of his voice, there was no anger in his eyes, just confusion. And fear.

She stood and grabbed her robe from the floor where it dropped when he attacked her after her shower.

"I thought this was what you wanted."

"Of course, I want this. I want to drink from you so badly my mouth waters virtually nonstop."

She pulled her robe tighter, the cool silk offering a shield against the storm brewing within him.

"Then why are you acting like this? I'm telling you I'm ready for you to bite me again, and you act like it's the worst thing in the world."

"Because you're not just asking me to bite you, Ellie, which, as much as I want it, still scares the fucking hell out of me. You're asking me to do it in the place I drained you."

He turned away from her and walked out of the bedroom to the bar in the living room. She followed him and sighed as he gulped down not one or two, but three drinks.

"Fuck! When you want someone to confront their fucking demons, you don't do it half-assed. Do you have any idea what this is going to do to me?"

"Yes."

She did. And part of her hated herself for asking. But she needed this as much as she needed to go back to that room.

Aden spun around and faced her. "Then why do you want to do this? If you're ready to share your blood with me, I'll take it. I'll take you up on it in a heartbeat. Right now. Tonight. But don't ask me to do it there. I'll go with you, and I'll go in that room again, but I don't know if I can do what you're asking. I'll give you anything, but, please, I'm begging you... don't ask me for this."

The sheer terror in his eyes was so foreign it tore at her heart. Despite his three-century-old, formidable vampire exterior, inside he remained a twenty-five-year-old new vampire tormented by the most horrific act of his life. He'd never gotten over it, even though they found each other again. And she finally understood he never would, regardless of what they did or how much time passed. It would be a part of him for eternity, and Ellie's heart broke for him all over again.

"I'm not trying to hurt you, Aden."

"Then how can you ask me for this? What the fuck are you thinking?"

She stepped closer and pressed her hand against the warm skin of his bare chest. He shuddered beneath her fingertips. Before she gave up her hope of them doing this, she had to tell him the truth.

"I love you, and I want to share my blood with you. And yes, I'm asking you to do it in that room. Because then nothing will be left. We can leave the past behind us. I want eternity with you, Aden. But I don't want to spend it constantly trying to outrun what happened. It's something neither of us will ever forget, but it shouldn't overshadow our future. If you're not ready and you can't do it there, then we won't, but please think about it. I'd never want to hurt you or ask you to hurt yourself for my sake. That would break my heart."

"Did you just say you want eternity with me?"

A soft chuckle escaped her lips at his shocked expression. "Yes, you knuckle-head. Of course, that's what I want."

"But you never told me that before right now."

The adorable mixture of bewilderment, a touch of fear, and barely concealed longing on his face was so endearing it made her heart melt.

"How could you even doubt it?" Her voice was gentle.

His throat bobbed as he swallowed. "You know what it means."

She nodded, saying the words she wouldn't be able to take back. "Yes. I have to become either a half-breed or a vampire. Or a half-breed first and then a vampire. I don't know which one I want, Aden. And I'm not ready for it yet, but, sweetheart, of course, I'll do whatever it takes to be with you forever."

He stumbled, and she held her hand out to him, alarmed.

"Are you okay?"

"I think my brain just shut down."

A grin pulled at her lips. "That's me, not you."

"Do you really mean it?" His voice, full of hope, made him sound centuries younger than his actual age.

She opened her robe and pressed her naked body against him, reaching up to cup his face in her hands. "With everything I am."

He gripped her tight, lowering his head, burying his face in her neck. Ellie wrapped her arms around his waist and hugged him, feeling him harden, pressing into her belly as she brushed a kiss to the side of his throat. Her breath ghosted over his skin as she reached between them, sliding her hand down the front of his boxer briefs.

"Feels like your hard-on is back," she murmured.

He pulled away, and she hid her surprise behind a neutral expression. He never pulled away when she touched him like that, but she saw the lingering reluctance in his eyes, a simmering intensity that betrayed his inner struggle.

"I need to think about this, Ellie," he said, his brow furrowed.

"That's my line," she teased even as she nodded. "I can live with that."

Some of the tension eased from his shoulders.

"Now come on, stud, take me back to bed and lose yourself in me."

His eyes shifted, changing from bright blue to almost black in an instant, and she sucked in a soft breath.

God, sometimes she felt like he could make her orgasm from just that look.

He licked his lips, revealing what he was thinking without a word.

"Uh-uh." She shook her head as she led him back to the bedroom, walking backward until her legs hit the mattress. There was no way her abused clit could take any more. "You've spent enough time with your head between my thighs today. It's time you take some of your own pleasure."

"Don't you know how much pleasure I derive from being there? I'd spend half my life there, with the other half buried inside you, if you let me."

Ellie gulped, the heat of his words igniting a fire within her. "But then you'd have no time to do your job protecting the world."

"Fuck my job. And fuck the world."

She inhaled a sharp breath before the tinkle of a laugh escaped. His words, raw and honest, didn't surprise her. She knew he'd do anything for her, even if it meant sacrificing everything. The exhilarating yet terrifying weight of that fact pressed down on her, making her heart pound in her chest.

She dropped her robe and lay back on the bed, looking up at him as she spread her arms and legs, her thighs falling open.

His nostrils flared, and he shoved his boxers down.

Ellie swept her eyes over him, gasping at how hard and ready he was for her.

"You didn't lose your erection for long."

"Ellie, I'm a walking hard-on for you. All the time."

"Aww, honey, you say the sweetest things sometimes." Her lips curved into a sultry smile, a slow, deliberate movement as she ran her tongue across them, the heat rising in her eyes. "Now come to me."

He crawled over her, moving up her body until he settled on top of her. She tilted her hips and moaned as he slipped inside her with one smooth, deep thrust, stretching her almost to the point of pain.

He held her eyes with his, and he leaned in, his lips finding hers, his tongue gently parting them. She moaned again, tasting a mixture of herself and the whiskey, and a fresh jolt of arousal speared through her.

He began moving, pumping, thrusting in long, deep strokes as Ellie wrapped her arms and legs around him. She clung to him, her fingers tracing down the warm skin of his back, relishing the sensation of his thick cock filling her. Everything else faded into a hazy blur, leaving only the feeling of him.

Aden pulled his mouth away, but only slightly, their lips still touching. When he exhaled, she inhaled, breathing him in.

Ellie held his gaze, rocking with him until her eyes fluttered closed and her body convulsed with gentle tremors that rippled through her. He slid his mouth over her cheek and down her neck. He pressed his lips to her scar before sliding them up to her ear.

"I'll give you anything you ask of me."

Ellie

"I'm going to the capital with you, Aden."

Ellie followed him out of the bathroom, the warmth of her shower still clinging to her skin as she tied her robe around her body. He walked into the closet and dropped the towel from his waist, grabbing a pair of boxer briefs.

"No."

She leaned against the doorframe, biting her tongue to stop herself from saying something she'd regret.

Despite their strained discussion before bed, she hoped he'd be in a better mood when he woke, especially after the intensity of their lovemaking once she'd lured him back to bed. And he was in the shower, but now he was being stubborn and unyielding, and it made her want to scream.

She hadn't planned to bring up the capital again until after Christmas, giving him time to adjust to everything else. But the offhand comment he made as he was brushing his teeth about her traveling back to Réimse Shíochánta with Keeley while the rest of them traveled to the Arcipelago forced her to respond.

"I want to see my dad and Carrie. It's been almost a year."

Aden slid his black pants up his legs. "Ellie, I said no."

She exhaled a long breath, crossing her arms over her chest. Why did she always have to be the reasonable one?

"Please, Aden. I miss them both so much. They're the only family I have."

The hurt look on his face made her cringe.

"That didn't come out right," she sighed, stepping into the closet with him. "You're my family. Your family is my family. But so are they. When I came here, I thought I'd never see them again. I didn't even know if I'd survive living here with you. I want them to know that even though I miss them, I'm happy here."

"Ellie, it's not safe for you to go back to the capital."

She walked to her dresser and selected a matching green lace bra and panty set. Sliding the panties up under her robe, she turned to face him.

"Why not?"

"Because Matthais stole you once." He grabbed a black shirt, shrugging it on. "I won't give him the opportunity to do it again."

His words, laced with tension, made her soften. "But I'll be with you. I'm safe with you."

"I won't always be around. I have a busy schedule of meetings and other events."

"You mean the games and slave auctions?"

Annoyance sparked in his eyes. "Ellie, don't start, okay? I'll figure out a way to skip the games, but I'll still need to attend at least one auction."

With a sigh, she shed her robe and slid her bra up her arms, fastening the clasp in the back. The heat of Aden's stare felt like a physical touch as she slipped into a navy blue sheath dress.

"Are you wearing that to BloodStone?"

She looked down at herself. "Yes. Why? What's wrong with it?"

"It's a little fucking short. I thought Keeley said to wear a thrall uniform."

"She did but then changed her mind. She gave me this last night and said to wear it."

"Fucking figures." Aden grabbed his socks and shoes and strode out of the closet.

Ellie followed, carrying her low heels. She didn't like dresses and heels, preferring pants and flats, but Keeley was the boss.

"Aden, I want to see my dad and Carrie. And I want to tell him about going back to our house."

He tied his shoes and then stood. "Ellie, you can't tell them about Matthais."

"Why not? I trust them implicitly."

"He's your father's sire."

She braced her hand on the back of the chair as she slipped on her heels. "But he's my dad. He'd never do anything to put me in danger. He probably thinks Aurick let him take us, and he needs to know he didn't."

"Why the fuck does it matter if he knows?"

"It matters to me. I don't want him to think you and your family are like Matthais."

"Ellie, I don't want you near the capital ever again."

"Aden, how much do I ask you for?"

He stepped around the coffee table, his posture rigid. "You mean besides asking me if our guards can terrorize and hunt you to teach you self-defense? Or how about asking me to go back to Bíonn súil le muir?" His voice grew louder with each sentence. "Or what about asking me to drink from you again in the room where I killed you?"

"Aden."

He stormed across the room. "Damn it, Ellie." He put his fist through the wall. "Fuck," he roared, shaking his hand.

"Let me see," she murmured, approaching him. He lifted his hand to her.

With gentle fingers, she traced the outline of his hand. He shuddered under her soft touch but flinched when she reached his knuckles.

"Sorry," she said, then, "Please, Aden?"

He yanked his hand away from her.

"Ellie, I said no! I've given all I'm capable of giving you right now. For once, will you think of my feelings first? For once, will you let your sense of self-preservation override your fucking need to get your way?"

He turned and strode toward the door. For the second time in three days, his angry words echoed throughout their rooms as he stormed away.

The door slid open before he reached it, and Keeley stepped in.

"Hey, I'm here to steal your girl," she said with a smile.

"Yeah, you and every other fucking vampire on the planet!" He snarled as he pushed past her.

Ellie

Ellie watched Aden storm out, and her lip trembled. He was right. Her sense of self-preservation had always been a little fluid. Even when she lived in constant fear in Matthais' house.

But she thought of Aden's feelings first. Or tried to. Maybe she was so used to him agreeing to her wishes that she was taking him for granted. Perhaps she was asking too much, not considering the toll it would take on him or the way it might break him down.

A deep ache pulsed in her chest, urging her to follow him. But when he was like this, it was best to leave him alone for a while.

"What the hell was that about?" Keeley asked as she walked closer. "Okay, maybe joking about stealing you may have been in poor taste, but that's a bit of an overreaction. Even for him. It's not about Christmas, is it? I talked to him the other night, and he was still cranky about it, but not mad like that."

Stepping over to the mirror, Ellie checked her hair.

"No. It wasn't about Christmas. I'm sorry he yelled at you."

"Please. I'm used to it." She started for the door. "Come on, let's walk. We have to take the warp port from my living room to get to the BloodStone labs. You can fill me in on the way."

"Do I need a coat?" Ellie asked as she followed.

"No, we're not going outside. We'll go straight to the BloodStone lobby. That dress looks fabulous on you, by the way. I knew it would."

"Thanks, but are you sure I shouldn't wear my thrall uniform?"

"No. Screw that. You'll be in the labs with Hannah most of the day. No one will see you. We'll get you a lab coat when we get there," Keeley said as they exited the room.

Drake, who was standing in the hallway, fell into step behind them.

"Drake, you don't need to come with me," Ellie said as she looked at Keeley for confirmation.

"Oh, yes, I do," he replied. "Aden made it clear. I go where you go."

"Keeley?"

"I'm not contradicting that order. Not today. Besides, Mordechai will be with us, too."

Ellie huffed but decided not to argue. She'd done enough of that for one day.

Keeley turned toward Drake as they reached the courtyard. "Take the warp port from the foyer to the lobby of the BloodStone headquarters downtown. Then take the one from the executive level to the lobby at the labs. We'll meet you in the atrium."

"Got it," he replied before breaking off to head toward the east wing of the compound.

"Why isn't he using the warp port we are?"

"Because it's my private one. Even Mordechai doesn't use my personal one unless it's an emergency. He'll be waiting in the atrium for us, too."

As they entered the hallway to Keeley and Ryan's wing, Ellie scanned the art on the walls. She'd been studying more about it because it was such an important part of Aden's life, and he once told her that the artwork could help her identify the wings in the compound. While she preferred the figurative art that Aden loved so much, she also understood Keeley's preference for abstract pieces. She liked the feeling of controlled chaos it often invoked.

"So, should I come to your rooms every night to take the warp port to the labs?"

"Nah. If you decide this is what you want, I'll get the one outside your suite programmed to get you there. I usually go straight into my office, but today we'll go to the lobby so I can show you around. Now, do you want to tell me why Aden's head was about to pop off back there?"

"He really doesn't want me to go to the capital."

A soft murmur of understanding escaped Keeley's lips. "To be honest, I'm glad not to be going. I despise the annual council gathering. I missed it last year because of the AEON prep, so I haven't been in two years, but I'd much rather stay back with you and my boys."

"But I want to go, Keeley," Ellie said, biting back her frustration.

Aden's sister offered her a sympathetic look. "Hey, I don't blame you. And I think he should let you go, but you know Aden."

"I get he's angry about Master Matthais, and he's worried about me being there, but I have no idea what's got him so worked up."

Keeley's door slid open as they approached the suite.

"He flips out about the most ridiculous things sometimes, but the steam coming out of his ears was a little much."

"He's upset with me about a few things. I've been a little inconsiderate lately, but that has nothing to do with me going to see my dad and Carrie."

Keeley snorted. "Aden's middle name is inconsiderate."

"No, it isn't," Ellie said, a protective edge to her voice. "He's usually very considerate of me. But I ask him for a lot."

"As his girlfriend, you have every right to. What good are men who won't give us what we want?"

Keeley's attempt at humor failed to lessen her guilt over upsetting Aden, the weight of it remaining heavy in her chest.

"All we do is fight. About everything lately. Especially since I asked him—" Ellie caught herself before she said too much.

They stepped into the warp port in the corner, but Keeley held her hand over the keypad. "Since you asked him what?"

Ellie bit her lip. Damn. Why couldn't she keep her mouth shut?

"Since you asked him to go to the villa?"

"No."

"Take you to the capital?"

"No."

Keeley crossed her arms. "We're not going anywhere until you spill. Come on, out with it."

Ellie cringed. "I asked him to bite me when we're at the villa."

"Oh, shit." Keeley let out a long breath.

"Yeah."

"I've got to say, Ellie, you've got bigger balls than half the men I know. You don't do anything half-assed, do you?"

"Aden said the same thing." She shrugged, a wry smile curving on her lips. "Well, not the balls thing, but the half-assed thing."

"I'm not surprised." Keeley laughed and held her gaze. "Look, we need to drop this for now because it's time to focus on BloodStone, but let me just say one thing."

Ellie braced herself for Keeley to call her selfish and awful.

"I know I don't need to tell you this... Aden is complicated. But he's a big boy. A brutally broken boy inside the body of a fierce three-century-old vampire. He's got a lot of baggage, and he always will, but he can handle anything you throw at him. Loving him will never be easy, Ellie. And he'll always overreact because that's his personality. He'll try your patience every damn day, but loving him will be worth every tantrum, explosion, and oblivious, insensitive thing he does. No matter how much of a dick he is sometimes, when he loves, it's unconditional. It's intense, and I don't envy you being on the receiving end of that, but his love for you will make it all worth it."

Despite how moved she was by Keeley's words, she arched her eyebrow, a smirk playing on her lips. "That was one thing?"

Keeley snorted. "Yeah. Like I said... complicated."

"Thanks, Keeley. I was afraid you were going to call me an insensitive bitch."

"I don't know if you could be a bitch if you tried, Ellie. I love my brother, but I know what a pain in the ass he can be. If there's anyone on the planet who can handle him, it's you." Keeley swiped her hand over the keypad, entering the coordinates for the labs.

"Now come on, let's ditch the complicated brother stuff and dive into the awesome world of BloodStone!"

Ellie

Ellie spun slowly, her gaze following the elegant curves of the octagonal glass roof above the atrium. Diffused light from the moon and stars shining through the clear panels created a soft, twinkling effect against the night sky.

"Wow," she murmured, her mouth gaping open.

"I know, right?" Keeley said from beside her.

"It's magnificent."

"My dad designed it himself."

In the center of the gleaming white marble floor, a twenty-foot-tall brushed stainless steel abstract sculpture towered over them. A spiral staircase off to the right led to a balcony that encircled the entire space.

Hallways branched off the lobby in every direction, emphasizing the building's immense size. The atrium buzzed with activity as vampires and half-breeds went about their work.

Drake and Mordechai walked up.

"Oh, good. Let's head upstairs, and I'll show you where the real magic happens," Keeley said as she guided Ellie toward the stairs.

Unsure whether to act like a thrall or an employee, Ellie hesitated.

"Should I walk behind you?"

"Hell no! Don't worry about that here. We'll grab that lab coat for you when we get to Hannah's office, and you'll blend in just fine."

When they reached the landing at the top of the stairs, Keeley led them to the right and down a long hall. Drake and Mordechai followed a few steps behind.

"This is the main research wing. All the primary labs are located in this wing. My office is on the top floor, but Hannah's office and labs—she has several going all the time—are in the next hallway."

The LED lights above cast a soft sheen on the flooring, creating twin shadows ahead of them as they moved deeper into the building. At the end of the hall, they reached a door, and after a series of biometric scans on Keeley's face and fingers, it opened, and they entered another corridor.

Evenly spaced metal doors, marked with security clearances, broke up the stark white wall on the left.

"Those are the high containment labs, where some of the more delicate experiments are run. Those labs have very limited access."

On the right, floor-to-ceiling windows revealed scientists and lab techs in white coats working at rows of long tables covered in scientific equipment.

Keeley paused to wave at a woman who looked up from what Ellie knew was a microscope, returning the gesture with a gloved hand.

"That's Miranda. You'll meet her. She's almost as brilliant as Hannah."

Ellie's gaze darted around, absorbing everything she could. "It's a little overwhelming," she said with a small smile.

"It can be at first. But you'll figure it out. What I like about the hallways in this wing is the contrast between the two sides—one shrouded in necessary secrecy, while the other proudly displays the methodical magic of science."

"That was poetic," Ellie said with a gentle nudge of her elbow to Keeley's side.

"That's me. Where poetry meets science," Keeley said, drawing a chuckle out of Ellie and the two guards as they came to a stop in front of a door just shy of the end of the hallway.

After another series of biometric scans, the door slid open.

"You two can take a load off." Keeley waved Drake and Mordechai away as the door slid shut.

"Do they have to stand outside there the entire time we're in here? That seems kind of silly, considering how locked down this place is."

"No. The room across the hall has couches and chairs and a TV, as well as monitors to keep watch on who comes and goes. They'll hang there until we leave."

"Well, it's about freaking time someone brought you to meet me," a tall, beautiful woman with warm golden skin said as she walked towards them.

Her sleek black hair framed her face and fell past her shoulders in a perfectly straight line. With a heart-shaped face, high cheekbones, and expressive almond-shaped eyes, she was the most exotic woman Ellie had ever seen.

She stopped in front of Ellie, her eyes traveling slowly up and down, taking in her appearance with an intense curiosity, a slight smile playing on her lips.

"Damn girl, Sophie and Keeley weren't exaggerating when they said you were a knockout. No wonder you've got Aden all tied up in knots."

A blush crept up Ellie's cheeks as Keeley's laugh echoed beside her.

"Don't mind Hannah," Keeley said. "She has zero filter. She's as bad as Aden."

"I don't, and I am," Hannah agreed with a shrug. "Do you remember me at all?"

Ellie shot Keeley a nervous glance.

"Yeah, she knows who you are. She was the second person my mom told after me."

Ellie looked back at Hannah. "I remember meeting you on our wedding day."

"Well, shit. Leave it to me to stick my foot in it on day one. But who knew Sophie's crazy idea about you one day being reborn wasn't so insane after all? Welcome back!"

"Uh... thanks, I think."

"Okay, Hannah, stop tormenting her. She's here to learn. Let's show her what we do."

She threw her arm around Ellie's shoulders and led her toward the back of the lab. "You ready to have your mind blown, little girl?"

Ellie's head throbbed as she tried to absorb everything Hannah and Keeley had thrown at her over the past two hours. The holograms floating around the lab cast a faint glow across their faces as charts, diagrams, and molecular structures rotated slowly in the air.

"So, that covers the overview," Hannah said, closing one set of holograms with a swipe of her finger.

Grateful for the pause, Ellie rubbed her temples. She'd read about Blood-Stone's history in the books Keeley gave her, but nothing had prepared her for the complexity of their current research. The company's roster of existing drugs, those under development, and other research projects created a dizzying web of information that overwhelmed even her brilliant mind.

She glanced at the 3D model of the female reproductive system hovering to her left. "So, female vampires have viable eggs that drop into their uterus like humans?"

"They do." Hannah leaned back against the counter and crossed her ankles, her casual posture contrasting with the sophisticated technology surrounding them.

"So why can't they get pregnant?"

"The fundamental problem is metabolic stasis," Hannah replied. "Or more specifically, the cellular regeneration process that inhibits typical pregnancy-related physiological changes. If we can overcome that stasis, temporary alterations to a vampire's unique physiology may be possible."

"What do you mean by temporary alterations?"

Keeley walked over and sat beside Ellie as she scrolled through data on her tablet. "We need to make the female vampire's body more hospitable to the fetus," she said, holding it out to Ellie. The tablet showed microscopic images of vampire uterine tissue. "We've run thousands of experiments, but none have successfully created a contained pseudo-living uterine environment that suppresses vampiric reproductive stasis."

"What about?" Ellie paused, bit her lip as she studied the diagrams before gesturing toward one of the holograms. "May I?"

Hannah nodded, and Ellie stood up, moving toward the hologram. With hesitant fingers, she touched it, surprisingly feeling resistance as the tactile feedback technology responded to her touch. The system recognized her gestures as she scrolled through several charts and expanded one of the diagrams.

"I don't understand most of what I'm seeing, but—" She paused again, manipulating the floating model to show the blood supply to the uterus.

"But what?" Hannah urged, moving closer.

"Give her a minute," Keeley said. "We've been studying this for centuries, and she's only had a couple of hours."

Ellie zoomed out on the model, then brought up a comparison chart showing metabolic rates between humans and vampires. She tilted her head as she put her thoughts together.

"So you basically need a human body environment, but inside a vampire?"

"Yes," Keeley said. "I knew you'd get it."

Ellie gave her a small smile. "We'll more than half the books you had me read the last few weeks were about female reproductive health and regenerative stem cell biology."

"How many of the books Keeley gave you did you read?"

"All of them."

Hannah snorted out a laugh. "You weren't kidding about her, were you?"

Keeley shrugged. "There's a reason my dad approved of having her here. She's smarter than all of us combined."

"Hey, I take offense to that. No offense to you, Ellie."

"None taken," Ellie said, her attention still focused on the diagrams. "So, have you ever been able to create an artificial womb in a lab? Grow the baby outside the vampire's body?"

"Yes," Hannah replied. "Back before the Great Vampire Wars, there were a handful of successful human births in a lab. But the human scientists started dabbling with gene editing, trying to create the 'perfect' child, and things went haywire. So, vampire scientists stepped in, and that's how the half-breed breeding program was launched."

"None of the books you gave me mentioned anything about the breeding pro-gram. I don't know how that works. I only know how Master Matthais changed my dad. He almost drained him, then fed him his blood."

"You don't have to call Matthais master anymore. He isn't your master," Keeley said.

"But he's a vampire. All vampires are humans' masters."

"Ellie—"

"Keeley, you can educate her about her station later," Hannah said, cutting her off with a wave of her hand before turning back to Ellie. "To answer your ques-tion, for the breeding program, we used the artificial womb technology for the half-breeds and performed our own gene editing using vampire blood, creating the largest and strongest male specimens. We cherry-picked all their physical and mental traits, ensuring their physical and mental dominance. They're bred to be soldiers and warriors, born and raised in half the time it takes a human to mature."

"But why? What was the purpose of creating them in the first place?"

"To win the Great Vampire Wars. But that's a story for another time. It has nothing to do with science and everything to do with power and world domina-tion."

Ellie frowned, wanting to ask more, but Hannah just moved on.

"So, back to overcoming vampiric reproductive stasis. Our thought process has always been to create a drug, similar to how LIBER restores vampire sperm motility. A combination of synthetic hormones and modified stem cells that would essentially trick a vampire's body into supporting life."

"But that's where we get stuck," Keeley jumped in. "The issue has never been about making pregnancy possible. We've done that. The challenge is how to sustain it."

"Vampires' bodies naturally reject rapid cell division," Hannah said. "And our static immune system, the source of our immunity and immortality, typically attacks developing tissue. Thus, attacking the fetus. It views it as an invader and destroys it. Also, vampires' slower circulatory systems prevent an adequate blood supply to the fetus, which is needed to maintain an optimal temperature for growth. So, as you so eloquently put it, we need a human body environment inside a vampire. Despite centuries of testing, we haven't been able to achieve that yet."

A weary sigh escaped Keeley's lips. "We've been researching this for so long, we can no longer see the forest through the trees. We could use a fresh set of eyes. Maybe you'll see something we're missing."

Ellie nibbled on her bottom lip, her gaze lingering on the hologram, her mind already racing with possibilities. "I'll have to study this a lot more before I can even begin to form an opinion."

"That's what you're here to do, if that's what you want. You'll work directly for Hannah and have access to all her data. Maybe your brain can see what we haven't been able to."

Ellie glanced around the lab. "I'll give it a try."

"I told you she'd want to do it." Hannah elbowed Keeley in the arm before she turned to Ellie. "Girl, we have so much to teach you. Are you ready to change the world with us?" A grin spread across Hannah's face.

With a smile of her own, Ellie nodded, the thrill of the challenge simply too tempting to resist.

"Let's do it."

Aden

"**F**ucking start them again, Roderick!"

Aden stood on the edge of the training field watching Roderick put the newest recruits through their paces, their movements casting long shadows across the moonlit, snow-covered ground. The crisp winter air vibrated with the sounds of swords clashing and the exertion of their practice. Fresh snow fell, coating their dark uniforms with specks of white that melted against their overheated bodies. Despite weeks of training, they showed little improvement.

"These fuckers are useless," Aden muttered with a scowl.

Kane stood beside him, his face equally annoyed. "When will the next batch of half-breeds be ready?"

"Two weeks. Roderick will start working them while we're in Arcipelago."

Genetically engineered as the strongest and fiercest warriors, half-breeds from the breeding program were raised by the VWC. Upon maturity, they were divided between each region's militaries and trained as soldiers.

"I hope they're better than this group," Kane said, shaking his head.

The tension in Aden's jaw had nothing to do with the incompetent recruits in front of him but with the constant replay of his fight with Ellie in his head. She wasn't wrong. She had every right to want to see her father and friend, but, as usual, he acted like an ass, using his anxiety about the trip to refuse her. His anger towards Matthais and frustration with Aurick were always simmering beneath the surface, and she was the one who bore the brunt of his frustration most of the time.

It was unfair to her, but she'd also been provoking him lately. The things she was asking of him weren't outwardly unreasonable, but fuck if she wasn't determined to make him face every one of his fucking demons all at once. He was just barely able to think of or hear Aly's name without losing his shit. You'd think she'd fucking give him time to adjust.

Beside him, Kane remained silent as Aden's internal monologue distracted him from the drills.

A hologram of Matthais appeared, and Aden growled under his breath. Holograms had an auto-accept feature, but fortunately, Matthais wasn't on his automatic acceptance list.

His jaw ticked as he swiped the hologram to accept the call. Matthais was seated behind the desk in his office.

"Aden." His smooth voice made Aden want to punch something.

"What can I do for you, Matthais? I'm a bit busy at the moment."

"Always one to get right to the point."

Aden remained silent, prompting him to continue.

"I need your assistance in Sever Sib-Ir. Anatoly has encountered some...complications that require support."

"What kind of complications?"

The hologram flickered, the weather interfering with the signal, as Matthais waved his hand dismissively. "A situation involving certain elements that could prove destabilizing if not handled properly."

Aden narrowed his eyes. "Is there a reason Andrei can't handle it? He's closer."

"Andrei is occupied with other matters. I would consider this a personal favor, but if you prefer, we can also call it me collecting on the debt you owe for biting Elliana."

Well, that was unexpected.

He assumed Matthais would leverage that debt for centuries, but clearing it would better protect Ellie. Aden had zero desire to do him any favors, but they both knew his request was anything but. As second in command of the world's military, Aden had a responsibility to heed the call for assistance from the commander generals in other regions.

"I planned a brief trip there next week," Aden said. "Can whatever he needs help with wait until then?"

"I'm afraid not. It should only take a few days. You'll be home well in time for the Christmas I know Sophie is planning."

The reminder made him want to delay his trip even longer to avoid going to the villa. But disappointing Ellie wasn't an option. It never was. Which meant she was fucking going to the capital with him, too.

He let out a sigh. "I'll leave tomorrow night."

"This matter is quite pressing." Matthais' tone cooled several degrees. "It would be best if you left tonight."

Aden ground his teeth, but he kept his voice neutral. "I'll be wheels up in an hour."

"Excellent," Matthais said, his lips stretching into a smile that didn't reach his eyes. "I look forward to seeing you at the gathering in two weeks."

The hologram closed, leaving Aden alone with Kane and a growing knot of unease in his gut. He'd have to leave before he had time to make things right with Ellie.

"Could that have been more cryptic?" Kane asked, a slight edge in his tone.

Aden grunted, irritated by the demand that he leave right away.

The snow fell harder now, obscuring the distant tree line, leaving him with an unsettling feeling of being watched. He turned away from the training field, his boots crunching in the packed snow as he headed to his SUV. He needed to prepare for his departure while also finding a way to apologize to Ellie.

Time and the universe, it seemed, were not on his side tonight.

Ellie

Ellie walked into the suite, bracing herself for another fight, yet also eager to share her night at BloodStone with Aden. Instead, she found Sophie and Vlad sitting on the sofa, reading and napping.

Sophie looked up and smiled. "Hi. I hope you don't mind that I waited in here for you."

"Of course not." Ellie sat, and Vlad stretched before leaping over to the chair to greet her. "But why are you here?" She looked around. "Where's Aden?"

"He had to leave for Sever Sib-Ir earlier than expected."

"Oh."

A thick wave of disappointment washed over her as she rubbed the cat under his chin. He responded with a purr and a headbutt.

"It was very last minute. He had to get on a plane right away, so he didn't have time to stop by BloodStone to see you. He asked me to tell you he'll see you at Bíonn súil le muir when he's done."

Ellie frowned. A quick hologram message would have been easy, but he was probably still angry at her.

"I'm sorry. What was that you said?" She asked as she shook her head.

"Bíonn súil le muir?" Sophie asked with a smile.

"Yeah. That's what Aden and Keeley called it. Is that the name of the west coast villa?"

"Yes. It's an old Irish proverb."

"I don't remember that. Is it Gaelic? What's the translation?"

"There is hope from the sea."

"What does the proverb mean?"

"That even in the darkest of times, there's always reason for hope."

"That's kind of ironic," Ellie said. "Considering what happened there."

"The irony is not lost on any of us, but you're living proof there's always reason for hope," Sophie said, smiling. "So, Keeley tells me you had a productive night."

Ellie nodded, meeting her gaze. "Yes."

"She and Hannah are both incredibly impressed with you."

"I think so. I'd really like to work with them."

Sophie folded her hands in her lap, letting out a soft sigh. "I guess I've lost you then."

A painful lump tightened in Ellie's throat. "Sophie—"

"It's okay, Ellie. I knew this day would come. It's clear you're destined for BloodStone. I'm very happy for you. You'll learn so much from Keeley and Hannah. But I'll miss spending time with you."

"I will too." Ellie shifted Vlad from her lap to the cushion next to her. "I asked to start after the new year so I can train whoever you pick to replace me."

"Oh, sweetheart, you don't need to do that."

"I want to. Please. I don't want to abandon you with no one to help. It also gives them time to come up with a plan to keep me inconspicuous and avoid attracting attention."

"They'll find a way. And thank you. I'll enjoy our last few weeks together."

"Me too."

Sophie rose from the sofa. "Well, I'll let you settle in for the day. You must be tired."

Ellie stood, her lower lip caught between her teeth. She wanted to hug Aden's mother, but she was hesitant to be physically affectionate with anyone but him. As Sophie walked past, Ellie embraced her.

"Thank you so much," she said against Sophie's shoulder.

Sophie squeezed her gently. "Oh, Ellie." A soft sniffle reached Ellie's ears. "I'm the one who should thank you, sweetheart. You brought my son back to life and completed my family."

Ellie held on, clinging to her longer than was necessary, relishing the first real maternal hug she'd had since age five. Even Sophie holding her after her past life confession felt different.

"Sorry," she said, her face flushing with embarrassment as she pulled away, her grip lingering even then. "I don't know where that came from."

Sophie blinked, and Ellie was sure she saw a glistening in her eyes.

"Hey, hugger here." Sophie pointed at herself. "So never apologize for that. I didn't want to crowd you, but anytime you need a hug, or even if you don't, I'm here."

Ellie laughed, her eyes stinging with emotion. "You might regret that."

Sophie rubbed her arm. "Never. Now, I think Vlad plans to stay with you today."

She looked over and saw him sprawled in her chair, fast asleep, with his feet in the air, mouth open, and whiskers twitching.

"I guess so."

"Okay, I'll see you at the hangar tomorrow night at six."

She nodded, and then Sophie left.

Ellie walked into the bedroom, suddenly exhausted, not even sure she was up to eating dinner. In the center of her pillow were two flowers—a long-stemmed red dahlia and a red honeysuckle bloom. Having worked in the greenhouse for almost a year, Ellie's love of flowers was no secret. And dahlias were her favorite.

She picked it up and buried her face in it. Dahlias produced little to no scent detectable to humans, though Aden told her that vampires could smell what he described as a clean, green scent, similar to cut grass. It was a smell Ellie faintly remembered from her childhood in her village.

She loved the flower for many reasons. She liked how the lush, intricately packed petals created a sense of order and symmetry. Also, depending on the kind, she liked how they ranged from rounded and overlapping to pointed and starlike, which were her favorite because they made them look both delicate and dangerous. But most of all, she loved that a single dahlia bloom could have hundreds of individual petals.

A small smile curved her lips. Sophie didn't leave these flowers. Aden did. He may not have reached out to her before he left, but he couldn't go away without assuring her she was on his mind.

The second flower was his favorite. Honeysuckle.

She brought it to her nose, breathing deep. He told her once that it reminded him of her natural scent. He described it as a mix of jasmine and honeysuckle—fresh and clean, floral and complex, mostly sweet but slightly spicy, with vanilla-like undertones.

To her, he smelled like a warm blend of vanilla and cinnamon. Could drinking his blood have changed her scent or at least mingled their unique scents into one?

The two flowers, together, represented eternal love, devotion, and fiery passion. Red dahlias also symbolized inner strength, even in dark times, to persevere and overcome.

A wave of love, so intense and powerful it stole her breath, washed over Ellie, forcing her to sit, the ache of missing him already settling deep within her chest.

Aden

Aden stepped off the plane inside the hangar in Severograd, the capital of Sever Sib-Ir. He was fucking pissed he had to travel here early, taking him away from Ellie.

While Aden's search for information about unregistered rogues entering Réimse Shíochánta was no secret, he tried to downplay his planned visit as a casual inquiry. But something wasn't right with this urgent need for assistance coinciding with his trip next week. Matthais calling in his favor and releasing the debt he owed for Ellie only strengthened his suspicions.

But here he was, in the cold, desolate tundra that was the capital of Sever Sib-Ir, freezing his ass off, thousands of miles away from her, when all he wanted was to bury himself inside her body and beg her to forgive him for being an asshole.

Again.

This better be worth it because if he left her without making things right, heads were going to fucking roll.

Kane stepped up beside him. "I heard from Drake. He just dropped Ellie at your suite. Apparently, she blew your sister's and Hannah's minds, and they've officially poached her from Sophie."

"I knew that was going to happen." Pride swelled in Aden's chest. Now he was even more pissed because he wasn't there when she got home, even though hearing the details of it would've probably made his eyes cross.

"Sophie's going to be bummed out," Kane said with a knowing look. "You know what that means."

Yes. His mother was losing yet another daughter to BloodStone, so that meant she would throw herself into renovating one of their compounds, her usual coping mechanism when she was upset.

"Where the fuck is Anatoly? Why isn't he here to meet us?"

"Hey, man." Aden turned at the sound of Andrei's voice. "I'm the welcome brigade."

What the fuck was he doing here?

"Anatoly is meeting with Yuri, so he asked me to pick you up. Come on. It's fucking cold out here."

They exited the hangar. A line of five armored military vehicles lined the sidewalk. He and Andrei took the first one, while Kane and the rest of Aden's guards followed in two more. Andrei's security detail brought up the rear in the last two trucks.

"Why are you here?" Aden settled into the seat. "I thought you were occupied with other matters."

"Yeah, I finished up early. I was nearby, so Matthais asked me to drop in."

"Nearby?"

"What can I say? I get around."

Aden didn't find him remotely amusing. He glanced sideways at his friend, seeing him in a new light. He had to have known about Ellie and her father's abduction. He was privy to nearly all of Matthais' activities.

But stealing another vampire's humans was an act of treason. Had he been there that night? Ellie only mentioned Lorcan, but that doesn't rule out Andrei's presence.

Aden had exactly one person he considered a friend, after Keeley and Kane. Andrei. He trusted him with his life in military matters, but now, with this new knowledge, could he still consider him one?

He'd assess his friend's loyalty later.

"So, why would this problem need both of us here? Do you have any idea what it's about?"

Andrei sighed. "Yeah. I don't know the details, but it appears we've got another uprising on our hands."

"Does it have to do with my mysterious rogue problem?"

"Not exactly. But I think he might have an update about that for you, too. Matthais mentioned Aurick brought it up to Yuri a while back, and he had Anatoly investigate."

Aden gazed out the window at the passing scenery. Snow stretched for hundreds of miles in all directions.

"That was a couple of months ago," he said, turning back to Andrei. "And why would he need us both here? Is Anatoly incapable of dealing with an uprising on his own? This better not be about needing to train another fucking military. I don't want a repeat of Paolo."

"No. This isn't about that either." Andrei frowned. "You seem cranky. Is everything alright?"

"I just have a lot to handle before the council gathering, and I didn't need to be summoned here like some lackey for something that Anatoly should be able to take care of on his own."

"I thought you were planning to come here to meet with him, anyway."

Andrei's knowledge about his plans was unsettling.

"I was, but not until next week."

"This shouldn't take long." Andrei lowered the car window, and a blast of snow rushed in.

"Fuck, Andrei. Shut that damn thing. It's like an icebox out there."

Andrei rolled it back up, but a chill lingered that felt unrelated to the weather.

"So, are you ready to get your ass kicked in the HEW games?"

Human Extinction Warfare was a live-action game of deadly combat, pitting humans against each other and wild animals handpicked by Matthais. The games were brutal and bloody, a spectacle Aden had relished in his younger years, a dark escape from the crushing weight of guilt and grief for accidentally killing Aly.

Now he had no desire to play, realizing how sick and twisted they were. A wireless console controlled a collar embedded in the human's neck, allowing the vampires to manipulate their actions at will. Humans' lives were always at the mercy of vampires. Violent tournaments weren't necessary to emphasize the point.

"Matthais brought in a pack of arctic wolves this year."

"Instead of the bears?"

"No. In addition to. It's going to be a bloody mess." Andrei flashed him a cocky smirk. "It would be a shame if you were too out of practice to beat me."

The vehicle came to a stop at the entrance of the military facility adjacent to Yuri's compound, saving Aden from having to continue the conversation. Entering the building, they found soldiers engaged in a variety of drills.

Anatoly stood off to the right. With thick arms covered in tattoos crossed over his chest and hair cropped in a harsh buzz cut, he looked every bit the rigid career military leader he was. Four centuries of commanding troops in the hard, cold Sever Sib-Irian countryside had etched deep lines around his mouth and between his pale gray eyes. A long, jagged scar ran from under his right eye, down his cheek and neck, disappearing into his shirt collar, from a wound he received before becoming a vampire.

He was a condescending, arrogant dickhead who believed Aden's position was nepotism. Their mutual dislike was well known.

Anatoly walked over, getting right to the point without so much as a greeting.

"So, we have common problems. Let's hit yours quickly, then we can move on to mine, which are bigger."

Asshole.

He turned and walked toward an office at the back of the facility. Aden and Andrei shared a look before following him.

"Let's not dick around," Aden said. "Why don't you enlighten me? What are my problems?"

"We didn't send unregistered rogues into your region. If they were Sever Sib-Irian, they acted on their own."

"Is that so?"

"Yes. So now that's out of the way, let's get to why you're here."

Aden stepped in front of Anatoly, blocking his path.

"That's not a satisfactory answer. You've been investigating this for months, and that flimsy response is all you have. Unacceptable."

"It's all you're getting."

Aden snarled, a low growl rumbling in his chest, his fists clenched, ready for a fight, but Andrei stepped between them.

"For someone who's looking for our assistance, you're acting like an ungrateful prick, Anatoly. Aden's right. That's a bullshit answer. If you can't figure out why you have rogue vampires defecting and wreaking havoc in other regions, then I'll do it for you."

Anatoly's body went rigid. "And how exactly do you expect me to investigate this adequately when he executes all the suspects?"

"How the fuck do you know that?" Aden snarled again, trying to push past Andrei.

"That's enough. Knock this shit off. Both of you. Tell us what your problem is, Anatoly, and let's get this thing done. Then you will give us more details about your investigation and what you found out. Now tell us what the fuck is going on here."

"Fine," Anatoly said after an unusually long stare at Andrei. "You're not the only one having a rogue problem. I've had half a dozen covens pop up throughout my region."

"Why haven't you cut them down?" Aden folded his arms across his chest.

"It's not just rogues."

"What does that mean?" Andrei asked, his rigid posture mirroring Aden's.

"They've teamed up with humans."

"How are they teaming up with humans and not slaughtering them?" Aden asked.

"Because they're not feral. They're as sane as you and me."

Anatoly's sanity was questionable. As was his own sometimes, but they were both fed and healthy.

"They've made a blood swap arrangement. The humans agree to provide blood, and the rogues provide protection and are leading uprisings, testing our defenses."

"A human-vampire alliance? Are you fucking kidding me? How long has this been going on?"

"Almost a year."

"Was it happening during the last council gathering?" Andrei asked.

"It started up shortly before it."

"Why didn't you or Yuri bring it up at the meetings?" Aden snarled, his teeth bared.

"Because Cecilia's problem was much more severe. And we didn't realize the extent of it at that point or the humans' involvement. We thought it was a simple rogue infestation wreaking havoc. We didn't know how widespread it was until later."

"Does Aurick know about it?"

"Only Matthais as of right now. Yuri will brief the council this week."

So, his father was also in the dark.

"How big is the problem?" Andrei asked.

"Six covens of a few hundred rogues each."

"How many humans?"

"Six villages."

Getting information out of Anatoly was like pulling teeth.

"How many humans per village?"

Anatoly averted his gaze.

"How many?" Aden pressed.

"All our villages have five thousand residents."

What! The! Fuck!

"You have a thirty-plus-thousand-strong rogue-human uprising on your hands, and this is the first you're telling us about it? What kind of fucking moron are you?"

"Fuck you, man." Anatoly rushed at Aden, but Andrei pushed him back. "Not everyone has access to the resources the great son of Aurick Westcott has."

"Back off," Andrei warned. "You're fucked for not informing us about this sooner. Do I need to call in some of my troops, or do you have enough?"

"I have enough."

"Then let's get this thing done, and then we're going to talk about the importance of communication."

Andrei stomped off toward Anatoly's office, pulling up Matthais on a hologram as the door closed.

Without another word to Anatoly, Aden crossed the room to Kane.

"Did I hear that right?"

"Yeah. Another fucking moron failing to manage a rogue problem."

Aden surveyed the troops from his position half a mile away as they surrounded the village on all sides. This was the fourth one they'd captured in as many nights.

Wave after wave of relentless snow fell from the Sever Sib-Irian sky, blanketing the ground. The night air crackled with tension as activity behind the village walls ramped up. The humans were outnumbered, but to their credit, they held their position, unwilling to surrender even when Anatoly gave them the chance.

Aden offered to call in a contingent of his own men to supplement Anatoly's troops, but the vampire declined. So, he and Andrei's presence was only to ensure everything went smoothly, with Matthais insisting that Anatoly was to take point.

He felt decorative, useless, like a fucking ornament, serving no other purpose than to stand there and look pretty. How had his fucking life come to this?

Andrei approached, brushing snow off his shoulder.

"Why are we even here?" Aden asked.

"I don't know, man. Anatoly's troops are doing fine."

Aden looked at him like he'd lost his mind. "He's yet to leave one human or rogue alive. Was he instructed to exterminate them all?"

"Yes."

"Why? Without the rogues' assistance, the humans would fall back into line."

"Matthais' orders. No one who takes part in the rebellion is to be spared."

"You realize how extreme that position is, don't you? They're killing children, for fuck's sake."

"I carry out the directives of my chancellor."

Disgusted by his flippant response, Aden raised a dark eyebrow in a silent challenge.

Andrei shook his head. "You weren't alive during the Great Vampire Wars. Humans are never more dangerous than when they're cornered."

"T-minus five," Anatoly's voice crackled through the earpiece, partially drowned out by bursts of storm static.

"This is the largest village so far. How long do you think it will take?" Aden asked. "I want out of this fucking snow. How do they live here year-round? No wonder Anatoly is such an asshole. His balls have got to be frozen all the time."

Andrei chuckled. "That sounds about right."

"T-minus one," came another voice through the earpiece. "Get into positions."

The first explosion lit up the sky like lightning in a cloud, turning the snowflakes into glittering diamonds. A gaping hole ripped through the village's stone wall, allowing Anatoly's soldiers to flood in.

Human and inhuman shrieks filled the air as Helios rang out in the night. Helios guns fired bullets infused with UV light, making it easier for the half-breed soldiers to overpower and kill the weakened vampires.

"Who's got a camera on their helmet?" Aden asked.

"All of them. But if you want to see the front line, we should check Dimitri's."

Andrei projected a hologram of Dimitri's camera feed, giving him and Aden a close-up view of the action.

The sight of the UV bullets streaking through the sky reminded Aden of the aurora borealis, wavy ethereal streaks of bluish-green light.

Where the bullets struck the rogues, flesh sizzled and steamed in the freezing air. Anatoly's soldiers fired semi-automatic weapons at hundreds of humans who scurried away like rats trying to flee. Many fell where they stood. Others stumbled along for a few feet before dropping into the snow, staining it crimson.

"Are they wearing armor?" Aden asked, unsure if his eyes deceived him.

"Where the fuck did they get armor?" Andrei seethed, his eyes following the conflict spreading through the streets.

Restricted to military use only, armor wasn't readily accessible to civilians, each piece marked with unique serial numbers for tracking.

"Anatoly needs to collect and catalogue those to trace their origin," Aden said. "I'll speak to him."

"You might want to talk to him before he throws all of them on the pyres while they're still wearing it."

The battle raged for hours, with the villagers proving unexpectedly resilient.

The rogues also didn't go down easily. A group took to the high ground at the northern edge of the village. They coordinated with remarkable precision, holding their position for most of the night.

But in the end, Anatoly's troops prevailed. All that remained was a village in ruins, soaked in blood and littered with the dead.

As the first remnants of dawn peeked over the horizon, church bells rang out, barely audible over the wind's howl, the sound eerie in the almost otherwise quiet stillness.

For the first time in centuries, humans proved they were more than docile prey. They were fighting back against an unbeatable enemy with unexpected courage born of desperation.

The unsettling picture left Aden questioning if it signaled the beginning of a more ominous trend.

Aden reclined on the sofa in the plane's main cabin, while Aurick spoke to Matthais on a hologram. He and his father met up at the compound after returning from their separate trips, deciding to fly to Bíonn súil le muir together.

Restless and eager to see Ellie, he fidgeted, the seconds stretching into eternity, each minute a painful reminder that it had been over a week since he'd seen or talked to her. Well, he'd seen her, checking on her via hologram. But he hadn't called her, despite how much he ached to, not wanting to taint her with his fury and disgust over the Sever Sib-Irian situation.

Aden still had to brief Aurick on the details of the mission, and part of him dreaded it, knowing his father's views on military tactics.

So, he listened, waiting to hear Matthais' assessment of the events.

"Aden said he and Andrei got everything handled," Aurick said. "Though I haven't heard the full story yet."

"Yes, Andrei briefed me. I'm very pleased with the outcome."

Of course, Matthais was pleased.

Thirty thousand rebellious humans and over two thousand rogues who dared to defy vampire rule had been wiped out.

"We'll need to address this at the meetings. This kind of thing can't be kept quiet in the future, Matthais. I'm sure Anatoly took his retribution too far. That's how he operates. I hope the number of innocent casualties was minimal."

"Those humans weren't innocent, Aurick," Matthais said, his voice tight, his words clipped and sharp. "Their defiance sealed their fate."

Anger sparked in Aurick's eyes, but Matthais only ended the conversation.

"We'll discuss this more at the meetings. See you in a week."

The hologram disappeared, and Aurick turned to Aden, his eyes holding the familiar haunted expression that appeared whenever he learned of human casualties.

"Tell me what happened, Aden. I want to know exactly what Yuri and Anatoly did."

Ellie

E llie surveyed the communal living area at the heart of the villa. The layout here differed from the main compound, which didn't have any shared living spaces. Only the courtyard connected the private family wings.

The room was vast, stretching almost one hundred feet in length with thirty-foot ceilings. Sophie, Keeley, Ellie, and a team of five thralls and four half-breeds spent four days decorating it. What had once been an immense living room was now a twinkling winter wonderland.

A dozen twenty-five-foot balsam fir trees circled the perimeter, each one decorated with its own distinct theme, yet all complementing Sophie's white and silver color scheme. Beneath them, wrapped presents in blue and silver sat on beds of artificial snow.

Twinkling white lights that cascaded like falling snow draped the towering floor-to-ceiling windows overlooking the cliffs and ocean below. Real pine garlands wound around large marble columns and over the four arched entrances to the room.

Each corner of the room boasted a massive stone fireplace. Their hearths crackled with roaring fires, filling the room with warmth, their mantles transformed into miniature snow-covered villages, complete with tiny lit houses and minuscule ice skaters on ponds that reflected like mirrors.

Although celebrating Christmas was new to Ellie in this life, the recovered memories from her past life made the holiday familiar. She remembered being here with Aden and his family, especially this room. They were married in this room. The sight initially overwhelmed her, tightening her chest and squeezing her heart like a fist. But the constant activity of the last few days, the blur of motion and sound, kept her distracted while she waited for him to arrive.

She dropped to the carpet next to Keeley and Iain, holding her arms out. "Can I give you a break?"

"Thanks." Keeley handed the almost three-month-old baby to her.

Sophie sat nearby, engrossed in her book on one sofa, as Ryan scrolled through his tablet on another.

"Hi there, handsome," Ellie cooed as she snuggled him against her chest. He rubbed his face on her breasts, and she laughed. "There's nothing there for you, little guy."

"The wet nurse just fed him fifteen minutes ago." Keeley leaned back on her elbows with a sigh. "But he's always hungry. And obsessed with boobs just like his father," she teased, looking at Ryan, who smirked.

Ellie placed Iain on his back on the rug in front of her, tickling his feet as he kicked his legs in the air. Vlad slinked over and sat beside the baby, sniffing Iain's head. Keeley reached out, stroking her fingers down the cat's back.

"Be gentle with the baby, Vlady."

The cat flopped to his side, purring as he kneaded Iain's diaper and head-butted Ellie's thigh.

"Oh Aden, why didn't your dad call to tell me you were on your way?" Sophie asked as she stood from the sofa.

Ellie's lips curved into a smile, her heart quickening with a mix of excitement and yearning. She missed him so much, their stupid fight before he left seeming trivial now.

Iain let out a squeal, kicking his arms and legs as Ellie tickled his and Vlad's bellies.

"Aurick wanted to surprise you. I guess I ruined it," he replied, his tone gruff. She didn't need to see his face to know he was scowling.

"Yes, he did," Aurick said as he walked in. "But Aden couldn't wait another minute to see Ellie."

The urge to jump up and hurl herself into Aden's arms was almost overwhelming, but Ellie resisted, instead lifting a giggling Iain and blowing raspberries on his belly.

"She's beautiful holding a baby, isn't she?" Sophie murmured, and Ellie stiffened. She lowered Iain onto his back again, and Vlad curled up against his side. Keeley sat up and slid him and the baby closer to her.

Aden growled as Ellie sensed him approaching. Her body was so attuned to him now. When he was right behind her, she tilted her head back and looked up at him, her lips again curving into a smile.

He pinned her with his intense gaze, and her breath caught in her throat. He looked like he wanted to eat her alive.

Literally.

Then his eyes softened.

Ellie pushed to her feet, turning to face him. He was on her in an instant, cupping her face in his hands. Her fingers curled around his wrists, a warmth spreading through her as her smile widened.

"Hi." Her breath hitched as their lips met, a tender kiss that grew deeper as their tongues intertwined.

Ellie's soft moan mingled with the sound of their breathing. His kiss spoke of longing and desperation. She let go of his wrists and grabbed the front of his shirt, wanting, needing him closer. Aden ran his hands down her body, gripping the back of her thighs, lifting and pulling her legs around him.

"Aden, what are you doing?" Ellie murmured against his lips, but he just deepened the kiss further, stealing her breath as he turned and strode toward the door.

"We're getting this fucking nightmare over with once and for all," he growled as he pulled his mouth away from her.

"Yeah, we're not gonna see them again for a while," Keeley drawled.

"Ahhh, to be young and in love." The sound of Aurick's laughter joined hers, reverberating in the large room.

"Don't forget, tomorrow night is Christmas Eve," Sophie said, her voice trailing off as Aden walked through the archway.

"I think that ship has sailed, Mom, carrying her out of here like a caveman."

Ellie chuckled as their words faded into the distance, threading her fingers into Aden's hair.

"It's not fucking funny," he huffed, but it morphed into a moan as she nibbled a gentle path over his chin and down his neck. He flexed his fingers into the soft curves of her ass as he pulled her closer.

"I missed you," she murmured, the words a feather-light touch against his skin. "Thank you for the flowers."

"I was an asshole."

Ellie lifted her head and looked at him as he turned the corner into the hallway leading to his wing.

"I shouldn't have argued with you. Sometimes I don't know when to shut up."

He met her eyes, his gaze fierce.

"That's no excuse to take my anger out on you. Never on you."

She tilted her head, puzzled by his ability to navigate the path to his suite while looking at her. With gentle fingers, she traced the rough stubble on his jaw.

"I'm sorry we've been fighting. It's all my fault."

"You're not the one who explodes and yells when she doesn't get her way."

"Still, I've asked you for too much."

"No, you haven't." He pulled her closer, his grip tightening. "There's nothing I won't give you, Ellie. It might take me time to come around to it, but I will."

Before she could answer, Aden stopped outside the entrance to the suite, the one she had died in, and looked at the doorway over her shoulder. Ellie followed his gaze. The long hallway leading into the room was a menacing tunnel of dark shadows. His muscles tightened, and she turned back to look at him, touching his face and feeling his tension ease, but only slightly. She unwrapped her legs from around his waist, and he let her slide down his body until she was standing in front of him.

"I haven't been in there yet."

His eyes whipped to hers. "You haven't?"

"I wanted to wait for you. So we could go in together."

"Where have you been sleeping?"

"In one of the guest suites."

His hands moved on her hips, fingers tightening and loosening in an anxious rhythm against her. The heat of his palms felt both urgent and uncertain.

"Are you sure you can do this?"

"No. But there's nothing I won't fucking do for you."

Ellie reached up and traced her fingers down the line of his face, from his temples to his chin, and along his neck. He shuddered and relaxed in a single fluid motion.

"We've got this."

Her heart beat like a jackhammer in her chest. As brave as she was trying to be for Aden, a thin sheen of sweat slicked down her back. She grabbed his hand, turned, and tugged him into the room. The lights in the hallway illuminated their path as they walked deeper, each step feeling ominous.

They reached the end, and Ellie stopped. Her breath hitched as she looked around the suite. It looked nothing like it did that night almost three hundred years ago. But the ghosts of the past slithered over her skin like snakes, leaving her cold and trembling. Aden pressed the front of his body to the back of hers, wrapping her in his arms, pressing their joined hands against her stomach.

"I've got you, mo ghrá," he murmured, his voice strong and confident, but she could feel the tension in his body, despite his attempt to sound reassuring. She flexed her fingers under his.

With his arms encircling her, feeling his heartbeat against her back, she knew she could do this.

They both could.

Aden

The subtle change in Ellie's body was obvious, her brave facade crumbling. A fine tremor radiated through her frame, vibrating against Aden's chest where she pressed against him, even her fingertips trembling beneath his. His muscles tightened in response, his arms instinctively pulling her closer as they stood facing the room. She kept her chin up, but the fearless mask she'd worn a minute earlier was slipping.

Why the fuck had he let her talk him into this?

He'd been bracing himself for this moment for almost two weeks. From the second she told him what she wanted, he knew he'd do it for her. Even if it destroyed him, he'd come back into this room to face the horrific act he'd been running from for nearly three centuries.

A throbbing fist of tension clenched his gut. His eyes swept over the room, a room he vowed to never step foot in again, but he had to give his mother credit. Nothing looked the same.

Both the layout and footprint were different. What had once been one large open space was now very similar to their newly configured suite in the main compound, with multiple rooms and spaces. Where there had been solid walls, doors now opened into a private bedroom, dual closets, a bathroom, and what looked like an art studio.

"Everything is different." Ellie's voice shook as hard as her body, mirroring his own trembling. "She said everything was different, but I didn't know what to expect."

The hair on Aden's arms rose where her trembling form pressed against him, his body responding on a primitive level to her distress. He deliberately slowed his breathing, lengthening each inhale and exhale, hoping she might unconsciously match his rhythm. He rubbed his thumb in small circles on her stomach, a gesture meant to comfort him as much as her.

His gaze was drawn to where the bed had once stood. There was now an archway leading into a room resembling Ellie's private library at home. It was clear that his mother had made some more recent changes to cater to her love of books and reading.

"I completely destroyed this place. After my meltdown, the villa's foundation on this end had to be shored up. The entire right side of the room caved in."

"Oh, Aden." Ellie spun in his arms, wrapping hers around his waist, pressing her forehead to his chest.

The words "Don't fucking pity me" were on the tip of his tongue, but he held them back. This wasn't about him anymore.

"I'm not the one who died."

She tilted her face up to look at him. "Yes, you did. Part of you anyway."

Aden tucked a strand of her hair behind her ear, his fingers lingering against her earlobe, as he let out a tight breath. "Okay. We did this. Can we get the fuck out of here now?"

With a shake of her head, she grasped his hand, bringing it to her mouth for a tender kiss. "No."

He scowled. "Why the fuck not?"

Her lips curved into a seductive smile, but a hint of uncertainty still lingered in her eyes.

"Because you're going to take me to bed. And you're going to bite me."

"Ellie, we don't have to do this here. We've proven we... I... can come in here, and the world won't end. But I really don't think I can do that here. You want me to bite you? Let's do it." He stroked her bottom lip with his thumb. "I'm not afraid I'll lose control again. I'm not. Yes, I'm nervous, but—don't look at me like that."

"Like what?" Her eyes now held a gentle twinkle.

"Like you trust me completely."

Her face turned serious. "I do trust you completely."

Closing his eyes, Aden breathed deeply before reopening them. "The first time we share blood, I'm going to be anxious. Like I was the first time we had sex. But my control is unwavering now. You never have to fear me again."

Ellie tugged him toward the bedroom. "So, what's the problem, then?"

Fuck! Where did she get so fucking brave?

"I don't want to do it here. I don't want to taint it with that memory."

"But everything is so different. It feels like a whole new place."

"It's the energy in here."

"So, let's change the energy."

She released his hand as they stepped into the bedroom. Turning to face him, she pulled his shirt out of his jeans, her fingers moving to unbutton it. He watched her, accepting his fate, his arousal spiking with each button she unfastened despite his reluctance. She pushed the fabric open and trailed her hands up his chest, the warmth of her fingers searing his skin.

She leaned forward and pressed a gentle kiss over his heart. Aden glided his hand up the back of her neck, sliding it into her hair. He wrapped his fingers around the soft strands, tilting her head back, his eyes skimming over her face, looking for any sign of hesitation. A faint trace of it remained, but the intensity of her longing for him was palpable. It shone in her eyes, and he bent down, his lips softly grazing hers.

Ellie smiled and stepped back, pulling his hand out of her hair before lifting her sweater over her head, revealing her black lace bra. She tried to hide it, but her trembling hands betrayed her nerves. Her spirit was a captivating paradox of strength and fragility—brave as a lioness, yet as delicate as a flower, their combined resilience evident in everything she was.

Reaching behind her back, she unhooked her bra and let it slide down her arms, tossing it away. A groan escaped Aden's lips as his cock hardened, adding to the already overwhelming rush of mixed emotions.

"Ellie, stop."

"Nope."

A low growl rumbled in his chest.

"I love it when you do that."

She reached for him, dipping her fingertips into the front of his jeans, tugging him forward.

"Come on, handsome. Don't keep me waiting. I've been aching for you for a week, and we can't do this if you're dressed."

His eyes locked with hers as he stared, a long moment passing before he finally pulled her fingers from his waistband. He unfastened the top button and tugged the zipper down, then lowered his pants over his hips.

She grinned and followed suit, leaving her in only her panties.

He paused, swallowing hard as he gazed at her. "You are so fucking beautiful."

A blush spread over her body, and he groaned again, his mouth watering at the prospect of tasting her blood. There was no way he could resist what she was offering. He wasn't that strong.

He shed the rest of his clothes, flinging them across the room as she giggled, finally standing in front of her, completely naked. His cock stood erect, hard and thick, his tip weeping.

Ellie licked her lips, grabbing his hand and pulling him to the bed. She sat down, looking up at him as she reached out and took the length of him in her hand. The heat of her fingers seared his skin as they wrapped around him. With each beat, his heart's pounding rhythm pulsed through his body, all the way to his throbbing and twitching cock in her hand.

"Let me take the edge off," she said with a sultry smile.

"Ellie," he groaned, nodding, his entire body shuddering. If they were going to do this, he needed to be in complete control. After seven agonizing days without her, without the scent of her skin or the taste of her lips, or the feel of her tight, wet body wrapped around him, he wanted to devour her. And devouring her was not an option when she offered her blood so willingly as a sacrifice to his beast.

The first touch of her tongue sent a shockwave shooting up Aden's spine. Wet heat traced along the underside of his cock, and the world dissolved around him. His vision blurred, narrowing until all he could see was Ellie, her lips engulfing him, her eyes looking up at him.

"Fuck!" The word tore from his throat without thought, his voice foreign to his own ears.

His fingers found her hair, wrapping the long, silky strands around his knuckles. He needed something to ground him, anchor him to reality, as the feeling of drowning overwhelmed him. The thunderous beat of his heart obliterated all other sounds except the soft, slick noises she made.

Aden's legs threatened to buckle. Every muscle in his body seemed to melt and reform in rapid succession, leaving him breathless and trembling, making even his fingertips tingle. He couldn't think, couldn't remember his own name. There was only her.

Ellie's moan vibrated through him, ripping a groan from deep in his chest. Each swirl of her tongue built pressure at the base of his spine, a coiling tension that spread through him. He gasped for breath, unable to pull enough oxygen into his lungs.

Sweat beaded on Aden's skin, trickling down his back. His hips moved of their own volition, his body operating on pure instinct now, conscious thought obliterated by waves of ecstasy.

"Fuck, baby. Just like that." The words scraped past his lips, barely audible, as he watched her, mesmerized.

A dizzying rush of pleasure built, layer upon layer, each more intense than the last, making the room spin. He flexed his fingers in her hair, but he needed more.

More connection.

More of her.

Aden kept one hand in her hair as he reached down with the other, pinching and tugging her nipple. When she whimpered around him, the vibration nearly sent him over the edge, his hips bucking involuntarily.

Time lost meaning.

He wanted to fuck her mouth for hours, but it had been too long, and he was hurtling toward release with frightening speed. The intense need to be inside her consumed him, even as the pleasure threatened to overwhelm him. A burning heat flushed his skin as desire pulsed through his veins, making him feel feverish.

Every nerve ending screamed with sensation. Waves of ecstasy so intense they bordered on pain washed over him, his eyelids fluttering and his breath coming in short, stuttering gasps. The faint sound of Ellie gagging registered, but he couldn't stop the movement of his hips, couldn't regain control of his own body as it chased release.

The telltale tightening in his balls was the first warning he'd reached the point of no return. His entire body tensed, every muscle contracting in anticipation. Both hands gripped her hair again, anchoring him to reality when he might have otherwise surrendered to oblivion and collapsed to the floor.

"Here it comes, baby," he managed to groan before his world exploded, coming with a roar so loud it echoed throughout the room.

Pleasure crashed over him like a tidal wave, radiating outward, engulfing him, and wiping his mind clean. His vision darkened at the edges as his body convulsed. The sharp sting of Ellie's nails digging into his ass cut through the ecstasy, somehow intensifying it.

As the intensity ebbed, his legs shook, his chest heaving with labored breaths, sweat cooling rapidly on his skin. His mind pieced itself back together, thoughts returning in fragments as he gazed down at her, overwhelmed by how completely she had taken him apart.

He loosened his fingers in her hair, gently massaging her scalp as she let his cock slip from her mouth with one last swirl of her tongue over his sensitive tip. Reaching up with her thumb, she wiped the come from the corner of her lips, her tongue darting out to catch the lingering trace.

With a gentle curve of her lips, she smiled, her eyes soft and warm as she looked up at him. "Feeling better?"

Aden choked out a laugh. "You're a goddess," he whispered, his voice thick with awe. "You know that?"

She wrinkled her nose at him, revealing a brief moment of insecurity, before she smiled again.

"Are you ready for this?"

"Hey." He cupped the side of her face, forcing her to meet his eyes. "You're a fucking goddess."

She pulled his thumb to her lips and nipped the tip. "All that matters is you think so. Now, are you ready for this?"

He held her gaze a moment longer, wanting to argue, wanting to demand that she believe how truly fucking amazing and beautiful she was. But he wanted to be inside her more, so he nodded, and she reached for his hand as she lay back, scooting up the mattress.

Aden slid her panties down her legs, tossing them over his shoulder before he crawled over her, lying in the cradle of her thighs. Ellie sighed as he settled his weight on her. He buried his face in her neck, breathing her in, reaching between their bodies, his fingers caressing her. She was warm and wet, ready for him. She arched her back and moaned, her lips pressing against his ear.

"I love you, Aden."

His body shuddered, and he raised his head from her throat to look down at her. He rolled onto his back, flipping them over so she was on top, and she let out a surprised squeak. He lifted his knees for her to rest against, his cock trapped beneath her ass.

Ellie took his hands, her fingers lacing through his.

"Tell me what it's going to feel like."

Confused, Aden frowned. "I thought you remembered."

"I do. But the memory is fuzzy. I know in theory how venom affects the body. And briefly in practice because you bit me once, but I was in so much pain from my whipping that my brain didn't really register the feeling. Explain to me what your venom will do and what will happen when it paralyzes me. The thought of not being able to move is a little..." She trailed off.

She was stalling, but he didn't mind. Although he was already hard again, beneath her, he shared her hesitancy and was more than willing to take it slow. And they'd never talked about this, even in Aly's lifetime.

"Are you afraid of being paralyzed and helpless against me?"

"I'm helpless against you, whether I'm paralyzed or not. And no, I'm not afraid of you or what your venom will do. I just want to know what to expect."

His thumbs moved in gentle circles across the back of her hands, the soft skin a soothing contrast to the throbbing pulse of his cock between them.

"As soon as my venom enters your veins, you'll come instantly, hard and fast. But you'll also be completely paralyzed for about fifteen seconds, and your orgasm will last as long as the paralysis."

"Will I feel it? If I'm paralyzed?"

"Oh yeah. It will be the most intense orgasm of your life."

"Really?" she purred, a sultry smile curving her lips, her eyes darkening as a shiver ran through her. Aden bucked his hips, his body reacting to the sudden rush of arousal that coated his cock.

"If you want to finish the conversation, you'll behave yourself." His growl, a low, rumbling purr mirroring hers, vibrated in the air like a dark promise.

"I'd say sorry, but I'm not," Ellie breathed as she circled her hips, teasing him like the fucking minx she was.

"How is that possible, though? How can my body be paralyzed and still orgasm?"

Determined to stay focused on answering her, Aden fought the urge to move her just an inch to the right so he could slip his cock inside her. Her subtle shifting and wiggling didn't make it easy.

"Venom doesn't affect the brain or most of the nervous system, just the body's physical motor functions. A paraplegic can have an orgasm, even if they can't feel it. But the paralysis venom causes doesn't take your ability to feel away. It just prevents your body's ability to move."

He recognized the look in her eyes as her brain processed his words. She had such a magnificent mind, always driven by an innate need to understand.

"If I were to bite you here." Aden pulled their joined hands toward him and pressed his teeth to the inside of her wrist, causing her breath to hitch, but not in fear. "You'd have an orgasm." He brushed a soft kiss against her skin before lowering their hands to his abdomen. "But it would be a gentle, slow, rolling one that makes you shudder. It'd be pleasurable but not super intense."

"That's what happens to thralls when you drink from them?"

"Yes. But if I bite you during sex and we're both already aroused, my venom is more potent. It has a stronger effect on your body, and the orgasm you'll have will be a screaming, heart-stopping, mind-wiping one."

She swallowed, the movement a visible ripple in her throat, drawing his eyes to her jugular vein.

"Are you sure I'll survive it?"

His gaze met hers again, and he smirked. "Humans have been doing it for millennia. So have half-breeds."

"Your mom tried to explain the intensity of it when we talked about compulsion."

"You'll never experience anything more intense."

"But why does venom paralyze?"

"Like a snake's, vampire venom is designed to incapacitate its prey temporarily so it can't escape."

"That's an awfully sinister answer."

"Vampires are sinister creatures by nature." He let go of her hand and traced his fingertip down the column of her throat. "Are you sure you want to do this tonight?"

Her eyes softened as she looked down at him, a gentle warmth spreading across her face, before flaring with the same fierce desire from earlier.

"I've never been more sure of anything in my life," Ellie replied, sliding herself along his cock, drenching him in her arousal.

Clearly, their conversation was over.

Still hard and ready, he surrendered to her, grasping her hips to lift her as he guided his cock inside her. The tight warmth of her body as it wrapped around him threatened to consume him.

Ellie's squeal of surprise morphed into a groan as her eyes fluttered closed.

"Look at me," Aden demanded, and her eyes whipped open. "I need you on top for this the first time. I need you in control."

He'd been on top with Aly, his weight and strength pinning her down, and he couldn't bring himself to be in that position again. Not yet. Not until he knew his control would hold.

Ellie leaned forward, bracing her hand on his chest as she sank further, taking him deeper, making them both groan.

"I can take control," she gasped as her body gave way, adjusting to his girth.

She rocked her hips, her eyes fluttering each time he lifted her, then pulled her back down on him, plunging to the hilt. Aden watched her, his fingers gripping her, the scent and feel of her filling his senses as the battle between desire and restraint raged within him.

His fangs descended, and he allowed the venom to flow from them for the first time since he'd been with Ellie, making no attempt to stop it. His throat rippled at the slight burn. He looked up to see Ellie's eyes darken as she stared down at him.

She moved over him, guiding him deeper with every rotation of her hips, and Aden's craving for her blood intensified. With each passing second, his confidence grew.

She pulled his hands away from her waist and tugged them to her breasts. Her nipples pushed against his palms like hard pebbles. The soft flesh yielded beneath his touch, his fingers sinking into their warmth, and her head fell back as a low, guttural moan vibrated from deep within her throat.

Helpless to resist, Aden sat up, taking a nipple in his mouth, biting gently before pricking it with the tip of his fang. Ellie's body jerked, and she grabbed his head, pulling him closer.

"Please," she begged, and he gave in. He sunk his fangs into her nipple as she cried out. Her body froze, his venom hitting her bloodstream, sending her into an instant orgasm. The paralysis prevented her from moving, yet she pulsed around him, gripping his sensitive cock tighter as if to pull him further inside, drawing a low growl from his throat. The rippling of her wet walls was like tiny velvet fingers clutching and massaging him.

He lowered his hands, gripping her hips, holding her steady against his thrusts beneath her. Aden sucked her nipple hard, and the first drop of blood that touched his tongue nearly undid him, his venom ensuring a continuous flow. The flavor exploded in his mouth, a symphony of sweetness and spice. His eyes rolled back as he lost himself in the taste.

Every nerve ending in his body seemed to light up simultaneously. His hands trembled where they touched her, his skin hypersensitive to the softness of hers beneath his fingers. Only one thought echoed through his mind. He never wanted any other blood for the rest of eternity.

He was instantly and hopelessly addicted to her.

A wave of relief washed over him when the urge to drain her didn't come. The monster inside him remained sated with this brief taste.

But they were only just beginning.

When the paralysis lifted a few seconds later, Ellie's cry pierced through his blissful haze. Her fingers tangled in his hair, yanking so hard that sharp pricks of pain mingled with his pleasure. The contrast only heightened his arousal, making him groan against her skin.

He reluctantly released her nipple, flicking his tongue over it gently, a silent apology and promise combined. Before he could say anything, she pulled his head up, crashing her lips to his. The taste of her blood still lingered on his tongue as she kissed him, and the thought that she was tasting herself sent a jolt straight to his cock.

Her hips moved again, rocking in a rhythm that threatened to push him over the edge with each motion. He could feel every inch of her surrounding him, the slick heat of her walls fluttering, a sign that she was as close as he was. That he could bring her to this point again so fast sent his desire into overdrive.

Ellie kissed him, slow and deep, her tongue seeking his in a tender exploration that left him breathless. His chest ached with emotions too big to contain. Her taste, her scent, and the feel of her overwhelmed all of his senses until there was nothing in his world but her.

"Aden, please," she begged, her voice vibrating against his lips. "I need you to bite me."

A light chuckle escaped him, his mouth still pressed to hers. "I just did, baby."

She halted her movements, and the sudden stillness was its own form of exquisite torture. She leaned back and whispered almost shyly, "I need more."

"Look at me, Ellie," he said. When her eyes met his, he saw trust, desire, and love reflected back at him. He pulled her close, feeling her heartbeat thunder against his chest. Her hands flew to his shoulders, her fingertips pressing into his skin.

"I swear to you I'll stop this time. I'll never hurt you again. I vow it on my life."

The weight of the promise settled in his bones, a vow he would die before breaking.

She pulled his mouth to hers, whispering against his lips. "I know. Get out of your head and lose yourself in me." Then she guided his face to her neck. "I trust you."

Aden groaned, and his fangs descended again. He pressed a kiss to her jugular vein, feeling the strong, steady rhythm of her life beneath his mouth.

"I love you," he whispered against her skin, the words inadequate for the depth of his feelings for her.

Before doubt could creep back in and he could overthink it, Aden surrendered to instinct and sank his fangs into her flesh.

The world exploded into color and sensation, and he was lost.

Ellie

T ime stopped.

The world narrowed to pinpricks of sensation as Ellie's muscles locked, and her breath caught in her throat. Every nerve ending in her body screamed with delicious agony as the orgasm tore through her like wildfire, consuming everything in its path as sparks of white light danced behind her eyelids. The initial pain from his bite gave way to waves of intense pleasure, each pulse more powerful than the one before.

Her skin tingled with warmth everywhere their bodies touched, but beneath the physical sensations pulsed something deeper—a feeling of finally...finally being able to give him everything she was. Everything she had. This wasn't just physical. It was a surrender and acceptance that went soul-deep.

She'd felt the exact moment when the first taste of her blood hit his system. His entire frame shuddered against hers, and a low moan rumbled through his chest. The sound vibrated through her body like a caress. She wished she could tell him how beautiful and right this felt, how perfectly they fit together in this moment.

Each heartbeat pushed her blood into his mouth, and with it flowed every ounce of faith she had in him, every time she'd glimpsed the vulnerable man beneath his carefully constructed defenses, every silent promise that she'd never fear him, no matter what. This was her gift to him, trust made tangible, flowing from her veins into his body.

The world tilted as he moved with unexpected speed, and Ellie found herself on her back, pressed against the sheets. Though she was unable to move, he continued his rhythm above her, moving over her, inside her. The contradiction was exquisite torture, her body immobile while her senses burned white hot.

Her lips couldn't release the sounds building in her throat, but her soul cried out with each perfect movement. Her thoughts swirled in kaleidoscopic patterns as the pleasure built to impossible heights. Every cell in her body came alive, awakened as if she'd been only half-living before this moment.

Time stretched slowly as her pulse throbbed in time with his drinking and the pumping of his hips, creating a rhythm that was ancient and primal. This wasn't feeding. This was a sacred sharing, a gesture of acceptance and trust for them both. Each pull of her blood felt like healing, every swallow he took from her erasing another scar from their past, washing away centuries of self-loathing and doubt, and replacing them with certainty and love.

This was nothing like that first desperate bite in Master Matthais' suite, when pain from her wounds overwhelmed everything else. No, this was like their wedding night, but deeper, richer, and more profound. That night had been their beginning. And their end. But this was their rebirth.

Ellie's memory of their wedding night hadn't prepared her for the reality of this soul-deep connection. The intensity of the moment was almost too much, of finally sharing this with him, of proving that he wouldn't hurt her, that his control was stronger than his fear.

Why had she waited so long to let him bite her?

The question floated through her mind as pleasure continued to pulse through her paralyzed body.

After what seemed like an eternity, when the paralysis finally released its grip, Ellie's mouth fell open, a scream escaping her lips as sensation flooded back, the fading echoes of her orgasm leaving her breathless and trembling with aftershocks.

"Aden," she breathed his name.

Flexing her fingers, she threaded them through his hair, the strands feeling like silk as she cradled him closer. He growled against her throat, the sound dark and possessive, drinking deeper. The vibration of that growl sent fresh tremors cascading through her. Her nails dug half-moon crescents into his scalp as his arms tightened. There was something exquisite in the pressure, in being held so tightly that she could feel every inch of him against her.

Shadows started creeping at the edges of her vision, her thoughts growing fuzzy, but she didn't want it to end. The room spun, her mind swimming with the need to give in to the darkness, but there was a strange peace in the dizziness, a willingness to surrender herself completely to him.

She called to him again, pushing on his shoulders with hands that felt heavy as lead. A pang of regret shot through her.

"You need to stop," she managed, her voice a hoarse whisper. Even as her body recognized the danger, the words broke her heart because she wanted to give him more, everything, wanting this connection to last forever.

"Aden, stop."

He tore his fangs from her neck, blood misting the air and sending a spray of warmth against her skin. The sudden disconnection felt like a physical blow, like a part of her was ripped away.

He wrenched away from her with such force he tumbled from the bed, hitting the floor with a dull thud. The horror in his wide eyes cut her deeper than any bite. Centuries of self-loathing rushed back, threatening to drown their perfect moment in shame and regret.

No!

She wouldn't allow it. Not after they'd come so far.

Ellie's heart hammered against her ribs as she scrambled after him, dropping beside him, ignoring the sticky warmth trailing down her neck. Every protective instinct inside her flared to life at the sight of him sprawled naked on the marble tile, her blood painting his lips, his eyes distant with panic.

This moment could define them.

If she showed even a flicker of fear, it would confirm every dark thought he'd ever had about himself. But all she felt was love, fierce and proud, a triumphant feeling that vibrated through her whole body.

They'd succeeded.

"Aden, it's okay." She cradled his face in her hands, her thumbs tracing gentle circles on his cheeks. "Come back to me. We did it."

He blinked, and awareness flickered back into his eyes. They raked over her, sharp and intense, checking every inch of her. She held still, letting him see the truth—that she was whole, unharmed, and more alive in this moment than she'd ever been.

Relief flooded his features as the enormity of his accomplishment sank in.

He hadn't lost control.

Hadn't hurt her.

Hadn't killed her again.

A smile spread across her face, her heart swelling, feeling too big for her chest. Each beat, slightly weakened but steady, pulsed with love for him.

"We did it, baby," she murmured, kissing him, tasting her blood on his lips. The copper tang didn't disgust her. It was proof of their triumph over fear. In that kiss, she tasted their future.

He gently pushed her back just far enough to study her face, his eyes again devouring every inch of her, swimming with emotion.

"We did it?" he asked, and she gave a gentle nod.

"You did it."

His laugh, bright, unfettered, and real, filled the room as he pulled her close. In all their time together in this life, she'd never heard him sound so free, so unburdened. They clung to each other on the floor, her blood drying on their lips, their hearts beating in sync.

Even with the lingering light-headedness, a single thought emerged in Ellie's mind with perfect clarity. They were finally free of their past.

The chains that bound them—her death, his regret, their shared tragedy—had been broken by this act of ultimate love and trust.

Aden

Aden slid the needle from Ellie's vein, and she sighed, leaning back against the headboard as the BloodStone, laced with an extra dose of his blood, worked through her system.

Fresh from the shower and with clean sheets on the bed, no one would know the bloody mess they'd both been a short time ago.

"I think we freaked Mina out when she saw the blood everywhere." He tossed the syringe away.

Ellie laughed, and the gentle sound wrapped around him.

"Tell me about it. You know she went straight to your parents when she left here."

Kneeling between her thighs, Aden licked the puncture in the crook of her arm, his tongue swirling over the skin, sealing the tiny hole. The taste of her hit him again, and he felt his eyes roll back. Her blood was perfection, and now that he tasted it again, indulged in it, he'd never live without it.

"Uh-huh." Aden's lips traveled slowly down Ellie's forearm to her wrist. She quivered beneath his touch.

"So, how do you feel?"

He looked up at the slight hesitation he heard in her voice. There were so many undertones to her question. And so many answers. He gave her the simplest and most truthful.

"Like I'm alive again."

"Care to elaborate?"

A small smile played on her lips as she tilted her head, her question a soft murmur in the quiet room.

He moved to lie beside her on the newly changed sheets. She turned to him and took his hand, her fingers lacing through his as he tugged her down next to him.

Aden drew Ellie closer against his chest, the fingertips of his other hand trailing over the fresh puncture marks on her neck. Her skin was warm, her pulse a steady rhythm beneath his touch, and the taste of her blood lingered on his tongue, sweet and potent.

"The moment I tasted you, it was like being struck by lightning," he finally said, frowning at the memory. "Everything in me wanted to drown in you. The darkness was there, clawing at me, begging me to consume you."

"But you didn't." Her voice was gentle.

"No." A smile touched his lips. "This time, I controlled it. This time, I remembered what it felt like to lose you."

Ellie pressed a gentle kiss to his chest, right over his heart.

"I told you, you were strong enough."

Tilting her chin up, he looked into her eyes. "I never thought I could have this. I've spent centuries mastering my control, learning to cage the beast that took Aly from me. But nothing prepared me for this. For the reality of tasting you again and being able to stop." He leaned in, brushing his lips over the marks on her neck. "The monster in me still craves more, but when I felt myself starting to slip, giving into the bloodlust, I focused on your heartbeat. I heard your voice and felt your hands on my skin. Your touch, your trust in me—it anchored me."

She pressed closer, and he shuddered at the warmth of her.

"I can still feel your venom coursing through me."

"I can still feel your blood coursing through me. It makes me feel... alive. Whole."

"And sated?" She teased.

A low chuckle rumbled through his chest. "Thoroughly." He tucked a stray lock of her hair behind her ear, his fingers tracing the curve. "How many times did you have to say my name before I stopped?"

"Only twice." Ellie reached for his face, her fingers grazing his cheeks as she pulled him closer, pressing a kiss to his lips. "I knew we'd be fine."

He sank into her, rolling her onto her back, ready to lose himself in her again when the door to the suite buzzed and then opened. Reluctantly, Aden pulled back, covering her with the sheet as he stood. He grabbed his pants from the floor and tugged them on.

"That's your food. Don't move."

He strode out of the bedroom as a male thrall came around the corner, into the living room, pushing a cart with covered plates.

"Leave it. I'll call when it needs to be picked up."

"Yes, Sir." The thrall scurried out just as the bedroom door slid open and Ellie stepped out, wearing Aden's shirt.

"I told you to stay put."

"I'm not a dog."

Aden tilted his head as she walked closer. He loved the way she looked in his shirts after sex, the oversized fabric engulfing her small frame, her hair a mess, her skin flushed. It made him instantly hard. His eyes followed her as she stepped up to the cart and uncovered the plates.

"I'm so hungry," she said as she grabbed a turkey sandwich with chips and walked over to the sofa.

"Is that all you're going to eat?"

"It's what I'm starting with."

"Well, you better plan to have more because you're going to need your strength. We're only getting started."

"Even with your blood lacing it, the BloodStone will take a little while to replenish mine."

A pang of disappointment filled him. "As much as I want it, no more blood tonight. But I'm far from finished with your body."

Aden sat next to her, twisting her so that he could pull her feet onto his lap.

The raw hunger for her blood clenched his stomach, a fist of need pulsing in every cell of his body. But he wasn't about to tempt fate.

He'd have her blood again. And again. And again.

But not tonight.

He watched Ellie eat, caressing the bare skin of her calf, traveling up over her knee, and teasing the inside of her thigh.

"Aden, stop it. I'm trying to eat."

"What?" He gave her his most innocent smile.

"Nice try. There's nothing innocent about you."

He pressed his fingertips against her femoral artery, feeling it pulse as her blood flowed through it, and his fangs tingled.

"I'm going to bite you here. Do you want that?"

She nodded, her breath hitching as Aden's finger wandered further up, brushing over her sex, making her tremble.

"Can I ask you something?"

"Always," he replied.

"I don't want you to get upset."

"I fucking hate it when you say that. It means I'm going to lose my shit."

"It shouldn't."

She shuddered as his fingers fluttered over her clit, almost choking on her sandwich, before she pushed his hand away. He refused to be deterred but gave her tender flesh a rest and caressed the soft skin of her inner thigh instead.

"But considering everything we've done tonight, everything we've succeeded in doing, I don't want to ruin it. But I really need to know."

"Just ask me, Ellie."

"What happened to my parents?"

Aden's fingers stilled, and he met her eyes.

"After, I mean," she rushed on. "How long did they live? Where were their ashes spread?"

All humans were cremated when they died, their ashes spread and mixed with the dirt in the village where they lived. In the case of city thralls, their remains were mixed into the soil in the city flower beds.

"They both lived another sixty years or so."

"They died young."

BloodStone enabled humans to live an average of one hundred and fifty years.

Aden rested his fingers on her thigh. "Neither one of them got over what happened. They couldn't bear to be around me, so Aurick and Sophie sent them to live out the rest of their lives on her island. That's where they're buried."

Ellie's eyes grew wide. "They're buried? Why weren't they cremated?"

"You'll have to ask Sophie. It was her decision. I wasn't in any condition to decide anything at that point, but they asked to be buried next to Aly."

"I was buried too?"

Aden felt restless and uneasy at the thought of Aly's burial. He couldn't attend because he was locked in the vaults, but he wouldn't have gone, regardless. It would have broken him even further.

He shifted Ellie's legs from his and stood up. He paced, creating a tense energy that vibrated in the air.

"Of course, you were fucking buried. Do you think I would've let them burn you? I broke you, but I told Sophie I'd never speak to her again if she had your body burned. I don't think she would have, anyway."

Ellie sat forward, dropping her feet to the ground, and setting her half-empty plate on the coffee table.

"Where on the island are they buried?"

"The family cemetery at the northern tip."

The Westcott family graveyard was small. Miraculously, as his mother put it, her parents' and brother's graves in what had once been the northeastern United States survived the tectonic shift. So Aurick had their bodies exhumed and reburied on Sophie's island. Aside from his mother's family, Aly and her parents were the only others buried there.

"You buried my parents in your family's cemetery?"

"They were your parents. They were family."

Ellie stood and walked closer to him.

"Can I visit their graves?"

Aden stopped pacing, his eyes finding hers, and the hope he saw there pierced him like a knife.

Of course, she would fucking ask that.

Ellie

The headstone was larger and more beautiful than she thought it would be. Her parents were human, after all. Humans weren't important enough to warrant headstones. Their bodies were burned, and the ashes scattered or mixed in the dirt, the earth swallowing them without a trace, leaving behind only the silence of an unmarked grave.

But Sophie made sure her parents' existence was acknowledged for eternity, images of their faces carved into the stone, and Ellie held her breath as her eyes drank them in. The likeness was uncanny, reflecting her memories with unsettling precision, right down to the faint lines around their eyes and mouths.

The last time she saw them alive was on her and Aden's wedding night before they retreated to their suite. She'd hugged them both, promising to see them for breakfast the next evening. But she never saw them again, and they died heartbroken and alone after the brutal loss of their only child, murdered by the man who loved her.

Ellie extended her fingers, tracing them over her mother's face, so similar to Alysia's. More memories came unbidden to her mind, times spent with a woman from another life, not the woman who gave birth to her in this one. A brief flash of guilt, sharp and sudden like the edge of a knife, flooded through her, a feeling of betraying the mother who birthed her twenty-three years ago. A woman who didn't have a headstone with her image carved into it, who, like all other humans, was forgotten after she was dead, except by Ellie and her dad.

A thin layer of snow covered the top of the stone. It was a stark contrast to the deep snow she stood in, halfway up her calves. The recent heavy snowfall had been cleared away. Sophie, no doubt, handled everything once she learned of their planned visit.

From the corner of her eye, she saw Aden motionless in front of an almost identical monument.

Aly's headstone.

Her headstone.

She asked so much of him. And he gave it freely, regardless of the heavy toll it took on him. The depth of his love compelled him to confront his darkest demons.

For her.

She wasn't sure she warranted that kind of unconditional devotion, but she was grateful for it.

With one last glance at her parent's faces, Ellie closed her eyes and said a silent goodbye before stepping closer to Aden. The ocean waves lapping on the shore in the distance were the only sound in the otherwise soundless night.

She removed her gloves and reached for his hand, letting the warmth of her skin envelop his cool fingers. He didn't seem to notice, his gaze fixed on the headstone, his face etched with a solemn expression. She was hesitant to look at it. Not sure she wanted to. When she asked him to take her to her parent's grave, she ignored the fact that she'd be confronted with Aly's nearby.

Despite her recent need for closure, the uncertainty of the moment unsettled her, unsure she was ready for it.

She squeezed Aden's hand, watching him instead. His face was a mask of pain and sorrow, his jaw tight as he fought to contain the emotions overwhelming him. She released his hand and stepped in front of him, pressing her body against his and wrapping her arms around his waist as she looked up at him.

"Hey, are you okay?"

He finally tore his eyes away from the stone and looked down at her as he enveloped her in his arms. He nodded, but his eyes betrayed him. She tightened her grip on him to stifle the slight tremble in his otherwise rigid body.

"We can go if you want."

His brow furrowed. "Don't you want to see it?"

Ellie shook her head. "Nope. No need. I saw what I came to see."

He looked at her, then back at the stone over her head.

"Sophie didn't tell me she had Aly's face carved into the headstone. Then again, I refused to let anyone talk about her."

"She didn't tell me about theirs, either." Ellie gestured to her parent's gravestone.

Aden glanced over, seemingly surprised by its presence.

"Even in death," he said, a wry twist to his mouth, "Sophie has to make it about the art."

The truth of his words hit her, and Ellie chuckled, a sound that felt both light and freeing, before burying her face in his chest. He was going to be alright. They both were.

"Thank you for bringing me here. I know how hard this is for you."

"Story of my life this week," he replied, but there was no heat behind his words.

She pressed a kiss over his heart. "I love you, you know."

"I know." His breath ghosted over the skin of her forehead as his arms tightened around her. "And I worship you. Even when I want to wring your neck, I worship you."

She couldn't help but laugh. "That's a lot of the time lately, isn't it?"

"Fuck yes, it is."

Tilting her head back, she gazed up at him. "I guess I should be brave and look now, huh?"

"You're the bravest woman I know."

"I'm not nearly as courageous as I try to act. But with you beside me, I feel like I can be."

"Then turn the fuck around."

Her eyes narrowed, a glint of defiance in their depths, as he raised an eyebrow.

"If I can do it, so can you."

Ellie took a deep breath, then braced herself before dropping her arms and turning.

She gasped, staring at a face, not her own, yet somehow intimately familiar.

While her parents' faces were simply etched into the cold, white marble, Alysia's was a vivid, lifelike carving, the stone itself dyed with vibrant colors. The image was as sharp and clear as a photograph, capturing the warmth of her honey-toned skin, the striking emerald green of her eyes, and the rich auburn tones of hair that framed her face.

"Your mother doesn't half-ass anything either," Ellie said, trying to lighten a moment that threatened to overwhelm her.

Aden wrapped his arms around her from behind. The hard muscles of his chest against her back, combined with his intoxicating scent, grounded her.

"How does it feel to you? To look at it?"

It took her almost a minute to reply, her gaze fixed on Aly's face. "Surreal. Strangely familiar, yet foreign. If that makes any sense."

"It does."

Sensing that he was holding back, she looked over her shoulder at him, silently encouraging him to continue.

When he didn't, she said, "And?"

He cringed ever so slightly.

"Sometimes I feel that way when I look at you. When I see your eyes."

Her lips curved into a half smile. "Why does telling me that make you cringe?"

"Because I don't want you to think I'm still in love with her. Or that I love you because you have her eyes."

"They're my eyes too." Ellie turned back to the gravestone. "How about because I'm the same soul and it's the other half of yours?"

His gentle but firm squeeze and the kiss to the top of her head were the only answers she needed.

"It hurts to look at," he said quietly.

"I know, baby." She let the endearment slip out as she threaded her fingers through his on her stomach. "I'm sorry."

"She was so fucking beautiful."

Aden tensed. He clearly hadn't meant to say that out loud.

She murmured her agreement, and his body relaxed. His love for Alysia in the past was as much a part of him as his love for her in the present.

"You know, I sometimes wonder if my lack of jealousy towards a dead woman is normal. Considering how deeply you loved her. But I'm not. Although I have to say, she had great hair."

She hoped to make him laugh, but he stiffened behind her again.

"You have no reason to be jealous of anyone, Ellie. Ever. Especially not Aly."

"It's not easy to compete with a memory."

He spun her around, his face furious. "You're not competing with a fucking memory." And just as quickly his anger abated, his expression softening into a plea. "The love I feel for you eclipses anything I felt for her. And I know that sounds crazy because you are her. But you're not. Not really. Fuck! I don't know how to explain it. Sometimes I wish you never remembered."

Ellie shook her head. "I don't. I was already falling in love with you before I got my memories back. And, our wedding night aside, I'm glad I have those memories again. It doesn't make me love you more, but I think it helps me understand you better." She traced his lower lip with her thumb, and he kissed it. "And when I look at you, I don't see the young man or vampire I loved in the past. I see the vampire, or old man, I love in the present. Does that make sense?"

"No." A scowl flashed across his face briefly before disappearing. "But I'll take it. I'll take your love any way you'll give it to me, even if you just called me an old man."

With a laugh, she shrugged. "Can I ask you something else?"

He tucked a loose strand of her hair behind her ear, nodding.

"Do you ever wish I had red hair, not brown?"

He dropped his hand like he'd been burned, and he took a step back. "Why the fuck would I wish that? I told you, I don't want you to be Aly. And I know I said she was beautiful, but there's no comparison, Ellie."

"You don't have to say that."

"I don't fucking say things I don't mean!"

"I could dye it if you wanted me to."

A horrified look crossed his face as he stared at her. A few seconds later, overcome with mirth, she breathed a laugh into the stillness of the night.

A furious snarl replaced his horror. "That's not fucking funny!"

"It's very fucking funny," she replied, still giggling.

After a minute, Aden's lips twitched. "Can we be done with this past life shit now?" His voice was rough as he tugged her against him. "It's exhausting, and vampires don't get tired."

She nodded. "I think we hit all the highlights, conquering all our demons."

"In one fucking week, no less."

Ellie shivered as a chill ran through her.

"Why are you shivering?"

"My feet are getting cold."

Aden crouched and scooped her up, wrapping her legs around his waist.

"Oh," she gasped.

"Come on, let's go take a bath and warm up."

"Do you want to say goodbye?" She asked, motioning to the headstone.

He shook his head, a grin spreading across his face. "No. I have everything I'll ever want and need right here in my arms."

His heartfelt words warmed her. This was why she loved him so much—her fierce, brutal, beautiful vampire with a tender heart.

No one else saw this side of him. She was the only one.

Leaning forward, she captured his lips. "You're my whole world," she whispered as their lips parted.

"I better be. Because I'm never fucking letting you go."

Aden turned, and Ellie looked over his shoulder at Aly and her parents' graves one last time. She expected to feel something more, faced with not only her own mortality but that of the people who had once given her life. But all she felt was detached from a life that was no longer hers.

This life she was living was hers. This life. As Ellie.

And as he strode away, she buried her face in his neck, brushing her lips over his cool skin, bidding that life a final goodbye.

Aden

The sound of his personal comm buzzing beside the bed woke Aden from his light sleep. He reached over and grabbed it before it could disturb Ellie.

"What?" His growl was low.

"Aden, did I wake you, son?"

"It's the middle of the day. What do you think?"

"I'm sorry, but we leave for the capital this evening, and there are a couple of things we should discuss before we go."

"Can we talk about it on the plane?"

"I'm going to be taking a separate plane. I have to stop at Cathair an Lae Amárach on my way."

Aden sat up, pushing the sheet away. "So, why aren't we all just stopping?"

"That's part of what I want to speak with you about. Can you spare me a few minutes?"

Aden looked over at Ellie and sighed. "I'll be there in ten."

"I'm in my office."

The line went dead, and he looked at his comm before tossing it onto the bedside table.

He rolled back over and looked down at her sleeping beside him. She was on her stomach with her face turned toward him. Her long, dark eyelashes rested against her cheek, and soft, shallow breaths escaped her lips, barely disturbing the quiet air.

She looked stunning but so fucking young when she slept. It made him feel like the pervert she once teasingly called him.

But it wasn't enough to stop him from leaning down and brushing his lips across her bare shoulder. His lips were a whisper over her skin, but she still stirred and moaned in her sleep.

His fingers brushed her hair aside as his mouth traced a path over her shoulder blade, then down her spine. He tugged the sheet down to her waist as he explored her warm skin. The rough texture of her scars beneath his lips made him frown. The feel and sight of them continued to fuel his guilt and anger, as he knew he was partly to blame.

Ellie squirmed as his lips reached the small of her back. A breathy laugh escaped her.

"You can't possibly want more already."

He smiled against her skin, and his lips traveled back up to her neck, then her ear.

"I always want more," he whispered as his tongue circled the shell. She moaned and turned on her side, pressing closer to him.

He grunted, and she looked at him with sleep-filled eyes.

"But not right now." His regret was palpable. "Aurick just called, and he wants to talk about the trip to the capital."

Her eyes narrowed. "It better not be about leaving me behind. I'm going, Aden."

"I fucking know," he snapped, having lost that argument on Christmas night when Ellie, his mother, and Keeley all ganged up on him.

"I love you," she breathed, her soft words instantly melting his irritation.

"Telling me you love me isn't going to always get you your way."

Ellie smiled, arching against him, and he groaned. Pulling her closer, he placed a gentle kiss on the base of her throat.

"Don't start something I can't finish."

She pulled back, rolling onto her stomach again, burying her face in the pillow. "Well, go then. I need my beauty rest."

Though muffled, he heard the teasing tone in her voice and grinned.

"I won't be long."

"Do you want me to stay, or do you want to do it alone?"

"Stay, he listens to—"

Aden overheard his parents whispering as the door to Aurick's office slid open. His father was seated at his desk, and Sophie stood next to him, leaning against it.

"So what's this about, Aurick?" He asked as he stepped inside. "Why aren't you flying to the capital with us?"

Sophie turned and smiled before walking around the desk to sit in a chair. Aden dropped into the one next to her.

"I've asked Katsumi to stop by Cathair an Lae Amárach on her way to Arcipelago."

"Why? Can't you just speak to her there?"

"No. This conversation needs privacy. We can't risk being overheard."

The tension mounted as he looked from his mother to his father.

"Okay. What's with all the secrecy?"

Pausing, Aurick took a deep breath before resting his folded hands on his desk.

"Aden, there are many things about my job and what I do that you're not privy to. Even though you're my Commander General, there are some details I keep from you because they don't impact you or the job you do. And there are others that until now you've been better off not knowing."

Aden cocked his head to the side. "So, are you finally going to explain why you haven't confronted Matthais about Ellie and her father?"

"I told you he was suspicious." Sophie gave Aurick a meaningful glance.

"Look, Aden—"

"You don't trust me. Is that it?"

"Your father and I trust you implicitly," his mother said, leaning forward. "It's been in your best interest to keep you out of the loop."

"Until certain things were in place," Aurick added. "But it's now time to tell you everything. And we will as soon as we return from the capital."

Aden's body tensed with annoyance. "If you weren't planning to tell me now, why the fuck did you drag me out of bed?"

"I want to make sure you understand it's crucial you keep your temper in check in Arcipelago. Especially with Matthais."

Annoyed by Aurick's insinuation that he couldn't control his anger, Aden gripped the arms of the chair.

"I've spoken to him twice since we found out, and I haven't lost my shit. Why are you so worried about it now?"

"Because you're going to have Ellie with you in the capital, and I know you're on edge already about it."

There were times he wished his parents didn't know him quite so well. This was one of them.

"Are you sure taking her is the right decision?"

"Aurick, don't start problems where there are none," Sophie warned.

"If I don't bring her to see her father, I'll be sleeping alone in my office for the next year."

His mother chuckled beside him.

"Why is that so fucking funny?"

"Because my six-foot-five vampire son is afraid of a five-foot-six human woman."

"I'm glad you find this so amusing."

"Aden," Aurick said, his face serious. "I need your word you'll stay calm and act like you don't know anything."

"I don't know anything."

"Matthais will likely try to bait you about Ellie, particularly because she'll be staying in the concubine suite. Don't let him. I've promised you we'll get restitution for her and her father. Have I ever gone back on my word to you?"

That answer was simple.

"No."

"I won't start now. He will face the consequences of his actions. It's just going to take some time. You'll understand more when we talk after we return."

"Is this related to Matthais' policy to eliminate anyone who dares to rebel?"

"That's one aspect of it," Aurick replied, his voice low and thoughtful.

"And Katsumi is part of whatever it is you're doing?"

"Yes."

"Are any of the other Gerents involved?"

Aurick and Sophie exchanged a look.

"Yes."

"Could you be any more fucking vague?" Aden shook his head, exhaled, and forced a smile. "Fine. We'll talk when we return. And I'll try not to cause any chaos in the capital. But if Matthais so much as sniffs around Ellie, all bets are off."

"I don't think he will," Aurick replied. "You've repaid the debt you owed for her, so he has nothing to hold over you and no reason to interfere with her."

"Just make sure you keep her in your suite, and she'll be fine," Sophie said.

"Yeah, knowing Ellie, I'll have no problem at all doing that," Aden scoffed as he stood.

"When you ask Matthais' permission for her to see her father, insist he come to the suite. Drake will be there in case anything happens."

Aden nodded in agreement. "I plan to leave Kane outside the door most of the time, too. What about this friend of hers?"

"Ellie said her name is Carrie," Sophie said, standing. "I'll have the thralls discretely inquire about her and arrange for her to visit Ellie in your room. Keeley will stop by and see her a few times, too, so she's not lonely while you're busy."

"Keeley's coming now? What about her spawn?"

"Yes," his mother said, giving him a sharp look. "Ryan's staying back, but she's traveling home with your father to get him settled with the nannies. Then she'll fly over with your dad. I'll be on the plane with you and Ellie."

"Okay." Aden stepped toward the door. "I need a couple of hours of sleep before we leave."

He looked at Aurick, the lines around his father's eyes more prominent.

"I guess I'll see you when I see you," he said, then walked out.

The first sound Aden heard when he entered their bedroom was Ellie's heartbeat, slow and steady. She'd gone back to sleep. Though still lying on her stomach, she'd rolled onto his side of the bed, her face buried in his pillow.

Eager for her, he stripped off his clothes and slid under the few covers she left for him. His lips, warm and insistent, grazed her neck and shoulders as his fingers, light as a feather, swept her hair aside. He pulled the sheet off them, straddling her and planting his knees on either side of her hips on the mattress.

He should let her sleep. A less selfish man would have. But he was aching for her, and his busy schedule in the capital would leave him with little time with her.

Aden swirled his tongue over the salty-sweet curve of her back, causing her to stir. His cock swelled, thickening and lengthening, and he pressed it against her ass.

"Aden," Ellie murmured before burying her face deeper into the pillow.

Any remorse he might have felt at waking her vanished the instant he tasted her skin. A smile played on his lips as they trailed lower, tracing a path down her spine.

She came awake beneath him, squirming and arching her back, a moan escaping her. He slipped his fingers between her thighs, finding her warm and wet, the remnants of their earlier orgasms still present, like a mark of his claim on her. His cock surged against her ass, insistent and aching, yearning to be inside her again.

Ellie murmured his name again, her voice raspy with sleep.

He rose to his knees above her, his fingertips continuing to tease her, relishing how responsive she was even in her drowsy state. She lifted her head and turned her face to look at him, her eyes heavy-lidded and curious.

"What are you doing?"

"If you don't know, I'm not doing it right." He chuckled, the sound a low rumble in his chest, trailing his lips over her skin, leaving a trail of goosebumps in their wake. "Now shut up and let me fuck you."

Ellie's sultry smile in response to his words sent a fresh surge of desire through him. She spread her thighs, inviting him in as his fingers slipped inside her. Her soft groan echoed in the quiet room as he delved deeper into her warmth, his thumb pressed against her clit.

"Aden," she moaned, long and low, rocking her hips.

"Shh," he whispered, his breath ghosting over the shell of her ear.

Ellie arched her back deeper, pushing up on her hands. Each thrust of his fingers into her drew another ragged breath from her lips. He wrapped his other arm around her waist, drawing her up to her knees.

She whimpered as she pushed back.

He withdrew his fingers, sliding them over her ass, lingering on the curve, leaving a wet trail over her flesh. He leaned down, swirling his tongue through her arousal, the flavor of her sweet and musky, before nipping her cheek with his teeth.

A soft squeal escaped her lips, a shudder running through her, but it turned into a moan as he used his tongue to soothe the bite that didn't break the skin.

Aden gripped her hips, pressing just the tip of his cock into her welcoming heat. Ellie quivered beneath him, her breath coming in short, breathy pants as he entered her slowly.

"Fuck Ellie," he choked as he felt her wrap around him.

It only took a few thrusts, and he was seated inside her, his fingers sinking into the softness of her waist. She wriggled, trying to work him deeper, and Aden's hips bucked of their own volition. His movements started slow and measured, deep but gentle thrusting motions, as her body yielded to him. His hand skimmed down the flat plane of her belly. He pressed his fingertips against her clit, teasing her as her body eagerly swallowed him.

She rocked with him, their bodies moving in sync. Each time he pushed forward, she pushed back with equal force, colliding with heavy, wet thuds, punctuated only by the rasp of their breaths.

"Please," she begged softly, and that was his undoing.

What began as a slow, lazy, sleepy rhythm soon turned urgent, increasing in speed and strength. Aden pumped with long strokes, withdrawing almost completely before plunging back in again, making her gasp. His fingers abandoned her clit to grip the soft flesh of her hips harder, leaving more bruises, holding her steady against his powerful thrusts.

Each of Ellie's gasps, quiet at first, built upon the last, until she was crying out beneath him, her voice raw with desperation, begging and pleading for him to never stop. She met his every thrust with equal fervor.

Minutes stretched into an eternity of sensations as they moved together in the darkness. His grunts, her pants, and the slick sounds of their flesh slapping reverberated through the room, heavy with the scent of sex. Aden encircled her waist again, his fingers splayed across her lower belly, her muscles tense beneath his touch.

He held her captive against him, feeling every tremor that passed through her body, keeping her anchored to him as pleasure threatened to sweep them both away. Bracing his other hand on the mattress beside hers, he pressed his forehead against the center of her back, focusing entirely on the feel of her surrounding him, thrusting steady and deep.

"Ellie," he chanted her name. "Come for me, baby," he croaked, his voice a ragged whisper, knowing he wouldn't last much longer.

Her scent deepened, perfuming the air, and her arms shook as her head fell forward, Aden watching in awe as she surrendered completely.

"Oh Aden." Her quiet sob echoed through the room as her body convulsed beneath him.

He tightened his arm around her to keep her from collapsing onto the mattress. Each shudder of her body resonated through his own, her muscles clenching, gripping him in pulsing waves that threatened to unravel his control. He pressed his lips to her ear and whispered his love for her.

The exquisite sensation of her orgasm, slick and tight and perfect, was enough to set him off. Ellie lifted her head and tilted it back against his shoulder, baring her throat to him.

"Let go," she breathed, giving him permission.

Humbled by her submission, he accepted her offering, sinking his fangs into her neck. The dual sensations overwhelmed him, the intoxicating taste of her blood flooding his mouth as his cock erupted inside her.

She stiffened, her body freezing. Aden's orgasm ripped through him as a second one tore through hers. She clamped down on him so hard, that his eyes crossed. The venom he pumped into her bloodstream prolonged her climax, trapping her in a state of bliss despite her inability to move.

Finally, the paralysis released its hold, and with a sudden jerk, Ellie's body went limp, her arms giving out. She collapsed onto the bed. Aden moved with her, unwilling to remove his fangs or his cock just yet, but he stopped drinking. He savored the sweet, metallic taste of her blood on his tongue, trickling past the fangs still embedded in her neck.

Careful not to crush her, he rested his body on hers, reveling in the warmth of her skin against his, as she whimpered his name before succumbing to sleep.

Aden

Aden sat on the sofa in Matthais' great hall, the buzzing of the activity around him grating on his nerves.

Andrei settled in his usual spot across from him, his thrall on her knees at his feet. Aden didn't bring one with him tonight. Ellie would murder him if he did.

He left her behind in his suite, with both Kane and Drake standing guard outside the room. She wanted to accompany him, hoping to see her friend or her father, but he insisted she wait until he assessed the situation. That didn't go over well. He tried to entice her into bed for a quickie before he left, but she refused, retreating to the concubine suite to put her clothes away rather than have sex with him.

Her excited chatter on the plane about seeing them convinced Aden that keeping her confined to his room for the entire trip would be almost impossible. But he needed to evaluate the situation and figure out how to keep her protected, especially since he couldn't be with her all the time. Matthais' city was not, and never would be, a safe place for Ellie. Of that, he was sure.

Everything she brought with her was teal or teal and white, combined with the family crest necklace Sophie lent her, which identified her as his pet. That alone would offer her more protection than an ordinary thrall, so he didn't object to her clothes this time.

His scent on her, intensified by the blood she now shared with him, would mark her as forbidden to all other vampires. Even Matthais. But Aden had zero trust in him, feeling nothing but utter contempt for the vampire now.

Sophie was chatting with Indira on one of the other sofas across the room, but Aurick and Keeley had yet to arrive. Impatient and restless, Aden wanted to leave but chose to wait for them.

Vincent strolled in, leading his pet on a leash, the blonde he outbid Aden for the previous summer. She looked much worse than the last time he saw her. Despite her expensive outfit, the marks on her body were obvious.

Aden frowned. Vampires rarely abuse their pets. Most received better treatment than other thralls, but there were always those deviant vampires who ignored societal norms. Vincent was one of them.

He gave Aden and Andrei a subtle nod, his eyes lingering for a moment before he moved across the room to speak to another vampire.

"What's Vincent's deal?" Aden asked as the girl struggled to keep up with his long strides.

"What do you mean?"

"He's always creeping around here during gatherings. He's a civilian, so there's no need for him to attend."

"Matthais has taken a liking to him. He comes in from Roathune every few weeks."

"Sometimes I wonder about his choice of companions."

Andrei laughed. "You and me, man. Vincent is kind of an asshole, but he's alright."

Aden grunted his disagreement.

"So, as usual, Kira's been talking about you. You planning to see her again?"

Aden's face twisted in disgust as he shook his head. "I'm done with her batshit crazy."

After her treatment of Ellie, Kira was lucky she still had a fucking head.

"Yeah, you always say that. Then you cave when she walks into a room looking like every vampire's wet dream."

"If you think she's so hot, you're welcome to her."

"Are you kidding me?" Andrei's eyes widened in mock horror. "She's a viper. You don't get into bed with the devil unless you want your throat slit."

"And you just proved my point," Aden said, his gaze catching sight of Vincent pushing his pet to her knees beside him. Her grunt of pain echoed across the room.

"You're the only one who's ever been able to tame her," Andrei said, drawing Aden's focus back to him.

"No thanks. Like I said, I'm done."

Andrei paused, studying him. "Matthais mentioned you took a pet this summer."

Fuck!

Aden stiffened, his muscles tensing, but he hoped Andrei hadn't noticed. "Why is that so noteworthy?"

"It's the first time."

Fuck! Fuck!

How did he respond without revealing Ellie's importance to him?

"I finally found one to my liking, I guess."

"You reek of her. Is it Myles' daughter? You set off a hell of a shitstorm last year when you claimed her."

"Why? It's not like it was the first time I bit a thrall that wasn't mine."

Andrei leaned down and sunk his fangs into his thrall's neck. When he released her, she collapsed against the sofa.

"True." He wiped the blood from the corner of his lips. "But she's the daughter of Matthais' favorite guard. Don't ask me why the fuck he values Myles so much, but he does. And apparently, he had plans for her you ruined."

Aden's stomach plummeted with a sickening lurch.

"What plans?"

Andrei shrugged. "Fuck if I know. But he was pissed for months. I think he eventually got over it when Dietrich gifted him with a new pet. Larissa, I think her name is. He's become a bit obsessed with her."

Until that moment, Aden had never felt sorry for a thrall.

Aden considered jumping out the window more than once tonight. For the last three hours, the first meeting of the annual council gathering consisted of one argument after another.

But this was one blowup he expected.

"Matthais," Aurick spoke, his voice laced with controlled anger. "The annihilation of thirty thousand humans was an excessive response to that situation. Why didn't Anatoly simply eliminate the rogues and spare the villagers? He could have sanctioned them, a punishment that would have been harsh but fair, instead of resorting to a brutal act of murder that violates our core principles. Or the ones we once agreed to uphold."

Anatoly bristled where he sat behind Yuri, his jaw tightening and his hands clenching into fists.

"That's easy to say when you've had no rebellion inside your borders." Yuri's snarl came from the other end of the long conference table.

"And why is that, Yuri? Maybe because we treat our humans with kindness and compassion. We're morally obligated to ensure the well-being and protection of every human under our care."

"Aurick," Matthais said, his patience strained. "Given your frontline experience in the Great Vampire Wars, you know full well that restoring order and ensuring safety sometimes require sacrifice." He turned to Aden. "What is your assessment of the tactics taken during this mission?"

Aden stole a quick look at Aurick, and the grim set of his father's jaw and the caution in his eyes spoke volumes—a silent command to proceed with care.

Before Ellie entered his life, he would have sided with Matthais on principle. Post-Ellie, Aden's once rigid and often inflexible views on the treatment of humans had softened considerably. But Aurick's warning from two days earlier echoed in his mind. Keep his changed opinion of Matthais and his shifted perspectives hidden for now.

He chose his words carefully.

"This clearly wasn't a hastily organized uprising. This had been a long time in the planning, coordinated with non-feral rogues. Rebellion can't be tolerated, but humans are easily influenced. They can hardly be blamed for being impressionable when they're uneducated. The situation necessitated some losses, but the scale of the extermination was excessive, in my opinion, and far beyond what was necessary to suppress the revolt."

From the corner of his eye, his father gave a subtle nod of approval.

A bitter twist formed on Yuri's lips. "This coming from the man who blatantly commandeered another vampire's humans, an Ancient One's, no less, without permission, to bait feral rogues. Excuse me, if I don't give your opinion very much weight."

Aden growled under his breath, his anger flaring to life at the reminder of his actions the previous year.

Now he wanted to fucking throw Yuri out the window.

"Yuri," Matthais said in a conciliatory tone. Why hadn't Aden noticed how fake he always sounded? "That one incident aside, Aden's military strategy is above reproach."

Cecilia scoffed, and he shot her a sneer, the memory of having to grovel to her still bitter.

"Tell me, Anatoly," Aden addressed the man directly. "Did you trace that armor? Where did those rogues get it?"

Anatoly glanced at Yuri before replying, jaw clenched. "The serial numbers were melted off."

"How convenient."

"What are you insinuating, Aden?" Yuri demanded, his eyes blazing.

"I don't know, you tell me," he snarled in response. "Maybe if they hadn't been tossed onto those pyres along with the humans, we'd have—"

"That's enough," Matthais interrupted, with a rare snarl of his own. "Both the rogues and humans paid the price for their deeds. They actively conspired to commit open rebellion. That cannot and will not be tolerated. Not as long as I am Chancellor."

"We must choose between upholding our principles or descending into chaos," Aurick said. "If history has shown us nothing else, it's that."

Matthais ignored his statement and moved on to the next topic while Aden stared out the window, calculating the drop to the jagged rocks and water below, trying to decide whether the pain would be worth escaping this fucking meeting.

Ellie

Consciousness came to Ellie slowly, something soft and wet swirling on the skin of her stomach. She stretched, sighing as she realized it was Aden's tongue. A low moan escaped her lips as he dipped it into her belly button.

"Mmmm, is it evening yet?" She asked, her voice sleepy.

How could it be night already? It felt like she'd just fallen asleep. Aden had been insatiable earlier, almost desperate, after he returned from his meetings. He was on edge. They both were about her being back under Matthais' roof, and their anxiety manifested in their frenzied lovemaking.

But there was nothing frantic about what he was doing to her body now.

He didn't answer her question, so she lifted her head and looked down. He was looking up at her as his lips skimmed over the sensitive skin below her navel. His eyes were hooded and dark, almost crimson, and full of lust.

The look was one Ellie was intimately familiar with now, a predatory glint that sparked a thrill of anticipation and made the spot under her belly button clench.

He flashed his signature sexy smirk, pushed her thighs wide, held them down, and moved his face closer to her, breathing her in. A low growl rumbled in his throat before his tongue swept over her.

"Aden," she whispered as her head fell back onto the pillow and her eyes rolled back.

The first touch of his tongue against her sensitive flesh sent shivers cascading through Ellie's already fluttering stomach, gentle at first, a whisper of sensation that quickly transformed into something far more consuming. Each stroke sparked new waves of pleasure that radiated outward from her core. When her hips bucked instinctively toward the source of that intense feeling, Aden's hand pressed firmly on her abdomen, the weight of it both restraining and reassuring.

Her thighs quivered around his head as he traced swirling patterns over her clit. But when he drew it into the wet heat of his mouth, stars exploded behind her eyelids, and Ellie's world narrowed to nothing but feeling.

She reached down, her fingers brushing against the soft, dark curls of his hair. The silky texture against her fingertips was a stark contrast to the intensity building in her core, and she tugged on the short strands.

His tongue delved deeper, and she pulled harder, the rumbling growl that vibrated through her soaked flesh making her breath hitch. The pressure of his fingers on her thigh, hard enough to bruise, only heightened her awareness of every sensation. The marks he left on her skin were badges of honor, physical reminders of the intense passion they created together.

A sound of protest formed in her throat when his tongue left her, only to dissolve into a sigh as his attention shifted to the sensitive juncture where her pelvis met her thigh. His hands sliding beneath her, cupping and lifting, made her feel both vulnerable and worshipped.

She arched her hips as he drove her body closer and closer to the edge. She knew his intention when he started sucking on her skin, drawing blood to the surface. It took all of her strength to lift her head again and look at him. There was something profoundly beautiful about seeing him there, his face between her thighs, his entire focus on the most intimate part of her.

His eyes silently asked permission, and she nodded before letting her head fall back. As his fangs pierced her femoral artery, he slid one long finger inside her, creating a perfect balance of pleasure and pain that had her body seizing in ecstasy. The familiar paralytic effect of his venom flooded her system, rendering her motionless but heightening every sensation to an almost unbearable degree. He pulled her blood into his mouth, and her orgasm slammed into her so hard it blurred her vision.

She wanted to thrash wildly, arch into his touch, cry out, but his venom held her captive. Unable to escape or evade the intensity, the mind-numbing bliss lasted what felt like an eternity before her paralysis ceased. Every muscle contracted and released in waves as his name tore from her throat, her body convulsing, sinking into the mattress.

Before she could gather her scattered thoughts or catch her breath, he moved over her, licking the blood from his lips. He sank inside her in one hard, deep thrust, filling her completely, stretching her to the limits, and forcing the air from her lungs in a long, drawn-out groan. It didn't matter how aroused she was, how ready her body was for him; it still shocked her every time he entered her.

"Yes, goddess," he groaned as he kissed her, the reverence in his voice making her heart swell.

The taste of her arousal mingled with the metallic sweetness of her blood on his lips created an intoxicating flavor. She sucked on his tongue hungrily, craving more of it.

Aden pinned her to the bed, each thrust of his hips building on the lingering sensations of her previous climax, pushing her toward another orgasm that was just out of reach.

Ellie whimpered into his mouth, wrapping her legs around him, pulling him deeper, seeking to eliminate any remaining space between their bodies. This closeness was everything, and the thought of it ending ignited a desperate need within her to hold on to the moment, to stretch it into eternity.

He trapped her wrists above her head, and the restraint only heightened her desire. She arched her back, her breasts bouncing, her sensitive nipples grazing his chest. Combined with the insistent throbbing in her clit, Ellie's body buzzed like a live wire.

Aden broke the kiss, eyes squeezed shut, a low groan escaping his lips as he rasped her name.

Ellie kept her eyes open, watching his face. He was so beautiful when he let himself go like this, losing himself inside her. It was in these unguarded moments, when all pretense fell away and his guard dropped, that she knew without a doubt she made the right choice. Sharing her blood with him deepened their love for each other. Just like the first time, it felt sacred, a merging of their souls.

Every forceful thrust of his cock pressed her hips deeper into the mattress, her body yielding beneath him as ecstasy built beyond what she thought was possible. Her fragile human body could only take so much, trembling on the edge of what it could endure, the intensity almost frightening.

His relentless rhythm pushed her to a place where pleasure and pain blurred into one overwhelming sensation, and when her second orgasm crashed over her, it felt like being swept away by a tidal wave.

Ellie convulsed violently underneath him as he drove into her one final time and came inside her.

"Fuck, yes," Aden roared, and Ellie tilted her head, inviting him to sink his fangs into her neck.

The twin pinpricks breaching the delicate skin of her throat were the last feeling she registered before darkness claimed her and everything went black.

Aden

"**M**o ghrá," Aden murmured against her skin as his lips trailed down her chest. "Wake up for me now."

He nuzzled her breast before taking her nipple into his mouth, flicking it with the tip of his tongue. He nicked it with his fang for another brief taste of her blood because he couldn't get enough. She arched her back and stretched, and he released her, grinning as her eyes fluttered open.

Ellie's lips curled, and she sighed.

He couldn't resist kissing her again. In a soft murmur against her lips, he professed his devotion before burying his face in her neck to lick the oozing puncture wounds. He always bit her on the same spot, the spot of his first bite, to prevent any further scarring of her otherwise flawless skin.

"You have to stop blacking out on me."

The first time she did that on Christmas morning nearly shattered Aden, consuming him with the horrifying, gut-wrenching fear that he'd killed her again. But her strong pulse and the fluttering behind her eyelids reminded him she was prone to losing consciousness. It only happened after her most intense orgasms, but he reveled in it now, taking pride in his ability to make her come so hard she passed out.

Ellie turned her face and kissed his ear, nuzzling as she laughed softly. "I can't help it. God, I don't know how I'm gonna be able to walk."

"If I had my way, you wouldn't even get out of this bed." Aden pushed up on his arm, his fingers tracing a path down her body, making her shudder. "But you need BloodStone."

"I think I need more than BloodStone. You were pretty greedy."

"But you taste so fucking good," he said. "You should have breakfast delivered, too." He glanced at the clock on the bedside table. "I have to leave for the games in a half hour."

Ellie pushed on his chest, scooting out from under him. "Why do you have to go? I thought you weren't going to."

"I won't play, and I won't attend the rest of the week, but I have to go to opening night."

She got out of bed and reached for her robe, wrapping it around her. She tightened the belt, closing herself off from him.

"Why?"

Aden stood and headed to the bathroom. "Ellie, cut me some slack, will you? I have to go."

He turned on the shower and stepped in before the water even heated up. He didn't want to wash off her scent, but going to the games smelling so strongly of her and sitting next to Andrei was out of the fucking question.

She followed him into the bathroom, leaning against the counter, a frown pulling at her lips. He wished she'd follow him in so he could have her one more time, but her face revealed the impossibility of that hope.

"How long will you be there?"

"I'll leave after the first round. Anything before that, Matthais will get suspicious."

He showered quickly, instantly missing her scent on his skin, then toweled off before stepping out.

"Why do you care what he thinks? Why is it bad you don't attend? Your dad doesn't."

"He never has. But I have." Aden walked into the adjacent closet, grabbing a clean pair of boxer briefs, sliding them up his legs before pulling on a pair of his usual black pants. "And I don't give a fuck what Matthais thinks, but I won't put you in danger by acting any differently. He'll know it's because of you. And no one outside the family can know how I feel about you. Not yet."

Ellie watched him from the doorway, anxiously twisting her hands. "I know. I just hate that you have to go. It makes my stomach ache. I was so heartbroken when you went to the summer games."

"I didn't play then, either."

"You didn't?" she asked with a mix of surprise and relief on her face.

Aden slipped his arms into his shirt and fastened the buttons. Why the fuck was she so surprised about that?

"No. I was too upset over what happened at the beach house. And I'm trying to be a better fucking man for you."

Ellie approached him, sliding her arms around his waist and tilting her face up to his for a kiss.

He fell into it, and into her, deepening it until she pushed him away, needing breath.

"Aden, when can I see my dad and Carrie? It's already our second night here."

"I have to speak to Matthais. Protocol requires that I ask his permission."

"Why didn't you ask him at the meeting earlier?"

Aden grabbed a pair of socks and walked out of the closet, Ellie trailing behind him.

"Because it wasn't the time or place. It got pretty heated, and he walked out as soon as it was over. I'll try to talk to him before tomorrow's meeting."

Ellie bit her lip, furrowing her brow. "What if he says no? What if he keeps my dad away?"

"I doubt he'll do that. Courtesy dictates that a request like that be granted."

"But what if he does?"

Aden scowled as he looked around for his shoes, finding one under the bed.

"Then I'll deal with it. Fuck, Ellie, have a little faith in me to do this for you?"

"I do." She grabbed his other shoe from beside the sofa and handed it to him as he sat in the chair. "But what about Carrie? He shouldn't care if I see another thrall? Can't I just go see her?"

"No. Sophie is having her thralls ask about her so she can come visit you here. I'll talk to her about it when I see her later."

"How long will you be?"

"A couple of hours. And you're to remain in this room at all times. Kane will stay here with Drake while I'm gone."

Aden stood up after he finished putting on his socks and shoes.

"Why aren't you taking him with you??"

"I want him here with you."

"But Aden," she protested. "He's always supposed to be with you."

"I can take care of myself. I've left him behind plenty of times. Just don't fucking argue with me. Not here. I have enough to deal with without having to worry about you."

Ellie nodded, apprehension etched on her face. "I don't like the idea of you going without him."

"I'm a big boy, Ellie."

The neckline of her robe slipped off her shoulder, exposing the skin of her collarbone, drawing Aden's gaze.

"Fuck, why did I get dressed already?"

"Huh?" She looked at him, confused.

He pulled her into him, his hand tugging at her robe's belt. Suddenly, she swayed a little.

He grabbed her arms, his touch firm but gentle, to steady her. "What's the matter with you?"

She shook her head. "Just a little dizzy. I definitely need more than Blood-Stone tonight. You took a lot of blood from me."

"Call Mina and the kitchen. Get BloodStone and food. No more orgasms for you until I get back."

She pouted, pulling her robe closed as she moved to sit on the sofa. "I can't initiate a hologram, so can you call for them?"

Ignoring her question, he walked over and tilted her face up to look at him. "You're a little pale."

Why hadn't he fucking noticed that?

She caressed his cock through his pants. He grabbed her hand and pulled it away with a groan.

"Behave!"

She smirked. "Yes, Sir. I need to get used to calling you that again while we're here."

"No, you don't. You won't be in anyone's presence that would require you to address me like that."

Anger flared in her eyes. "So, I'm just going to be locked in this room like a prisoner the entire time?"

"Ellie, you knew you wouldn't be able to roam free. Don't act like it's a surprise."

He held her gaze, his eyes burning with a silent challenge. She picked up her tablet from the table. Settling against the cushions, she tucked her feet beneath her and dismissed him with an aggravated wave.

"Fine. Go to the games. I'm going to read the books Hannah gave me."

Not wanting to fight anymore, he turned and headed to the door.

"I'll be back in a few hours."

Kane and Drake were standing on the other side when the door slid open.

"Order Ellie some food and have Mina bring her a BloodStone IV."

Without waiting for an answer, he strode down the hallway, wondering when he'd suddenly become the fucking bad guy.

Andrei was already in the Westcott's private skybox when Aden arrived for the HEW games.

Modeled after the Colosseum of Rome, the capital's outdoor arena, a massive circular structure of weathered limestone and granite, dominated the snowy landscape outside Arcipelago.

The games were a brutal spectacle where humans fought each other to the death. Not that they had a choice. Players were forced to compete.

As usual this time of year, snow blanketed the arena's dirt floor. The temperature was frigid. Though cold temperatures didn't affect vampires, humans froze easily in them.

He dropped into the seat beside Andrei, who looked up from the hologram projecting his players for the night. He was Matthais' gamer, and he and Aden had a centuries-long rivalry, swapping the championship back and forth. After holding the title for almost a century, Andrei dethroned him last year thanks to the distraction that was Ellie.

"Matthais loaded you up." He motioned to the console on the chair next to Aden.

"Yeah, I don't know if I feel like playing tonight."

"What the fuck, Aden? What's up your ass about the games lately? First, you tanked the championship last January and then again over the summer. Don't get me wrong, I love winning, but I don't want it handed to me. I'm starting to think you're no longer into this."

Aden brushed off Andrei's words with a shrug. "It's lost its appeal."

"Come on, man, without you, my next closest opponent is Vincent. And I'd despise losing to him."

"There's no way he'd beat you."

"He did pretty well last summer. Gave me a run, but in the end, I kicked his ass. Why are you not into it anymore?"

Aden cast a quick glance at the hologram of the arena projected at eye level with the Gerent's skyboxes. The polar bears and arctic wolves Andrei told him about in Sever Sib-Ir paced in their cages, their warm breath forming swirling patterns in the frigid air around their heads.

"I'm just not. Let it go, man."

"You need—" Andrei began, but his words were cut off by the roars of the crowd as Matthais stepped out to the glass platform in front of his skybox.

"Welcome, my friends, to the opening night of the winter Human Extinction Warfare Games, where we celebrate our triumph in the Great Vampire Wars. Humans once dared to call us inferior, even after we saved them from extinction.

Twice. We gave them BloodStone, eradicating their second pandemic and curing their pathetic mortal diseases. When the comet hit and their continents shattered, we rebuilt civilization from the ruins. Yet they still denied us the respect and gratitude we deserved. So we claimed it and broke free from their tyranny. Tonight, as we have for nearly five centuries, we celebrate our freedom."

Matthais recycled the same speech every year, though it sounded like he mixed it up this time. But Aden was listening to it with fresh ears. Although his parents taught him history as a child, he wondered what, if anything, they'd omitted. He'd have to ask Sophie at some point, when they both had some time.

"I am once again offering my lovely Zurina for your enjoyment while you play," Matthais said.

His prized polar bear loped around the arena, led by her guard, roaring at the sound of her name. The crowd cheered for the deadly killing machine.

"And I have a special treat for our opening night, a pair of arctic wolves, specially bred for these games."

The two wolves, almost as large as Zurina, elicited even louder cheers from the stands. Aden scoffed under his breath, disgusted with himself for ever having enjoyed this spectacle.

"So, without further delay, let us begin our annual week-long celebration."

Matthais returned to his skybox as guards led the human players, ten from each region, both men and women, onto the field. Bound by chains, freezing, frightened, and barely clothed, each wore a metal collar embedded into their necks that enabled the vampires to control their actions via wireless consoles. Branded across their skin were their region's crests.

The guards herded the players into assigned cages by region, including the Westcott's. Matthais provided ones for Aden because Aurick refused to allow their humans to take part. But that was where Aden's players remained when he didn't pick up his console. They would likely die from exposure, but it would be a more merciful fate than being ripped to shreds.

He watched the first two rounds, the arctic wolves making the already brutal game even more vicious as the humans fought to survive each other and the animals. The sound of the bears and wolves tearing the humans apart, shrieks echoing in the freezing night, used to thrill Aden. Now it just made him sick.

He stood when the third round began, having been there long enough. All he could think about was being back in his suite with Ellie, buried deep inside her body and her vein, letting her quiet breaths and moans drown out the screams.

"I'm out. Have fun kicking Vincent's ass."

Andrei sighed. "See you tomorrow night. We'll go to my new training facility. I modeled it after yours, the one you used to train Paolo's troops."

"Alright. I'll catch up with you."

Aden turned to leave and caught Matthais' disappointed frown.

And an unsettling shudder of unease ran down his spine.

Matthais

Matthais approached the door to Aden's guest suite. Two guards stood at attention in the hallway. He recognized Kane, Aden's longtime bodyguard, and while the other was familiar to him, he couldn't quite place him.

"Master Matthais, Sir," Kane said. "Master Aden is not here. I believe he's in a meeting with Master Aurick."

"I'm not looking for Aden." He gave the two men a cursory glance and a cruel sneer as the door opened and he walked through.

The scent of blood and sex filled the room. His eyes landed on the girl in the bed, a thin sheet barely concealing the lower half of her naked body. She lay on her stomach, the jagged raised scars he'd inflicted on her visible like pale rivers across her back, though less prominent than he expected. Fresh bruises marked her hips and ass. Her dark hair, a tangled mess, splayed across the pillow, and dried blood crusted over the puncture marks on her neck.

At least Aden was using his gift. And by the looks of it, he was enjoying her.

She stirred, a soft sigh escaping her lips as she rolled onto her side.

"Hello, Elliana."

The girl bolted upright, and the sheet fell away from her body, revealing her to his gaze. She gasped as her eyes flickered upwards, only to drop quickly. She grasped the sheet, pulling it around her as she shifted to her knees, bowing her head.

"Master Matthais." Her voice trembled as she said his name.

He was impressed by her immediate submission.

At that moment, Aden strode through the door, his eyes blazing with fury, the sound of his heavy footsteps against the polished marble floor echoing in the tense silence.

"Matthais," he snarled. "What the fuck is the meaning of this?"

The girl's body sagged with what looked like relief even as she remained in a prone position.

"Ah, Aden, there you are. I was looking for you."

"Ellie," he barked at his pet. "Go to your room. Now!"

Elliana scrambled off the bed, almost tripping over the sheet, before scurrying into the concubine suite.

His eyes still blazing, Aden turned to Matthais, his jaw visibly tense. "Is there something I can help you with? If you needed to see me, you could've used a fucking hologram."

"Your holograms are blocked."

"I always block them when I'm with my pet," he replied through clenched teeth. "I guess I forgot to turn them back on."

"Yes," Matthais said with a chuckle. "I heard you stopped breaking your thralls, but the bruises on Elliana were fresh and glorious to see. And her submission was immediate when she realized I was here. You've trained her well. I'm impressed. Though I don't think you've ever kept a thrall in the concubine suite here. She's clearly... different from your other thralls."

"Is there something I can do for you, Matthais?"

An undercurrent of controlled fury resonated in Aden's tone, but Matthais ignored it.

"I just wanted to make sure you were settling in. You left the games early last night."

"I had more pressing matters to attend to."

Matthais glanced toward the concubine suite. "Yes, it appears so. Your scent is incredibly strong on her. You either spend an extraordinary amount of time pumping your venom into her, or you've shared your blood with her."

"Ellie doesn't drink my blood. After we returned home with her last year, she almost succumbed to her injuries, so some of my blood was necessary to ensure she survived."

"It seems fresher than that."

"Well, I use her to excess, so Mina usually has to amp up the BloodStone with a couple of drops of my blood. It's often given to her via IV." Aden gestured to the stand in the corner.

"Ahh, I see."

Aden cleared his throat, his body still vibrating with suppressed anger. "Actually, since you're here, it saves me a visit to your office. Ellie asked permission to see her father. I don't have a problem with it. I assume you don't either."

Matthais narrowed his eyes. Aden's concern for Elliana was uncharacteristic of him.

"A happy pet is far more likely to be eager to please. I'll tell Myles he can see her tomorrow night while we're at the meeting."

"I appreciate the consideration."

"Of course, Aden. Do I need to worry about her condition? I don't want one of my favorite guards to find his daughter broken."

Aden's lips curled into a defensive sneer, a low growl rumbling in his chest. "As you said, I don't break my thralls anymore."

"Well, we'll see about that," Matthais said, the words hanging in the air like a threat. "In fact, I'd like to show you something. Come to my office tomorrow night after the party. You do plan to attend the annual ball?"

"Yes."

"Good." Matthais smiled. "I have something I'd like to share with you."

Aden

Matthais left, and Aden flipped the coffee table into the air. It crashed onto the floor, sending splinters scattering across the floor toward the door he'd just exited.

"Fuck!"

He clenched his teeth until he felt they might crack. He wanted to destroy something, anything, to keep him from going after Matthais and ripping his heart out.

The sight of him looming over a nearly naked, trembling Ellie made Aden's blood run cold. A furious, bone-chilling rage flared within him. He'd barely restrained himself from attacking the vampire on the spot.

Though fury burned in his chest, a knot of worry twisted tighter. He needed her, needed to make sure she was alright. He walked to the door of the concubine suite. It slid open, revealing her seated on the bed in her robe.

"Ellie," he said gently. "He's gone. You can come out now."

Her eyes whipped up, relief flooding them as she exhaled a breath. She rushed over to him.

"I heard the crash. Are you okay?"

"I'm fine. Are you okay?" His teeth and fists clenched again. "He didn't do anything to you, did he?"

"No." She shook her head, wrapping her arms around herself. "He had just said my name, and then you came rushing in. Why was he here?"

"Because he's a fucking pervert."

"But why would he come here when he knew you weren't here?"

Aden stomped back to the middle of the room. "To show us he could. I knew I shouldn't have let you come."

The sound of her soft steps was almost inaudible as she trailed behind him.

"Be careful of the wood," he cautioned as she stepped around the broken table.

"Aden, I'm fine. A little creeped out, but okay. Where were Kane and Drake?"

"They were outside, but they couldn't prevent him from coming in. They called me immediately." She was trembling despite her brave face. "Come here."

He pulled her into his arms, and she melted into him.

"I asked him about your father. He said you can see him tomorrow night."

Ellie lifted her gaze to meet his. "Really?" Her eyes welled. "Oh, Aden, thank you."

She rose to her tiptoes, reaching up to pull his face down to hers, kissing him and stealing his breath. He clutched her closer, relieved she was safe in his arms.

When the kiss broke, she grinned. "I'm so excited. I can't wait to see him. What about Carrie? Does your mom know anything about her?"

"I haven't seen her. She's been in meetings with Indira and Katsumi, but I'll ask her when I see her in a little while."

Ellie frowned. "Okay."

"If she doesn't have any news, I'll get Keeley to nose around. She'll find her."

She smiled again, and Aden let the sight soothe his still frayed nerves. He glanced at the clock on the wall. His meeting with Aurick was over, but there was at least an hour before he had to meet up with Andrei at his training facility.

He needed her. He needed to reassure himself she was safe, and a fierce longing for her surged through him, a burning desire that drowned out everything else.

"Ellie, I have to put more of my scent on you."

"What" She looked at him, confused. "Why, I don't understand."

"It needs to be unmistakable that you're mine."

"Aden, there's no mistake about that. Even I can smell you on me."

"I need to pump more venom into you."

She placed a hand on his chest. "Aden, I realize you're upset. So am I, but you just drank from me a couple of hours ago. You've taken a lot of my blood and pumped a lot of your venom into me already today."

"Didn't Mina bring you BloodStone?"

"Not yet. I just rolled over and fell back to sleep when you left."

"Damn it, Ellie." A deep scowl etched itself into his face as he looked down at her. "Then I won't drink. I'll only take enough to get my venom moving through your veins."

Her eyes softened, and it made his dick hard.

"Aden, you're not going to just bite me and pump venom into me. That isn't what we do."

She untied her robe and let it drop to her feet.

Aden's growl was a low, dangerous rumble as his eyes soaked in the sight of her. Ellie ran her palms up his chest, further calming his frayed nerves with her touch.

"We agreed you can drink from me when we're intimate. I share my body and blood with you as part of our lovemaking, and I won't let Matthais or your fear for me taint that."

"Turn around."

Her eyes curious, she did as he asked. He placed his hands on her, matching his fingertips to the bruises on her hips and ass. He gritted his teeth, a louder growl rumbling in his chest.

"You need to tell me when I'm hurting you."

Ellie turned to face him again. "I don't feel it. I'm usually too caught up in more intense sensations to feel when you're bruising me."

"Ellie, I have to know you'll stop me when I'm going too far."

"I trust you, Aden. I know you won't hurt me. We talked about this. Human flesh is pliable, and bruises are inevitable."

"They fucking shouldn't be," he snarled as he stepped back. "I know you trust me, Ellie, but I need to trust you, too. I have to trust you'll tell me if I hurt you. I can crush your bones with a flex of my fingers, and I can break your pelvis with a simple thrust of my hips. You need to remember that."

"I do. A few times it's been a little painful—"

"Fucking hell!"

"But you don't hurt me, Aden. It feels good."

He let out a sharp breath before lifting her face to meet his gaze.

"I lose myself in you, Ellie. This is just as new to me as it is to you. All I've done for centuries is fuck, but that isn't what we do." Her lips curved as he echoed her words. "I need you to keep me grounded. I think we should have a safe word."

A look of surprise flashed across her face. "Like a BDSM safe word?"

Of course, she knew about BDSM. She read too many of his mother's fucking books.

"That's not something that will ever happen between us, at least while you're still human, but we need something you can say to me when I'm going too far, something that I know means 'Stop immediately!'"

Ellie picked up her robe and slipped it on, tying it loosely around her waist. "The times I've said no to you, you've always stopped."

"Yes, but sometimes you don't mean it. Then you get mad at me when I do."

"I don't get mad. I pout." She sat on the sofa, nibbling on her bottom lip, lost in thought. "Okay, so we need to pick a word that's unmistakable. Something that will make you realize something isn't right."

"Yes."

"Like banana?"

"Why the fuck would you ever say banana when we're having sex?"

"Exactly."

Was she out of her fucking mind?

"Ellie, if you said banana while I was inside you, I'd probably think you were having another seizure."

"But you'd stop."

"Ellie!"

He glared at her, but her sincere expression melted his irritation.

"Okay, okay." She thought for a minute. "How about hibiscus?"

"Ellie, you need to take this seriously. We need a word that I will never mistake."

She stood up, and her robe fell open. Magnificently naked, she arched a brow at him. "Like 'stop?'"

He shook his head, unsure if he'd heard her correctly. "Stop?"

"Too obvious?"

"That's not exactly a safe word."

"I don't think we need a safe word. Besides, anytime I've said it to you, you've stopped."

He thought about it. Could it really be that simple?

"I guess that could work. You can say no to me all you want, but that won't mean you want me to stop."

"Well, sometimes when I say no, I mean it."

"Then you'll have to start saying stop. And I promise you, when you say it, I. WILL. STOP."

She took his hand and walked backward, leading him to the bed.

"How much time do you have before you have to leave again?"

"An hour."

"That should be enough time."

"For what?"

"To test out our new safe word. But I hope you're okay with me not using it and you possibly being late for your meeting."

"Fuck my meeting!" he said as he tore his shirt open. Andrei could go fuck himself.

A soft, tinkling laugh escaped Ellie's lips as she dropped her robe. "Do you want me on my back or my knees?"

He'd already taken her from behind twice today. And while he knew she loved that position, he preferred her lying on her back. He loved the feel of her beneath him, his body pressing down on hers as he lost himself inside her.

"Back."

She smiled knowingly, expecting his answer, and climbed onto the bed, lying back, her thighs falling open.

Aden removed the rest of his clothing and settled on top of her, feeling the warmth of her skin, letting his body finally relax. She pulled his lips to hers, moaning as she kissed him, wrapping her legs around him. Savoring the taste of her on his tongue, he kissed her deeper as he pushed inside her.

Everything in his world righted itself in that moment. It was as if the universe spiraled off its axis the second Aden saw Matthais standing over Ellie, and only now, as he sank into her, it realigned. The swirling chaos in Aden's mind dissolved, leaving only her.

He fucked her with long, deep strokes as she arched her back and clawed his ass. Every nerve ending in his body sang with relief and desire at the feeling of her around him—warm, soft, and welcoming. It wasn't just physical gratification, but something deeper, as though some innate part of him recognized that this was where he belonged.

The sweet pain of her nails against his skin reminded him that this was real. She was real. All the burdens he'd carried for so long lifted away with each synchronized rock of their bodies. Here, wrapped in Ellie, he wasn't a monster. He was simply a man who was loved and wanted.

Aden tore his lips away from hers, burying his face in her neck.

"No drinking," she groaned, her hips lifting to meet his.

Determined to only taste, he sank his fangs into her again.

Aden turned the corner and walked down the hallway towards his family's guest suites. Following Andrei's tour of his new training facility, he went to the slave auction. He promised Ellie he wouldn't buy any more thralls, so he wasn't there to shop, but having left the games early the night before, he thought he should at least show his face at the auction for a short while.

But he spent only an hour, his eagerness to see her overriding everything else. He hoped Mina followed his instructions, giving her a transfusion. He drank so much of her blood earlier. BloodStone wouldn't have been enough. At this rate, Ellie was going to be anemic in no time.

After warping from the arena to the entrance of Matthais' compound, he decided to walk to the guest wing where his family was staying.

He heard her heels clicking even before she spoke, but Aden would recognize that walk anywhere.

Fuck!

He was not in the mood for this.

"There you are," Kira purred, and, against his better judgment, he stopped and turned. "You're a hard man to find."

"Maybe you should take the hint, Kira," he said, his voice sharp. The images of her assaulting Ellie seared too deeply into his memory, making it impossible for him to be civil to her.

She glided toward him, impeccably dressed as always, her fiery red hair falling in long, flowing waves over her shoulder. Her emerald green dress clung to her curves, and her sultry smile left no doubt of her intentions.

"You're not still holding a grudge about our little run-in last year, are you? You need to get over it, Aden. I have."

"I don't hold grudges, Kira." That wasn't exactly true. He could hold a grudge better than his mother. "I'm just not interested in seeing you."

Now that was the truth.

"You can be such an asshole," she said in a teasing tone. Her confidence was so unwavering that his words didn't even register as offensive.

"That's who I am."

Aden walked away, but she followed.

"Are you kidding me? You're still pissed over that little bitch thrall? Tell me, have you drained her yet?"

He spun around, his body flooded with rage.

"Don't you fucking call her that!"

Kira's lips curved into a cruel smile.

"Oh, isn't this just perfect?" She taunted. "Matthais said you took her as a pet, but I figured she'd be out of your system by now."

"Kira, walk the fuck away before you say something you regret."

"Is her pussy so magical that you think you've developed feelings for her?" Her scoff was a brittle, humorless laugh, laced with disdain. "You've fucked enough human pussy over the years to know they can't compare to a vampire's."

Aden grabbed her by her throat and pushed her against the wall, his fingers tightening.

"I mean it, Kira. Shut the fuck up before—"

"Before what?" Kira leaned forward and sniffed him, then gagged. "God, you stink of her."

As tempted as he was to taunt Kira about the reason Ellie's lingering scent was so strong on him, he wouldn't disrespect Ellie.

"Fuck you, Kira. Get out of my sight."

He released his grip on her neck and turned to walk away.

"You fucking—"

Kira lunged for him, catching him off guard, grabbing his face, and yanking it down to hers. With a fierce growl, she slammed her lips to his, her fangs sinking into his bottom lip.

"Fuck!" Aden roared and shoved her away from him. She stumbled into the wall, her maniacal laughter filling the air.

"I bet the little whore thinks she's in love with you. What a fucking pathetic pair you make. Now, why don't you scurry on back to her and let the cunt see your betrayal?"

Before he could grab her by the throat again and choke the life out of her, she spun and walked away. He swiped his hand over his bleeding lip.

While normal wounds healed on their own, vampire bites required blood to heal. Just as with a human, the venom kept the blood flowing. But it also prevented it from clotting, so he would continue to bleed until he drank human blood.

He should call Georgina and have her send him a thrall so he could feed before he went back to his room.

That was what he should do.

But the thought of keeping this from Ellie, or worse, lying to her about it, wasn't an option.

Fuck!

Now he'd have to confess his complicated history with Kira, a conversation he never wanted to have with Ellie.

That thought alone had his palms sweating.

Fucking Kira!

Aden

With a hand pressed to his bleeding lip, Aden approached the door to his suite. Kane and Drake stared, wide-eyed, at his blood-soaked fingers.

"Fucking Kira!" He snarled for the fifth time in as many minutes, only this time, it wasn't in his head.

Kane grunted his agreement, a sneer twisting his lips. He loathed her almost as much as Sophie did.

As the door slid shut behind him, Aden heard Drake growl under his breath, "Why the fuck were her fangs that close to his mouth?"

If he wasn't so fucking pissed, he might have appreciated Drake's defensive reaction on Ellie's behalf. But he had bigger problems to deal with at the moment, specifically, the love of his life. Except for a handful of times, she rarely overreacted, and Aden hoped this wouldn't be one of them.

He stepped around the wall, and even with the anxiety coursing through him, just the sight of her calmed him. She was freshly showered, tucked into bed, surrounded by a slew of pillows. Her tablet, its screen glowing, rested on her lap as an IV drip pumped BloodStone into her vein.

She looked up, and her eyes met his, a smile curving her lips, but it vanished as her gaze zeroed in on his lip.

"Oh my God, Aden."

Tossing her tablet aside, she scrambled out of bed, ripped the needle from her arm, winced, and slapped a bandage from the bedside table over the puncture. The sweet, rich, metallic scent of her blood filled Aden's nostrils, igniting an overwhelming urge to sink his teeth into her neck.

"What happened to you?" She asked, her fingers closing around his wrist as she reached him.

He swiped at the mouth again. "Fucking Kira."

Apparently, those were the only words he could find at the moment. He braced himself, the silence heavy and thick in the air, waiting for her to react.

A myriad of emotions—shock, confusion, disbelief, and aggravation—swept across her features. Then her eyes narrowed, and a flicker of suspicion settled on her face.

What the fuck was she suspicious about?

But at least she wasn't freaking out.

That was a start.

Aden sighed and walked into the bathroom. Ellie followed him and leaned against the counter, arms folded across her chest, her eyes guarded as she watched him inspect his lip in the mirror.

"You wanna explain what happened?"

"She fucking ambushed me in the hallway."

With an incredulous look, she raised her eyebrow at him. "How does a woman half your size ambush you?"

"I don't know. You tell me," he snarled as he grabbed a towel from the hook and pressed it to his lip.

"Why was she anywhere near your mouth?"

"She wasn't," he roared and slammed his hands down on the sink. The marble cracked, leaving a long, jagged fissure in the stone.

To calm himself, he inhaled deeply. This wasn't her fault, and she had every right to question him.

"She wanted to have sex, and when I refused, she lunged at me and bit me. It caught me off guard."

"Excuse me?" Ellie's eyes flashed angrily, and her voice sharpened.

"Oh, for fuck's sake, Ellie, don't make me say it again."

Aden stomped out of the bathroom and over to the bar, pouring a drink. By the time he'd downed his second one, she stood beside him.

"Why won't your lip stop bleeding?" Her voice turned soft again.

"Because venom prevents vampire blood from clotting. It'll keep bleeding until I have some human blood."

"Okay, I think you need to start at the beginning and tell me what happened."

While keeping the towel pressed to his mouth, he gave her the highlights, leaving out that Kira called her a whore. Her expression softened, a calm settling on her face as she listened. Some of Aden's tension eased.

"Why are you so calm about this? I thought you'd freak out. Maybe lock yourself in the concubine suite."

Ellie let out a soft snort, and Aden felt a little more of his tension fade away.

"Aden, how often do I freak out?"

"There have been a few times I can name." He set his drink down, then pressed the towel to his mouth again.

"Okay," she conceded. "Maybe I have once or twice. But why would I be upset with you about this?"

"You mean aside from Kira wanting to have sex with me and then biting me to make it look like I betrayed you?"

With a tender look, she put her hand on his chest, over his heart. "Aden, I know you'd never betray me."

"I never fucking would." He gripped her hip, his fingers digging in as he tugged her closer.

"Besides, I know how much she hates me. She deliberately sent you back to me like that. Pets often fall in love with their masters, and she wanted me to see her bite on you because she thought it would hurt me."

"She's a fucking psycho bitch. I should tear her heart out for what she did to you."

Ellie stepped back, tilting her head to look at him. "That's a little excessive."

"No, it isn't."

"Believe me, I know how psychotic she can be. She tormented me for years, but she isn't worth starting something with Master Matthais. Now that I'm yours, she can't harm me. She wouldn't dare."

Ellie clearly didn't know how truly evil and twisted Kira was. Kira would target Ellie simply *because* she was Aden's.

"I don't know why she hates me so much."

"Did you miss where I said she's a psycho bitch?" He cringed, dreading telling her the next part, but he knew he had to. He couldn't keep it a secret from her. "But there's more to it you need to know."

With a sigh, she took the towel from his hand and held it to his lip herself. His eyes closed at her gentle touch.

"You mean that you and she used to have sex?"

Aden shook his head, unsure if he'd heard her correctly. "How did you know that?"

"I saw you once. Years ago. It was a year after my dad and I got here. I was six, I think. Anyway, I was looking for him, and I wandered down the wrong hallway. I still didn't know my way around very well. You were at the end of the hall. You were having sex against the wall."

"Fuck me." Aden blew out a long breath.

"You didn't know I was there, obviously. And I didn't know what you were doing. Not then. I thought you were fighting. It looked like you were attacking each other. So I ran and told my dad. He said to never go into that wing of the compound again." Ellie let out a little chuckle. "Wow, I forgot all about that until right now." She flinched and drew back a little. "I wish I didn't remember that."

"You and me both."

She could have died that night, coming upon two vampires in the frantic throes of brutal sex. Most would have turned on her, lost in the maddening frenzy of it, and drained her dry.

"Aden, you're getting blood all over us." She rolled the bloody towel and pressed it to his lip again. "Why didn't you have a thrall brought to you before you came back? I never would've had to know about it."

"Because I don't fucking lie to you. And I don't want any other blood but yours to heal me."

Her entire body softened then, and her scent deepened. "I don't know how much I can give you." She motioned to the IV stand. "Mina gave me a transfusion, and that's the second drip she brought because I was feeling dizzy earlier."

He grasped her wrist. "Again? Why didn't you tell me you were dizzy?"

"I wasn't until after you left."

He tilted her face up so he could look into her eyes. "Fuck, Ellie."

"How much do you need?"

"Not a lot, but I probably shouldn't take it from you."

"I can handle a little. But that means we have to have sex."

He reached for her, but she stepped back, handing him the towel.

"But first, you have to go wash your face and mouth because I'm not letting it anywhere near me until she's off you. In the meantime, I'm going to put my IV back in and finish that bag."

Without waiting for an answer, she turned and walked to the bed. He smirked but did as she asked. He even took a shower to give her a little more time to finish her drip. And to get all traces of Kira off him.

Ellie briefly entered the bathroom, using a washcloth to clean the blood he'd dripped on her, but then left, much to his disappointment. When he reentered the room, she was pushing the IV stand into the corner. A robe was her only clothing.

Aden dabbed his lip with a fresh towel as he approached her from behind. "I won't take much," he murmured. "I only need a little to get the bleeding to stop. It'll heal quickly once it does."

Turning, she pulled him towards the bed. He liked the thrill of letting her lead, the way his anticipation built until his control snapped and he had to take over.

"I can't kiss you until the bleeding stops."

"Why not?"

"Because I'll get blood in your mouth."

"So?"

"Ellie, I can't share my blood with you."

She shed her robe, and a low growl rumbled in Aden's chest, not a conscious sound but something from deep within him. The sight of her smooth skin and soft curves made his blood surge hot and violent through his veins.

"I share mine with you. Tit for tat, Aden."

"Ellie."

With a tug, she removed the towel from around his waist, the fabric brushing against his hypersensitive skin as it fell to the floor.

"Aden, I'm not looking to drink yours like you do mine. But I want to kiss you." A possessive gleam shone in her eyes as they met his. "I won't let her leave a mark on you I don't replace with my own. If I get some of your blood in my mouth, so be it."

His cock surged, hardening to the point of pain. He'd been surprised by her lack of revulsion when he fed her his blood to heal the wounds from her whipping. But she always managed to surprise him.

"Fuck, Ellie! You can't say something like that and not have me lose my mind."

Her eyes dropped to his cock, a seductive smile curving her lips.

"And don't fucking smile like that, or you're going to end up flat on your back with my fangs in your jugular."

"Isn't that the plan?" The sultry challenge in her voice made his skin prickle with need.

"Your father will smell that you've had my blood when you see him."

Ellie climbed onto the bed, settling cross-legged in the middle. "I don't care."

Those three simple words shattered the last of his resistance. He'd give her anything she wanted.

"That's not flat on your back."

"We'll get there."

She extended her hand, and he took it, joining her on the bed. Crawling towards her, he sat in front of her, mirroring her position. Ellie moved closer, shifting to her knees.

She took the bloody towel from his hand, tossing it aside, before she reached up, cupping his face in her hands. Blood dripped on her chest, leaving a crimson trail over her breasts and down her stomach. Aden looked down. The sight of it staining her skin gave him a possessive thrill. He rested his palms on her thighs, his fingers sinking into the soft flesh.

"Look at me, Aden."

At her quiet command, he looked up. Her gaze was gentle, but her eyes burned with intensity as she leaned in, her lips softly grazing his, the blood smearing across both their mouths. She pulled back, and with a quick flick of her tongue, she licked it away, swallowing it without hesitation.

It was the hottest fucking thing he'd ever seen.

One of Aden's hands slid up her thigh and gripped her ass as the other reached between them, slipping between her thighs. He brushed his fingers over her clit.

"You're not wet enough."

"Just shut up and kiss me."

Her command stripped away any last pretense of his control, and he yanked her closer. Her lips enveloped his lower one as she kissed him, soft and deceptively tender. The sweet pressure made his chest ache with longing.

Then she bit him.

Hard.

Aden's groan was muffled by her mouth as her teeth sank into his flesh. The moment they broke the skin, a sudden rush of her arousal flooded his fingers.

He pushed her onto her back, settling on top of her. The soft cradle of her thighs welcomed him. Every muscle in his body tensed, fighting the urge to just impale her, wanting instead to savor this experience with her.

He sank inside her slowly, her body welcoming and slick. And so fucking tight, her inner muscles gripping him with a perfection that bordered on agony. Letting out a gasping breath, she released his lip before fusing their mouths together as Aden moved, burying his cock inside her in long, slow strokes. She wrapped her legs around his hips, the heels of her feet digging into his ass. The shift in angle let him sink deeper into her heat, and the drag of her inner walls against his cock was almost unbearable.

Aden pinned her hands above her head, trapping them in one of his own as he pulled his lips away, gazing down at her. Blood smeared her mouth, cheeks, and chin, and her eyes were wild. She looked like a goddess of war and lust combined, fierce and beautiful in her bloodied state.

Unable to wait a second longer, he buried his face in her neck, sinking his fangs into her jugular. Her body froze as she clamped down on him. He took several quick pulls of her blood before he retracted his fangs, licking the punctures, his venom soothing and sealing the wounds.

The bleeding from his lip stopped as the bite closed. He lifted his head just as she regained the use of her body. His name tore from her lips in a sound that was half sob, half prayer, and she continued to orgasm around him, gripping his cock like a hot, wet vise.

"Kiss me," she begged, her voice breathy and desperate. He lowered his mouth to hers, a fleeting thought crossing his mind that he should let her wipe the blood from her face first. But she showed no hesitation or disgust as she nibbled around his mouth, dipping her tongue between his lips to taste their shared blood.

Sharing blood like this was illegal unless Ellie was marked as his mate. But only Matthais could approve a mating bond between a vampire and a human.

Fuck Matthais!

She was his fucking soulmate, and if he wanted to share his blood with her, he was going to fucking do it.

"Aden," Ellie whimpered into his mouth, and he felt her tighten around him again, her body on the precipice of another climax. That was all he needed to set him off. With a groan, Aden plunged deep and exploded, his orgasm pulsing in hot waves as she clamped tight around him again.

Releasing her wrists from his grip, he pulled out of her and rolled to his side. He gazed down at her, his eyes tracing the smeared blood across her breasts, neck, and face.

She looked fucking magnificent.

Ellie exhaled a long breath, her body melting into the mattress, the tension visibly leaving her body.

"I think my heart stopped."

Aden smirked. "It did for half a second while you were paralyzed."

He leaned over her, drawn by an irresistible urge to taste her again. He kissed her, soft and deep, before swirling his tongue over her skin, licking their combined blood off her face and neck. She let out a giggle that trailed off into a moan.

"Are you okay?" he asked, pulling back, a little wary of her reaction now that the orgasmic effect of his venom was wearing off.

"Yup."

Ellie brought her hand down from above her head and traced her nipple with her index finger, the casual sensuality of the gesture causing Aden to growl low in his throat. His body's reaction was instant, a Pavlovian response to her very existence, despite his recent orgasm.

"You're not disgusted?"

"Nope."

He gave her a dubious look. "But you're smeared in vampire blood."

"It's yours," she said, touching her finger to her lips and licking his blood off, her eyes never leaving his. She laughed softly as his eyes widened.

"How do you feel?" He asked.

"Like I have an electric current running through my body, but in a good way."

Reaching over, he swirled his fingertip around her belly button, mesmerized by the crimson against her pale skin. With a gentle smile, she took his hand, lacing her fingers through his.

"You wish it was my blood, don't you?" There was no judgment in Ellie's voice.

"Yes." When she only looked at him with that steady gaze that seemed to see the darkest parts of him, he continued. "Then I could lick every drop off you."

Pulling his fingers to her lips, she kissed them before sitting up and tugging him out of bed. The unspoken absolution in that tender kiss made his throat tighten with emotion.

"Come on. Let's take a bath."

He followed, allowing her to lead him wherever she pleased. He'd follow her anywhere—into water, into fire, into the sun—trusting her in a way he'd never trusted another living soul.

"But you said no baths here."

"I changed my mind. I'm a woman, and it's my prerogative."

After turning on the tap and testing the temperature, Ellie climbed into the oversized jetted tub. Aden had never used it before. Not once in almost three hundred years.

Climbing in after her, he leaned against the side, pulling her into his arms as the warm water lapped gently around them.

"You're so fucking perfect, you know that."

She snorted, settling in his arms, her back to his chest. "Hardly. But as long as you think so, that's all that matters."

She often said that, and it made him wonder if it stemmed from insecurity or confidence.

He grazed his lips over the closed puncture marks on her throat while she cleaned the rest of the blood from her face and neck with a washcloth. The water in the bath turned a light shade of pink.

"I'm sorry about Kira." His words had double, perhaps even triple, meaning.

"Being sorry doesn't serve a purpose, Aden. You can't change the past."

Her blunt practicality sometimes bordered on indifference and was slightly unnerving. Shouldn't she be more upset about Kira because of what that viper did to her? The lack of apparent anger or jealousy confused him, making him wonder if she truly understood the depth of his sinful past.

"But she was so fucking cruel to you."

"That's not your fault." Ellie shrugged as she soaped up the washcloth again and cleaned her arms and breasts. "Just because you slept with her before we met doesn't mean I hold that against you. Although I don't really understand how you could be with her when you can barely stand to be touched by anyone. What was it about her that made you tolerate touch?"

The subtle tensing in her body suggested she wasn't as indifferent as she seemed.

"I didn't. I just wanted to fuck." He looked away, not wanting to see her reaction to his next words. "I mastered the skill of fucking my thralls without touching. But Kira wouldn't adhere to my rules, so it ended as quickly as it started. I knew she was batshit crazy, but from time to time, it didn't matter."

Ellie didn't respond to his words. Instead, she turned in his arms and washed his face and neck with gentle strokes, the tenderness of her ministrations drawing a sigh from him.

"How did I ever live without you and your touch?" Aden closed his eyes, reveling in the soft pressure of her fingers. "I wasn't. I was barely existing."

Ellie pressed a kiss to the hollow of his throat.

"And that's why Kira doesn't matter to me," she murmured against his skin. But then her teeth sank into his clavicle, biting him again. Although relatively painless, it still startled him.

She pulled back and looked into his eyes, hers flashing with something that made his cock hard. Again.

"But if you ever come back to me with another woman's bite on you..." She wrapped her hand around his cock and squeezed. "This will never find its way inside me again. Ever."

He didn't doubt her for a second, and he throbbed in her palm in response to her fierce declaration.

"Do you understand, Aden?"

He nodded, his breath catching in his throat. She was so fucking glorious as she was laying claim to him. Her hand softened its grip, and she stroked him with deliberate slowness, gliding up and down his rigid shaft. His entire body trembled, a tremor that started in his cock and spread to the tips of every limb.

"I can't take any more of your blood today."

"No blood this time. Just us," she murmured as she climbed onto his lap and sank down on him in one fluid motion, groaning into his mouth as she fused her lips with his in a deep kiss.

The sensation of being enveloped in her warm, wet walls once more made his mind go blank. Water splashed around them as she moved, rocking her hips, holding his gaze until he was shuddering beneath her and she was convulsing in his arms.

Afterward, his legs could barely hold their weight as he carried her back to bed, but he managed the short journey through sheer force of will. Collapsing onto the mattress beside her, he pulled her close, falling into an exhausted sleep.

Ellie

Ellie leaned against the headboard, her head falling back as Mina slipped the needle into her arm. Her head spun, but the dizziness eased as the blood flowed back into her veins.

"Why are you giving me another transfusion instead of just a BloodStone IV?"

"Have you looked in the mirror? You're pasty, and Aden is worried you're becoming anemic."

"It feels different from the other day. I feel a tingling sensation throughout my body, like when I drank his blood."

Mina didn't need to know she'd done it again last night, but her heightened half-breed senses probably figured it out.

"That's because I added more than just a few drops of his blood to the bag. Though it smells like you had some of his blood already," she said with a curious arch of her brow.

Of course, Mina knew.

"You need an extra boost. This is what happens when vampires take too much blood too fast."

Mina's tone dripped with disapproval and rebuke.

"He's not taking more than I'm willing to give him, Mina."

"What you're willing to give and what your body can handle are not the same thing." She sat on the edge of the bed and adjusted the IV line. "Ellie, I know compulsion can be overwhelming at the beginning. Everything is incredibly intense, and the pleasure goes beyond anything you ever imagined. But—" She lifted Ellie's arm to display the fading bruises around her wrists. "You have to set boundaries. He's greedy and just as overwhelmed as you, but he'll abide by them."

Ellie yanked her arm away. Thankfully, Mina couldn't see her hips and butt or the deep puncture in her thigh above her femoral artery. "There's no need for boundaries. We're adults and can decide what's right for us."

"That's what you both thought before."

Her eyes widened as Mina referred to her past life. But she wasn't surprised the woman knew. Not much was a secret in the Westcott household.

"It will destroy him if he hurts you." Mina's quiet voice held a steel edge. "He'll never come back from it this time."

Ellie's heart clenched. "I know, Mina. I know. Is there enough of his blood in there to get rid of my bruises completely?"

Ellie didn't want her father to see them, and he was due there soon.

Mina nodded. "Probably enough to fade them significantly. Your love for Aden can't be stronger than your sense of self-preservation, Ellie. That's how thralls die."

Mina was never one to hold back, even when the truth was harsh.

"You've made your point."

"I hope so, because I meant what I said. He won't survive it this time. It will destroy this entire family."

Ellie felt the sting of her words but knew Mina was right. Her death would mean Aden's this time. And that would devastate the rest of them.

When her transfusion was complete and Mina left, she took a shower and got dressed, ignoring the tightness in her chest. She and Aden had been arrogant once. The memory of their mistake needed to be seared into their souls, a burning brand ensuring they never again risked repeating it.

Ellie grabbed her tablet and curled up on the sofa to finish her book. A short time later, she looked up as she heard the door slide open. She hid her tablet under the cushion. After what happened with Matthais, she didn't want to get caught unaware again.

"Dad!" she choked, leaping to her feet when her father turned the corner to the living area.

"Ellie Bellie."

Her father wrapped her in his arms as she flung herself into them, not caring that he used her stupid childhood nickname. Tears stung her eyes as he lifted her off her feet, tightening his grip around her. She couldn't believe she was with him again.

After a minute, Ellie coughed softly. "I can't breathe, Dad," she chuckled.

He released her but grasped her arms as his eyes swept over her. "Ellie, you're alright. You're alright." He pulled her against him again, this time more gently.

"I'm okay, Dad. Really," she assured him as she rested her head on his chest, arms clutching him tight, listening to the strong beat of his heart. "I missed you so much."

"I missed you too, Ells. I've been so worried about you."

"Me too. I worry about you all the time."

"You don't have to, kiddo. I'm fine."

Ellie pulled out of his arms and tugged him further into the room. "I can't believe Master Matthais let you come see me."

"Before everyone got here, I asked him if I could see you if you came, but he said no. He surprised me last night, saying he changed his mind."

She turned back to look at him. "Aden asked his permission for me."

A small gasp escaped her father's lips. "Ellie, be careful what you say. Someone might hear you use his name like that."

She gave his hand a gentle squeeze. "It's okay, Dad. I'm allowed to call him Aden. How's Carrie?"

A knot tightened in Ellie's gut at the look that crossed his face.

"What? Is she okay?"

"She's not here anymore, Ells."

Now her stomach plummeted, an icy dread washing over her as if the ground itself had opened up under her feet.

"What? Where'd she go?"

"She was auctioned off last summer."

Tears sprung to her eyes, and her vision blurred. She grabbed her father by his forearm. "No!"

"I'm sorry, baby." His voice cracked. "I tried to keep her safe, but Master Matthais put her up for auction. I failed both of you."

Ellie shook her head as she blinked back her tears. "No, Dad. You always did what you could to protect her like you did me."

"It obviously wasn't good enough."

"Who bought her? Was it a vampire from here?"

"No. It was a vampire named Vincent. He doesn't live in the capital. I see her sometimes, though, because he brings her with him when he visits."

A wave of nausea washed over Ellie. She knew of Vincent. He was known for his cruel treatment of thralls.

"Is she alright?"

"She's his private pet."

"Oh God. Is she here this week?"

"Yes, I saw her arrive with him a few days ago."

"Does she look okay?"

He didn't answer right away, and she knew her worst fears for Carrie had been realized. Her father stepped closer and lifted his hand to her face.

"I was so worried he would hurt you, but you look alright."

With a deep breath, Ellie forced herself to push her thoughts of her friend aside for a minute, focusing instead on reassuring her father.

"I am, Dad. I promise. He doesn't hurt me."

He let his fingers slip down her cheek and brush against the scar on her neck. The BloodStone had sealed and healed the mark from Aden's fangs, but it was still a little raw and red since he'd bitten her when they made love before he left.

"But he feeds on you?"

"No, that's not what that is."

"Those marks are fresh, Ellie."

"I didn't say he doesn't bite me. Just that he doesn't feed on me."

"You said he doesn't hurt you."

"He doesn't. It isn't like that. He loves me."

His eyes flared with anger. "Oh, Ells, don't tell me you're a willing pet? So many girls fall into that trap."

"I'm not his pet."

His gaze swept over her teal outfit, then he grabbed her arms, his grip firm and insistent. "I know you don't have a choice but to submit to him, but you can't possibly enjoy it."

Ellie heard Aden's roar and felt her father's hold slip before she stumbled. She gasped as he hoisted her enormous father into the air by the neck as if he weighed nothing.

"Get your fucking hands off her!"

"Aden, no!" Ellie cried as she saw her father struggling to breathe in Aden's tight grip. Though he was nearly a foot shorter, his rage made him seem larger than her unusually tall father. "That's my dad!" She grabbed his arm and tried to pull him away, but it was like trying to move a mountain. "Aden, please stop. That's my dad!"

His eyes, blazing red with fury, snapped to her. She took a step back, as always shocked by the rage that his eyes could display.

"What?" He shook his head, his eyes fading back to blue.

"Let him go, Aden. Please, he's my dad."

With a sharp jerk, Aden dropped Myles and turned to her.

"Why the fuck was he manhandling you?"

"We were just talking, Aden." She walked over to her father and stood in front of him.

"He shouldn't have touched you that way. No one has the right to touch you."

"He wasn't hurting me."

"It fucking looked like it."

Satisfied he posed no threat to her father, Ellie stepped closer to him.

"Why did you come back?"

Aden shot a glare at her father, his eyes blazing before softening as he looked at her again. "I wanted to tell you that Sophie found out your friend is no longer here."

"I know." She grasped him by the front of his shirt. "My dad said she was sold to a vampire named Vincent. You have to get her away from him."

"Excuse me?" He did a double take as he put his hands on her hips, visibly relaxing even as his eyes flashed. "What did you say his name was?"

"Vincent. Aden, he hurts his thralls. You have to get her away from him. Please?"

He ran his hand roughly through his hair. "Fuck! What does she look like?"

"She's a little taller and a little heavier than me. Or she was. And she has short blonde hair."

"Her hair is longer now," her father said.

"Fuck!" Aden said again. "I think I almost bought her last summer."

"What?"

"When I was here for the games. I got into a bidding war with him over a short-haired blonde girl."

Her brow furrowed in confusion. "Why would you do that? We agreed you wouldn't buy any more thralls."

"That was before our agreement, and I wasn't really shopping for thralls. I saw her, and she looked scared, so I decided to bid on her." He lifted his hand to her face. "I'm sorry, mo ghrá, if I'd known she was your friend, I wouldn't have conceded so easily."

Ellie felt her father watching them, his intense gaze burning into her back as Aden caressed her cheek.

"I have to go. We'll talk about this later." Aden dropped his hand and stepped back. "Fuck, the ball is tonight. We'll talk when I get back from that."

"I want to go with you. He'll probably bring her, right?"

"Absolutely not!"

"I need to see her, Aden." She grasped the front of his shirt again. "I'm going to that party with you."

"Ellie, don't fucking start with me right now."

She felt her father's eyes still on them. His gaze didn't feel as heavy but more incredulous now.

"I have to go. We'll talk later."

Aden stepped around her and up to her father. "I jumped to conclusions when I walked in. You would have reacted the same way if you saw what I did."

That was the only apology Aden was capable of giving, and Ellie loved him fiercely for it.

He strode out of the room without looking back at her. Still feeling her father's eyes on her, she met his questioning stare. She had a lot to explain to him.

"What did he call you?"

"Huh?"

"What did he call you? Mo something?"

Ellie's mouth turned upward into a small, almost imperceptible smile. "Mo ghrá. It's Gaelic."

"What does it mean?"

"My love."

"I don't understand, Ellie."

Taking his hand, she led him to the sofa.

"Come sit down. I have so much to tell you, Dad."

When her father left about an hour later, Ellie felt lighter, despite the heavy weight of her worry for Carrie.

She'd told him about Aden and her life in Réimse Shíochánta. Well, almost everything about her life. She omitted the details about her past life and being reborn. There was no need for him to think she'd gone crazy. Maybe she'd share it with him someday, but she dumped enough on him. Her normally stoic father looked a little shell-shocked when she finished telling him about the last year of her life.

He surprised her by revealing that he knew they once lived in the Westcott's region. He'd never told her because it was irrelevant. As Chancellor of the VWC, Matthais would face no consequences for his actions. Despite Aden's warning, Ellie admitted to her father that he was furious and demanding restitution, which seemed to alarm him. But before she could ask why, a persistent call on his earpiece called him away.

As she watched her father turn the corner at the end of the hallway, Kane snickered beside her from his position just outside the door.

"Did I hear what I think I heard? Did your father call you Ellie Bellie?"

"Shut up, Kane." She turned to Drake, who was also laughing. "Et tu, Drake?"

He held up his hands in mock surrender but continued to chuckle.

"It's a cute name, Ellie Bellie. Suits you, I think," Kane mused through his laughing.

She crossed her arms tightly over her chest, glaring at him with narrowed eyes. "I swear if you two ever call me that, I'll tell Aden."

"You're no fun," Kane huffed, his lower lip jutting out in a disappointed pout. Drake wisely remained silent.

With a triumphant smirk, she walked back into the room, plotting her strategy for convincing Aden to take her to the party.

Ellie

"**I**s this really necessary, Keeley?" Ellie asked, her neck muscles tight as she tried and failed to keep her head from jerking back with each pass of the brush through her long locks.

"Quit your complaining," Keeley scolded as she handed Ellie the brush before styling her hair into a French twist. "You're the one who asked for my help."

"With convincing your brother to let me go to the party tonight, not dress me up like a Barbie doll."

"How do you know about Barbie dolls?"

"You had them when you were a kid. I remember stealing them when you weren't looking."

"Shit, that was you?" Keeley snorted out a laugh. "I blamed Aden for that."

Ellie grinned at her in the mirror. "I can't believe you never figured it out."

Keeley met Ellie's eyes in the mirror. "It must be so strange having memories of a different person like that."

Ellie shrugged. She and Keeley had never talked about this. She shared it with Aden, but only when a significant memory resurfaced.

"It's not so strange anymore. I think I have most of them back, but every once in a while one resurfaces, and that surprises me."

"What do you do when it happens?"

"Let them merge so they feel like the memories of the same person, rather than two different people." She shook her head. "I don't know. That probably doesn't make sense."

"Quit moving your head, or I'm going to have to start over. But that makes sense, I guess."

She remained still while Keeley finished her hair before standing back to peruse her handiwork. Ellie turned her head, examining the sleek twist from different angles. Keeley had left a few strategic wisps of hair free around her face. They softened the look, falling in gentle curves that highlighted her cheekbones and drew attention to her eyes.

"Damn, you look incredible. Aden's gonna lose his shit."

"Hopefully not so much that he refuses to take me."

"You know there's only a fifty-fifty chance of succeeding at this, right? Taking you to the party has risks. Especially since you smell like you've been gorging yourself on his blood."

Ellie's eyes snapped up to meet Keeley's in the mirror, horror filling them. "Does it really smell that strong?"

Keeley nodded. "What the hell are the two of you thinking, anyway?"

"He came back with a bite on his lip from Mistress Kira. He needed my blood to heal, and things got a bit carried away."

"He what?" She screeched, but then she stopped, and her lips curved into a sly smile. "What did you two deviants do?"

"Nothing you need to know." Ellie cursed the blush that crept up her neck. "I just got a little of his blood in my mouth before it was fully healed."

"Smells like a lot more than just a little."

Ellie let out a sigh. "Why do vampires have to have such a strong sense of smell?"

Keeley laughed and pulled her out of the chair.

"Come on, let's get you in this dress before Aden gets here. You want to have the full effect on him when he walks in."

Keeley reached for an elegant charmeuse dress draped over the sofa. The teal fabric caught the light like liquid jewels, creating subtle shadows that rippled with each movement.

"Why did you even bring this with you?" Ellie asked, running a finger over the soft silk, her gaze lingering on the shimmery fabric. Once again, she lamented that the color teal was reserved for pets.

"A woman always has to be prepared. And I had a feeling something like this would happen. Now, drop the robe. And your panties and bra. You can't wear them with this."

"I can't go braless, Keeley. I need more support than that. Or without panties. Aden will definitely lose his mind and not let me go."

"There's a built-in bra. And your panty lines will show if you have them on. Don't worry, it'll be fine. Now, come on. We're running out of time before he gets back."

Ellie obeyed, walking closer, removing her robe, and tossing her bra aside. Covering her breasts with her hands, she lifted one foot after the other, stepping into the dress as Keeley slid it up her body. A soft gasp escaped her lips at the sight of Ellie's scars, but she said nothing, for which Ellie was grateful.

The material was impossibly soft and cool against her bare skin. Once it cleared her hips, she pushed her panties to the floor. Sliding her arms into the sleeves, she held the dress to her chest as Keeley fastened the tiny buttons behind her neck.

A low whistle escaped Keeley's lips. She turned Ellie to face her, hands moving over the fabric at Ellie's hips, her eyes traveling the length of her body.

"Shit. Aden is going to swallow his tongue when he sees you."

Catching her reflection in the mirror on the dressing table, Ellie's eyes widened in surprise.

The dress was exquisite. Its bodice was form-fitting, softly gathered at the waist, and featured delicate pleats cascading from the left hip, creating an elegant, understated, and subtly asymmetrical design.

The neckline plunged between her breasts, showing off her natural cleavage, but it wasn't too revealing. The dress fit her perfectly, hugging her curves without being too tight or too loose, but Keeley was right; her panty lines would have been visible.

Ellie stepped closer to the mirror and turned to the side. The hem swayed just below her knees, the silk whispering against her skin with every movement. A hidden panel of slightly darker teal created a shadow effect when she walked, only noticeable in motion. Where the light hit it, the teal deepened to almost aqua. In the shadows, it darkened to the color of a forest pool.

"Wow."

"He'll never be able to deny you when you look like that."

Ellie opened her mouth to contradict her because Aden could say no to her when she was naked if he was angry enough. She doubted the dress would influence him, but she hoped that being already dressed would make him more agreeable to letting her go.

But then Aden's voice sounded as the door slid open.

"No, Kane. I want you to stay here with Drake. I don't need a fucking babysitter."

He turned the corner into the suite and stopped short. His eyes revealed a whirlwind of emotions—surprise giving way to shock, then anger, culminating in a desire so hot, Ellie thought it would melt the dress off her body.

Maybe Keeley was right.

His gaze whipped to his sister, eyes narrowing. "What the fuck is this?"

"I'm helping Ellie get ready for the party."

Aden stalked over to Ellie as she brushed her fingers over the silk. "Do you like it?" she asked with a smile, and his eyes softened, any lingering anger fading out of them.

He reached up, his touch feather-light as he caressed one of the stray wisps of hair curving around her face. "You don't play fair, you know."

"That's me not playing fair," Keeley said with a chuckle as she sat on the sofa. Ellie's grin widened.

"Keeley, go away. I'll deal with you later."

"No. I didn't spend the last hour on her hair and makeup for you to keep her locked in this room. She wants to see her friend. If you say no, then you're a dick, and I'll never talk to you again."

Keeley's words were hollow, and they all knew it. Even if she stopped talking to Aden for a little while, she'd cave like she always did.

He turned his head and glared at his sister, but Ellie reached up and redirected his gaze back to her.

"Please, Aden. I have to see her with my own eyes. I know I'll have to act like your pet and kneel on the floor in front of you, but I'll do anything to see Carrie."

He closed his eyes and inhaled a deep breath. "You can go for a little while, but that's it. And you're not wearing that fucking dress. Keeley, get her another one."

His sister stood. "No. She looks gorgeous in it. And people will expect your pet to dress a certain way. She just needs to put her collar back on before she goes. It's on the dressing table."

"Keeley," Aden ground out through clenched teeth.

"I can take it from here." Ellie took him by the hand and led him to the sofa.

"You can't have sex with him right now, Ellie. You two are like freaking rabbits, I swear."

"Go the fuck away, Keeley," Aden said as he let Ellie push him to sit.

"Don't you dare defile her and ruin all my hard work."

"We'll be okay." Ellie kept her gaze fixed on Aden.

"Fine. This is the thanks I get," Keeley muttered to herself before heading to the door.

Aden kept his eyes on Ellie as she slid the dress up her thighs, straddling him, positioning her knees on either side of him, and draping the soft fabric over them both. He reached for her, but she slapped his hands.

"No. You'll wrinkle it if you touch me."

His eyes burned into her, but he rested his hands on the sofa cushion. She cupped his face in her palms, and the lines around his eyes softened.

"Thank you for letting me go. In this dress," she added, and his lips dropped into a scowl.

"Every vampire in that room will be staring at you. That was my sister's fucking plan, no doubt."

"I don't care about them. And I think you're making her out to be more devious than she is. But she's right. Everyone will expect me to dress a certain way."

His face betrayed his emotions, and she couldn't help but feel a little sorry for him. She needed to get him out of his own head.

"I'm not wearing any panties," she said, and his eyes flashed crimson.

"Why the fuck not?"

"Because the panty lines would show."

"Why are you telling me this if you won't let me touch you?"

"Because you not being able to touch me doesn't mean I can't touch you. But I'll let you if you make me a promise."

"What?" Aden growled low in his throat.

"If you promise to behave yourself, you can touch me, but only here." She took his hands and slid them up under the silk. "Only under the dress, so you don't wrinkle it."

He flexed his fingers on her hips.

"And no biting me. We can't risk getting blood on it."

"I want to fucking kiss you," he growled, and she shook her head, reaching for the zipper of his pants. With practiced ease, she freed him, and he lifted his hips so she could shove them down.

He moved one hand between her thighs, and she gasped as his fingertips brushed over her.

"No." She pulled his hand back to her hip.

"What the fuck am I supposed to do if you won't let me touch you?"

"Watch me." His eyes grew dark and his breath hitched as she rose to her knees, scooting forward, before lowering herself onto him, the weight of her body pressing down. Slowly, his cock pierced her, filling and stretching her to the limit as her wet heat enveloped him. "And just feel me," she breathed, a gasp escaping her.

With her gaze fixed on his, she circled and rocked her hips, her fingers caressing his face and neck. Aden's eyes, sapphire pools rimmed with fiery red, flashed with desperate longing as his lashes fluttered. He trembled beneath her, his hands flexing into her hips, the only place he could touch her, low rumbling growls vibrating in his chest as he struggled to obey her.

The power of this man and the control he placed in her hands was humbling. He dug his fingers into her flesh so hard she could feel the bruises forming, but she ignored them and rode him until they both orgasmed.

When he came, Aden roared, snapping his teeth shut.

With a shaky exhale, she rested her forehead against his, their breath mingling as they gasped for air.

"Thank you," she whispered against his lips, feeling the rapid beat of his heart beneath her palm.

"Mo ghrá."

A half-hour later, after cleaning up and putting on panties at Aden's insistence, Ellie kneeled on the floor in front of Aden, her head down as he sat on the sofa, talking to Andrei, Master Matthais' Commander General.

The tension radiated off him as he shook his leg in an anxious tic, one only she noticed. Her fingers were wrapped around his ankle, letting her touch ground him, the angle of her body concealing the subtle contact.

Keeley sat beside Aden, chiming in occasionally, and Ellie was glad to have her close by. Vincent and Carrie had yet to arrive, and she was growing increasingly nervous about their absence.

"You should have seen Vincent melting down last night," Andrei said with a laugh, and she flinched, a fresh wave of worry washing over her at the sound of his name. "I had all his players out in a matter of minutes in every round. He threw a hissy fit over a hologram, and I thought his head was going to explode."

"He always crumbles under pressure," Aden said, his tone casual, but Ellie knew better. Having her in a room full of vampires had his anxiety soaring.

"Speak of the devil," Andrei said, and she stiffened, fighting the urge to whip her head up to see if Carrie was with him. In her peripheral vision, Ellie saw the flash of black heels and slender calves, and she nearly wept with relief.

"I wasn't sure you were coming. Figured you'd be hiding your face in shame after your ass-whipping last night," Andrei taunted him.

"Sit the fuck down," Vincent snarled, and Carrie's knees slammed into the tile beside Ellie. She grunted but didn't cry out. "And you fucking wish, Andrei. I'll have my revenge tonight."

"Jesus, Vincent," Keeley said, her voice sharp. "You don't have to push the girl to the floor."

He dropped onto the sofa next to Andrei, and his voice softened as he spoke to her. "Don't worry about her, Keeley. Carrie likes it rough." His tone hardened as he addressed Carrie. "Don't you, pet?"

A hollow "Yes, Master," fell from Carrie's lips.

He petted her head like she was a dog. Carrie's hand curled into a tight fist, only inches away from her own, and Ellie ached to reach out to her. Dark purple bruises marred her hands and wrists.

"Yeah, she looks like it," Keeley scoffed in disgust. "Abusing your thralls doesn't make you a man, you know."

Ellie dug her fingernails into the back of Aden's calf, but he didn't react.

"He's apparently never learned proper social etiquette," Aden said, the words dripping with contempt.

"Oh, shut the fuck up, Aden. I've seen the state of your thralls over the years. At least I haven't drained her yet. Yours barely lasted months before you bled them dry."

Aden's entire body tensed, and a wave of anxiety washed over Ellie. To calm him, she discreetly slid her hand beneath the hem of his pants, her touch soft against the skin above his socks. Skin-to-skin contact was always the fastest way to soothe him.

Carrie's hand twitched, a tremor running through it, fingers flexing and stretching as if to reach for her. Ellie resisted the urge to yank Carrie into her arms, her knuckles white on her thigh.

How was she going to do this? How was she going to speak to Carrie? It was obvious she was being abused, but what could Ellie do? Overwhelmed with desperation, she wanted to beg Aden right then to buy her from Vincent. Her impulse was to snatch Carrie and flee. But all she could do was sit there trembling with silent fury and devastating grief for her best friend.

"You're looking lovely as always, Keeley," Vincent said, his voice a low, smooth purr that made Ellie's skin crawl.

Aden placed a comforting hand on her shoulder, his touch a gentle caress against the skin of her neck with his thumb.

"Where's your husband tonight? Ryan's his name, right?"

"You know his fucking name, Vincent," Aden answered for her.

"Not that it's any of your business, but he's at home with our son," Keeley said, her tone clipped.

Vincent reached down and released the leash from Carrie's collar. "Get me a glass of O Negative."

"Yes, Master," she replied as she rose on shaky legs, hurrying away.

Again, Ellie dug her nails into Aden's ankle, silently pleading for him to understand. Keeley got it first.

"Aden, why don't you have Ellie get you a glass of blood, too?" She suggested.

Before he could reply, she stood. "Here, I'll go with her since I feel like stretching my legs and know you don't like her wandering around alone. Come on, Ellie. Let's get Aden a drink."

"Fine," He gritted his teeth as Ellie scrambled to her feet.

"Yes, ma'am. I'll be right back, Sir," she said, playing her part.

Ellie rushed over to the banquet table along the north wall. Carrie waited in line for the thrall in front of her to be bled into a glass. She grasped Carrie by the hand and pulled her aside, finally pulling her friend into her arms.

"Carrie, I'm so glad to see you."

A soft cry escaped Carrie's lips, her body spasming in obvious pain.

Ellie released her. "I'm sorry. I'm sorry. I didn't mean to hurt you."

Carrie's eyes filled with tears. Her lower lip trembled, and then she grabbed Ellie, yanking her into a fierce hug that made her squeak.

"Alright, you two," Keeley said in a hushed tone. "Don't draw attention to yourselves."

With a sharp gasp, Carrie let go and stepped back. "I'm sorry, ma'am. I shouldn't have touched your thrall."

"It's okay," Ellie said quietly. "How bad is he hurting you?"

Carrie stepped further back, shaking her head. "I'm fine, Ellie. I need to get Master his blood now."

She turned, but Keeley's voice stopped her. "Is this the first time he's hurt you like this, or does he do this often?"

With no choice but to respond, she turned back. "Like Master said, I like pain. He enjoys reminding me every day."

"Jesus Christ," Keeley said under her breath.

"Why are you lying?" Ellie asked, finally getting a good look at Carrie.

She was thin, too thin. Her emaciated frame was clear to see—face drawn and pale, eyes dark and shadowed, whispering of starvation. Dark purplish bruises marked her throat, and more welts, angry and red, ran along her right cheekbone. Her once-short hair was now long and wavy, the curls framing her face, but it looked as unhealthy as she did. She was still beautiful, but the haunting emptiness in her eyes revealed a fractured spirit.

Most horrifying, though, were the deep slashes across her abdomen, visible through a gap in her dress. The sight was sickening.

Deep cuts, red and raw, stood out against her pale skin, several crusted with dried blood. Ellie placed her hands on Carrie's hips, her touch light and cautious, keeping her fingers well clear of her stomach.

"What has he done to you?" She choked through a sob.

"Carrie, hurry the fuck up," Vincent called from the sofa, and Carrie jumped, spinning around, rushing to the table to get his glass of blood.

Ellie wanted to run after her, but she worried about the consequences for Carrie. Instead, she spun to Keeley. "We have to help her," she pleaded, her voice clogged with emotion.

"Ellie, get it together," Keeley snapped. "Let's go back to Aden. I'm going to tell him you aren't feeling well, and I'm taking you back to his suite."

"I can't leave Carrie."

"You can't do anything to help her here. Or now. We have to come up with a plan, and we need to get you out of here before you have a meltdown."

"I'm already having one."

Keeley softened. "I know. We'll figure out how to get her away from him. Let's just go back. Aden will follow quickly because he'll be worried about you."

Carrie rushed by them with the glass of blood, heading back to Vincent, and giving it to him with shaking hands. They followed and found her kneeling on the floor, head down.

"Aden, Ellie isn't feeling well. I'm going to take her back to your suite. I suggest you stop taking so much of her blood unless you want her to pass out in public."

His eyes tightened, and he frowned. "I'll be along shortly."

With each step away from Carrie, Ellie felt a fresh wave of agonizing loss, as if her heart were being ripped out.

When they reached the hallway, she whispered under her breath. "Why did you say that to him? About taking too much of my blood?"

"Because I could. He isn't sure what's wrong with you now, so he'll hurry the hell up."

Aden

Aden excused himself a few minutes later, eager to find out just what the fuck that was all about. It was obvious that Vincent was abusing Ellie's friend. Anyone with eyes could see that. And while he watched Ellie as she and Keeley talked to her, Vincent's incessant chatter about nothing distracted him from being able to eavesdrop on them.

As soon as he entered the room, Ellie threw herself at him, clutching the front of his shirt, her eyes wild and frantic. Her hair had come loose from its elegant style. It was now a tangled mess around her face as if she'd been anxiously running her fingers through it.

"Aden, she's being brutalized. We have to help her. He's hurting her. Please, you have to get her away from him."

She was shaking so hard he feared her bones might break.

He gripped her arms. "Ellie, take a breath. Tell me what the fuck happened back there. Did you almost pass out, or was that a ruse?"

"Of course, she didn't almost pass out," Keeley said from where she sat at the dressing table.

"Aden, please, I'm begging you, you have to get her away from him."

His next words filled him with more regret than he could express. "Sweetheart, as much of an asshole as Vincent is, Carrie is his thrall."

"But he's cutting her."

A frown tugged at the corners of his mouth. "How do you know that?"

"Because of her dress. I could see the cuts. They were fresh."

"Less than a year ago, one of the first things you would've noticed was that her midriff was bare in that dress." Keeley stood and walked toward them. "I didn't notice them when she first arrived because she had her arms wrapped around her abdomen, but I saw them too, Aden. They're brutal."

"Can you buy her from him? Please," Ellie pleaded, her eyes full of desperation.

"Ellie, no one would believe I'd be interested in purchasing a tainted thrall." He cringed at his own words. "That sounded worse than—"

"No, it sounded exactly as bad as you meant it." She moved away, hugging herself.

"I tried to outbid him for her once. I don't think he's going to give her up, no matter what I say."

"Offer him double what he paid for her," Keeley suggested. "Vincent is a money-grubbing creep, so he'll probably take it. You're a persuasive guy. Surely you can convince him."

"There are a few pressure points I can exert, but he'll likely refuse just to be an asshole."

Ellie stepped closer and placed her hand on Aden's chest. "Can you please at least try? He's going to kill her. I know it."

Aden cupped her face with gentle hands. She was trembling. "I'll offer whatever it takes."

She buried her face in his chest, her voice muffled when she spoke. "Thank you."

"Okay, I'm going. Let me know if you need any help pushing Vincent's pressure points. I'd be happy to assist."

He nodded over Ellie's head.

"Night, Keeley," Ellie said as his sister left.

"You're shaking." Aden led her toward the bathroom. "Come on, let's get you into a warm bath."

She yanked her arm away. "Aden, no. I can't even think about that right now."

He gave her a sharp glare. "I'm not trying to fuck you, Ellie. Your skin is as cold as ice. I just want you to take a bath and warm up."

"When are you going to see Vincent? Can you buy her tonight?"

Aden guided her to the bathtub and turned on the water. "I can't. I have to meet Matthais shortly."

"Why are you meeting him?" She shivered, rubbing her arms.

"He asked me to meet him after tonight's party. He said he wanted to show me something. Why aren't you getting naked?"

Ellie turned her back to him. "I need help."

He unfastened her dress, and she slipped out of it, letting it fall to the floor and pool around her feet. She turned back to him.

"What does he want to show you?"

Aden pushed her panties down her thighs, letting them fall silently to the floor beside her dress. "Fuck if I know."

"How long will you be gone?"

Her anxiety poured out in her barrage of questions, reflecting her despair and nervous energy.

"I don't know, sweetheart, but I'll get back as soon as I can. If I run into Vincent again, I'll offer to buy her. If not, I'll find him first thing tomorrow, I promise."

"What if he hurts her tonight?"

Her eyes, wide and pleading, shone with unshed tears, their vulnerability nearly breaking him.

"I'll find him after I finish with Matthais."

Ellie slipped her arms around him, clinging to him, and for once, her naked flesh didn't tempt him. Not when she trembled so violently.

"Come on, baby." Taking her hand, he helped her into the bathtub.

She climbed in, sinking into the hot water, leaning against the side, looking completely drained and demoralized.

He sat with her in silence for a few more minutes, his fingers running through the soft, long strands of her hair as the tips floated in the water. Her eyes drifted closed, and the gentle rhythm of her breath filled the quiet room. When he couldn't put off leaving any longer, Aden leaned down and kissed her forehead, then stood.

"I'll be back as soon as I can."

A barely audible "okay" escaped her lips, but her eyes remained closed.

The door slid open with a hiss, and Aden walked into Matthais' office, nearly colliding with Ellie's father. With a subtle nod, he moved aside, allowing Aden to pass.

"Ah, Aden. There you are," Matthais said as he looked up from his desk. "Do you know Myles? Elliana's father?"

"We met earlier." Aden glanced at Myles, then returned his attention to Matthais.

"Master Westcott," he said before walking out.

Ellie assured him that her father wouldn't reveal anything about them to Matthais, but Aden remained skeptical. He knew the fierce loyalty half-breeds felt towards their sires. Still, he had to trust Ellie's instincts and unwavering belief in her father's love and loyalty to her.

Matthais rose and walked around his desk. "I was starting to think you weren't coming."

"I had something I needed to deal with."

"Yes." His nose twitched, a sign he was smelling Aden. "I saw your sister escort Elliana out of the party tonight after she had an encounter with Vincent's thrall."

Of course, he noticed.

"She was upset over seeing her friend in such a battered state," he said, figuring he might as well lay the groundwork in case his plan to buy Carrie went sideways.

"Those two were inseparable growing up. Carrie never got over losing Elliana when she left with you. She became unbearable." Matthais headed to the door. "I had to punish her multiple times and then just put her up for auction when Vincent inquired about her. He'd wanted her for a few years."

"He looks to be brutalizing her."

"His pets don't tend to be long for this world."

Aden's anger flared at Matthais' apathy, but he managed to keep his temper in check.

Barely.

"So, what do you want to show me?"

"Come, follow me."

Matthais led Aden into a warp port in the corner of his office. It opened into a stone corridor at least half the length of the east wing of the compound. Like the vaults in Réimse Shíochánta, the scent of damp earth permeated the space. But the unmistakable, cloying smell of blood, sweat, sex, and tears hanging heavily in the air overshadowed it.

"Welcome to the dungeons."

"What is this place?"

Matthais seemed pleased with his question.

"A collection of playrooms for vampires to play with their pets. Similar to those clubs you frequented on the lower levels of my city in the past."

"I'm sorry, what?" Aden's eyes flickered to him, a frown creasing his brow. The dungeons didn't surprise him, but Matthais' knowledge of his familiarity with the city's underbelly did. Apparently, he hadn't been as discreet as he thought.

"Surely you didn't think I was unaware. I know everything that goes on in my city."

"This looks nothing like those clubs. And sounds nothing like them either. All I hear here is crying and pain."

"Well, my dungeons cater to a specific type of vampire. One with a very discerning taste."

Aden folded his arms across his chest. "And what taste is that?"

"As you said. Pain. Let me show you around." Matthais led him down the center corridor. "These cells are carved out of the basalt bedrock and are replicas of the cells in the Carcere Mamertino."

The Carcere Mamertino was an ancient Roman prison in the Comitium, whose lower dungeon served as a holding cell before executions. According to legend, Saints Peter and Paul were imprisoned there, awaiting execution by Nero, the last Roman Emperor of the Julio-Claudian dynasty.

"It was no longer in use when I was born in the mid-fifth century, but my sire kept me captive in one of those cells for the first one hundred and fifty years of my new life." Matthais halted and faced Aden before they reached the first rooms. "Did Aurick ever tell you my history?"

"No."

"I was turned in 476 A.D. It was a leap year. The year the Western Roman Empire fell and what, centuries later, many considered the end of ancient times and the dawn of the Middle Ages." He gave Aden a knowing look. "I know Aurick and Sophie taught you the forbidden history."

Aden's expression remained neutral, betraying nothing of his parents' actions.

"My sire was a sadist. For a century and a half, he kept me in chains, starving me, keeping me weak, and subjecting me to unspeakable horrors. But he imparted to me the one essential truth about vampire existence." Matthais paused. "It's defined by pain and pleasure. And both can be exquisite when combined."

Aden frowned at his words but remained silent.

"But not just any pain. The kind of pain that etches itself into victims' memories, leaving them trembling and haunted long after the physical wounds have healed. He taught me to enjoy pain. Revel in it. Endure it. And most importantly, inflict it."

"What the fuck, Matthais?" He said, no longer able to keep quiet.

Matthais gave him an indulgent smile.

"Come now, Aden. You've inflicted pain over the years. Every little red-headed, green-eyed thrall at Soraya's club that you drained." Off of Aden's look, Matthais added. "I told you, there's nothing that happens in my city that I don't know about. Come, let me show you more."

Matthais motioned for Aden to continue walking, and against his better judgment, he complied.

Circular cells lined both sides of the walls, each with floor-to-ceiling viewing windows. The walls and floor were primitive, with rough stone in a herringbone pattern, slanted, with a grate in the center.

"We drain the blood into cisterns below. Though it's tainted, there's no reason to waste blood. We feed it to prisoners or other undesirable vampires."

Thick metal chains hung from the ceiling at the center of each cell. A stone table sat off to one side, covered in a variety of instruments, designed more for pain than pleasure.

"The cells are fitted with opaque glass panels that can be activated to provide privacy, but most of us like to be watched." Matthais gestured to a row of over-sized stuffed chairs, placed back-to-back in the corridor, seating for viewers to watch the horrors within.

Vampires and pets occupied most of the rooms, many of the latter strung up and bleeding. The gruesome sight made Aden swallow thickly, his stomach churning with revulsion.

"Why can't we hear them?"

Not that he wanted to, but after seeing the horrors happening in the cells, the screams should have been much louder.

"Every cell contains a sound filter. It would be too overwhelming otherwise. If we want to listen, we can simply turn it up. I've spared no expense in these playrooms."

Aden needed to get out of there before he fucking lost it. The deeper they went into the dungeons, the more nauseous he became. As a vampire immune to all ailments, the sensation was unfamiliar. But this sick feeling, a deep, dark revulsion, settled in his gut like a cold, heavy stone.

"Matthais, why would you think I'd be interested in these rooms? I don't inflict pain on my thralls. I fuck and feed from them. That's it."

"I know you haven't shown an interest in this, but I've always seen a darker side to you, beneath the surface. Only those who have experienced extreme personal pain have the ability to inflict it. And I know your young bride's death was the most agonizing thing you've endured."

"That topic is fucking off-limits," Aden snarled. "And I have no desire to inflict pain on my thralls."

"Not even Elliana? The bruises I saw prove you're far from gentle with her."

"Excuse me?" Aden snapped, the urge to grab him by the throat and choke the life out of him overwhelming, but Matthais merely seemed amused by his reaction.

"Vampires bring their pets down here, not their everyday thralls. The most exquisite kind of pain is sexual." Matthais stopped in front of one room and motioned for Aden to look. "Vincent and his pet spend quite a bit of time here when they visit."

A prickling sensation, like a thousand spiders crawling, formed on the back of Aden's neck, combined with a gut-wrenching dread, urging him to ignore the horror unfolding behind him. A year ago, he just might have. But unable to stop himself, he turned, his muscles tense, each movement deliberate. A vein throbbed in his temple, a furious pulse mirroring the storm of rage building inside him as he braced for the inevitable, horrific scene.

The sight that greeted him was more sickening than he imagined.

Ellie's friend hung from the ceiling, her hands and ankles bound above her. Vincent was standing behind her, raping her, as he used a long serrated knife to slice her breasts and stomach. She was crying, screaming, and thrashing against the pain as her blood flowed down her body and onto the floor beneath them.

Aden stepped forward, about to intervene when Matthais' hand came down on his shoulder.

"It's an exquisite sight, isn't it?"

Aden shook him off with a sharp jerk.

Vincent's eyes met his. A wild, feverish insanity reflected in them. Why the fuck hadn't he continued bidding last summer until Vincent gave up? He was far wealthier, and Vincent would have ultimately had to concede.

Even if he had, another unfortunate girl would be in Carrie's place. But she wouldn't be Ellie's best friend.

Matthais deactivated the sound filter.

"Want to join us, Aden?" Vincent asked as he pulled out of Carrie and walked over to a table with more knives and a row of syringes of BloodStone.

Carrie's cries turned to whimpers as she hung there, her long blond hair covering her face.

"You can't fuck or bite her, but you can cut her and feast on her blood if you want."

In that instant, Aden knew he would do whatever it took to take Carrie from him.

Whatever. The fuck. It took.

And then he would make sure Vincent suffered such unimaginable pain that what he was inflicting on that girl would pale in comparison. When Aden was done with him, he'd never be able to inflict pain on another thrall again.

And Aden wasn't about to wait another second.

For Ellie's sake and the sake of her friend, he buried his rage deep inside him, drawing on every ounce of self-control he possessed, and he stepped into the cell.

"Actually, I have a proposition for you, Vincent."

Vincent turned from the table with a syringe of BloodStone in his hand, completely unfazed by his nudity. "Oh yeah. And what's that?"

Aden swallowed back the bile that threatened at the sight of Vincent's blood-soaked cock.

"I'd like to buy her from you."

"Fuck you, Aden." Vincent walked over to Carrie and plunged the needle into her neck. She was so weak from blood loss that she barely even flinched.

"I'm serious. How much do you want for her?"

"No fucking way," Vincent replied, a smirk playing on his lips. "You tried to outbid me last year. And you lost. What makes you think I'd sell her to you now?"

"Because you're a businessman. I'm offering you a premium on your property. How much?"

"Why do you want her?"

"Why the fuck do you care?"

Vincent tossed the syringe onto the table. "Because I waited years to get her. Sorry, man, no deal."

"I'll pay you triple what you paid for her."

"No," he snapped. "If you want to have a go at her, you're welcome to stay. Kira is supposed to join us in a while. Otherwise, you can get the fuck out. I'm done with this conversation."

Vincent lifted Carrie's face and slapped her cheeks a few times.

"Time to wake up, pet. We're only getting started."

"Please, Master, no more."

With a snarl, Aden grabbed Vincent's arm and spun him around. "If you won't accept my offer, then I challenge you for her."

Vincent's eyes widened, and he looked over Aden's shoulder at Matthais, whose hard stare burned into his back.

"What the fuck, Aden?"

"Aden." Matthais' smooth voice came from behind him. "You'll want to think this through. Once a challenge is accepted, it can't be revoked."

To challenge a fellow vampire for a thrall was an extreme action. The most extreme in their world. A challenge was a fight to the death between two vampires who claimed the same human. Once the challenge was accepted, neither vampire could withdraw. Only one would survive, and Aden intended to be that vampire.

"I have no intention of revoking the challenge I've issued," he replied to Matthais before addressing Vincent again. "Now, do you accept, or are you going to agree to my monetary offer to buy her?"

"You're out of your fucking mind, you know that?"

"No. I'm a man who wants what he wants. And if you won't give it to me willingly, I'll take it."

After a long look at Carrie, Vincent finally met Aden's gaze again.

"Fine. I accept."

Aden turned to Matthais. Rage was simmering in the older vampire's deep gray eyes. "I'd like to request the use of the arena, either before or after the games tonight."

The length of Matthais' pause hung heavy in the air. When he answered, his reply was a low, menacing murmur.

"You can use it before."

Aden turned back to Vincent. "Now rules dictate that once a challenge has been accepted, the thrall in question cannot be harmed until the challenge is fulfilled. So I suggest you take her down and to the infirmary. If she bleeds out before tonight, your life is automatically forfeit, and your manner of death is at my discretion." Aden's voice darkened. "You don't want that."

"You can't tell me what to do with my thrall while she's still mine," Vincent snarled.

"Matthais," Aden said calmly. "Please explain the rules of a challenge to Vincent. He seems to be ignorant of them."

Matthais' furious gaze remained fixed on Aden. But only his eyes betrayed his anger. Everything else about his outward demeanor was his usual calm, composed self.

"Aden is correct. Rules are rules. You cannot play with or harm a thrall that is the subject of a challenge. Take her down and get her medical attention."

Vincent lunged at Aden with a guttural yell, but Aden sidestepped him with ease, a smirk playing on his lips.

"How about I challenge you for your pet, huh?"

Reaching out, Aden seized him by the throat and shoved him against the stone wall, sending debris from the ceiling crashing to the floor.

"I fucking dare you. Threaten that again, and I won't wait until tonight. I'll rip your heart out right here."

"Now, now, Aden," Matthais said. "He's accepted your challenge. He can't make any new challenge of his own. Just put him down, and why don't you head back to your suite? Clearly, my dungeons are not something that interests you."

Aden tossed Vincent to the side with another hard shove, sending him crashing into the table, scattering knives and syringes across the floor.

"Can I trust you'll ensure he abides by the rules today and doesn't lay another finger on her? Otherwise, I'm staying and will have my medical team take possession of and treat her."

"Aden, don't test my patience. Vincent wouldn't dare disobey rules I put in place. Would you, Vincent?"

Vincent's sharp nod, eyes blazing with barely contained fury, was his only reply.

"Very well. I'll see you tonight at sunset. I'll give you until that time to change your mind and take me up on my offer to pay you triple for her. If not, I'll see you in the arena."

Aden strode down the hallway, furious that Vincent refused his offer. Now he was going to have to kill the fucking prick. Not that the world would miss him.

But Aden knew he was doing the right thing. Not only for Ellie and her friend but for himself and the atonement he still owed to the thousands of girls who died at his hands.

Now he had to tell Aurick that he broke his word and failed to keep his temper in check.

Aden

"Are they still awake?" Aden asked Horatio as he approached his parent's guest suite.

"Yes," his father's guard nodded, the smooth slide of the door echoing in the quiet hallway.

He found Aurick and Sophie sitting on the sofa, still dressed in their formal outfits from the party. Aurick was sipping from a glass of blood-laced whiskey, and Sophie was drinking a cup of tea.

"I don't mean to bother you so late, but this couldn't wait until evening."

Sophie sat forward, her keen gaze sharp as she looked at him. "What happened? Is Ellie alright?"

All at once, the last half hour melted away, and Aden was flooded with love for his mother, as her first instinct was to worry about Ellie.

"Ellie's fine."

"Sit," Aurick motioned to the chair. "What's on your mind, son?"

Aden dropped heavily into the seat. "I don't want you to freak out, Sophie." He addressed his mother first before his gaze shifted to meet his father's. "But I've done something that can't be undone."

She set her tea on the table. "I don't like the sound of that, Aden."

Aurick's eyes narrowed, reflecting the firelight. "What did you do?"

"I've challenged Vincent for Ellie's friend."

"What?" Sophie let out a high-pitched shriek, making the hairs on the back of Aden's neck stand on end.

"Aden," Aurick said, his tone sharp as he downed his drink. "I suggest you explain yourself now."

"I offered to pay for her, but he refused. So I challenged him."

"You don't challenge a vampire over such a minor infraction. What's really going on?"

He glanced at Sophie before meeting Aurick's eyes again. "Has Matthais taken you to his dungeons?"

"How do you know about those?" His father asked.

"He introduced me to them tonight."

"Why would he do that?" Sophie asked, clearly as knowledgeable about them. Interesting. His father apparently kept nothing from his mother.

"I have no fucking idea why he thought I'd have any interest in them. But after he gave permission for Ellie to see her father, he asked me to come to his office tonight so he could show me something. Then he escorted me down. When the fuck did he build those?"

Aurick stood and walked over to the bar, pouring two drinks. "He's had those dungeons for centuries. Since he built his compound. But he recently renovated them and has been showing them off this week."

"And what does this have to do with Ellie's friend?" Sophie reached for her tea again.

Aurick gave Aden a drink, which he gulped down.

"Ellie saw her tonight. She arrived with Vincent, looking pretty beaten up. Ellie asked me to buy her, and I promised her I'd do what I could to get her out of his clutches."

"And you felt challenging him was the only option?" Aurick sat on the sofa beside Sophie. "Certainly, he could have been persuaded by money."

"It's a long story, and I have no patience to get into it right now. But needless to say, he rejected my very generous offer for her."

"But why a challenge?" His father asked. "There are other options that can be sought when two vampires want the same human. Ones that don't include a death match."

"He had her down in those dungeons." Aden shot out of the chair, the image of Carrie and what Vincent did to her burned into his memory. "He was brutalizing her in the most inhumane way. I snapped. I would've killed him right there if Matthais hadn't been lurking behind us."

"But the risk of a challenge... it's too dangerous," Sophie said, wringing her hands until Aurick caught them in one of his.

"I'm not worried about beating Vincent," Aden scoffed. "He'll put up a decent fight, but he won't win. But I couldn't walk away from what I saw. Fuck! What am I going to tell Ellie?"

"The truth." Aurick's words hung heavy in the silent room.

"But it'll devastate her."

"Yes." Rising to her feet, Sophie approached him and rested a hand on his arm. For once, he didn't rebuff her, his time with Ellie having made touch more tolerable. "But she'll be more devastated when she finds out, and you hadn't told her."

"You don't keep secrets from the woman you love," Aurick said from the sofa.

Sophie returned to her seat next to him. "Take your father's advice in this, Aden. He knows the harsh consequences of keeping things from the woman he loves."

"Doesn't look like he's suffered harsh consequences to me," Aden said with a pointed look at where Aurick's thumb caressed Sophie's hand on her lap.

Aurick brought her hand to his lips. "That's because your mother has an incredibly forgiving nature. You and Keeley wouldn't be here right now if she didn't."

Aden had never been bothered by seeing his parents express affection, but he didn't need a front-row seat to it.

"Okay, enough, you two. Child in the room." Aden smirked as he sat again.

"Aurick, we need to tell him now," Sophie said a moment later. "This can't wait any longer."

"There are ears in all these walls, Soph."

"Then let's take a ride to see the aurora borealis. He needs to know."

Aden shook his head. "No. I can't leave Ellie in this city alone. I won't. Whatever you need to tell me can wait."

Though clearly unhappy, Sophie nodded. "When will the challenge take place?"

"Tonight after sunset. Matthais gave his approval to use the arena before the games start."

"Of course he did." Sophie's face showed her disgust. "He can make a spectacle of it."

"I want the world to see when I rid it of that piece of shit." Aden stood up. "I need to get back to Ellie before she falls asleep."

"I know you don't want to upset her further, but she needs to know the truth about this," Aurick said. "The risks in it. Don't keep her in the dark."

"I won't." He sighed. "Fuck! I would apologize for going back on my word of not causing chaos on this trip, but I'm not. I couldn't leave that girl at his mercy and be able to look Ellie in the eyes."

"You did the right thing," Aurick said.

"Even though you're taking a very grave risk," Sophie added.

"I'm not. Vincent is no match for me."

"I'm sure he isn't," Aurick agreed. "But don't get cocky in that arena. You have a woman who loves you, relying on you to come back to her."

With his father's words heavy on his mind, Aden excused himself and headed back to Ellie.

"What?"

Ellie screeched louder than Sophie had when Aden told her about the challenge. She stood over him as he sat on the sofa, her face a mask of horror.

Upon returning to the suite, he found her asleep in the tub, her encounter with Carrie having taken its toll. The tub's heater had kept the water and Ellie warm, but he was furious because she could have easily drowned. She hardly stirred when he lifted her, her body almost weightless in his arms, and carried her to bed.

So he decided not to wake her, instead settling on the sofa with another glass of Jameson. But as if sensing his presence, she woke fifteen minutes later and sat up. When he explained what happened, what a challenge was, and what it meant, she leaped out of bed, tugged on her robe, and stomped over to him.

Despite knowing he was in for a hell of a fight, Aden couldn't help but admire how fucking beautiful she was. With the fury radiating off her, her skin flushed and eyes flaring, she simply took his breath away.

"Ellie, you don't have to worry. He won't win."

"I want him dead," she hissed, turning and walking away, her hands twisting together. "For what he did to her, I want him dead." She spun back around to face him. "And I don't doubt you'll win, but how could you be so reckless?"

With a sigh, Aden stood and walked over to her. "Reckless? You asked me to save her, and that's what I'm doing."

Her eyes, wide with panic, met his. "But he could kill you."

"He won't."

"Aden, I can't lose you." Her anxiety made her voice tremble. "I want you to save her, but I can't lose you."

He'd known she'd be upset, but this was more than he expected. He tucked a lock of her hair behind her ear to calm her.

"Ellie, nothing is going to happen to me. But even if it did, Sophie and Aurick would protect you. You don't have to worry about ever going back to Matthais."

Her furious emerald eyes blazed, and he recoiled, taking a step back. What the fuck did he say to make her so mad?

"Is that what you think? That I'm worried about going back to him if you die?" Her small fists pummeled his chest. "How dare you, you jerk!"

Her actions stunned Aden. She'd never hit him before. Although her blows weren't gentle, they didn't cause him pain. But it reminded him she needed to use the weights in his gym when they returned home. She wasn't weak, but she needed to be stronger.

"If you die, I don't care what happens to me," she raged as she kept hitting him. "He can kill me for all I care."

"Don't you ever fucking say that!" Snarling, he seized her wrists to stop her hits.

She struggled in his grasp, tears wetting her lashes as she fought to break free from his hold.

"I can't lose you because I can't live without you, you idiot."

Though she fought him, Aden pulled her into his arms, his embrace surrounding her as she thrashed against him.

Gone was the calm, collected woman he loved. In her place was a whirlwind of frantic anger, her usual composure shattered.

"You're not going to lose me, I promise," he murmured, pressing his lips to her hair.

She slumped against him, her forehead resting on his chest, a quiet sniffling sound escaping her.

"I can't," she repeated as she wrapped her arms around him and clutched him desperately.

"You won't. I'll never leave you." He rubbed his hands up and down her back, his touch gentle and soothing. "You know, when you act like this, I think you might actually love me as much as I love you."

A sharp pinch to his side was her retaliation, and he yelped, though it didn't hurt.

"Don't joke about this." His chest muffled her voice.

"I'm not joking. Now can we get some sleep? I have a fight in a few hours."

Her breath hitched, and she pulled out of his arms, reaching up to brush the moisture from under her eyes. Ellie rarely cried, and he hated seeing it. He despised being the reason for it even more.

"Do your parents know about this? What did they say? Isn't there something your dad can do to step in?"

Aden led her toward the bed. "No. Challenges can't be revoked. Ellie, I promise it will be alright."

"How are you not afraid?"

He wasn't afraid of Vincent or losing to him. The only thing he feared was losing Ellie. Every day, he lived with the ever-present fear of losing her.

Aden unbuttoned his shirt, as the last few hours caught up with him. "Because I have everything to fight for. And everything to live for. So, don't worry about me, mo ghrá. I'll come back to you. Where are your pajamas?"

She slid out of her robe and gripped the front of his open shirt. "I don't need them. And you better come back. Because I'll come after you if you die on me. We promised to never leave each other again. I won't live without you."

The sight of her naked had the usual physical effect on him, but her words chilled him.

"Ellie, I told you not to fucking say shit like that!"

"Then don't you dare die on me."

Clasping her to his bare chest, he felt her tremble again.

"Have a little faith in me. I won't let you down."

"I'm sorry," she murmured against his chest.

"What for?"

"For endangering you. I never meant to do that."

He cupped her chin in his hand, tilting her face up to his. "You didn't, Ellie. After what I saw tonight, even if you hadn't asked me to save her, I would have."

Anguish flickered in her eyes as she bit her lip. "Was he hurting her that badly?"

"Don't ask me that. I don't want to lie to you. But now that I challenged him, he can't hurt her anymore. He had to get her medical attention, and he can't harm her again unless he survives the challenge. And he won't."

"I can never thank you enough for this." With a gentle tug, she brought his face down to hers as their mouths met softly.

When the kiss broke, he whispered against her lips, "You just did."

Ellie

Ellie paced like a caged animal in front of the sofa, tugging the IV stand along with her as Keeley scrolled through her tablet. Aden was in the shower, without her, because his sister showed up a half hour ago, just after they finished making love.

After they woke, he fed from a half dozen of his thralls, but then she dragged him back to bed, insisting he drink from her again, to maximize his strength. Thus the need for the BloodStone drip hanging out of her arm at the moment.

"Ellie, will you sit down already? You're going to wear a hole in the floor."

Keeley appeared calm, but Ellie knew better. She couldn't help but ask, anyway.

"Aren't you worried about him?"

"Not really," Keeley shrugged as she set her tablet aside. Her eyes betrayed her. "Vincent is a pussy. Aden's going to wipe the arena floor with him."

Ellie dropped onto the sofa beside her, removing the needle now that the BloodStone bag was empty. "You're as terrible a liar as I am."

"No, I'm not. You have an honest face and can't hide anything. Me? I kept Ryan a secret from my parents and Aden for a decade."

Fastening the bandage over the puncture, Ellie lifted her arm, elevating it so the bleeding would stop.

"How did they not smell him on you?"

"I avoided being in the same room with them."

"For ten years?"

"A girl in love does what she has to do."

Sophie and Aurick walked in. Ellie's eyes welled as she met Aden's mother's gaze.

Sophie held her arms out. "Come here, sweetheart," she murmured, and Ellie rushed into them. "Everything's going to be fine."

Ellie felt Aurick's hand on her shoulder, squeezing gently, and she inhaled a shaky breath, never having been touched by the ancient vampire. He didn't speak to her. He didn't need to. His touch said it all.

"You ready for this, son?" he asked Aden, who came up behind her and maneuvered her out of Sophie's arms and into his.

"Let's get this done. I'm already over it."

Ellie clutched him, her fingers digging into the solid muscle of his back, every cell in her body rebelling against the idea of letting go.

"I had Mina go to the infirmary to check on Carrie," Sophie said in a low, serious voice that sliced through Ellie's desperate focus on Aden. "But she wasn't there. She'd never been brought in."

The words landed with a heavy thud in her stomach, and Ellie's eyes snapped to Aden's face.

"I'm going to kill that motherfucker slowly," he snarled.

"Aden, just focus on prevailing at any cost," Aurick said. "I'll inquire with Matthais where she was taken. If he assured you she wouldn't be harmed, it's unlikely he let Vincent take another shot at her. But you need to concentrate on the task at hand."

The roar in Ellie's ears made Aurick's words almost unintelligible. "What do you think he did with her?" She choked over the lump in her throat.

"I'll find out, Ellie," he said. "Now, son, it's time to go."

Ellie tightened her arms in a desperate attempt to stop him from leaving.

"Hey," Keeley said from behind Aden. He turned to face his sister, taking Ellie with him, because she refused to release him. "Don't play with your food. Get in. Tear his fucking head off. Then get out."

He barked out a laugh, the sound rumbling through his chest against Ellie's cheek. "I love when you use the word fuck! See how good it feels."

She grinned, but it didn't meet her eyes.

Aden looked down at Ellie, and his eyes softened in a way that made her heart squeeze painfully. "I love you."

"You're the love of my life, Aden Westcott. You better fucking come back to me unscathed."

The entire room laughed at her rare curse, but Ellie barely registered it. All she could see was Aden's face, his eyes dark with emotion. He bent to kiss her, lifting her off her feet as he fused his mouth to hers. The kiss was all-consuming, a silent promise and reluctant goodbye all wrapped into one.

She clutched at him, wrapping her arms and legs around his neck and waist, not caring that his family was watching them. Let them see how completely she belonged to him and how thoroughly he had claimed every part of her. His mouth moved against hers with a hunger that matched her own, their hearts pounding in sync, a frantic rhythm echoing their awareness of the danger that awaited him.

"That's the hottest fucking thing you've ever said to me," he groaned, releasing her lips.

She loosened her arms and legs, sliding down his body to stand in front of him. His cock was hard against her stomach, his body instinctively responding to her proximity, oblivious to their audience and the potential jeopardy he was facing. All Ellie wanted to do was drag him back to bed and stay there forever. She felt his hesitation in his stiff posture, a palpable tension mirroring her own, and something about their shared reluctance comforted her.

As was his way, he turned without a word and strode out, but this time the abruptness of it left her feeling hollow. One moment he was there, solid and real in her arms. The next, he was walking away, taking a piece of her with him.

With an encouraging nod to her and Keeley, Aurick and Sophie followed.

"Why does he do that? Is it so hard to say goodbye?" Keeley draped her arm over Ellie's shoulder.

"It's not goodbye," she said fiercely, unable to tear her eyes away from the door.

He was only doing this for her. But he was strong. He was fierce. And he would come back to her.

Keeley gave her a quick squeeze. "Come on, let's distract ourselves by calling my boys. Maybe Vlad will even be around. Ryan said he's been sleeping in Iain's crib with him."

"He doesn't like to sleep alone," Ellie murmured as they moved to the sofa, grateful to Keeley for the distraction.

Aden

Aden strolled into the arena, his feet crunching on the frozen ground. A layer of undisturbed snow covered the dirt, broken only by the tracks of the two other men standing in the center. It fell in thick, lazy flakes, illuminated by the torches around the perimeter of the fighting pit.

The surrounding stands overflowed with a crowd of vampires, half-breeds, and humans, all there to see the first challenge in almost four centuries. The last one was a century before Aden was born, between Matthais and Alaric, the original Gerent of Erebu. However, they coveted the same thrall, a girl named Mia, and their inability to reach an agreement led Alaric to issue a challenge.

But Matthais was older, by over six hundred years, and he was stronger. A vampire's strength increased with age, and with that to his advantage, he triumphed. Alaric died, and Matthais took Mia for himself. She only lived a short time. His personal thralls rarely lived past thirty.

Aden reached the pair, his eyes blazing. He stepped into Vincent's face, snarling, his hands gripping the front of his shirt.

"Where the fuck is she, Vincent?"

"I don't know what you mean." A slow smirk stretched across Vincent's lips.

"Aden, what are you going on about?" Matthais asked with a puzzled expression.

"His thrall never showed up in the infirmary last night. It seems your assurances hold little weight."

A dangerous glint flickered in Matthais' eyes. "Vincent, is this true?"

"She's my pet. I'll do whatever I want with her."

"You will obey my rules," Matthais' aggressive tone surprised Aden. He was typically more composed. "Now, where is she? The thrall in question is required to attend the challenge."

"She's tied up in my concubine suite, where she belongs," Vincent spat. "And she's not in any condition to attend."

A harsh laugh burst from Aden's lips. "You need to get your house in order, Matthais. If losers like Vincent are openly defying you, what's next? Anarchy?"

Matthais' composure slipped further as he pushed between the two men, facing Aden. "I assure you, my house is in order, Aden. You'd be well advised to remember that."

He spun, thrusting a finger in Vincent's face. "And if you win this challenge, you will be held accountable for your disobedience. Your actions have consequences, and you'll be lucky if I don't drain that whore myself." His composure returned as suddenly as it vanished, and he stepped back. "Now, you both know the rules."

"Perhaps you should review them with him," Aden suggested, his eyes sweeping over the spectators in the stands. The turnout was larger than he anticipated. "Vincent clearly didn't brush up on them since last night."

"Your impertinence is wearing thin, Aden," Matthais cautioned. "There are only two rules. One—no mercy. This is a fight to the death, gentlemen. Only one of you will walk out of here alive, so I suggest you fight as if your life is on the line because it is. Two—nothing is off-limits. You can use anything at your disposal inside this arena, but it must be declared before the fighting begins."

"Wait a minute," Vincent said, his hand outstretched. "No one told me I could declare anything."

"Should've read those rules," Aden chuckled just as Kane walked up behind him and dropped a canvas bag at his feet before walking off.

"What's that?" Vincent asked.

"My swords," Aden said, his grin as fierce and sharp as the blades at his feet. "I'm declaring them."

"That's not right. I didn't know I could bring anything."

Aden considered bringing a Helios gun but decided against it. If Vincent got a hold of it, he could easily use it. He could kill Vincent with his bare hands, but it wouldn't be quick. And he was heeding Keeley's words to get in, tear Vincent's fucking head off, and get out.

His swords would be more than sufficient.

"If I have a right to have my own weapons, I demand the opportunity to get them."

"You needed to walk in with them." Matthais shook his head in disgust. "As Aden said, you should have read the rules, so the answer to your demand is no."

"He didn't walk in with them. His fucking guard brought them in."

"Kane walked in with me but was just standing off to the side. That is within the rules. Don't worry, Vincent, I brought one for your use. I don't want anyone to say it wasn't a fair fight, after all."

"Jesus, Aden. Why the fuck are we doing this?" Vincent threw up his hands.

"Just let me buy the girl, and we don't have to."

"You have no right to her," he snarled. "Why would I sell you my favorite pet?"

"Because I asked nicely. And offered you a fuck ton of money for her."

"Time for negotiating is past," Matthais said. "My games start in two hours, so let's begin."

He glided away, and Aden leaned down, opening his bag and tossing a sword at Vincent. He reacted as expected, slashing out before Aden could grab his own.

Dodging the attack, Aden swept his leg up, striking Vincent in the abdomen, in the exact spot he'd sliced Carrie. The impact sent him reeling backward, his sword flying from his hand, a metallic clang echoing as it hit the ground.

"You're such a fucking sleaze, Vincent, ignoring the rules of engagement." Aden grabbed his sword and turned to face him, his arm tensed, poised to strike. "Come on, asshole. Pick up the blade and show me what you've got."

Scrambling across the snowy ground, Vincent picked up the fallen weapon. Aden circled, and Vincent followed, his eyes wild, his breath ragged, as he watched Aden's slow and steady movements.

"You only wanted to use swords because you have the advantage."

With a grin, Aden raised his hands in mock surrender. "We can go hand to hand if you prefer."

"I'm not as inexperienced as you think I am."

"Alright, let's see it then."

A thrill surged through Aden, a warm rush that felt exhilarating, making his heart pound and his senses heighten. He hadn't been in a fight like this, one-on-one, in a long time. Most of his sparring sessions involved fighting with at least a dozen recruits. Group combat, with its flurry of blows and adrenaline-fueled intensity, kept Aden's fighting skills razor-sharp.

Weeks of anxiety and stress had been building up inside him, simmering beneath the surface and erupting in arguments with Ellie. But now he could unleash his pent-up frustration on Vincent, saving an innocent thrall from torture, and making Ellie happy in the process.

Aden needed this outlet more than he realized.

Vincent lunged first, crossing the distance between them in a blur, the speed that only a vampire could travel. His initial attack was a feint—a high slash that whipped through the air before it transformed into a low sweep aimed at Aden's legs.

Aden leaped over the sword, its edge scraping against the snow, carving a deep gash that exposed the dark earth below.

The slick slush was treacherous under his feet, but Aden kept his movements smooth and efficient. He shifted his weight, his boots finding purchase in the dirt beneath the snow, as Vincent charged again. Aden's skill, honed over centuries of rigorous and disciplined training, showcased his experience as a military leader—something Vincent lacked, thus making him no match.

His blade came down hard, striking Vincent's shoulder. A howl of pain, raw and ragged, tore from his throat.

"Fuck, Aden!"

"Being sliced open hurts like fuck, don't you think?"

Vincent snarled, the sound reverberating through the arena. "I'm going to slice her to ribbons when I get my hands back on her."

Aden's blood pounded in his ears, a furious rhythm echoing his rage. He knew Vincent was an asshole, but how did he not realize what a sick, fucking, sadistic bastard he was?

Aden felt his parents' and Kane's eyes on him from the sidelines. He instructed Kane not to interfere, no matter the outcome, something that went against his very nature as Aden's guard. But Aden needed to make sure Kane survived, in case he didn't, to guarantee Ellie's safety. As he promised her, Aurick and Sophie would care for and protect her, ensuring she never went back to Matthais. But Aden's faith in Kane's ability and commitment to keep Ellie safe was absolute.

But that meant he had to let Aden die if things went sideways. Aden didn't think it would happen, not with the way Vincent fought, but he couldn't take the chance of Kane's last-minute interference. So, he extracted a blood oath from him, the second one of their lifetime, a demand Kane resisted at first but fulfilled out of his unwavering loyalty.

For the next half hour, Aden and Vincent's swords clashed in a furious clang of steel that rang through the arena, forcing Aden to admit the other vampire's skill.

The roar of the crowd was like a relentless pounding in his head, making him regret asking Matthais for the arena's use. In his moment of distraction, Vincent's sword plunged into his side, eliciting a pained roar and a spurt of dark blood that stained the snow. Despite the excruciating pain, for a second, he was almost impressed by the unexpectedness of the blow.

But the moment passed, and Aden's fury exploded as he launched a counterattack by seizing Vincent's wrist, spinning him around, and throwing him across the arena, sending him crashing into the stands. The stone structure groaned and trembled from the impact.

He was over the swordplay and wanted to get back to Ellie, who he knew was going out of her mind with worry. Aden tossed his blade aside and waved his fingers.

"Come on, let's end this."

Snarling, he stalked toward Vincent, who charged into him. Their collision sent them both sliding twenty feet through the snow. Aden held his ground as he reached for Vincent's neck, raking his nails across his skin, spraying blood into both their faces. Vincent snapped his head forward, the impact breaking Aden's nose. A crimson torrent burst forth and soaked their shirts and the earth below.

"Fuck!"

With a roar, he sent Vincent reeling backward with a powerful shove. As soon as Vincent hit the ground, Aden slammed his heavy boot down on his throat with a sickening crunch.

He much preferred the thrill of hand-to-hand combat. It was exhilarating.

Aden raised his foot, but as it came down again, Vincent rolled away at the last moment, narrowly escaping. Then a knife plunged into Aden's calf, the pain immediate and sharp. With a guttural snarl, he ripped the bloody blade from his leg as Vincent stumbled to his feet, coughing violently.

"Hidden knife?" A sneer twisted Aden's lips. "I believe you were required to declare that."

"I thought you'd appreciate—" cough. "The irony since it's the one I used—" cough. "To leave permanent scars on that tainted, used-up thrall—" cough "You want."

"Well, why don't we let you find out how it feels, shall we?"

He grasped Vincent by the front of his shirt, yanking him closer, and plunged the knife into the side of his neck.

Vincent screamed as he stumbled back. "You fucker," he gurgled as blood filled his throat.

While he was distracted, Aden tackled him to the ground in a flurry of motion and muffled grunts. Vincent's jaw shattered, quickly healing even as Aden followed with a combination of strikes against his face.

They grappled in the deepening snow, their supernatural strength leaving craters on the arena floor. Blood froze on their skin, creating macabre patterns of red ice.

Bones cracked and healed with unnatural speed as they clashed, their almost evenly matched skills unnerving Aden. The snow beneath their feet turned into a slushy mess, making it difficult for them to keep their footing.

Vincent dropped and rolled on the ground, grabbing his sword again. "You want to end it? Let's end it," he growled as he lifted it with a vicious slashing motion.

Aden caught Vincent's blade between his palms, drawing gasps from the crowd. The edge bit deep into his hands, but he ignored the pain, using Vincent's momentum to pull him forward into a knee strike to his balls, causing Vincent to double over in agony.

Stumbling back, Aden shook his bloody hands, picking up his sword, but Vincent's voice made him turn around.

"Hey, fucker!"

Aden's arm shot up, poised to strike. But then blackness spotted his vision as Vincent's sword came down, slicing through flesh, sinew, and bone, severing his left hand at the wrist.

A raw, guttural roar tore from Aden's lips, the sound utterly inhuman. Like a wounded beast. He felt his eyes flashing crimson as his sight returned. Driven by desperation and centuries of combat, he seized Vincent's sword arm with his intact hand, twisting it with a sickening crack that echoed in the night. Vincent's blade fell into the snow, and Aden's follow-up strike drove him to his knees. In the same motion, Aden retrieved his sword, pinning Vincent's head with his forearm and pressing the blade to the vampire's throat.

"Any last words?" Aden's voice vibrated with the thrill of victory and the chilling promise of death.

"Fuck you!" Vincent snarled, but the words died in his throat as Aden's sword sliced through his neck. His head tumbled away, a grotesque mask of shock and disbelief. Vincent's body convulsed, dropping to the ground, his blood forming a dark pool in the snow.

With the bloody stump of his arm pressed against his side, Aden swayed as the world swam and blurred before his eyes. Ellie's name slipped from his lips as the ground rushed up to meet him.

The last thing he saw before the world went black was Kane's dark silhouette rushing towards him.

Ellie

Ellie continued to pace, as she'd been doing for the last hour.

"Keeley, can't you call Aden up on a hologram? Just to see how it's going?"

Keeley looked up from where she sat on the chair, scrolling through a report from Hannah on her tablet. "Do you really want to distract him right now?"

"Can't you just look? You don't have to contact him. He checks on me all the time without me knowing."

"Do you want to risk seeing what's happening?"

"How about your parents?"

"Ellie, if they had something to tell us, they'd call us."

"What about Drake? Drake, can you come in here?" She asked quietly, but she knew he could hear her. With a soft hiss, the door slid open. He came around the corner and stepped into the suite.

"Everything okay?" he asked, and she offered a strained smile to the guard, who was now also her friend.

"Have you heard anything from the arena?"

"No."

"Can you call Kane on a hologram? I can't activate one."

Thralls couldn't use holograms. Anytime she wanted to reach Aden, she had to ask someone else to contact him. She'd have to talk to him about it when they got home. She was done always being at the mercy of others.

"He won't answer right now unless it comes through as an emergency call. Those were the instructions when they left. I don't know if it's a good idea to distract them if it isn't truly an emergency."

"Fine," Ellie said, her voice tight. She didn't want to alarm Aden and risk him getting hurt. "Thanks, Drake."

He nodded and walked out of the room.

She resumed her pacing. "It's been too long, Keeley."

Setting her tablet aside, Keeley looked up. "I know you're worried, but you need to chill."

"I can't lose him. I won't survive it." Her heart pounded so hard in her chest, she felt it might burst.

Rising to her feet, Keeley crossed the room and stood in front of her.

"You're getting hysterical. Do you need me to slap you? I'll do it if you need me to."

Keeley's offer, delivered with a straight face, cut through Ellie's hysteria, making her laugh.

"Okay. I get it. Thanks. I needed that."

"Happy to be of service." A grin briefly touched Keeley's lips before disappearing. "I'm worried too. But I know Aden. He's been undefeated for centuries. He took down twelve feral vampires and barely broke a sweat. This is easy for him."

"I think it was a little more than a sweat. And those rogues were weak. Vincent isn't."

"But there were still twelve of them. Twelve, Ellie. He'll—"

Her words were cut off when the door opened and Kane came striding around the corner, carrying an unconscious Aden in his arms. Thick, dark red blood soaked his clothes, matting his hair. Jagged, angry gashes marred his exposed skin, pulsing with fresh blood, leaving a crimson trail across the pristine white marble.

A choked cry escaped Ellie's lips as her legs buckled. Keeley reached for her as she collapsed to the floor.

"Ellie!"

Sophie, Aurick, Mina, and Drake came rushing in behind them in a whirlwind of activity, followed by one of Master Matthais' surgeons and a floating medical bay that differed from the ones used for humans.

Kane laid Aden on the examination table inside the medical bay as Mina hurried to his side, lifting his arm. Only then did Ellie see that his hand was missing.

"Where's his hand? What happened? Where's his hand?" She screeched, her voice growing louder and more hysterical with each question.

"Sophie," Mina snapped. "Get her out of here and give her a sedative before she has a breakdown. And where is that damn hand? If we don't get it reattached quickly, he'll lose the use of it."

With a cooler in hand, the doctor stepped into the medical pod, and the door slid shut.

"Keeley, help me get Ellie into the bathroom." Sophie urged Ellie to stand. "Come on, sweetheart."

Ellie shook her head, thrashing it back and forth, chanting Aden's name. A loud buzzing filled her head, blurring her vision and making it impossible to focus.

Aden lay motionless on the examination table, his breathing shallow, as Mina and the doctor worked on him. His stillness was unnatural, a stark contrast to his brooding, volatile personality.

Sophie and Keeley coaxed and cajoled, their voices gentle yet firm, as they tried to get her to stand. But Ellie wouldn't budge. She could see Aden from where she was, and she didn't want to move.

"Drake, can you help me?" Sophie asked beside her. "We need to get her into the bathroom."

"No! Don't touch me." She fought against him as he attempted to pull her up.

"Ellie!" Sophie's voice, sharper than she'd ever heard it, sliced through the air. Ellie froze. "Aden would want you to stay calm right now. Please let Drake take you to the bathroom."

"I can't see him from the bathroom," Ellie said, tearing her gaze from Aden and begging Aden's mother to not take her away.

"We'll be just a minute, I promise," Sophie said, gesturing for Drake to lift her.

Feeling like she was going into shock, Ellie didn't fight him this time. He pulled her to his chest, and she buried her face in his shirt, its rough material scratching her cheek as he walked past the medical pod and into the bathroom.

Ellie

Ellie sat on the bed beside Aden, her hand clutching the fingers of his hand, the one that hadn't been detached ten minutes ago.

She stopped spiraling once the sedative Sophie forced on her kicked in. Keeley tried to distract her while Mina and the doctor reattached Aden's hand. But Ellie insisted on standing outside the medical pod, her gaze locked on them as they worked on him.

With the doctor's help, Mina pressed his severed hand against the ragged stump of his wrist, keeping it aligned as invisible threads of tissue reattached to each other. First, the bone knitted together with a sharp crack, sounding like breaking ice. Then, the tendons, white cords resembling writhing snakes, connected. Next, his dark blood vessels, pulsing and throbbing, stretched toward each other, intertwining like grasping roots. Finally, the skin closed over the severed area, leaving jagged white scars and raised, puckered flesh in its wake.

Ellie watched awestruck as Aden's body healed itself in what could only be considered a miracle of cellular evolution. When they finished, the doctor put a cast on his arm to immobilize it.

Aden woke once while they were working on him, but Mina injected him with a powerful tranquilizer that Keeley said could knock out a polar bear—the only one of its kind that worked on vampires.

Now Ellie waited for him to wake, her chest feeling tight and breathless. Everyone said he'd be fine. It was the severe blood loss that caused him to lose consciousness. Mina assured her he'd wake up when the drug wore off, but Ellie wouldn't be able to breathe freely again until he opened his eyes.

Sophie and Aurick were across the room, seated on the sofa, talking to Mina, while Kane and Drake stood guard inside the door.

"At least it wasn't his dominant hand," Keeley said as she sat on the other side of Aden. "That would've seriously pissed him off."

"Will he really get full use of it back?"

"Yeah. They got it reattached quickly enough. It'll take a week or two to fully heal and for him to get full range of motion back. But the more blood he drinks, the quicker it will happen."

Aden stirred, and Ellie reached out to touch his face as Keeley leaped off the bed.

"He's waking," she called out. "Ellie, get back."

Ellie looked up at her confused. "What's the—"

Interrupted mid-sentence, she squealed when powerful arms lifted her off the bed, her back pulled to a solid chest as she strained against the hold. A glance over her shoulder revealed Aurick, the sight causing her to stiffen in surprise because he was touching her again. She opened her mouth to ask him what he was doing when Aden's roar filled the room.

"Fuck! What the fuck! My hand! Someone get my fucking hand. Where is it?"

Ellie's gaze whipped back to Aden, her heart pounding against her ribcage. He sat bolt upright, his eyes wild and blazing crimson. He surged to his feet, his head snapping back and forth, a frantic motion that made him look like a blind man searching for direction.

Then he unleashed a string of "fucks," a torrent so long and creative that Ellie felt like she needed to wash out her ears.

Aurick spun, shielding her from Aden's sudden movements as she turned in his arms to face him, lifting her eyes to his face.

"Aurick?" she asked, using only his name for the first time. "What's happening to him?"

"He'll be fine, but he's disoriented right now. We have to give him a minute."

Despite his casual tone, his protective actions contradicted his words. Clearly, this wasn't the first time something like this happened.

Ellie peered around him. Aden was trashing the room, flipping the bed, and throwing the IV stand beside it, his "fucks" growing more inventive.

Was it even possible to do that with a sword's hilt?

Beyond him, Kane shielded Sophie, Keeley, and Mina from Aden's chaotic outburst. It didn't appear to worry them.

"Where the fuck am I? I can't feel my fucking hand. Where the fuck is Vincent? Is he dead? I'm going to kill that fucker again! I'm going to tear—"

"Someone needs to calm him down before he detaches that hand again," Mina said as she watched Aden carefully.

"Ah, Kane," Aurick said over Aden's shouting. "Do you want to step in here?"

"Should he go near Aden when he's like this?" Tears welled in Ellie's eyes, her heart aching as she watched Aden's agitated confusion.

"Was that Ellie? Where is she?" He roared, and Aurick froze, his grip tightening as she struggled against his hold, her focus solely on reaching Aden, oblivious to her own safety.

"No, Ellie."

"But—"

"You can't go to him right now."

"Calm down, boss. Ellie's fine," Kane said in a firm tone.

"Where the fuck is she? Ellie!" Aden bellowed her name, and her breath hitched in her throat.

"Please let me go to him," she begged Aurick, his arms a tight, inescapable cage around her.

He looked down, his kind eyes filled with gentle understanding. "Not until he's in control. He'd never forgive me if I let you near him now."

"Get your fucking hands off me," Aden bellowed again, and Kane's body flew across the room, slamming into the wall. The impact made the entire room shake.

"Drake, take her," Aurick hissed, thrusting Ellie toward him. It was a gentle handoff, but still jarring as Drake's arms encircled her, blocking her from Aden's view. Sophie and Keeley hurried over and formed a half-circle behind her.

"It's okay, Ellie," Sophie said, her voice a small comfort to Ellie's frayed nerves. "Aurick will bring him back."

"What's happening to him?"

Before she could answer, another louder crash echoed through the room, followed by Aden's roar. "Get off me! Fuck! Why does my fucking hand hurt?"

Aden wasn't making sense. First, he asked where his hand was. Then he said he couldn't feel it. Now he was demanding why it hurt.

Ellie peeked around Drake to see Aurick pinning Aden to the wall, his throat in a tight grip, just as he had done to Aden the last time they were all in this very room. His furious eyes burned red as he shoved against his father, struggling in his grasp, to no avail.

"Fuck, that hurts." Aden shook his hand as he shouted, "Let me go!"

"Not until you stop," Aurick replied calmly. "Ellie is here, but you're scaring her."

He was scaring her. He was completely out of control, a whirlwind of flailing limbs, wild eyes, and screaming obscenities. But she didn't fear him.

She feared for him.

Aden froze, his fiery red eyes seeking hers, the intensity of his gaze pinning her in place. His aggressive posture eased, fierce eyes softening, morphing back to their usual calm blue. A shuddering sigh escaped his lips as the tension visibly left his body.

Aurick stepped back and released Aden's neck. "Let her go, Drake," he said.

Ellie didn't hesitate, darting past him when he released her. With four long strides, Aden covered the distance between them, and she threw herself in his arms. His name tore from her in a sob as she clung to him. His arms tightened around her, and he buried his face in her neck. "It's alright, Ellie. I won't hurt you."

With a sharp jerk, Ellie's head snapped back. "Don't you dare say that. I'm not afraid of you."

"You really should be," he said, though the tenderness with which he held her contradicted his harsh words.

He'd said that to her several times recently, and she planned to set him straight when he felt better. She had complete, unwavering trust in him to never hurt her, and he needed to stop saying otherwise.

"I'm just so happy you're alive," she breathed, the relief washing over her like a wave, silencing the urge to argue with him right now.

Ellie felt his body sag, and she wrapped her arms tightly around him.

"Are you going to fall on me?" she teased, masking her anxiety with a light tone.

"No, but I think I should sit down," he said, his voice tight with a rare admission of vulnerability.

A barely perceptible tremor in his body worried her as she led him to the sofa. He dropped onto it, and she climbed up next to him, pulling her knees to her chest and pressing into his side.

"I need blood."

Sophie gestured to the door, and Drake walked over to activate it. A dozen of Aden's thralls entered when it opened. He stepped into the hall, and the door slid closed.

Aden reached up with his good hand and caressed Ellie's cheek. "You can go into the other room if you don't want to see this."

Although she loved him for it, a surge of anger filled Ellie, and she glared at him, her gaze sharp.

"Aden, just drink," she growled under her breath as his thralls dropped to their knees in a line in front of him.

He frowned. "But you don't like—"

"Drink!"

He raised a questioning eyebrow before nodding. Leaning forward, he grasped the first thrall's wrist, his fangs tearing into it.

Ellie had to look away. Now, having experienced the intense pleasure of Aden's bite and the overwhelming ecstasy of his venom coursing through her, it made her possessive. She couldn't bear to see him bite anyone else, especially his female thralls.

He went through three before he sat back with a groan, opening his eyes, his irises fading back to blue. "Fuck! Why is this fucking thing on my arm?" He ripped off the cast. His hand flopped, and Mina scoffed with disapproval as she helped the thrall he'd just released to stand.

"That was meant to keep your wrist immobilized so it could heal faster."

"I don't fucking need it."

"But you do need more blood," Sophie said, standing nearby.

"I know. Give me a second, though." He glanced around. "Why are all of you still here? Go away. I'm fine." Everyone remained, and he scowled. "I said go the fuck away. I'm fine."

"Stop being such a baby," Keeley said as she walked out of the bathroom, carrying a wet cloth. "Here. Your face is still covered with blood."

Ellie took it from her and lifted it to his cheek. His head jerked, and she froze before he sighed and pressed his face into her hand. She smiled as she gently cleaned his face. That he let her do it in front of others showed how out of sorts he still was.

Aden beckoned the next thrall in line forward and drank, going through five more thralls before he sat back again.

Ellie bit the inside of her cheek, averting her gaze, until he finished.

"We have to get you home. You didn't bring enough thralls with you for the amount of blood you need," Mina said as she tugged the twisted IV stand toward the bathroom.

"Yes, I think our time here is done," Sophie said.

"Yeah." Keeley nodded in agreement. "I'm ready to leave."

"I'll need to stay for a couple of meetings tomorrow night, but then I'll follow," Aurick said.

As Sophie, Aurick, and Keeley talked logistics, Aden drank from the last four thralls before they left. Ellie breathed a sigh of relief. She cuddled up against his side again and brought his head to her breasts, stroking her fingers through his hair. A low growl rumbled in his chest as he sank into her.

The door to the suite slid open again. It was like a revolving door tonight.

"You don't need to announce me in my own house," Matthais said to Drake, his voice dripping with contempt.

Ellie inhaled a sharp breath and shoved away from Aden, dropping to her knees on the floor in front of him just as Matthais turned the corner.

"What the fuck!"

She shushed him with a subtle shake of her head before looking down, a silent plea not to make a scene. If Matthais found her cuddled up to Aden, it would prove she was more than just a pet.

The air crackled with tension.

"What are you doing here, Matthais?" Aden snarled, and despite everything tonight, Ellie's lips curved into a small smile.

His snarling was a good sign. It showed he was recovering.

"I wanted to check on your condition. It's good to see you revived."

His smooth, almost oily tone betrayed the insincerity of his words. He glanced around, taking in the splintered wood, shattered glass, and overturned furniture left in the wake of Aden's tantrum.

"Your temper has left my suite in shambles once again, Aden." Ellie felt Matthais' eyes flick to her, a cold, calculating gaze that sent a shiver of fear and revulsion through her. "This is becoming a tiresome habit."

"I'll pay for it as always. And I'm fine," Aden said, his voice tight with irritation. "No thanks to that fucker, Vincent." He sat forward. "Fuck! That reminds me, Carrie is tied to the bed in his concubine suite. I don't know what kind of condition she's in, but someone needs to get her."

His words were a blow that sent Ellie's heart leaping into her throat. A strangled gasp escaped her lips. Matthais' heavy gaze settled on her again, making her skin crawl.

"Oh my, with everything else, I forgot about her. Kane, will you go?" Sophie asked, looking at him. "I don't know if Vincent's guard will be there or if he'll cause an issue for whoever comes to get her."

"On it," Kane said, heading to the door.

"No one will prevent you from taking his thrall. You earned your spoils," Matthais said.

"Kane, wait up. I'll go with you," Keeley called after him.

Pausing, he turned to her, eyebrow raised.

"If a huge gorilla like you shows up and tries to take her, she might freak out. After what she's been through with Vincent, she's probably terrified of men."

Sophie hummed in agreement. "Take her to the infirmary, and Mina will meet you there."

A wave of guilt washed over Ellie as she realized she hadn't considered Carrie's situation while preoccupied with Aden. Relieved he was going to be alright, she could breathe again, and she wanted to go with them. If Carrie's reaction last night was any clue, she'd be terrified of Kane and even Keeley. But Ellie couldn't ask in front of Matthais.

"Maybe Ellie should go with her," Sophie suggested. "So it's someone Carrie knows."

The subtle shake of Aden's head as he locked eyes with his mother made Ellie's stomach clench. Just what kind of condition was she in, and what did Aden know about it?

"She'll be fine. No need to send your pet wandering around my compound," Matthais said, and Ellie felt Aden tense above her. "Vincent's thrall doesn't need to be coddled. After surviving him, she ought to be exceedingly resilient."

Ellie fought back the whimper his words provoked.

"She's my thrall," Aden bit out through clenched teeth.

"Yes, of course. She is now," Matthais said. "Regardless, your performance tonight was impressive, Aden. Though I must say I'm rather annoyed about losing Vincent. I was grooming him to be my protégé."

"Vincent's behavior did not adhere to the principles we agreed to abide by, Matthais," Aurick said.

"What a vampire does in private is his own business, Aurick. We don't police what people do behind closed doors."

"It wasn't behind closed doors," Aden said.

Matthais waved his hand dismissively. "Semantics. It's of no importance any longer now that he's dead, but I would suggest you remember I allowed this challenge. I allowed you to take over my arena to carry it out, and I'll be dealing with the aftermath of his coven's wrath on your behalf."

"I don't need you to deal with their wrath. I'm happy to reiterate what an asshole he was."

"I approved the challenge," Matthais said, and Ellie knew he was emphasizing his control over the events tonight. "I'll handle his coven, but I expect you will remember my generosity."

Aden stiffened again as a look passed between Sophie and Aurick. It had been so long since she had to avert her gaze in anyone's presence that Ellie forgot how much she saw in her peripheral vision.

"Now, I'll leave you to recover," Matthais said. "You look well already. Will you attend the games this evening?"

"Aden needs more blood than we have available here, so we'll be leaving the capital tonight," Sophie said.

"What about the final meetings tomorrow?" He asked, looking at Aurick.

"I'm staying," Aurick said. "I'll fill Aden in when I get home."

"I have plenty of feeders who can provide blood for you."

"I prefer my own."

"Of course, your pet can provide for you, too." Matthais gestured to where Ellie sat at Aden's feet. "Surely her blood is preferable."

"Matthais, let me worry about where I get my blood."

"Very well. I'll be in touch soon. Enjoy your new thrall."

Matthais left, and as soon as the door slid closed, Ellie climbed back onto the sofa, pressing against Aden's side. She cradled his injured wrist between her palms, trying to ignore the lingering unease from Matthais' visit.

"That was rather ominous," Sophie said with a frown.

Mina came out of the bathroom, dragging the IV stand behind her. She'd been lurking in the background, and Ellie forgot she was there.

"He was issuing a warning," Aurick said. "He expects something in return for what happened tonight."

"What else is fucking new?"

"Mina," Ellie said, tracing Aden's wrist, "I want to give him some of my blood."

"I figured." Mina pulled the IV stand closer. "That's why I grabbed this." She hung a bag of blood on the hook. "I've already added some of Aden's blood to yours and boosted it with some BloodStone. It will replenish your blood faster, as he's drinking from you. But you have to be careful not to give too much. This is the last of your blood I have here. Your daily transfusions have used it up."

"You've been getting daily transfusions?" Sophie's frown deepened.

"They're both a little caught up in the compulsion," Mina replied, her voice a low murmur.

"Okay, you know what? You three need to fucking leave now." Aden turned his face into Ellie's neck and nuzzled just beneath her chin. "Baby, I can't have sex with you right now. I'll try, but you'll have to do all the work."

She pushed his head away. "Aden, we're not having sex. But you are going to drink from me."

"But you only let me when we have sex." A flicker of hope shone in his eyes, but Ellie shook her head.

"No sex, but you need blood. And until we get you home to your other thralls, you're taking it from me." She held her arm out so Mina could attach the IV. "How much can I safely give him?"

"No more than half a pint right now. After your transfusion, another half pint. But that's it. And we should leave as soon as possible."

"I'll have the jet readied," Aurick said, heading to the door.

"I'm coming with you," Sophie said before she addressed Mina. "You should head to the infirmary. Let Keeley know we're leaving, and I'll have Georgina get the thralls ready."

"Okay." Mina pointed at Aden. "No more than a pint total. I mean it."

"Go away, Mina," he grumbled. "We fucking heard you."

She placed a syringe of BloodStone on the coffee table. "And take that when you're done, Ellie. It's laced with Aden's blood and ferrous sulfate. It should keep the dizziness at bay."

When they were finally alone, Aden yanked Ellie onto his lap. She protested, but he just pulled her closer, burying his face in her neck again.

"I don't want to hurt you." Despite her words, she tightened her arms around him.

"I'm fine. Fucking pissed off more than anything."

"Thank you for saving her," Ellie whispered against the side of his face, her breath hitching.

"I don't know if she'll feel the same way, Ellie. She's free of Vincent, but she still has to live with what he did to her."

The look in his eyes, dark and shadowed, sent a wave of icy worry through Ellie, making her stomach cramp. But he didn't know Carrie like she did. If anyone had the strength to come back from what Vincent did to her, it was her. And Ellie would do whatever it took to help her.

"She's stronger and braver than me."

His eyes showed his doubt. But Carrie could wait just a little longer. Ellie trusted Kane, Keeley, and Mina to take care of her.

She took Aden's face in her hands and pressed it against her throat. "Now, you need to drink."

He brushed a kiss against her skin before lifting his face. "Why are you doing this? It's only supposed to be—"

"It's supposed to be an act of love. That's what this is. That's what this always is."

A different kind of darkness filled his eyes now. One of adoration, lust, and utter devotion, as his gaze locked onto the pulsing vein in her neck.

When his sharp fangs sank into her, Ellie surrendered to the intense, bittersweet ecstasy of her love for him.

Keeley

The door to Vincent's suite was unguarded.

"I guess a dead man doesn't need a guard." The gravelly timbre of Kane's voice betrayed the barely suppressed anger simmering beneath his calm exterior.

A slight tremor ran down Keeley's spine. As much as Kane might be a secret softie on the inside, and Keeley didn't fear him at all, his exterior was terrifying.

He glanced at her, and Keeley frowned. "Shouldn't it automatically open for us?"

"Not if it's programmed to only open for him. I knew I should have grabbed his head."

"Kane, please, that's an image I could've lived without."

His sneer, a chilling twist of his lips, revealed a flash of teeth. "His cold dead eye would have at least opened the door."

"You spend too much time with my brother."

The door remained stubbornly closed, and a tense silence hung between them as they looked at each other.

"How do we get in there?"

"You could always contact Matthais by hologram and ask him to open it," Kane suggested.

"That would be a hell no. Can you break it down?"

"Not sure if that's a good idea after what Aden just did to his suite. Again."

With a hiss, the door opened, as though someone had been listening to them.

"That was weird," Keeley said, but neither of them moved. "If we find her dead in there, Ellie's going to be devastated."

"I can hear her heartbeat, but it's faint."

Keeley nodded, summoning her courage, and entered the suite with Kane close behind. The room was a mess, with bloodstained sheets scattered on the bed and a set of knives on the bedside table. A wave of nausea washed over her as she gagged, then a horrified gasp escaped her lips when the concubine suite's door slid open, revealing the unconscious girl inside. The room smelled faintly of lavender and the coppery, sickening scent of old blood.

Just as Aden said, they found her tied to the bed, her wrists and ankles bound so tightly with rope that her skin was turning blue. But that was the least disturbing aspect of the horrifying scene before them.

Cuts and bruises covered Carrie's naked body, with nearly every inch of her skin marred in horrific ways. Incisions on her torso and legs were deep and fresh, blood welling up around their edges. Her swollen eyes were shut tight, her lips cracked and dry from dehydration. The dried blood and fluids pooling between her thighs confirmed she'd been brutally raped. A long, bloody gash across her cheek exposed her cheekbone.

"Fuck!" Keeley breathed.

She glanced at Kane, his eyes blazing with a fury unlike anything she'd ever witnessed from Aden's calm, yet serious, bodyguard.

"He deserved to die a hundred times for this."

"We have to get her to the infirmary," Keeley said. "She's barely breathing."

Kane walked to the bed, snapped the ropes binding her, and freed her limbs, while Keeley released the sheet from the corners of the mattress and wrapped it around her body.

Carrie's eyes fluttered, and she sucked in a sharp breath. When they opened and locked onto Keeley and Kane, she struggled and screamed.

"No! Please, no! Just let me die."

Keeley kneeled beside the bed, a lump forming in her throat.

"Carrie, it's me. Keeley." Her words were barely audible over the screaming, but she hoped they registered. "We're here to help you."

Carrie shook so hard that Keeley was surprised her bones didn't shatter. The ones that weren't already broken.

"We're not going to hurt you," she said, a little louder. "Ellie sent us."

Carrie's screams cut off, her eyes widening in shock.

"Ellie?" Her voice was a hoarse whisper as she licked her dry lips.

Keeley nodded. "We're here to take you to the infirmary. We're going to get you help."

Carrie shook her head. "No. It will only make Master madder. He'll hurt me more."

"He's fucking dead," Kane snarled, a low, guttural sound that vibrated in the air. Keeley felt Carrie freeze beside her, and both their eyes snapped to him in unison.

Keeley gave him her best glare. "You want to dial down the rage a little? Not needed right now."

Carrie's gaze remained locked on Kane, her wide, fearful eyes betraying a flicker of disbelief tinged with hope.

"Let's get you to the infirmary, huh?" Keeley pushed to her feet and leaned down to lift Carrie from the bed.

But Kane stepped forward, moving her aside. He crouched, gently scooping Carrie's broken body into his massive arms. Keeley braced herself, expecting Carrie to start screaming again, but she just shuddered and whimpered before sagging in his arms.

Keeley watched in surprise as he turned and strode out the door.

Ellie

Ellie entered the infirmary to find Mina sitting at a desk off to the right. The last time she was here, Zach deactivated her tracking chip. The door to the examination room Ellie had visited was behind and to the right of where Mina sat. A door on the opposite wall led to the room where patients slept. She occupied that room for a few days while she recovered the use of her body.

Mina looked up. "Do you need some BloodStone?"

"No. I'm here to see Carrie."

Aden and Keeley refused to let her see Carrie on the plane. Kane joined their blockade by blocking the door to the thrall's cabin. She was in such terrible shape, Mina had to place her in a sealed medical pod until they returned home and Zach could treat her more extensive injuries. Ellie argued with all of them, but they wouldn't budge. Even Sophie backed them up. Ellie was so upset, she refused to talk to any of them for the entire flight.

"I had to give her a sedative," Mina said. "She was refusing to sleep."

Ellie knew what that was like. It could only be one thing keeping her from wanting to sleep.

"How badly did he hurt her?"

"It's not my place to discuss her injuries or how she got them, but I will say her physical ones are healing rather quickly. I added a few drops of Aden's blood to her BloodStone drip. But her emotional wounds are going to take much longer."

Ellie swallowed back the bile in her throat as she nodded.

"Does Aden know you did that?"

"Yes, he instructed me to."

Ellie fell in love with him all over again for his tender thoughtfulness.

"Can I see her?"

"She'll be out for a while."

"I don't care. I just need to see her."

"Go on in, then."

Ellie entered the room, and her eyes found her friend. Carrie lay motionless, draped in a stark white sheet, her arms resting beside her. Ellie's eyes filled as she took in the state of Carrie's injuries. At least the ones she could see.

The black and blue bruises around her eyes were fading but still visible. As were the marks around her wrists—rope burns, cuts, and fingerprint bruises. A jagged line of stitches, glaring against her pale skin, ran along her right cheek near her mouth to almost her ear, marring her beautiful face. Given Carrie's condition and the fact that Aden's blood was aiding her recovery, Ellie could only imagine how severe her injuries had been.

She sat in the chair next to the bed, reaching for Carrie's hand, entwining their fingers. Carrie didn't stir, so Ellie rested her forehead on the cool, smooth skin of her hand, needing the physical connection with her friend. She sat like that, listening to Carrie's soft, even breathing until Mina came in a while later.

"Don't you have to head to BloodStone tonight? I doubt she'll wake up before you leave."

Ellie lifted her head. "Keeley gave me a few nights off. I'm not leaving until Carrie wakes up."

"I'm heading to check on Aden shortly. How is he?"

"His hand still aches, but he can move it again."

"Okay. Have the nurse call me on a hologram if anything happens. Don't be surprised if she wakes up screaming."

Ellie nodded. She knew what that was like, too.

Once Mina left, she climbed onto the bed beside Carrie, the mattress so narrow she barely fit. She pressed closer, hoping the warmth of her body would be a comfort against Carrie's fragile frame, a silent promise to reciprocate the years of care Carrie had given her.

The next night, Ellie returned to the infirmary. Carrie had never woken the previous evening, before Ellie's eyes lost their fight, and she drifted off to sleep. Carrie tossed and turned, plagued by periodic nightmares, but remained asleep. Ellie offered the only comfort she could, moving closer, her grip on Carrie's hand tightening until she calmed.

When Ellie woke again, she was in their bed, Aden wrapped around her and Vlad purring on the pillow beside her head. He fetched her when she never returned to their suite, but she wished he'd left her there. She felt sick thinking about Carrie waking alone.

But Ellie found her awake when she entered the room. Carrie's face crumbled when she saw her, her eyes welling with tears. Running over, Ellie threw her arms around her.

"I'm so sorry I wasn't here when you woke up."

Carrie flinched, a strangled gasp escaping her lips, then hugged Ellie close, her body wracked with sobs. Ellie climbed onto the bed, tucking Carrie's head under her chin, letting her cry.

"Thank you," Carrie whispered repeatedly against Ellie's neck, her tears soaking her shirt and skin as she wept.

It was almost a half hour later when Carrie's sobs ceased, and she drew back, wiping her fingers under her eyes. The faded bruises left her skin looking thin and delicate. Ellie reached over and grabbed a handful of tissues from the side table.

"Here. Wipe your snot. If there's anything left after you used me as a human tissue."

Carrie laughed, and Ellie smiled, dabbing her neck with a couple of tissues, pleased her teasing worked.

"You do know how many times you've snotted on me, right?"

Ellie held out the wet tissue. "I think this makes us even."

"Not even close."

Ellie offered her a bottle of water from the table, and Carrie drained it before placing it on the mattress beside her.

"I'm so grateful you're safe now." Ellie's voice trembled as she grasped Carrie's hand.

A sniffle escaped as Carrie hiccuped. "It's only because of you."

A thick silence hung in the air as Ellie swallowed hard, her throat tight with emotion and unspoken words. How could she comfort Carrie, whose body and spirit had been ravaged by brutal torture? What could she say? Carrie would never forget what happened to her. Ellie understood the lasting power of violent memories well enough to know that.

With restless fingers, Carrie played with the collar of her thin cotton nightgown. The overhead lights cast shadows across her face, making her look even more fragile than she was.

"Mistress Keeley said you asked Master Aden to buy me, and when Master Vincent refused, he challenged him."

Ellie nodded. "I had to when I saw what he was doing to you."

Carrie flinched, her haunted gaze reflecting the horrors she'd endured.

"Is it true that Master Aden killed him?"

"Yes. That's what a challenge is. It's a fight to the death."

"Why would he do that?"

"Because I asked him to protect you."

Carrie picked at the light blanket over her legs. Normally unflappable, she was now a mass of nervous tics.

"But why? Why would he do that for you?"

A gentle smile touched Ellie's lips. "It's a long story. And I'll tell you, I promise. But it can wait. I want to hear about what happened to you." Ellie paused. "If you want to tell me, that is."

A fresh wave of tears filled Carrie's eyes.

Ellie sat up, a knot forming in her stomach, afraid she asked too much of her friend. "It's okay if you don't. Just know I'm here for you whenever you are."

Carrie inhaled deeply, her hands shaking as she lowered the blanket and unfastened her nightgown. Ellie held her breath, her throat tightening as Carrie pulled the collar down, revealing a network of silvery scars across her collarbone. Dozens of bite marks overlapped on her pale skin, creating a horrifying, savage pattern.

"He'd feed on me all the time, even when I had barely any blood left," she said, her eyes fixed on a distant point over Ellie's shoulder. "Then he'd shoot me up with BloodStone and do it all again."

Her fingers tugged the gown lower. Ellie blinked back tears as Carrie revealed her torso. More scars—long, deliberate marks, the ones she saw the night of the party, that could only have been made by knives. They tracked down over her breasts and stomach like terrible ribbons that told a tale of unspeakable cruelty.

"He'd cut me. Said my blood tasted sweeter when he cut me."

Carrie continued to reveal evidence of her torture, lost in the painful memories. She pushed the blanket off her legs, exposing more knife and bite scars across her hips and down her thighs.

"He'd rape me and feed for hours." Carrie's voice broke as she confirmed Ellie's worst fears. Ellie swallowed back the bile that rose in her throat, each new revelation a fresh blow to her heart. "Then he'd leave me there, too weak to move, bleeding. Sometimes for days. If I cried, he came back and started over. He said he liked it when I cried."

Carrie pulled her gown back into place and the blanket up over her. Her physical scars were horrific, but it was the invisible ones that truly devastated Ellie. She longed to take her friend's hand, but she didn't dare touch her at the moment.

"I thought I was going to die there," Carrie whispered. "Every day I wanted to. Anything to make it stop."

Ellie found her voice, though it was thick with tears. "You're safe now. He can never hurt you again." The words felt hollow, inadequate in the face of Carrie's suffering, but they were all she had to offer.

Carrie nodded, but shadows lingered in her eyes. Recovery would be a long road, and both her seen and unseen scars would take more than time to heal.

Watching her exhausted friend sink back into the pillows after sharing her story, Ellie vowed to support her every step of the way.

Much later, after dinner, Ellie noticed her fidgeting again, her telltale sign she wanted to ask something. Still sitting in the bed beside her, Ellie reclined against the pillow, gazing at her.

"Okay, I can see you're holding back, and you lasted longer than I thought you would. So just ask me already."

Carrie nibbled her bottom lip, then leaned back, her face a hair's breadth from Ellie's on the pillow.

"Why would Master Aden save me just because you asked him?"

Ellie intended to tell Carrie everything, but it wasn't the right time. She doubted her friend was ready to hear it yet.

She brushed a loose strand of hair from Carrie's face.

"Because he loves me."

Ellie led Carrie into the suite. She'd spent last night with her, sleeping with her, until Ellie again found herself waking up in her own bed, wrapped in Aden's arms. As he'd done the previous day, he returned for her after she and Carrie fell asleep.

She'd told Carrie little about her and Aden, only that they were in love, and promised a full explanation later. Exhausted, they slept, but it wasn't quite that simple. Carrie's screams woke her several times, but each time, Ellie's presence and soft touch soothed her back to sleep.

Carrie seemed better tonight when Ellie visited the infirmary, more like her old self, but Ellie knew part of it was her friend putting on a brave face. That's what she did, but Ellie hoped she would feel safe and comfortable enough to be herself here.

"Wow, this is nice," Carrie said as she stepped into the living room, with a slight limp.

"I helped design it. Aden let me decorate how I wanted as long as I kept his wood furniture. He said he needed something masculine to balance out the femininity."

Carrie nodded, but Ellie's hoped-for laugh never came. It was a lot to take in. Everything was different here, and it took Ellie weeks, if not months, to adjust. Carrie had only been here for two days, but Ellie wanted to show her how drastically her life here would change.

She looked around, her fingers trailing along the back of the sofa. "So you live here with him?"

"Yeah. Now. But I stayed in his concubine suite when I first got here."

"Did he make you his pet?"

Ellie watched Carrie's eyes linger on the nude watercolor portraits, wondering what she thought of them.

"No. Everyone assumed he did. But he didn't touch me until we fell in love."

Carrie met her gaze, those familiar hazel eyes alight with curiosity. "How the heck did that happen, Ells? This is Aden Westcott. The vampire with the eyes that haunted you all your life."

"Yeah, about that..."

"It's a long story," Carrie finished for her with an arched eyebrow. "So you've said. Am I ever going to get that story?"

"Here, come into this room."

Ellie wasn't sure why she was so hesitant to tell Carrie the truth. Maybe because revealing it would make her sound insane. But Carrie was the one person she'd trust with it.

Ellie led her to Aden's gift, the private retreat that replaced the concubine suite, a small library of her own. The door slid open, and she stepped in, a smile gracing her lips. It always made her smile to enter this room. Carrie walked in and looked around as the door closed behind them.

On one side of the small room was an L-shaped sofa beside a miniature fireplace identical to the one in the library. On the opposite wall, a sitting area with a reading nook next to a window looked out over an outside garden Sophie designed just for her. Beyond the mass of flowers and trees was a twenty-foot-tall wall, blocking the view of anything on the other side. Ellie longed for a door that allowed her access to the garden, but security protocols prevented exterior access to any of the Westcott's private rooms.

Bookshelves lined the walls, filled with books Sophie gave to her, most of them favorites she'd read on her tablet.

"What's this room?"

"It's my private library. Aden had this room built because I love to read."

"They know you can read?" Carrie asked, surprised. Ellie confided her ability years ago, swearing her friend to secrecy.

She nodded and sat on the sofa. Carrie joined her, wincing as she took a seat. The BloodStone Mina gave her helped, but as Ellie knew from when Master Matthais broke her arm when she was fifteen, broken bones mended slowly, and Vincent had broken Carrie's pelvis, ankle and wrist.

"Aden caught me when I snuck into the family library one night. I was terrified he'd punish me, but he said I could visit it any time, as long as I only read the books Sophie approved."

"It's so weird that you call them by their names."

Ellie laughed as she settled deeper into the cushion. "Yeah. I know. It was weird for me at first too. I can only do it when no one else is around."

Carrie leaned back, a flicker of annoyance in her eyes, signaling to Ellie that her patience had reached its limit.

"You keep just dropping these cryptic hints about your life here and you being in love with him and him loving you. Now you're allowed to read and call them by their names. It's time you spit it out. What the hell, Ells?"

Ellie turned toward Carrie and tucked her foot beneath her. "I want to tell you. But I'm afraid you'll think I'm crazy, and I know how this is going to sound, but it's the truth."

"I know you'd never lie to me. Just tell me. I'll believe you."

"Okay, but you have to promise to hear me out. All of it. And no questions until I'm done because it's a lot."

Carrie crossed her fingers over her heart in a silent promise.

Ellie took a breath.

"I was married to Aden in my past life."

Aden

Aden swiped the hologram closed as he exited the courtyard, entering the hallway to his parent's wing. Ellie had brought her friend to their suite, and they were sitting in the library talking. He'd been tempted to listen in, but he resisted.

Their expressions were serious, piquing his interest, but she'd made it clear she didn't appreciate his propensity for eavesdropping. If she found out, she'd kick his ass. Not literally, but she sure knew how to make him atone for his indiscretions.

"Aden, wait!" Keeley called from behind him.

He turned to face her, his brow furrowed. "What are you doing here?"

"Mom and Dad asked me to come. They said they wanted to talk to us about something."

Aurick had summoned him earlier, saying it was time for them to speak, but he didn't say Keeley would also be there.

"Do you know what it's about?" She asked as she fell into step beside him.

"No. I take it you don't either?"

"Nope. How's Ellie?"

Aden scowled. "Spending all her time in the infirmary. I've had to carry her unconscious body back to our suite for the past two nights after she fell asleep there."

Did he sound as bitter and jealous as he felt? Judging by his sister's expression, he did.

"Can you even fathom what that girl has been through? Of course, Ellie's going to be there for her."

"I know that," he snapped. "But that doesn't mean I have to like being ignored for two days straight."

And now he just sounded spoiled and self-centered.

Horatio nodded as they approached. "They're both inside, waiting for you."

Aden shared a look with his sister as they entered the suite, the sounds of his father's beloved Celtic music in the background.

"Oh shit," she said under her breath. "The dulcimer is playing. It must be serious."

They turned the corner into the main living area and found their mother tucked on one side of the sofa, writing in her journal.

"Good, you're here." She looked up and smiled. "Aurick, they're here."

"What's this about, Mom?" Keeley sat on the opposite end of the couch, tucking her feet beneath her.

Vlad, who had been napping beside Sophie, stretched and yawned before slinking over to his sister for attention.

"This is your father's show. You'll have to wait for him."

Aden walked to the bar and poured a glass of whiskey. Since Ellie wasn't spending much time with him anyway, he might as well drink.

Aurick entered, his expression solemn. Whatever this was about, Aden had a feeling he was going to need even more alcohol.

"Have a seat, Aden," his father said as he moved to his favorite chair beside the sofa.

"Am I going to need this?" Aden asked as he held up the bottle of Jameson.

"Probably," Sophie replied, so he took the whiskey with him to his chair.

"What's with the dramatics?" Keeley asked, raising an eyebrow as she rubbed Vlad's belly.

A familiar look passed between Aurick and Sophie. Aden took a swig straight from the bottle.

"Keeley, you're likely unaware of the day-to-day challenges of running this region or the political machinations afoot, so you're going to be completely in the dark here. But Aden isn't." Aurick shot him a quick look before he continued.

"I've kept him in the dark on this until now because what I'm planning is a dangerous endeavor. But it's now time for you both to know because it will change everything."

"Stop talking in riddles, Aurick. Just spit it out already."

"Aden shut your mouth and listen for once." Sophie's voice was as sharp as a whip.

In response to his mother's scolding, he took another long swig from the bottle, the liquid burning slightly as it went down.

"We've always taught you true history, despite the watered-down version of it that's common knowledge and taught to vampires," Aurick said. "Only the ones who were alive then know the accurate history, and many of those vampires have been exterminated by Matthais. But there are a few things we've kept from you, nuances that there was no reason to burden you with."

"Like what?" Keeley asked.

"Well, for one," Sophie said, her voice devoid of any emotion. "That Matthais once wanted me dead."

"What?" Aden snarled as he leaned forward in the chair.

"After I saved your mother's life when she was eight by making her a half-breed, I hid her existence from Matthais and other influential vampires because what I did was illegal in our world. Creating half-breeds was always forbidden."

"For most vampires," Sophie said.

"Yes," Aurick agreed. "We later discovered that Matthais had been building a half-breed army for centuries, but that's a well-known fact now. Needless to say, keeping your mother's existence quiet was imperative to keep her safe. But he found out when she was nineteen and demanded I kill her. I refused."

"What?" Startled by Keeley's gasp, the cat hissed and leaped from the sofa. "Sorry, Vlady."

"Why didn't you fucking murder him on the spot?" Aden hissed as he surged to his feet, waving the almost empty whiskey bottle around.

"Aden," Sophie said, her voice soft. "Things aren't always as simple as they seem."

"They should be. He threatened you. Aurick should have killed him instantly."

"Your mother wasn't my wife yet. We weren't romantically involved at that point. But you have to understand, the world was different then. Matthais was older, stronger, and had an army he'd been building in secret behind him. But I still refused. I never would have killed her, no matter what he demanded."

"Aden, sit down," Sophie said.

He was still too furious but did as she asked.

"It's no secret the creation of BloodStone was the catalyst for vampires being revealed. And I carry the responsibility for that happening. I don't regret its creation. It saved your grandmother's life, but it led to the rise of a world I don't agree with. I've never agreed with it, and it's a world I no longer want to live in."

"What's that supposed to mean?" Keeley asked with a frown.

"Aurick, you're going on a tangent. Stay on topic," Sophie urged.

"You can't just say something like that and call that a tangent," Keeley replied, irritated.

"We're not going to rehash the history you already know—"

"Soph," Aurick interrupted. "I was going on a little tangent, but some of that is pertinent and provides context."

"Okay, fine. But I'm going to stop you if you go too far off-topic. You tend to do that."

"Yes, love," he said with a tender smile. "Now, where was I?"

"You don't want to fucking live in the world anymore," Aden said with a snarl. He was still stuck on and seething about Matthais once wanting his mother dead.

"In the mid-twenty-first century, after vampires came out and it was known that BloodStone was derived from vampire blood, the world devolved into chaos. Just as vampires had always feared, humans went on a killing spree, trying to rid it of the undead monsters they'd always thought were legends. It was a bloody few years."

Sophie scoffed under her breath. "That's an understatement."

"There had been a worldwide pandemic in the early twenty-twenties before BloodStone was perfected. But when another pandemic, worse than the first, hit in twenty-thirty, just months after BloodStone's release, everything changed. BloodStone cured the disease and all diseases. Humans were grateful, so grateful that vampires were not only accepted by most of society, they were invited to be active participants."

"We know this already," Aden said. "What's your point?"

"My point is, that's when everything changed. Matthais formed the Vampire World Council to represent vampire interests. He was invited to join the ICJ, or the International Court of Justice, which had always been solely a court interpreting international law. But, over the years, without the public's knowledge, it had turned into a body that was no longer just interpreting the law but setting and enforcing it with a world military behind it. A world military made up of half-breed soldiers Matthais had been creating in secret."

Aden downed the rest of his whiskey and placed the bottle on the floor.

"Humans were dumbed down. History was changed and no longer taught. In less than a decade, vampires infiltrated the highest levels of government worldwide, slowly and silently instilled in positions of power and influence. And humans were willingly and unknowingly giving up their freedoms. Democracies fell, starting with the United States, which had been fighting a civil war for years. Dictatorships rose, and those dictators were vampires, with Matthais at the highest level. In twenty-fifty, vampires seized full control of the ICJ, and he rebranded it. The Vampire World Council now controlled every government in the world."

"Again, Aurick, we know all this," Aden said. "Where are you going with it? And what does it have to do with Matthais wanting to kill Sophie?"

"Sweetheart, tangent," Sophie nudged her husband to make his point.

"Where I'm going with this, Aden, is that I was part of this downfall. Matthais used your mother to secure my loyalty and support for his plans. In my defense, although I knew he had some nefarious ideas, I didn't think he could pull it all off. I was wrong."

"We were all wrong." Sophie's sigh carried the weight of centuries.

"Before BloodStone, Matthais was the de facto leader of vampires because he was the oldest one in existence. Vampires followed him and bowed to him. By the time I was turned in 760 A.D., he was already the leader. My creation of BloodStone and the other advances we invented, including the UV-filtering polymer, gave me more power and influence than he would have liked. Vampire law at that time required the killing of illegal half-breeds, but he said if I supported his plans, he'd allow me to spare your mother. I accepted his offer."

Aurick shifted, and Sophie reached out, squeezing his arm in a gesture of silent support.

"As time went on, Matthais realized I was more influential over other vampires than he was, particularly the other Ancient Ones, so he offered me the position of Vice-Chancellor. It was to keep me under this thumb, and I knew that, but I agreed, hoping I could institute some changes."

"And you have," Sophie said. "Especially with improving the treatment of humans."

"Yes," he agreed. "But as we saw from the situation with Ellie's friend and Vincent, many of those laws are ignored. And Matthais merely humors any of the Gerents who question his rules. He's turned this world into a dark, violent, evil place. I lived in the world when vampires were secret—when they hunted us, torturing us when they discovered us, and I'd never want to go back to that. Humans are just as cruel as vampires when given the same power. Unfortunately, it's human nature. I don't think vampires should cede control, but there has to be another way. A way to live together. Matthais has gone too far, and it's time for his reign to end."

Aden didn't need Aurick to answer the question burning on his tongue, but he asked it anyway.

"So, what are you planning to do, Aurick?"

"We're staging a coup."

Ellie

Ellie leaned back, taking her first full breath in the last half hour, her gaze settling on Carrie's blank face.

She'd told her friend everything. From Aden biting her to her past life and falling in love with him even before she remembered. To Aden killing her on their wedding night and her seizure when her memories came back. How she had the exact same eyes as Aly and his initial refusal to believe Sophie's theory of who she was. And how, despite it all, he fell in love with her, too.

Carrie listened in silence, not once asking questions as she requested. But now that she was done, Ellie waited for the inevitable explosion.

"What the actual hell?" Carrie said as she blew out a long breath.

Ellie's lips lifted in an ironic half-smile. "I know. Crazy, huh?"

"Completely crazy."

"You believe me, though, right?"

"Of course I do. I wouldn't believe anyone else, but I know you wouldn't lie to me, Ells."

Ellie watched Carrie bite her lip, her expression betraying her racing thoughts. Even with Ellie's detailed account, her eyes swirled with unspoken questions.

"What?" Ellie asked.

"I mean, I believe you. I do. And it explains the freaky dreams you had about his eyes all your life. But past lives and soulmates and being reborn? And Aden Westcott falling in love with a human? Twice? How? Someone like him? How does he fall in love with a human once, never mind twice?"

Carrie didn't give her the chance to reply.

"Don't get me wrong, Ells. I know why he'd fall in love with you. You're amazing. And you're my best friend, and I love you more than anyone else in my life, but how could you love him?"

She just kept talking, and Ellie let her vent because it was a lot to process.

"A vampire? Of all people? And his reputation, Ellie. He's a monster who abuses and drains his thralls all the time. He's a monster like Vincent, and he—"

"No, he isn't," Ellie interrupted, her eyes flashing with anger. Carrie's words, while partially accurate, triggered a protective instinct in her, a surge of fierce, unwavering loyalty to Aden.

"Yes, he is," Carrie insisted as she pushed to her feet, agitated. "We've both heard the rumors over the years. And they didn't just come from some random thralls gossiping, but from *his* thralls. A vampire like that, who does those kinds of things, isn't capable of love."

"That's not fair." Ellie scooted to the edge of her seat. "And it's not true. Yes, he's done a lot of terrible things. I don't deny that. And it's not alright, but he was suffering so much pain and grief. He accidentally murdered me on our wedding night."

With a weary sigh, Carrie dropped back onto the sofa. "Hearing you say that so casually is making my brain hurt."

"I know, but it's true, Carrie. I won't defend what he's done in the past, but the man he is now... he's different. And he's the man I love."

"Ellie!" Aden bellowed her name from the other side of the closed door, startling them both.

Carrie jumped up, her eyes wide. "Are you going to be in trouble for me being here?"

Ellie stood, her gaze fixed on the door. "No. I can have anyone I want in here. Don't worry, he won't come in."

"He won't?"

"No."

"Ellie, I know you're in there. Get out here. Now!"

She sighed. Only one thing could have made him that angry. He listened in on her and Carrie's conversation. After last summer's incident with her and Finn, he swore he wouldn't do it again.

"He sounds really mad."

"It's his own fault. He shouldn't eavesdrop."

"Huh?" Carrie looked at her, confused.

"Don't make me come in there." Aden's voice was lower now, more of a growl, but still loud enough to carry through the door.

"I don't want to get you in trouble, Ellie."

"I'm not. And he won't come in unless I let him."

"Why not?"

"Because he made me a promise."

"Fuck!" Aden snarled, and Ellie heard him stomping away.

Carrie started to panic, twisting her hands together, anxiety radiating off her in waves. She'd always been Ellie's rock. The calm one. But Vincent's abuse left her a fragile, anxious shadow of her former self.

Ellie gave Carrie's hand a comforting squeeze. "Here, let me go talk to him before he has a complete meltdown. Sit and relax, and I'll be back in a few minutes."

"Are you sure? He won't hurt you, will he?"

"No, I won't fucking hurt her!" Aden roared from the other room, and Ellie closed her eyes, shaking her head.

"He'd never hurt me, Carrie. I promise," she said, taking a deep breath and approaching the door.

She expected the blazing fury in his eyes when the door slid open. His gaze snapped to Carrie before returning to Ellie's, hurt flashing behind the anger. Ellie stepped out, and the door closed.

"You were eavesdropping again, weren't you?"

She walked toward him, her gaze raking over him. All evidence of his fight with Vincent was gone from his body, though some lingering weakness remained in his wrist. Even the raised, puckered scar tissue where his hand had been reattached was no longer visible. And Ellie felt like she could breathe again. He came much closer to dying than he admitted to her, but Keeley let it slip.

Since their return from the capital, he'd been gorging himself on his thralls, needing the extra blood to heal. Sophie even brought girls from the other cities to supplement because his need exceeded their bodies' ability to replenish it. Still, he drank from her earlier, after waking up. He bit her almost every time they had sex now, and Ellie felt closer to and more deeply in love with him than ever.

Yes, she was angry at him for listening in, but she was more relieved and grateful that he was alive.

"I've hardly seen you since we got back," Aden said, his tone defensive. "And I was looking for you. I'm allowed to look for you via hologram. That doesn't violate my promise."

The sarcastic inflection in his last word made Ellie's lips quirk upward, despite her disappointment with him.

"But you agreed not to listen in."

"What is she even doing here?"

Ellie recognized his avoidance tactic as he headed to the bar, ignoring her comment.

"Shouldn't she still be in the infirmary?"

"Mina released her," she replied as she followed him. "I was showing her around before taking her to the thralls' quarters. I also needed to get some pajamas to take with me."

He spun, sending whiskey sloshing over the rim of his glass as he faced her. "Why would you need to take pajamas with you?"

"I need something to sleep in."

"That doesn't answer my question."

"I'm staying with Carrie tonight."

"No, you aren't." He turned to the bar and poured another drink. "Do you think my carrying you back here every night is just a suggestion? We sleep together, Ellie."

"Aden, she needs me. She's traumatized and having nightmares. She's afraid to sleep because she's reliving what that monster did to her."

He didn't turn back to face her.

"That's not my problem. And why does that require you to stay with her?"

Ellie sighed, trying to find the words to make him understand. "Aden, my entire life, I had nightmares. I dreamed of your eyes when I was little, but they didn't scare me at first. Only as I got older, when your eyes started changing from blue to red, did it terrify me." He flinched at her words. "But after my mother's murder, I relived it over and over again, and I'd wake up screaming almost every night. Carrie would crawl into bed with me and hold my hand. It was the only way I could sleep."

Aden turned, the weight of his gaze settling on her. "You've been with her in the infirmary for the last two nights. Isn't that enough?"

"There's no time limit on trauma, Aden." Tilting her head, she noticed for the first time that his eyes were glassy. "Were you drinking before you got here?"

He remained silent.

"Aden?"

"Yes," he snapped. "And don't start with me. I've had a shitty night."

"What happened? Do you want to talk about it?"

"No. And stop trying to change the subject. You're not going to the communal thralls' quarters to sleep with her, Ellie. It's not happening."

She folded her arms across her chest. "I'm not asking, Aden. You told me I don't need to ask your permission anymore."

"And you agreed we wouldn't sleep separately. Who's breaking her promise now?"

"That's not what this is. It's only until she's settled and feeling safe."

"I said no!" He roared just as Sophie's face appeared in a hologram beside them.

"Oh, I'm sorry," Sophie said, her eyes darting between them. "I didn't mean to interrupt."

Ellie sighed. "You aren't, Sophie."

"Yes, she fucking is." Aden turned to the bar and poured another drink.

Thankfully, only a truly staggering amount of alcohol could affect vampires. Otherwise, Aden would be perpetually intoxicated when they fought.

"Is there something you need?" Ellie asked.

"Well," Sophie's gaze lingered on Aden for a minute before she looked back at Ellie. "I just wanted to ask you if you would mind keeping an eye on Vlad for a couple of days. I'm heading to the beach house. I'd take him with me, but I'll be overseeing some renovations, and as you know, he's always underfoot."

Vlad was notorious for finding hiding places in construction zones. While their suite was being renovated, he frequently slept in the open walls, but one day he got trapped when the workers sealed a wall shut without knowing he was there. Luckily, he had a tracking chip. But he remained trapped for more than a day before Sophie and Ellie noticed he was missing.

"Of course," Ellie replied, but Aden whirled around and interrupted her.

"Sophie, if you don't mind, we're in the middle of a fight right now. Your nuisance of a furball will find his way to Ellie in your absence. It's a given."

"Aden, you're mad at me. Don't take it out on your mom."

"Well, I'll leave you to it." Sophie shot Ellie a sympathetic look.

"Sophie, wait," Ellie said before the hologram disappeared, an idea sparking. "You told me once that the private thrall level had personal rooms, right?"

"Yes."

"Are any of them empty?"

"Not at the moment." Sophie's gaze shifted between Aden and Ellie. "But I can free one up if you need me to."

"No fucking way! You're not getting around it that way."

"It's not for me," Ellie said, frowning at Sophie's assumption that it was for her.

"I said no! Fuck!" He threw his glass against the wall, shaking his head in frustration before taking a deep breath. "Sophie, can you instruct maintenance to deliver a double bed to Ellie's library and take her sofa away temporarily?"

"Okay," Sophie said, confused. "But can I ask why?"

"Because she's going to fucking sleep in the thralls' quarters with her friend, if I don't."

Even with Aden's tantrum on full display, an intense wave of love for him crashed over Ellie. Her heart pounded, and she wanted to throw herself at him and kiss him senseless. Was that normal when a grown man was throwing a fit?

She swallowed hard, her throat tight with emotion. "Carrie is having nightmares, and Mina just released her from the infirmary. I'd like to keep her company until they pass, but I can't stay in the communal thralls' quarters with her."

"Ahhh," Sophie said. "I'll get one freed up."

Aden threw his hands up. "Does nobody fucking listen to me anymore? I said she'll stay in Ellie's library."

"I'll still free up one of the private rooms. After what she's been through, Carrie will need some special attention, and privacy will help. Mina has already arranged therapy sessions for her."

"Thank you, Sophie."

"Of course, sweetheart," Sophie said with a smile. "Thanks for looking after the king. I'll be back next week."

Sophie's hologram disappeared, and the room fell silent.

Aden walked into the bedroom without a word. Ellie followed and found him staring out the window. The full moon, shining in the distance, cast an ethereal glow over him and on the swirling snow, its light a stark contrast to the deep shadows of the night.

Ellie wrapped her arms around him from behind. He stiffened, but she only tightened her hold as she kissed his back.

"Thank you, Aden. I love you."

He wriggled free of her embrace and turned to face her, his expression closed off, eyes narrowed, and his mouth a thin, straight line. That haunted, defeated look on his face was something she hadn't seen in a long time. Not since the night of her seizure.

"Until your friend convinces you I'm a monster just like Vincent."

"Aden..."

He shook his head and stepped back. "No. We both know she's right. I am a monster. One who killed his wife on their wedding night and then brutalized generations of girls who looked like her."

Stunned, Ellie watched him walk past her and out of the bedroom.

Ellie walked back into her library and found Carrie sitting in the chair beside the window. She looked up, relief filling her eyes.

"Are you alright? I heard him yelling at you."

"He wasn't yelling at me. He was just yelling. That's how he communicates sometimes."

"He sounded so angry."

Ellie's hand traced a small glass sculpture of an open book that rested on the table next to the sofa. It was a gift from Sophie, a childhood keepsake from her mother.

"Aden's emotions are intense, and he often has trouble controlling them, especially anger and hurt."

"Does he yell at you a lot?"

"Not as much as everyone else," Ellie said honestly.

"Did he hear our conversation?"

"Yes."

"I'm sorry if I got you in trouble for what I said about him," Carrie said, looking sheepish.

"You didn't. It wasn't just that. He's angry about something else." And hurt, Ellie thought, but kept that part to herself. "I don't make it easy for him some-times."

She had a lot of making up to do to Aden later. They both did. And while Ellie had hoped that returning to that room, facing the shadows of that night, would lift the heavy weight of guilt from him, letting them finally leave it in the past, it apparently wasn't that simple. His hurt expression just before he walked out of the bedroom haunted her, but she had to focus on Carrie right now. And he needed some time to calm down.

With a soft sigh, Ellie kneeled in front of Carrie, her hands resting on her knees.

"After everything you've been through, you have every right to feel the way you do, Carrie."

"I just don't understand it, Ells. You know what he's done. How can you be in love with him?"

"I know it's hard to grasp. And it's hard to see from where you are, but he's a good man. Yes, he's done some terrible things. And I don't condone them."

"What does that mean?"

"It means I don't approve of what he's done. And I won't defend them, but he's never done anything like what Vincent did to you."

"How do you know?" Carrie's voice was a hoarse whisper.

Ellie opened her mouth to respond but realized she didn't know. Not for sure. She still hadn't asked Aden about what happened after Aly's death. Or, in Sophie's words, what carnage he left behind.

"He forced his thralls," Carrie said, her voice a little stronger. "How is that any different from what Vincent did to me? Rape is rape, Ellie. And we all heard he drained them all the time."

Ellie couldn't argue against that. She reached out and rested her hand on Carrie's abdomen, causing her to flinch. She knew Aden had drained many of his thralls, brutalized them in his grief and pain, but she knew in her heart that he never inflicted the kind of wounds Vincent did, and he was incapable of Vincent's vicious, calculated cruelty.

"He never cut them, Carrie. He never bled them that way. Yes, he forced them, but all vampires force humans. It's wrong. And I won't make excuses for him.

But I know the man he is inside. He's not perfect by any means. But deep down, he's a man who feels deeply and loves fiercely. And he regrets what he did."

A long silence hung between them. "Are you sure you don't just think you love him now because you remember loving him in the past?"

It was a valid question. And Ellie was certain of the answer.

"I was already falling in love with him before I remembered. Yes, I was drawn to him, even with his volatile personality. And maybe that was tied to the memories of my past life that hovered beneath the surface. But I don't love him because we share a past. I love him for the man he is today. Not for who he was then."

Carrie traced the scar on Ellie's neck. "Did he ever force you?"

Ellie took her hand and squeezed it. "No. Never. I expected him to when I got here. But he didn't." She ran her fingers over her own scar. "And this is fairly new. It's only been a couple of weeks. When we admitted we loved each other, he let me set the pace. We didn't have sex until I was ready."

"I'm so glad you had that, Ells. I'd never want you to go through what I did. Or anyone."

Her knees began to ache, so Ellie shifted to sit cross-legged on the floor. "I'm so sorry Vincent hurt you."

"I knew he'd torture me to death, eventually. It was just a matter of time."

"You're safe now. You'll always be safe here."

Doubt flickered in Carrie's eyes, but also a glimmer of hope. Believing it would take her time, just as it had for Ellie.

The door buzzed.

"Come in," she said, and the door slid open, revealing two maintenance men, one leaning against a bed frame and the other balancing a mattress on its side.

"What's that?" Carrie asked.

Ellie smiled, a warmth spreading through her chest as her heart throbbed with love for Aden all over again.

"That's your bed."

Aden

Aden's eyes fluttered as he came awake, awareness filtering through his brain in increments. The feel of soft, warm lips brushing over the skin of his abdomen was both familiar and unexpected, given their earlier fight.

"Ellie," he moaned, reaching down and sliding his fingers into her hair. Her mouth formed a smile against him as her tongue swirled around his belly button.

She dipped her fingers beneath the waistband of his pajama pants, pushing them down his hips. He released her hair and pushed up on his elbows as she sat on her knees, shimmying his pants further down his legs. His cock, eager as always for her, sprang free, craving her just as much as he did.

"You wanna help me here?" She shifted his legs so she could strip him.

"I thought you were sleeping with Carrie."

"I was. And I will later. But right now, I need you." Love and remorse were oddly mingled in her gaze. She settled on her stomach between his thighs and smiled up at him. "Now lay back and let me have my wicked way with you."

With a slight arch of his eyebrow, he lowered his hand to trace the delicate curve of her cheek.

"I'm sorry for earlier."

Ellie turned her face to kiss his thumb, shaking her head. "No apologies right now. We'll talk after, okay?"

With her mouth inches from his aching cock, her warm breath teasing his sensitive skin, Aden could only nod in agreement.

Her small palm enveloped him, her fingers caressing as she lowered her head. Starting at the base, her tongue danced along the underside of his cock, each swirl making his spine tingle.

Mesmerized, he was unable to tear his eyes away as her lips wrapped around his tip. She flicked her tongue beneath his head, igniting a fire that shot down his shaft and coiled low in his abdomen. Aden's eyes rolled back, his body collapsing onto the mattress with a soft thud, the springs groaning under his weight.

He fisted his hands at his sides, wanting to reach down and grip her hair between his fingers, but he didn't want to guide her tonight. He wanted her to set the pace.

"Fuck, Ellie," Aden choked her name, the sound guttural and deep.

Her mouth engulfed his cock, the wet heat an exquisite agony that overwhelmed his senses. She moaned around him, her tongue lapping and teasing, and he felt the vibration all the way down to his toes.

Unable to help himself, he bucked his hips. As she repeated the motions, her lips and tongue worked together to take him deeper, making him forget his own name. His sense of time disappeared because it had no meaning when his cock was in her hot, wet mouth. Lost in the moment, held captive by her touch, everything else faded away. The pleasure was so intense, a shudder that felt like fire and ice at once rippled through him, pushing him closer to the edge.

Her fingers tightened, stroking him from base to tip, her hand moving perfectly in sync with her mouth.

Ellie placed her other hand flat on his stomach, her short fingernails digging into his skin. He welcomed the slight pinch, a stark contrast to the soft, yielding warmth of her mouth. Overwhelmed by the need to touch her, Aden reached down and grasped her fingers. She tugged his hand to her head, pushing his fingers into her hair. He lifted his head, gazing down at her. Their eyes met, hers blazing with a fierce longing, the unspoken desire crackling in the air as her fingers tightened around his.

He wrapped his fingers in the long, silky strands, tugging gently at first, but then harder as she hummed around his cock in approval. Using her hair to guide her, he pushed her head down until she gagged, the sensation making his eyes cross.

Sweat beaded on his skin as the heat of her mouth consumed him, drowning everything else out. He never wanted her to stop, but Ellie's hand gripping and squeezing his balls was his undoing. His hips shot off the bed, his back arching as a shiver, electric and intense, surged through him. His muscles spasmed, his skin prickled, and even his hair felt electrified.

"Ellie!" Her name tore from his lips with a low groan.

Spots flashed behind Aden's eyelids, his entire frame shuddering, his cock twitching and throbbing as he came into her mouth in long spurts. He gasped for air, his hips dropping back onto the mattress. His body jerked as Ellie's tongue swirled around his sensitive tip once more before releasing him.

Fuck! She was going to be the death of him.

Ellie crawled up his body, her lips a caress ghosting over his still-quivering stomach muscles. His touch was gentle as he pulled her naked form up his body. She leaned in, brushing her mouth to his for a tender kiss, pressing her palms to his chest for balance.

Even though she'd just sucked his soul out through his cock, it wasn't enough. He needed more. Aden gripped the inside of her thighs and lifted her above him, positioning himself at her entrance before lowering her onto him.

"Aden, stop," she whispered, her breath warm against his lips.

Her use of their agreed-upon safe word took him by surprise, dousing the fire in his veins, and he froze. Sliding her hands down the corded muscles of his abdomen, using his hard body for leverage, she pushed herself up. He met her gaze, and in the gentle, swirling depths of her emerald eyes, he saw a love so tender, so profound, it stole his breath.

"What's wrong?" He asked, holding her suspended above him, her warm, wet lips clinging to the head of his cock even as it deflated.

"This was for you, not me."

"This is exactly for me," he replied, his eyes dropping to where they were almost joined, then returning to hers.

Her soft laugh wrapped around him as she leaned down to kiss him again. He shifted her forward and set her on his stomach. She moved to drop onto the mattress beside him, and he rolled to his side, pulling her with him. She hiked her leg over his hip and pressed closer.

When the kiss ended, he leaned down, resting his head on her breasts.

"That's the first time you've used our safe word."

"And you stopped like I knew you would," she murmured against the top of his head, the words muffled in his hair as her fingers threaded through the thick strands. "I'm so sorry if you feel like I'm neglecting you."

He shook his head, his cheek brushing the soft curve of her breast. "You're not. I'm just selfish and greedy, and I acted like a dick."

He traced his hands over her body, reveling in the warmth radiating from her skin, its satiny smoothness a delightful contrast to his rough fingertips. Her body's gentle shudder spread through him, like a soft current.

"Yeah, you did," she agreed, and he felt her smile against his scalp. "But I don't blame you for being upset about what you overheard or for the time I'm spending with her."

"I'm not," he insisted before admitting with a sigh. "Well, yeah, I am. I don't like sharing you." There was no use lying to her. "And I know how that sounds. I'm a grown man who doesn't like sharing, but when it comes to you, I fucking don't. And I was in a terrible mood already and—"

She cupped his chin in her hand, tilting his face up to look at her.

"Why were you in a terrible mood? What happened?"

"Don't ask me that right now. I'll tell you, but I need to wrap my head around it first."

She held his gaze before nodding. "Okay."

He turned his face back, burying it against her breast, the familiar and much-loved honeysuckle and jasmine scent of her skin enveloping him.

"I don't want her to convince you I'm a monster." His body tensed as the words left his mouth. "I know I am, but for some reason, you don't see me like that."

Ellie released him, pushing herself up into a sitting position. Aden scowled, unhappy that she moved, but shifted to sit beside her. She turned and faced him.

"You're not a monster, Aden. You're a flawed man, yes, and you've done some terrible things. But your heart is pure. No one will ever convince me otherwise. Carrie just can't see anything beyond her own pain right now."

He shoved his hands into his hair. "But she's not wrong, Ellie. I've been monstrous for a long time. Killing Aly awakened a beast inside me that is irredeemable. I've never done anything like what Vincent did to her, but the things I did are beyond your comprehension, acts you couldn't even imagine. If you knew, you'd turn from me forever."

With a fierce look in her eyes, she cupped his face in her palms, her touch both tender and urgent. "Never."

She didn't fucking understand the extent of his monstrous nature, what he was truly capable of. She never would, because he'd hide it from her forever. He pulled her hands away.

"Yes, you would. And I know we agreed to leave the past behind us, but it's not that easy. I won't lie to you, Ellie, but I'll never tell you about it, even if it means refusing to answer your questions. My pain was so intense that I lashed out, wanting to inflict pain on everyone and everything, so I wasn't suffering alone."

With a tilted head and soft, understanding eyes, Ellie gazed at him. Scooting back down on the bed, she beckoned him to lie next to her. When he settled on his back, she snuggled close, pulling his arm around her and resting her head on his shoulder as she looked up at him.

"Aden," she said, her voice gentle but firm. "Yes, your reaction was extreme. But lashing out at others when we're hurting is sadly a very human trait. You're surprisingly human for a vampire."

Aden's fingertip traced a path down her side, lingering on the curve of her hip, making her tremble in response. Her skin, smooth as silk, was warm and soft beneath his touch.

"I don't know how you do that."

"Do what?" She asked, her voice a breathless whisper.

"Accept every dark and twisted thing about me."

She pressed closer, the warmth of her naked body against his, her breath ghosting over his lips in a near-imperceptible kiss.

"It's very simple. I love you."

Aden's fingertips danced up and down Ellie's back, a gentle rhythm over her skin as she slept, her snores a quiet hum against his chest. The sound was a soft snuffle, a tiny puff of air on his skin, a calming contrast to the turmoil in his mind.

After they'd talked, he used his most persuasive moves to convince her to let him reciprocate. He made her come twice, with his fingers, then his cock, before she promised to just rest her eyes for a minute.

But, in her exhaustion, she fell asleep, and he was too fucking selfish to wake her. He didn't sleep well without her in his arms anymore. And she slept better nestled against him, the nightmares that haunted her for her entire life finally silenced.

He really should wake her, let her go back to her friend, but every time the angel on one shoulder urged him to do it, the devil on the other told her to shut the fuck up. His poor, struggling angel always seemed to lose, until the warmth and love of the angel in his arms changed everything.

A slight movement of the bed made Aden jerk his head up to see his mother's irritating cat on the pillow beside Ellie's head.

"Get lost, you mangy furball," he whispered, careful not to disturb Ellie.

Ignoring Aden's reprimand, Vlad lifted his paw, licking it.

"This is my bed, not yours." He swatted out with his hand, but the cat responded with a hiss and a swipe of his extended claws.

Ellie stirred in his arms but didn't wake. The cat inched closer, kneading her hair splayed on the pillow, then curled up into a ball. Resting his head on his paws, Vlad gave Aden a long, silent stare, daring him to disturb Ellie and end his unwanted company. The air was thick with unspoken challenge.

"Don't look at me like that. She's mine."

Without blinking, Vlad reached out, claws retracted, and pressed his paw against Ellie's scalp. Aden's eyes narrowed.

"Oh sure, no claws for her, huh? You dare scratch her, and I'll pluck those out one by one."

Vlad took a deep breath, his small body expanding before settling, inching closer to Ellie's head, his green eyes flashing.

"Fine, we can share her," Aden snarled after a tense one-minute stare-down. "But I won't fucking come second. If it's a choice between us, they'll never find your body."

Where the fuck did his mother's cat get off challenging him like this? Didn't it realize Aden was the true apex predator?

The cat inched even closer, a gentle purr rumbling in his chest as he nestled into Ellie's hair, rubbing his face on the soft strands.

Aden sighed in defeat.

"She's everything, isn't she?"

Vlad blinked.

"As long as you love her, we'll get along. But you need to get your own girlfriend."

Extending his paw, Vlad rolled onto his back and rubbed his head on Aden's arm.

"Don't rub on me. Fucking hell."

Ellie stirred again, stretching her naked body against him, a soft yawn escaping her lips.

"Who are you talking to?"

"Your second biggest admirer," he said, a touch of jealousy in his voice.

She laughed, turning her face and nuzzling the cat's fur. He gave her forehead a lick. "Hi, Vlady. Is Aden being mean to you?"

"We've come to an understanding," Aden said, still annoyed he lost. To a fucking cat, no less.

Ellie turned back to his chest, tilting her face up to look at him. "What understanding?"

"I'm willing to share you with him as long as he knows he comes second."

She pressed closer, her hand lifting to Aden's face as her fingers traced his lips. "You're always first."

"Take that, you mangy furball," Aden taunted as he leaned in to kiss Ellie. She laughed against his mouth as Vlad hissed and moved to the edge of the bed.

"He's not mangy. He's handsome."

Aden scoffed. Ellie's amusement with his response was clear on her face as she yawned again, sitting up and checking the clock. "I have to get back to Carrie."

"Already?" A pout formed on his lips, unintended and somewhat pathetic, despite his attempts at a neutral expression.

"You let me fall asleep," she said, a small smile playing on her lips, letting him know she wasn't upset.

"If you fall asleep, who am I to wake you? That would be inconsiderate of me."

Leaning in, Ellie kissed the corner of his mouth.

"I'm going to BloodStone with Keeley tonight, but I'll come see you before I leave."

She eased herself out of bed, offering Vlad a quick pet, and gathering her pajamas from the floor, she headed to the bathroom.

A scowl twisting his face, Aden flung his arms above his head, the absence of her warmth leaving him feeling bereft. A few minutes later, back in her pajamas, she smiled and blew kisses to both him and Vlad as she walked through the bedroom on her way back to Carrie.

Understanding Ellie's reasons for needing to be with her best friend didn't make it sting any less that she was leaving him to sleep with someone else.

As if sensing and sympathizing with Aden's distress at Ellie's absence, Vlad inched closer to the pillow.

Aden

"How was the beach house?" Aden asked as he poked his head into Sophie's office.

"Good," she smiled, looking up. "The renovations are coming along nicely. They should be done in time for summer if you want to take Ellie there."

He stepped into the room. "She'll probably want me to."

"Don't you want to?"

"So she can spend all her time outside on the beach without me or sulking because I make her stay inside with me. Sounds like a blast."

His words were bitter, but he'd take Ellie if she asked. He and Sophie both knew it.

She leaned back in her chair. "You stopping by to see me today is a delightful surprise."

"I stop by several times a week."

"Not since Ellie went to work with Keeley."

His mother was adept at concealing her feelings, but a low hum of sadness over Ellie's departure vibrated beneath her words.

Aden sat in the chair in front of her desk, but not before his eyes drifted to the deserted work table. The faintest trace of Ellie's unique scent seemed to hang in the air.

"Don't worry, I don't take it personally. I know you weren't coming to see me."

He looked back at her. "That's not true."

"Uh-huh," she said with a gentle, teasing smile. "I miss having her here, too. But I have a feeling she's where she belongs."

"Why don't you have another assistant?"

"It's funny you should ask me that."

Standing, Sophie went to the window, rearranging the flowers in a vase on the windowsill. Aden's eyes followed her.

"Why do I feel like I'm going to regret it?"

She clucked her tongue. "Why do you always assume the worst?"

"Habit."

Moving to the credenza, she turned the flowers in the vase so they faced the window. It was unusual for her to be so restless.

"So?" He urged her to speak.

Sophie turned to look at him. "I was wondering what you plan to do with Carrie."

Was that all she was wondering?

Aden sighed. "I have no fucking idea."

"That was a pretty heavy sigh."

"That girl is keeping Ellie from me."

"How are the sleeping arrangements working out?"

He gave her a withering look. Allowing a thrall access to his private rooms was shocking, but letting her stay was unheard of. Only Ellie could get him to do it.

"They're getting old fast. So what do you want with her?"

Sophie crossed the room and sat on the sofa as Aden swiveled in his chair to face her.

"Well, I was thinking, when she's feeling better, she might be a good choice to replace Ellie. I visited her in the infirmary, and though she was terrified and hesitant, she seemed likable and smart."

"Why would you want a thrall who couldn't read or write to help you? You'd have to teach her, in addition to training her to use the technology. She isn't like Ellie."

"No, you're right. But Ellie thinks she'd learn things quickly."

The rhythmic drumming of Aden's fingers on the arm of the chair betrayed his annoyance. "You talked to Ellie about this before me?"

"She also stopped by to say hello earlier."

Aden scowled. "Why are you even asking me then?"

"Carrie is your thrall."

It didn't bother him that his mother spoke with Ellie first. And he trusted her judgment of whether her friend was right for the job with his mother.

"If you already have Ellie on board, what I think doesn't matter."

"Yes, it does."

With a dismissive wave of his hand, he rose and walked over to Ellie's old table, running his fingers along the edge. "I don't care, Sophie. If you want her as your assistant, take her. Maybe that'll keep her busy enough so I can have more than a half hour a day with Ellie."

He sounded like a petulant brat, but thankfully his mother ignored it.

"Thank you."

He felt Sophie's curious eyes on him, her gaze making the back of his neck itch.

"Why are you looking at me like that?"

"Like what?"

He pointed an accusing finger at her. "Like that."

"I was just wondering what your thoughts were, now that you've had time to digest our conversation the other night."

Aden walked to the chair opposite her and sat down.

"My thoughts are that I have one more reason to end Matthais."

A gentle smile curved her lips. "I appreciate your anger on my behalf, but it's unnecessary. It was a long time ago."

"I don't understand you and Aurick sometimes."

"What do you mean?"

"How have you spent the last five hundred years looking him in the face, knowing he wanted you dead?"

She gave a casual shrug. "I avoid being in Matthais' presence as much as possible."

"So, how does Aurick do it?"

"He's a consummate diplomat, prioritizing the collective good over his personal feelings."

"That's where we're completely different."

A soft laugh escaped Sophie's lips. "That's where you're wrong, Aden. He wasn't always like that. He was as hotheaded and volatile as you are, back when I first met him."

Aden scoffed. "I know he's a hothead, and he's alluded to his dark past a few times when we've talked, but somehow I doubt he and I have the same dark nature."

Sophie tilted her head as her gaze lingered on his face. "Do you know he set my grandfather on fire, killing him for abusing my mother? He did it without flinching or an ounce of remorse. And he'd only known her for fifteen minutes. Of course, he didn't see her again for almost eight years after that night, but that's how he reacted back then. With unrestrained anger and violence. And no regret."

"Fuck, Sophie. Why is it I know virtually nothing about your and Aurick's history?"

The question hung in the air, Aden wondering how well he knew the man he called father.

"Because we've chosen not to share the darker aspects of your father's past. By the time you and Keeley came along, he was a very different man. He'd let his darkness go, the same way you're letting yours go now that Ellie's in your life."

"I don't know about that. Mine is still there, hovering beneath the surface. But she does make me want to be better."

"And your father's darkness will always be a part of him, but he's re-embraced the humanity he lost for a long time. He would've killed Matthais the day he threatened me if there hadn't been an army of guards standing nearby. But he knew he couldn't protect me if he was dead."

Aden nodded as he considered Sophie's words, the parallel in his own life unmistakable. Keeping Ellie safe was more important than anything, even his own well-being, but he couldn't protect her if he died. Nothing would stop him from keeping her safe, no matter the cost. Including killing Matthais.

"I can't change what he did to her before we met, but if Matthais ever tries to hurt Ellie again, I swear I will unleash hellfire upon him."

Sophie nodded her head in silent agreement, her eyes reflecting her understanding. Though gentle and averse to violence, his mother was also a pragmatist. And she was just as fierce as Aden when it came to protecting her loved ones.

"Then you understand why this is necessary?"

"I'm still wrapping my head around it, honestly. I agree he needs to be removed, and that means killing him. There's no other way to remove him. And I get that you've been planning this for a long time, but there's a tremendous risk of failure. And if that happens, Matthais' retaliation will be swift and brutal."

"Yes," Sophie agreed. "But if we aren't willing to put it all on the line to rid the world of his evil, then we're no better than him. We've looked the other way for too long. It's exactly what you said about challenging Vincent. If we don't do this, we'll never be able to face ourselves again. And the crushing weight of our inaction will haunt us forever."

"For as long as we all live," Aden said, his words lingering in the air. "But if we fail, we're all dead."

"You're always so pessimistic. I thought Ellie was breaking you of that habit," she teased.

"She has her work cut out for her," he said with a smirk before adding. "I didn't know you were so involved in the backdoor politics of it all."

"You know what they say?" Sophie asked, a smirk of her own playing on her lips.

Aden arched an eyebrow.

"Great men often have even greater women supporting them."

Aden peered into Hannah's primary lab through the glass door. Ellie sat on a stool, smiling and talking to Keeley as she looked through a microscope.

"I told you glasses were sexy."

He only just restrained his startled jump at Hannah's unexpected voice.

"Fuck, Hannah, you shouldn't sneak up on people like that."

"What are you doing here?"

"I came to get Ellie."

"She didn't mention you were coming to get her." Hannah looked around. "What happened to Drake?"

"I sent him home."

Aden's gaze returned to Ellie, who was laughing, her face flushed with excitement, clearly in her element.

"You going to go in or just lurk out here like a stalker?"

He turned to Hannah, his face twisting into a scowl. "I'm not a stalker."

"Looks like it."

With a smirk, she leaned against the wall, tablet in her hands. She enjoyed annoying him too much.

"Why is she wearing glasses?" Aden looked back through the door. "She doesn't need them."

"They're magnifiers. Most of us wear them, even with our vampire vision. It makes it easier to see the microscopic cells."

A hologram of Aurick sitting on his sofa materialized beside them.

"Aden, do you have a minute?"

"Sure. I'll be right in," Aden said to Hannah, dismissing her.

"Oh, hey, Aurick." She popped her head in front of the hologram. "Do you plan to visit the labs anytime soon?"

"Hannah," Aden protested as she hijacked his call.

"What? This is saving me a separate hologram."

"I don't have any plans to," Aurick said. "Do you need me to come by?"

"Nothing urgent, but Keeley, Nicky, and I wanted to run a few things by you."

"I can make some time tomorrow night."

"Great. I'll tell Nicky." She stepped back.

"Oh, are you done hijacking my call now?"

"Yup. Thanks, Aurick. See you tomorrow night." She pointed to the door across the way. "You can use the security office if you want privacy. I'll tell Ellie you're here and were spying on her and Keeley."

"I wasn't fucking spying."

Hannah used her biometrics to get into the lab, chuckling. Aden walked into the office, the hologram following him.

"She irritates the fuck out of me sometimes."

"Because you let her," Aurick said with a laugh.

The room was larger than expected, featuring a seating area on one side and a long console table inlaid with integrated touch screens on the other. Holograms floated above, offering views of all the labs, including the one across the hall. He sank into one of the oversized chairs, continuing to watch Ellie. Maybe Hannah was right, and he was a creepy fucking stalker.

"What did you want to talk about?"

"First, I wanted to see how you were feeling after our discussion the other day. Your mother mentioned your chat."

Aden scoffed. "Didn't her play-by-play tell you everything you need to know?"

"I wanted to hear your thoughts directly from you."

"How do you expect me to feel? First, you tell me you're planning a coup against Matthais. And you have the support of more than half the Gerents. Then you tell me you've been planning this for decades and you're just telling me about it now. Did I sum that up right?"

Sophie poked her head into the hologram from beside Aurick. "That's a simplified overview, but that's the gist of it."

"Did Hannah teach you that trick?" Aden asked, scowling.

"What trick?"

"The popping into other people's conversations without asking. And I thought you were going to the beach house?"

"I'm at the beach house. So is your father."

Aden's gaze darted to the hologram with Ellie. Hannah pointed out something to her under the microscope.

"So you're literally on the same island as the BloodStone labs, and you can't make it over here until tomorrow night?"

Aurick glanced at Sophie, who just smiled at him. "You'll understand when you get married."

"Technically, he's already married," his mother murmured. "His wife is just in a different body. Oh, I hadn't thought of that before now."

A sudden stillness fell over Aden. That hadn't occurred to him either. He'd been thinking of Ellie as his girlfriend, but technically she was his wife. Reborn.

Fuck! He couldn't deal with that right now.

"Can we get back on topic?"

"Sure," Aurick said as he hushed Sophie's chatter about Ellie being his wife. "So, do you have any additional thoughts on our plans?"

"I told you Matthais needs to be taken out, and if you can pull it off, I think it's a good idea."

"But?"

"But while most Gerents support you, the ones with three of the largest territories and armies are not on board and likely never will be."

The sight of Ellie laughing and throwing her head back at something Kee-ley said caught Aden's attention, making him almost miss Aurick's words.

"Yuri and Dietrich will back Matthais, so they'll remain unaware of our plans. But Cecilia's position is yet to be determined. The timing hasn't been right to approach her. Though she attributes Paolo's dismissal to Matthais, her anger is more intensely focused on your role in provoking it."

"Too fucking bad. He was a hack. Marco is a far superior leader. He's successfully reformed and disciplined her military."

Sophie rose from the sofa and disappeared from the hologram.

"His and Cecilia's support for this could mean the difference between success and failure," Aurick said. "But let me worry about that. That brings me to my other reason for calling. I'd like you to take a trip to see Katsumi, Indira, Banjora, and Rashidi. They'd like your assurance you're on board for this. As the world's second-in-command military leader, you wield significant influence over the troops. They respect you."

"They respect Andrei too."

"But they respect you more."

That was news to Aden. As long as his troops followed his orders, he didn't give a fuck what they thought of him. The knowledge of their respect was preferable to their animosity, but they more likely just feared him because of the unpredictable and volatile nature of his moods.

"How have you kept something like this concealed for so long?"

"By keeping a very tight circle. None of the military leaders have been told yet. You're the first."

Aden stood, pacing, as was his habit when he was getting agitated. The lack of adequate time to process this idea, coupled with his dislike of uncertainty, irritated him.

"What if they won't support it? They could go straight to Andrei."

Sophie popped back into the hologram, sitting back on the sofa next to Aurick.

"That's why the others want your assurance," his father said. "They'll then notify their commander generals, and you can take charge of bringing everyone into line."

Fuck!

He had to take this trip. It would take him away from Ellie again, likely for a couple of weeks if he had to travel to all four regions. Now he was even more fucking irritated.

"I want to meet them all at once. Have them meet me in Terra Australis. That's the furthest away from Matthais, Yuri, and Dietrich."

"Fine. I'll make arrangements for you to go as soon as possible."

"I can't go immediately. Schedule it for the beginning of the month."

Aurick opened his mouth, but Sophie's hand on his arm and the meaningful look she gave him stopped him.

"Okay. I'll let you know when everything is arranged."

Aden headed toward the door. "I have to go before Hannah sneaks Ellie out of here, just to piss me off."

"Aden," Aurick said his name, and he turned back to the hologram. "Thank you, son. For understanding why we're doing this."

"I understand the risks of failure are as equal to, if not more than, success. We may all die in this."

"There is always a risk in doing the right thing," Aurick said. "But it's the only way to preserve what we've built and protect the people we love."

And that's why Aden would do this without question or complaint—protecting Ellie was worth risking everything.

Aden stepped into the hall and took a deep breath. Aurick was right, just as Sophie had been when they spoke the other night. What they were planning was the only way to safeguard their way of life and protect their family, the only people Aden loved.

His family extended beyond Ellie, his parents, Keeley, Ryan, and that spawn of theirs. Kane and Mina were too. And god help him, Hannah and Nickolas. Now that Ellie had her friend back in her life, Carrie was unofficially family, as was Drake because Ellie trusted him.

Fuck!

He had too many people he considered family now.

Protecting the people of his region—both vampires and humans—was a duty he took seriously. If this coup succeeded, his father's societal reforms would improve the world. Matthais had gone too far. He was unpredictable and dangerous, and Aden couldn't stand by and just do nothing.

His faith in his father was unwavering, so he'd support Aurick no matter what. But he'd fucking burn the world down to keep Ellie safe.

Burn. The entire. Fucking. World. Down.

Now he needed to figure out how to tell Ellie. He gave her his word that he wouldn't keep anything important from her anymore. Why had he made that promise?

Oh, yeah, because she was the fucking love of his life.

Peering into the lab through the glass door, Aden saw her sitting on the same stool. Only she was no longer looking in a microscope. Instead, her arm was outstretched, and Hannah was taking her blood.

His biometric scan cleared, and he burst into the room.

"What the fuck is going on here?"

The three women looked up at him, startled, but then Ellie's lips curved into a smile.

"We're drawing Ellie's blood," Hannah said like it wasn't obvious.

He crossed the room and took hold of Hannah's wrist. "I can see that. Why?"

"Because she said we could," Keeley said. "Human blood is rarely used in our testing now."

"There's a reason for that. Aurick forbids it."

Hannah shook Aden's hand off and slid the needle out of Ellie's vein, pressing a piece of gauze into the crook of her elbow to stop the bleeding. The smell made his mouth water.

"He forbids us to take and test blood from humans who don't willingly donate it. Ellie is," Keeley said as Hannah walked away with the half-full tube.

"Ellie's blood is mine," he snarled.

Ellie narrowed her eyes, the heat of her stare sharp and intense. "Actually, it's mine. I share it with you, but I can give it to anyone I want."

Her words hit him like a slap, and he felt his eyes flash red with fury before returning to their usual blue.

"Oh, shit. I think that's our cue to leave," Keeley said with a pointed look at Hannah.

"Yeah, let me show you that... ah... thing in my office," Hannah said as the two of them hurried out of the lab and the line of fire.

Ellie turned on the stool to look at him. "Aden, why are you so upset about this?"

"You're sharing your blood with someone other than me."

How could she not understand why he was so fucking angry?

"I'm donating my blood for scientific research, not passing it around to every vampire in sight."

A deep, menacing growl rumbled up from deep inside him. The thought of her sharing her blood with random vampires filled him with a furious, destructive rage.

She tossed the gauze on the counter and grabbed his shirt, pulling him close. He stood his ground for a minute, trying to shake off the unexpected reaction her words invoked, but relented when she raised an eyebrow.

"Aden, you're overreacting." The moment her hand touched his chest, his muscles visibly relaxed under her fingers, her touch always having an immediate calming effect. But her telling him he was overreacting kept his anger simmering beneath the surface.

He couldn't resist tasting her, so he lifted her arm and licked the puncture. "Ellie, this is not just some inconsequential act. You have no idea how precious your blood is to me. And it's not just because of how good it smells and tastes or how it makes me feel powerful and crazed and calm at the same time. It's because it's your blood, Ellie. It's the very essence of who you are, and you're everything to me."

A hint of warmth and understanding softened her eyes. "I'm sorry I didn't tell you first, but I didn't think it was a big deal."

"It is to me."

"Well, I'm going to donate any time they ask, so..." She trailed off, and Aden scowled. Clearly, his feelings on the matter were irrelevant. "What are you doing here, anyway?"

Her question was an evasion tactic she no doubt learned from him.

"I came to get you."

A gentle smile touched her lips. "I'm very happy to see you, but why?"

"Can't I pick my girlfriend up from work?" He snarled, then stiffened. The memory of his mother calling Ellie his wife washed over him once more. He needed time to reflect on her words, letting them sink in. "Why do you always smile when I snarl at you?"

She shrugged, her smile growing wider. "I don't always, but right now I am because I like it when you call me your girlfriend."

A loose strand of hair escaped from her ponytail. Aden tucked it behind her ear, feeling the softness against his fingers, eliciting a gentle shiver from her.

"I wanted to spend some time with you before you go off with Carrie for the day."

"I'm not seeing her until dinner."

"So you have time for me, then?"

Her fingers laced through his. "Aden, I know you're feeling ignored, but I promise it will only be for a little while. I've missed Carrie so much, and she needs me right now."

"I need you."

Ellie reached up and pulled his face down to hers for a gentle kiss.

"I always need you," she murmured against his lips.

Tugging her into his arms, he deepened the kiss, losing himself in her. Until his sister poked her head in, fucking interrupting them.

"Go the fuck away, Keeley?"

Arching an eyebrow, she crossed her arms, tapping her foot.

"You know, just because you're an owner of BloodStone doesn't mean you can commandeer my employees at your whim."

"She's done for today. You can have her back tomorrow night."

Ellie's shrug told Aden she was torn between going with him and staying with Keeley.

"Can Hannah at least finish drawing her blood? You're not really going to be an overbearing brute and refuse to let her donate, are you?"

With a defensive grumble, he conceded. "You can have one vial. And hurry the fuck up. You have five minutes, then I'm dragging her out of here."

"Okay, caveman," Keeley mocked as Hannah stepped back into the room.

"You know," Hannah said as she grabbed some fresh supplies. "They're a bit like Beauty and the Beast, don't you think?"

"Oh, I love that story," Ellie said as she stepped out of his arms and walked over to them. "The beast is just a big softy under all that bluster."

A quiet scoff escaped Aden's lips as Hannah and Keeley chuckled.

She did not just call him a softy!

Ellie

The overhead lights of Kane's workout room cast harsh shadows as Ellie circled with Drake. His eyes tracked her movements with predatory precision, though his expression remained patient. Across the mat, Kane stood with his arms crossed, eyes narrowed as he watched them.

"Remember," Drake said, "when someone grabs you from behind, your first instinct might be to pull away. Don't. Instead, drop your weight and create space."

He showed her by twisting her around and grabbing her from behind. Ellie lowered her center of gravity, tucking her chin and lifting her shoulders to protect her neck.

"Good," Kane called out. "Now hit him with the stomp and elbow combination I showed you."

Ellie drove her heel into the top of Drake's foot, throwing her elbow back toward his abdomen. He let her connect with him, but it felt like elbowing a brick wall—solid, unyielding, and completely unresponsive.

"Better," Drake said, releasing her. "The key is to cause surprise because you're just trying to buy yourself time to run. Go for vulnerable points—eyes, throat, and groin. Don't try that on me," he warned as he stepped back.

From her perch on a chair in the corner, Ellie felt Carrie's eyes on them. Hugging her knees to her chest, she flinched each time Drake or Kane put their hands on Ellie.

She'd invited Carrie tonight, hoping it would make her feel more at ease with the guards who were so often with Ellie. She remained nervous, especially around men, even a month after Aden saved her from Vincent. The Westcotts allowed very few vampires access to their compound, only a few higher-up advisers, but Carrie's fear seemed to extend to even the male thralls. The half-breeds, though, appeared to cause her the most distress because Vincent's guards had always just stood by, impassively watching her being tortured.

"You want to try it?" Ellie asked with a hopeful lift of her eyebrow.

Carrie shook her head, shrinking further into herself, pulling her long blonde hair over her cheek to conceal the jagged scar from Vincent's knife. Though lessened by Aden's blood, it was still visible and made her feel self-conscious. "I'll just watch," she murmured.

Kane's quick, troubled glance at her didn't escape Ellie's notice.

She moved to the center of the mat again, this time facing Kane. "Can you show me that choke defense again?"

He stepped up to her. "Ellie, you need to remember that what we're teaching you can only protect you from human attackers. Against vampires or half-breeds..." He trailed off, his expression grim.

"I know," Ellie sighed. "Run like hell and hope you two are nearby."

"We'll always be nearby," Drake said, and Ellie smiled. She trusted him as much as Kane now. Maybe more.

The rest of the session focused on showing Ellie knee strikes, palm heel strikes, escapes from hair grabs, and bear hugs. Carrie's eyes continued to follow her, alternating between fascination and fear.

When Ellie's body ached everywhere, she wiped the sweat from her forehead. "Okay, I'm done. Same time tomorrow?"

Kane shook his head. "It'll only be Drake. I have to go with Aden to Terra Australis."

Almost as if he knew they were talking about him, his face popped up in a hologram, his gaze flickering between her and the two guards.

"Why are you using Kane's workout room and not mine?"

"You were in a meeting with Roderick, so we didn't want to interrupt you."

"Are you done yet?"

Ellie nodded. "We just finished."

Aden looked at Carrie, his brow furrowing before he looked back at Ellie. Then a furious glint appeared in his eyes.

"Is that a bruise on your shoulder?"

"Yes, and I earned it," Ellie said, her tone warning him not to overreact. "Carrie and I are going to have dinner, then I'm showing her to her new room. After that, are you up for our ritual?"

His eyes snapped to hers, and she let her soft smile answer his unspoken question. Through the hologram, she saw his shoulders relax, even as his eyes flashed again, this time with heat that wasn't anger. It had been a month since their last shared bath, and he obviously missed it as much as she did.

She'd been spending almost every night with Carrie, but her nightmares had mostly subsided, so Carrie insisted she no longer needed Ellie to stay with her. She was ready to go to the room Sophie arranged.

Ellie hadn't argued because she missed sleeping in Aden's arms even more than their baths. But she made Carrie promise to tell her if they started up again.

"How long will you be?" He asked, his voice tight.

"An hour."

"If you're a minute later, I'm coming to find you," he said before he swiped the hologram closed.

Kane headed for the door, chuckling and muttering "freaking baths" under his breath.

"Shut up, Kane," Ellie called after him.

With a silent chuckle, Drake trailed behind. "See you tomorrow, Ellie."

Carrie walked up to her. "Why was Kane laughing? What ritual are you talking about?"

"Nothing." Ellie smiled and shook her head. Carrie looked suspicious, but Aden and her sex life wasn't something Ellie discussed with Carrie. Maybe someday they'd be able to share those kinds of details like best friends did. "Come on, let's go eat."

"If you don't have time, I can eat alone."

Ellie tucked her arm through Carrie's, leading them out of the gym.

"No way. I'm starving."

Ellie nearly spit out her drink, laughing as Finn buried his face in his hands. He'd been telling her, Carrie, and Mandi about the picnic he'd taken Lily on a few days prior.

Across the table, the two women laughed along with her, though Carrie's laugh was more subdued. She remained stiff and quiet, but at least she was sitting at the table with Finn.

Ellie had introduced them at dinner the previous day, and his easygoing nature and handsome face seemed to put Carrie somewhat at ease.

"Stop laughing! It completely ruined the mood I was going for," he groaned against his palms. "One minute the sandwich was there, the next that damn squirrel was running up a tree with it! And then that snake just appeared out of nowhere."

With her stomach muscles aching from laughter, Ellie pressed a hand to her abdomen.

"That squirrel sounds like a ninja."

"What's a ninja?" Finn asked, looking up at her in confusion.

Ellie sobered, remembering that he, like most thralls, couldn't read and wouldn't know about the feudal Japanese merccnaries she'd read about on her tablet.

"Never mind. Keep going. What was that about a snake?"

"It slithered across the blanket, and I couldn't help it; I screamed."

"Oh, Finn," Ellie said, wiping her fingers beneath her eyes as she caught her breath.

"It wasn't actually a scream exactly..." He mumbled. "More of a manly exclamation of surprise."

"Finn, don't," Ellie begged. "Don't make me laugh anymore. I'm going to pee my pants."

He scowled, but somehow it made him look even more handsome. But perhaps Ellie was just partial to scowls now.

"I'm glad you find my humiliation amusing."

"We're not laughing at you," Mandi said, also wiping the tears from her eyes. "We're laughing with you."

"I'm not laughing." Finn buried his face in his hands again.

"Well, Lily thought it was adorable," Mandi said. "I believe her exact words were, 'Thank god he didn't try to be some macho tough guy.'"

"Really?" He peeked through his fingers.

"Yes, really," Carrie said. "I was there when she said it."

Ellie smiled, a genuine warmth spreading through her chest, as Carrie joined the conversation, seeming a little more at ease with each passing minute. Finn and Mandi were the only two thralls Ellie was friendly with. They were the only ones who had ever been kind to her, and she wanted her friend to feel comfortable with them.

"Plus, she told us the snake scared her, too," Mandi added. "She said she was frozen in place, but you at least had the sense to grab her hand and pull off the blanket."

"I did do that, didn't I?" Finn sat up straighter. "But the squirrel thing was still humiliating."

"Finn, she's already agreed to go out with you again, right?" Ellie asked, and he nodded. "It sounds like your reactions just made her like you more. Not every girl wants some stereotypical tough guy who pretends nothing fazes him. Sometimes we just want one who'll shriek at snakes with us."

"It wasn't a shriek," he protested, but he finally smiled. "Fine, but next time, I'm taking her to an indoor restaurant on lower level three. No wildlife allowed."

"Except maybe that ninja squirrel. He's earned an invitation after stealing your sandwich."

"Ellie!"

"I'm just sayin'," she teased.

"I can't believe you're able to go outside the city at all," Carrie said. "We were never allowed out, were we, Ells?"

"The park is technically inside," Finn said. "But it's on the eastern edge with nothing much around it, so it feels like outside the dome."

"Still, dating was forbidden. And we never got time off." Carrie wrung her fingers, and Ellie reached over to squeeze her hand.

"It took me a while to get used to it, too," she said.

Mandi looked at the clock. "I've got to go. Master Aden is probably done in his office, so I can clean it now."

"Mistress Sophie will be looking for me soon, so I should go, too." Carrie stood and carried her dishes to the dishwasher. "Are you going to BloodStone tonight?"

"Yeah. I meet Keeley in a half hour," Ellie replied. "I'll see you later?"

Carrie nodded. "Come find me when you get back."

She and Mandi waved as they left, and Ellie took the last sip of her iced tea.

"Your friend is nice. A little nervous, though. I heard she'd been hurt, worse than you when you first got here."

"What I suffered was nothing compared to what she did."

"I'll keep an eye out for her," he said, and Ellie wanted to hug him, but if Aden found out, who knows what he'd do to Finn.

"Thanks, Finn."

"Are you sure I didn't make a complete fool out of myself with Lily?"

"No, I think you did. But it sounds like she likes you anyway."

"I really want you to meet her, Ellie. She wants to meet you, too."

"I'd like that."

"She has breakfast with me on Thursdays. Maybe you can stop by sometime."

"I'll be here Thursday."

The door slid open, and Aden stepped through, his presence filling the room with an almost palpable energy.

"Ellie?"

"Hi." She turned and smiled up at him as he approached.

"You need to turn the fuck around, Finn," he growled as he tugged her to her feet and away from the table.

"Yes, Sir," he said and spun in his chair.

It was pointless to scold Aden for being rude.

"I'm leaving for Terra Australis in a few minutes."

"Okay."

"I'm not sure when I'll be back."

"Is everything alright?"

He nodded, but his expression contradicted his words. He was keeping something from her, having been unusually distracted the last few weeks, even when they were alone. But she let it drop for now. Pressing the issue before his trip would only distract him more.

"Okay. Be careful."

"Always. Don't fucking give Drake any headaches while I'm gone."

"Only if you promise no creepy stalker holograms. If you want to see me, call me like a normal person."

He grunted, and she stepped into his arms. He buried his face in her neck, and a subtle nod was his silent agreement.

She pressed her lips to his ear and whispered too low for Finn to hear. "I love you."

"Mo ghrá," he murmured before kissing her soft and deep.

Ellie gasped, breathless, when he finally released her lips. Then he let her go, turned, and was gone as abruptly as he arrived.

She dropped into the chair as she swallowed. "You can turn around now, Finn."

"That was just too weird," he mumbled, a hint of amusement in his voice.

She burst out in a laugh.

"You have no idea."

"Hannah, can I ask you a question?"

Ellie looked away from the DNA sequence hologram hovering above her workstation. The double helix rotated slowly, the nucleotide sequences she'd been studying for the past three hours highlighted in pulsing red.

"Ooh, I like the sound of that," Hannah said, closing the centrifuge before tapping commands into the control panel, turning it on. "What do you want to know? Is it about Aden? I have lots of dirt on him. Far more than his family even knows exists."

A frown creased Ellie's brow. "I wasn't going to ask about Aden. But why do you have dirt on him?"

Hannah picked up her tablet, typing on it as she walked toward Ellie. "Because I can. One cannot have too much leverage over him." She glanced at the hologram above Ellie. "You're focusing too much on the telomeric regions. The key differences are in the mitochondrial DNA."

Ellie glanced up at the hologram. "Oh, I see what you mean," she said before swiping to a different sequence, then looking back at Hannah. "And I don't need leverage over Aden, Hannah."

"No. I imagine you don't," Hannah said with a thoughtful tilt of her head. "You're probably the only person who doesn't. I'd never use what I have on him. But I enjoy having it. It keeps us on a level playing field."

"That sounds a little disturbing."

"I know. That's the best part."

"You're dangerous."

A loud, unladylike laugh escaped Hannah's lips. "You have no idea, kid. Now, what do you want to ask? Because it obviously isn't about my blackmail material."

Ellie turned on her stool to face Hannah. "You told me about the breeding program, but how are half-breeds made?"

Hannah set down her tablet and gave her a puzzled look. "I thought you said you watched your father turn."

"I did. I had to sit next to him and watch all thirty hours it took for his transformation to be complete. It was agonizing, but not as bad as it was for him."

"Being turned into a vampire feels ten times worse."

Ellie bit her lip, a nervous habit she couldn't seem to break, as Hannah skipped right to the next question she wanted to ask.

"Is anything I've read about it true? The burning in your veins? The breaking and reforming of bones? The excruciating pain?"

"Fiction never got it completely right, but yeah, that happens, along with a lot of other things. But it's the hours of feeling like you're having a non-stop heart attack that's the worst. You think you recognize pain, but your pain receptors can't even process the agony. But I digress. You wanted to know about half-breeds?"

Ellie could feel the horrified look on her face as she swallowed. "Yes."

Hannah leaned against the counter next to her.

"So, historically, half-breeds were created the same way as your father. At least thirty percent of their blood has to be drained. But it can't exceed forty. Over forty percent is exsanguination. And that results in death or being turned into a vampire if fed blood before the heart stops beating. The timing has to be perfect. Otherwise, you're dead."

"What does it feel like afterward? Once the transformation is complete?"

"When becoming a vampire or half-breed?"

"Both."

"Like you're reborn when you become a half-breed. You feel like everything inside your body is new again because at the cellular level, it is."

"And as a vampire?"

"Invincible. That's the only word for it."

Ellie let Hannah's words sink in. "Is it worth it?"

"Being able to live forever?" Hannah raised an eyebrow. "Hell ya! Well, as long as the world doesn't go to shit around you. That's happened a few times since I was turned." She fixed Ellie with a stare so intense it felt like a physical touch. "Why are you asking? Are you and Aden talking about changing you?"

Ellie swiped the hologram closed and stood up from her stool. "You don't pull any punches, do you, Hannah?"

"Nope." Hannah grinned unapologetically. "No reason to. I'm nosy by nature, and I've lived long enough not to care if people are offended."

"I think that's what I like most about you."

"That and how I can give you the full, uncensored details about Aden that no one else has the balls to tell you," Hannah said as she walked to her desk in the corner where three monitors displayed the centrifuge's real-time data.

"I don't want the full, uncensored details about him. Please don't bad-mouth him to me. It's getting tiresome. I know you're just trying to get a rise out of me."

Her words hung in the air, mingling with the soft hum of equipment, leaving Ellie shocked by her own bluntness. A year ago, she wouldn't have dared to speak to a vampire like that. She wouldn't have spoken to a vampire at all unless spoken to first.

But things were different now. She was different, and she was growing weary of Hannah's constant insinuations about Aden's past.

Hannah turned from her monitors, a subtle look of approval crossing her face. "Keeley was right about you. You're intensely loyal and defend him fiercely against any criticism."

Ellie frowned, crossing her arms. "Of course I do."

"Good."

Ellie's jaw dropped in surprise, her arms falling to her sides. "Were you testing me?"

"Not really. I recognized the kind of person you were the second I met you and looked into those familiar green eyes. But I needed you to feel comfortable enough with me to tell me to back the fuck off."

"I don't think that's exactly what I said."

Hannah retrieved two tablets from her desk and returned to Ellie's side.

"Not in so many words. You're too polite, which is one hell of a balance for your boy. I don't think he knows the meaning of the word."

"Hannah," Ellie said, her voice sharp with warning.

"Okay. You're right," Hannah said with a dramatic sigh. "I'm just trying to get a little rise out of you. That's one thing Aden and I have in common. We like to get under other people's skin, especially each other's." She handed one tablet to Ellie. "But you and I can only work together if we're comfortable with each other."

"As long as you lay off Aden, we'll be fine."

"I like you, Ellie." A grin stretched across Hannah's face. "I give him shit, but I delivered him, and he's like a son to me. I'd never betray him or try to make you think badly of him."

Ellie nodded, then sat back down on her stool. "Thank you. So what does this tablet have on it?"

"More studies on vampiric reproductive stasis."

The tablet's bright screen seemed to mock Ellie. "More?"

"We've been working on this for centuries."

"Okay, I'll get started," Ellie said, already scrolling through the information.

She focused on the work, but from the corner of her eye, she saw another slow smile spread across Hannah's face.

"Why are you grinning like that?"

"You didn't answer my question."

"What question?"

"Are you and Aden discussing turning you into a half-breed?"

"No. I was just curious."

"Yeah, that was convincing," Hannah drawled but dropped the subject, resuming her work.

Aden

Aden stood at the wall of windows in Banjora's war room, overlooking the training field. Dheran, his general, was running his troops through rigorous drills. He wasn't yet aware Aden was in Terra Australis because Banjora wanted to keep Aden's presence confidential until after their meeting.

Kane stood beside him, arms across his chest. "They look better than they did the last time we were here."

"It was the right move to promote Dheran."

"You ready for this?"

"Yes. Why would you ask that?"

"Because you know they're going to try to put you through the wringer. To make sure you're up for this."

"Do you think I'm up for it?"

Kane scoffed out a laugh. "Please. You could do this shit in your sleep."

"This won't be some ordinary mission. The stakes are too high."

"They always are."

"They're higher now."

Aden's snarl cut off when the door behind them slid open. He turned away from the window.

Banjora entered, followed by Rashidi, the Gerent of Afara; Katsumi, the Gerent of Asu; and Indira, the Gerent of Vindhya. Aden watched as they passed through the room to one just beyond it.

Another door opened to reveal a private office, smaller and more intimate. Aden followed, leaving Kane to watch the training.

Banjora's war room was sleek and modern, filled with state-of-the-art technology. However, his office was ancient and earthy in design, reflecting his age and origin as one of only a handful of vampires to originate from Terra Australis.

The stone walls arched upward to a ceiling of granite, where skylights framed the moonlit sky. A heavy, ornate desk in the right corner took up more than a third of the room. An aged oak conference table on the left, also with a full wall of windows' view of the training field below, was inlaid with glass panels for holographic projections. Fire-lit sconces lining the walls cast a muted glow over the entire room.

As the door slid closed behind him, Aden took in the four Ancient Ones standing in the center of the room. He respected the Gerents. They ruled their regions firmly but fairly. And though they didn't always agree with Aurick, they favored his governing philosophy rather than Matthais'.

"Good to see you, Aden," Banjora greeted with a handshake. The others followed with their own greetings. As the others headed toward their chairs, Indira pulled him aside.

"Sophie tells me you have your hands full these days," she said under her breath, letting him know she knew about Ellie.

Fuck!

His mother and her big mouth. Indira was her closest ally outside the Westcott family. They'd been friends for centuries, having met before the Great Vampire Wars when Sophie was Indira's student at what was then Harvard Medical School. She shared Sophie's belief in soulmates, believing she and her husband, Rohan, to be such a pair.

Aden's grunt was a noncommittal response, neither confirming nor denying anything so close in proximity to the others.

"Please, come have a seat, Aden," Banjora said.

He sat on the left side of the table while the Gerents settled on the right. Aden smirked, understanding the unspoken message in the seating arrangement. He was here to be judged.

He relaxed in his chair, legs crossed.

"You put on quite a show at the capital a few months ago," Banjora said, his casual tone grating on Aden's nerves.

"I wouldn't call it a show. It was a necessary act to get rid of a piece-of-shit vampire."

"Dietrich's harboring a bit of resentment since Vincent was from his region," Rashidi said.

"I don't give a fuck how Dietrich feels."

"Your hand seems to be fine," Katsumi commented.

Aden held it up and wiggled his fingers. He had full use of it back, but his wrist still ached sometimes. He hadn't admitted that to anyone. Not even Ellie.

"Never better."

"Was the thrall worth it?" Banjora asked.

She was worth making Ellie happy.

But he kept his true thoughts to himself. "I wouldn't have issued the challenge if she weren't. Now are we going to dick around with small talk or get to the reason I'm here?"

"Your attachment to your new pet was more than obvious in the one night she accompanied you to the annual ball," Rashidi remarked.

Fury swept through him, freezing Aden in place. His gaze flicked to Indira, but her subtle head shake reassured him his secret was safe.

"What you do with her is your own business," he continued. "But I need to know that your coming on board here is about more than just one thrall."

"How fucking dare you question my motives!" Aden snarled as he leaned forward.

"No one is questioning your motives," Indira said, her demeanor reminding him of Sophie.

"It fucking sounds like it."

"We all have loved ones we want to protect from being collateral damage in this endeavor," Katsumi said. "But if we proceed with this plan, we all need to be aware of the risks."

"My job is literally to assess and eliminate risk. What I do in my personal life doesn't come into play."

"It did three hundred years ago," Banjora said.

Aden surged to his feet, blind with rage.

"Say that to me again, Banjora. I fucking dare you."

"Sit down, Aden," Rashidi said. None of them seemed overly surprised by his reaction. Three centuries were nothing to a vampire, so the memory of his actions after killing Aly was likely still vivid. But clearly, he needed to be less predictable. So, he remained standing.

"Deposing Matthais requires absolute certainty on all our parts," Rashidi continued. "We need your assurance that once you commit to this, you won't back out. Matthais is very adept at targeting the ones we love. I'm sure your parents informed you of that."

"I don't need a reminder that Matthais wanted to kill Sophie. When I make a commitment, I follow through. And he will pay for threatening her. You can count on that."

"Please sit back down, Aden," Katsumi said.

A moment of silence passed before he sat again, out of respect for her and Indira. It wasn't their fault Rashidi and Banjora were assholes.

"We're all putting not only our own lives on the line but that of the people we're committed to protecting," Indira said. "If we fail, they'll suffer exponentially. Matthais will simply kill us, but the ones we love, our families, the humans, and the half-breeds in our regions, he'll take out his wrath on them."

"But if we fail to act, things will only get worse," Rashidi said. "They've been growing graver for decades."

"Centuries, if we're being honest," Katsumi added.

"Matthais' instability threatens everything," Banjora said, and Aden shifted in his chair to glare at him, unwilling to let his previous remark pass. "We didn't fight over fifty years of war with the humans, only to watch what we fought for crumble under his arrogance and insanity."

"He's forgotten that even gods can bleed," Aden said, his voice laced with contempt. "Why the fuck did it take all of you so long to recognize his madness?"

"It didn't. We knew what we were getting into by following him."

"That's not entirely true," Indira contradicted Katsumi. "I never thought it would go this far."

"We wanted freedom to live without oppression," Katsumi replied.

"We wanted power," Rashidi said, his voice devoid of regret. "And to be completely honest with all of you, I have no plan to give it up. But the inhumane treatment of humans has reached unacceptable levels. It's extending to vampires and half-breeds now, too. Matthais wants to exterminate anyone who dares to challenge his authority in all matters. If we don't do something about it now, it'll be too late."

"I wasn't aware there were acceptable levels of inhumane treatment," Aden said.

"You sound like your father," Banjora said, and Aden sneered at him. Not because he resented the sentiment, but just because he could.

"Are you confident you can unite all your armies?" Aden asked as his eyes swept over the four of them.

"That's your job," Banjora replied. "But yes. Our generals will follow our instructions and yours."

"Are you sure you can trust them?"

"Yes," Rashidi said, answering for all of them.

"Good. Then we're done here." Aden stood, ready to get the fuck out of there.

"Wait," Rashidi said as he held up his hand. "How confident are you in Aurick's overall plan? He's a consummate military strategist, but it's been a long time since we've been in a veritable war. You're more familiar with the complexities of war games these days."

"It's solid. I have a few adjustments to propose, and meticulous planning will be essential, but I'd like to confer with each of your generals before I make any recommendations."

"Then we must bring them in now," Indira said as she stood.

Aden walked to the door and then turned. "This is going to take considerable time to organize and execute. We need to get started. I want to meet with them while I'm here."

"My general didn't travel with me," Rashidi said.

"Why the fuck not?" Aden snarled. "Do you think I'm fucking around with this, Rashidi? Get him here."

"You can be a real shit, Aden," he said, standing. "You forget who you're talking to sometimes."

Aden shrugged with a smirk. He didn't give a fuck if they didn't like how he spoke.

"You need to remember, Aden, challenging Matthais, and by default, Yuri and Dietrich, won't be a bloodless fight," Banjora said as he walked around the table. "There will be collateral damage. We're all taking an incredible risk planning this. If word gets out before we act, he'll strike preemptively. And he has the means to do it."

"I'm aware of his capabilities. I'm also aware of ours. Now get your generals here. I want to meet them tomorrow night."

Ellie

"**W**hat if you could create a microenvironment that mimicked the human body?"

Ellie looked away from the vampire cell mitosis hologram she was studying to glance at Hannah.

"Keep going," Hannah encouraged her as she turned her attention to Ellie.

"You need a womb environment that mimics the human womb—"

"Yes, but we don't want an artificial womb in a lab. The goal isn't to grow the baby outside the body. We want female vampires to be able to carry their own children."

"That's not what I'm suggesting," Ellie said as she stood and walked to a different hologram hovering over the table. A few quick commands brought up a model of the female reproductive system. A muted blue glow illuminated the expanding uterus as a simulated bloodstream pulsed through its intricate network of vessels. "What if you could implant a device in the uterine wall, similar to the implant half-breeds get to deliver AEON, that would allow you to maintain optimal conditions for fetal development?"

She traced the uterine lining with her finger. The hologram responded to her touch, highlighting the areas she outlined.

"One that could mimic human body temperature and circulation patterns, therefore protecting the fetus from the vampire mother's inhospitable physiology."

The room was deadly quiet. Ellie held her breath, wondering if what she suggested was just plain crazy, until Hannah pushed away from the counter, calling up Keeley on a hologram. Her fingers flew across multiple holographic interfaces, pulling up comparative genetic sequences and molecular modeling simulations.

"Get your ass in my lab now."

Keeley appeared in the corner via warp port a few seconds later.

"What's the matter?"

She glanced from Hannah's frantic activity to Ellie's uncertain expression. Ellie could only shrug as they both watched Hannah swipe through several more screens.

"Fuck! Keeley, look at this. She's on to something."

Keeley walked over, and the two women studied the simulations, swiping back and forth between several screens. Ellie sat there, nervously shaking her leg, unsure if her suggestion made any sense. But it appeared they thought her reasoning was logical.

"It's not just a drug, per se," Hannah said almost to herself. "It needs a delivery system that contains sensors that could detect any signs of rejection or incompatibility, automatically adjusting the temperature, hormone, and nutrient levels as needed."

Keeley and Hannah were quiet again while they pulled up a new molecular modeling simulation. It began running complex predictions of fetal development in different environments.

"A device that would adapt its output as the pregnancy progressed," Hannah continued as she paced, a manic look on her face. "Allowing the developing fetus to acclimate to the mother's biological profile."

"Holy shit," Keeley said. "Ellie came up with this?"

Hannah nodded. "Why the fuck didn't we think of this before? We've been so focused on modifying maternal physiology that we never considered creating a selective microenvironment. Have our heads been up our asses all this time?"

Keeley rushed toward Ellie, hugging her. "You figured it out. You really figured it out!"

"I did?" Ellie asked, her voice laced with uncertainty.

"Yes, you're freaking brilliant!"

Tears glistened in Keeley's bright blue-green eyes. She'd desperately longed for a child, and Ellie hoped her suggestion would actually work.

"We have to tell her about ICHOR, Hannah. Maybe she'll see something we've overlooked."

"What's ICHOR?"

Hannah swiped the holograms closed and turned with a conspiratorial grin.

"Oh, Ellie. You're going to love it."

Now in Keeley's private lab, Ellie stared at the three-dimensional holographic image of a blood cell, absently chewing on her bottom lip. Molecular structures and blood analysis data scrolled on separate holograms on either side, displaying everything from hemoglobin levels to white cell counts.

Perched on the stool beside her, Keeley explained the difference between real and synthetic blood.

"Human blood acts like a delivery service," she said, manipulating the hologram to highlight the different components. "Its functions include oxygen and nutrient distribution, infection control, and wound repair. That's why only human blood can sustain and heal a vampire. Our goal with ICHOR is to create an artificial equivalent that can handle the same functions."

"That's really possible?"

"Theoretically, yes. Synthetic blood was developed over six hundred years ago and was used as an emergency substitute for real blood when supplies were low. Those early versions could transport oxygen but lacked the complex immune factors and growth promoters found in natural blood. So, it could never fully replace human blood." Keeley manipulated the projection, zooming in on one molecular structure. "Vampires' need for blood isn't just hunger. It's a genuine biological necessity. We extract iron and proteins from hemoglobin. These components are vital for both cellular maintenance and satiating appetite."

"Okay. So blood delivers nutrients, but how does it help with healing?" Ellie asked, tracing the outline of a cell with her finger in the air.

"Our bodies have a remarkable ability to repurpose stem cells. Though present in human blood to aid healing, vampires' biology supercharges the process. We extract and reprogram them with amazing efficiency. Here, come look at this."

Keeley walked over to a counter lined with microscopes. She gestured for Ellie to grab a pair of magnifiers and look through the lens.

"That's Hannah's blood. The mitosis occurring is her tissue actively processing human blood. Vampire cells deconstruct the blood they consume into its base components—proteins, minerals, and stem cells—before perfectly reconstructing them. The iron in hemoglobin is crucial because it accelerates our healing process by up to five hundred times that of humans."

"That's incredible," Ellie said as she met Keeley's gaze.

"You want to know the most fascinating part? It's how our bodies store the energy from blood. Instead of using the glucose and proteins immediately, they're converted into a form of energy we still don't fully understand. This energy source fuels our strength, speed, healing, et cetera. It's why we can move faster than human eyes can track, yet we don't burn calories the same way."

"So why can't you replicate that?" Ellie asked, gesturing at the sophisticated laboratory equipment surrounding them. "With everything you can do, why can't you do that?"

"We can. Mostly," Keeley said, bringing up another hologram that showed a DNA double helix with highlighted sections and several gaps. "But there's a component missing we haven't been able to identify. Without it, we can't complete the genome."

"But if you can complete that sequence, ICHOR will—"

"Provide an alternative to human blood for vampires' sustenance," Keeley finished for her.

"Oh, shit," Ellie blew out a long breath, and Keeley laughed.

"You're starting to talk like me. At least you don't say fuck."

"Aden says it enough for all of us."

"So, what do you think? Want to help us try to find the missing piece?"

Ellie's face lit up. "Yes! Oh, my God, yes!"

"Good. I just know you'll see something we don't. Sometimes it takes someone who isn't set in traditional vampire biology thinking to spot what we're missing."

"Can I look at Hannah's blood again?" She asked, unable to contain her excitement. "I want to watch the cellular reconstruction process more closely."

Keeley gave a nod. "Have at it. Hannah should be back any minute, and then we can walk you through what we've tried so far."

Ellie

"**H**ey, Ellie Bellie."

Ellie growled as Kane's face appeared in the hologram Drake initiated for her. He snickered from his spot on the sofa where they'd been playing chess. She glared at him, but it just made him laugh harder.

Carrie accompanied Sophie to Bíonn súil le muir, where Aden's mother had been spending a lot of time since Christmas. With her friend away and Aden occupied, Drake was teaching her how to play chess. But she had yet to win a match, so she was already mad at him, and his snickering at Kane, calling her by her nickname, didn't help.

"Kane, I swear to god I'm going to rip your head off one of these days."

"I'd like to see you try that, Ellie Bellie."

"Where are you?"

"Training field watching your boy fighting with Roderick. Why?"

"Just curious. Do you know how long you'll be?"

"Probably a while, based on what I'm seeing."

"What are you seeing?"

"Lots of blood. Hey now, that's outside house rules. Gotta go, Ellie."

As he swiped the hologram closed, the last thing she heard him say was, "If you rip his arm off, boss, as you know, it'll be a bitch to reattach."

She shot Drake a worried glance, memories of Aden's severed hand causing her stomach to churn. "How quickly can we get there?"

He rose from the sofa. "That's the beauty of warp ports. I have to say, though, I definitely don't miss Aden kicking my ass in sparring practice."

Grabbing her coat, Ellie followed Drake out the door. After a warp port to the foyer, then to the exit gate, they loaded into an SUV. He drove like a madman, but he got them to the training field in less than ten minutes.

In the distance, Ellie counted six men fighting.

"I thought Kane said he was fighting Roderick."

"Aden doesn't ever just spar with only one person. It's always a minimum of five or six."

"He can fight them all off?"

"How do you think he single-handedly fought over a dozen rogues by himself?"

Ellie's perception of Aden's strength and skill after his fight with Vincent was incorrect. She knew he was fierce and strong, but seeing him in action was not only eye-opening but also a disturbing and breathtaking sight. He moved with a furious energy, a blur of motion and intensity, his every movement sharp and precise.

Drake stopped the SUV and lowered the tires. With a deep breath, Ellie stepped out.

"Drake, what the hell?" Kane asked as he strode over. "He's not going to want you to see this, Ellie."

Before she could answer, Aden's head snapped in her direction. Blood dripped from his mouth, nose, and ear, and an image of him unconscious and bleeding in Kane's arms flashed in front of her eyes.

His face and chest were a mass of bruises and cuts, his eyes blazing crimson. Although she no longer feared him and his red eyes, she still took a step back. She blinked, and he was in front of her, his body rigid and still in fight mode, but his eyes were now blue and flickered with worry.

"What are you doing here? Are you alright?"

Despite the gruesome condition of his face and body, she nodded and smiled up at him, though her gaze didn't quite meet his.

"I missed you."

His expression softened at her simple statement. He tugged her into his arms, the unexpectedness of it making her gasp. His grip was unusually tight, a sign of his continued tension.

"We're done," he called to his sparring partners, who dispersed quickly. "Why didn't you call me? I would have come back."

"I know. But I wanted to come to you."

She didn't admit she rushed to see him out of worry over his fighting. Though healed, she remained anxious about the hand he severed a few months ago. Kane's statement panicked her, and she overreacted, but Drake better keep his damn mouth shut about it.

"Go the fuck away," Aden barked at their guards, the only two remaining with them. "Leave me one car."

They both nodded, but Ellie doubted they'd go far. They wouldn't leave them out here alone, despite Aden's command. Not after what happened last time.

She gave him a quick once-over, her eyes lingering on the injuries that were already healing. Working at BloodStone provided her insight into the nuances of vampire physiology. She was grateful for the new knowledge of how his body worked and healed itself so efficiently.

"Why didn't you come find me before you came out here?" she asked.

"You were with Carrie."

"She left with Sophie tonight to go to Bíonn súil le muir. I was playing chess with Drake while I waited for you to come home. When you took too long, I came after you."

"Fuck! I should have checked with you first."

She inched closer to him, her anxiety already fading as he rubbed her arms. "Yes, you should have."

He'd just returned from his trip away that evening. He'd been gone for over a week, but they'd only been able to say hello before she'd had to leave for BloodStone and he had to debrief with his father.

"I missed you when you were away. It aches when I'm not with you," Ellie said.

"It fucking does." The truth in his words was reflected in the sapphire blue of his eyes. "Fuck! I got blood all over your coat." He released her, then gathered handfuls of snow, rubbing it against his exposed skin.

"Here you go, boss," Kane yelled from a few feet away. Aden caught his torn shirt in midair.

"I said go away, Kane." Aden wiped the blood from his face and chest. "There, not so scary anymore."

His questioning gaze met hers, eliciting a genuine smile as she looked up at him.

"You clean up quick. Aren't you cold?"

"Nope. Come on, let's get out of here." He lifted her, and she wrapped her legs around his waist.

"Where are you taking me?"

"Out of the sight and earshot of our annoying shadows. I can't fuck you with them here."

She laughed. "It's too cold out here for me to get naked."

"I'm not getting you naked."

"But you just said—" She started but decided she didn't care. She tightened her arms and buried her face in his neck.

"I'm the only person on the planet who will ever see you naked again."

"I can't even look at myself naked?" She teased as she nuzzled him.

"Don't be a wise-ass." He pinched her ass, and she let out a soft moan.

"Well, now I'm intrigued by how you intend to do this without stripping me."

"Just wait and watch."

He strode deeper into the trees. It was slightly less cold underneath the thick canopy as Aden walked to the center, where the overhead branches opened up and the moon shone down.

He lowered her to her feet before using his hands to scrape the bark from a tree, leaving just the smooth, bare wood behind.

"Don't want you to get splinters."

Tilting her head, she looked up at him. "What exactly are you planning?"

"I'm going to fuck you against this tree."

"I'll still need to get partially naked for that. I'm not wearing a skirt."

"I know. We have to talk about you wearing them more often."

"Don't hold your breath. I hate skirts and dresses. And I make it easy enough for you now. You don't need any additional advantages. So, how are we going to do this?"

"You're not going to do anything except feel. I'm doing all the work."

He kneeled and tugged her closer by her jacket. With breathtaking speed, he had her jeans unzipped and pulled to her ankles. A shiver ran through her as the cold air hit her warm skin.

He pushed her against the tree, lifting her by her calves. He ducked under and reappeared in the space between her and her jean-trapped feet. His mouth assaulted her, and she reached down, raking her finger through his hair. With rapid strokes of his tongue, he lashed at her, setting her body on fire.

A sultry smile curved her lips as she gazed down at him. His dark, intense eyes, filled with want, burned into hers as he groaned, his breath hot and ragged against her wet flesh. Giving her one last long lick, he stood up. With her legs around him, her feet still stuck in her jeans and boots, she looked down to see that he'd shoved pants down his thighs.

Damn, the man was talented.

She arched her back as he lined their bodies up, gasping out a delighted laugh. "That was a pretty neat trick."

"Thank you," he grinned. "This has to be quick because your body temperature is dropping. Just hang on."

He covered her lips, kissing her, swallowing her gasp as he pushed into her in one long stroke. The burning stretch she always experienced with his first thrust inside her took her breath away. But she had no time to dwell on it as his hands gripped her ass, pinning her against the tree. The cold was a distant memory as his powerful strides set her insides ablaze. All she felt was the rising heat between them, the pleasure building in her core pulsing with a rhythm that mirrored her racing heartbeat.

Breaking their kiss, he whispered in her ear. "You feel so fucking good."

Their frantic motions sent her body sliding along the tree trunk, and she was grateful for her coat. Despite his hand on her lower back, keeping her from touching the tree, she still worried briefly about splinters. But when he hit that particular spot deep inside her, it wiped her mind clean and made her eyes cross.

"God, so do you," she groaned.

"I'm going to bite you, but I won't drink. Just push my venom into you. It'll heat you up a little."

"Yes!" She tugged the collar of her coat down, turning her face and offering him her throat.

"Goddess," he murmured as he sunk his fangs into her.

Her body froze, seizing up as her orgasm slammed into her. Though paralyzed, the pleasure coursed through her, unabated, tearing through her in waves that made it impossible to breathe. She'd never get used to the feeling of his venom in her veins. It was like dying and being reborn simultaneously.

When she could move and speak again, she screamed his name, her body wracked with violent convulsions. Kane and Drake definitely heard her. She wouldn't be surprised if they heard her back in the city.

But in that moment, only the man in her arms mattered.

He pulled out of her neck and roared her name as she felt him surge into her once more—one hard thrust that she knew would leave a bruise on her back as her body slammed into the tree behind her. His knees gave out, and they sunk to the ground, but he slid his hands underneath her ass to keep her from hitting the snow as he held her above him.

"Kiss me," she begged, her breath hitching in her throat as his lips found hers again, their mingled breaths warm and urgent against each other, the faint metallic taste of her blood lingering on his tongue.

He pushed to his feet and lifted her off him. In a flash, he'd removed himself from between her legs and had both their jeans slid up and buttoned, shielding them from the cold.

"Wow!"

Her legs shook, and he grinned, his strong hands steadying her as she swayed.

"Told you it would be quick. Come on."

He grabbed her hand and tugged her forward, leading her out of the trees as she stumbled beside him.

"Give a girl a second to recover, will you?"

He scooped her up into his arms again, and she snuggled happily against his chest.

"You'll have time in the car. You'll catch a chill if we don't get you heated up."

"I'm fine." She replied, shivering.

"You will be once we get back and into a hot bath."

She nuzzled his neck, gently nipping at his chin. "Ohhh, I like the sound of that."

"Good. Because I don't plan to let you out of that tub for the rest of the night."

"My skin will get unattractively wrinkly."

He tightened his arms around her as he laughed. "Like that's even possible."

As they emerged from the trees, Ellie caught sight of Kane and Drake still standing guard, though they'd moved further away. Lifting her gaze, she met Aden's, his intense blue eyes soft with tenderness.

"I love you."

Her words were soft and simple, but she hoped he knew they came from the depths of her soul.

He tucked a stray strand of her tangled hair behind her ear. "You're my life," he murmured against her lips as he kissed her.

And she knew he did.

"Ellie, we need to talk about something."

She looked up to see Aden standing in the library doorway. She hadn't been back in here for months, usually reading in her own little library now. But she loved this room, with the fireplace, the chair beside the window, and the dim cave-like feel that just wrapped around her whenever she entered. It held a special place in her heart, with so many memories of this life and the last, and despite how much she loved the smaller one he built for her, she was always drawn back here.

Curled up on Ellie's lap, Vlad was fast asleep, purring.

"I didn't know you were back from training."

"I left it to Roderick."

He came closer, prompting Ellie to shift the cat to the cushion next to her before standing and setting down her tablet. He didn't lean down to kiss her, which was odd, because that was usually the first thing he did when he saw her.

"What do we need to talk about?"

He rubbed his hand across the back of his neck. "It's about Carrie."

"Okay. What about her?"

"Come here, sit down with me." Aden took her hand and tugged her to the sofa.

He ran his hand through his hair like he was nervous, and that wasn't like him. She reached out and replaced his fingers with hers, scratching her nails above his right ear. A low growl reverberated from deep in his chest as his eyes slipped closed.

"Hey, what's this about?"

"You know what Vincent did to her."

Ellie's throat tightened, and she let her hand fall to her lap.

"Yes."

"Well, his scent is incredibly strong on her."

"Okay. But won't that fade the more time that passes?"

"A little, but it will never fully vanish. All vampires and half-breeds will smell him on her."

"Okay," she repeated, urging him to continue, though she suspected where this was going.

"Now that she's my thrall, I should replace it with mine. For her protection."

He cringed, the tension in his body mirroring her own.

"So, you need to bite her?"

"Yes, so my venom can override his in her system."

"Would it also replace his scent in her scars?"

Aden shook his head. "She has too many bite scars, Ellie. I can't—no, I won't—bite over all of them. I don't want to bite her at all."

"Is there any way your venom could be injected into her instead?"

"Yes, but that will be more painful than a bite."

Leaning back on the sofa, Ellie bit her lip. He had to do this to protect Carrie. But the thought of him biting her best friend made her stomach churn. A wave of jealousy washed over her as she imagined Carrie experiencing the pleasure of Aden's venom coursing through her veins. It shouldn't have made her jealous, but it did, and she felt both angry and guilty for those feelings. It made her even more determined to help Keeley and Hannah find the missing piece of ICHOR, so Aden would never have to bite anyone but her again.

He reached for her hand, lacing their fingers together. "Talk to me, Ellie. I don't want to bite her, but what do you want me to do?"

Seeing Aden's struggle on his face, her heart ached with love for him. Her brutal vampire, feared by humans, half-breeds, and vampires alike. Her ferocious vampire, who killed the vicious monster who hurt her friend. Her complex vampire, who could snarl at her while telling her he loves her. And her tender, gentle vampire, the man who loved her so fiercely, it left her breathless.

He was struggling to do right by her friend because he worried it would upset her. But he was looking for her guidance because he'd do whatever she asked of him. Instead of answering him with words, Ellie pulled his lips to hers and kissed him, her tongue dancing with his before swiping it over the tip of his fang, offering her blood to him.

He groaned into her mouth, enveloping her in his arms as he leaned her back against the sofa. His relief was palpable, and she swallowed it, absorbing it into her, as her own filled her.

In that moment, Ellie realized she wasn't jealous of Aden biting Carrie. The very idea of being jealous of anyone was ludicrous, not when this man's heart and soul belonged to her. A feeling of lightness washed over her, and she couldn't help but laugh, the sound delicate and ethereal as it escaped her lips.

He pulled his head back, opening his eyes, grinning down at her, most of his tension now gone.

"What the fuck was that?"

"That was me telling you yes, you need to bite her, Aden."

He sat back, pulling her with him. She straddled his lap, her hips moving in a slow, deliberate circle, grinding against him until he groaned in response.

"Stop being a fucking tease."

"Who said I'm teasing?"

She brushed her lips over his, but hesitation lingered in his eyes and he drew back.

"It won't bother you that my scent is on her?"

"No." Then she was hit with another realization—of why he was asking. Another light laugh escaped her. "Wait a minute? Do you think I'll be jealous? Or are you afraid I won't be?"

His face twisted into a confused frown. "But you don't like it when I feed from my thralls. So, how can you be okay with me biting Carrie?"

Her fingers threaded through his hair as her hands slid into it.

"Aden, you won't be feeding from her. Just claiming her. Carrie is a sister to me, even though we don't share blood. If she has to have any vampire's scent on her, I want it to be yours because I know she'll be safe. No one will dare touch her if she's yours."

His head fell back against the sofa cushion, a sigh escaping his lips.

"Ellie, I have to push a lot of venom into her to override Vincent's scent. She's terrified, suffering from PTSD, and might freak out when the paralysis wears off."

"I'll be there. I'll keep her calm."

Raising his head, he looked at her. "Are you sure about this? It can't be taken back once it's done."

"Sweetheart," she whispered as she tilted her face down to his. "We're going to find Carrie. Then you're going to bite her. You're going to pump your venom into her, and she's going to be safe and under your protection for as long as she lives."

He gave a slow nod, his silence heavy with unspoken doubt, even as he agreed with her. He moved to stand, but she stopped him, resting her forearms on his shoulders. She leaned her face closer to his and trapped him in her gaze.

"Then when you're done. She'll go back to her room, and you'll take me to our bed and pump more than just your venom into me."

She watched his eyes darken as her words hit him hard. Without a word, he lifted her from his lap and stood before taking her hand and leading her out of the library.

Ellie pulled Aden into Sophie's office, where she found Carrie sitting on the sofa chatting with his mother. Sophie had a knack for making people comfortable, but Ellie picked up on Carrie's subtle nervousness, evident in the tremor of her hands. In time, she'd learn that Aden's mother's kindness was sincere and unconditional.

"Hi, you two," Sophie said as they entered.

"Hi, sorry to interrupt, but is it alright if we borrow Carrie for a while?" Ellie asked, smiling.

Sophie stood. "Sure. We were done for tonight. You can use my office. I'm going to find your father," she said to Aden with a questioning look. Ellie understood from his subtle nod that she knew what was going to happen.

"I'll see you tomorrow, Carrie."

"Yes, Mistress Sophie."

After Sophie left, Ellie sat next to Carrie and took her hand. Aden sat in the chair his mother vacated, allowing Ellie a moment to fill Carrie in.

"Is everything okay?" Carrie asked. "Did I do something?"

Ellie squeezed her hand. "No. You trust me, don't you?"

Carrie nodded.

"You know I'd never do anything to hurt you."

Carrie's gaze slid to Aden before returning to Ellie. She nodded again.

"And you know what Vincent did to you left his scent on you."

Carrie winced, a pained look twisting her features at the sound of his name.

"I'll always smell like him."

"Yes. But Aden can take most of that away."

"Nothing will take away what he did to me."

"No, it won't. But carrying his scent isn't safe for you. Now that Aden owns you, you need to have his scent on you for your protection."

Ellie cringed at those words. Despite it being the truth, no one should own another human being.

Carrie squeezed her eyes shut, processing Ellie's words. That was what she did when she needed to think something through.

"What does he need to do?" Carrie asked when they opened. A steely resignation, unlike her usual gentle gaze, settled in her eyes.

Ellie flicked her eyes to Aden, telling him silently he was up. He leaned forward in the chair.

"Carrie, look at me."

She looked toward Aden, avoiding his eyes.

"Look at me," he repeated, and Ellie squeezed her hand.

"It's okay to look at him."

With a deep breath, Carrie lifted her eyes, meeting his.

"I have to bite you. My venom will flood your bloodstream, and it will replace Vincent's scent. There will always be a very subtle lingering trace of his scent beneath, but mine will overpower it. And every vampire will know that you are mine."

Swallowing hard, she asked Ellie, "Are you okay with this?"

Ellie knew what her friend was asking because even though Vincent brutalized her, the pleasurable effect of his venom would still have flooded her system even as he was hurting her. She couldn't imagine the conflicting emotions Carrie must have felt as she endured both agony and ecstasy at Vincent's hands.

Ellie wished Aden could kill him again.

"Yes," she said. "His scent will protect you, and that's all that matters to me."

Carrie nodded. "I don't have a choice, anyway."

"Yes, you do." Carrie looked at her, confused. "If you really don't want him to do this, he won't. But I'm asking you to let him. It won't hurt like it did. He'll be gentle. He'll bite one of the scars on your neck. After you feel his fangs sink in, there will be no more pain. And I'll be right here."

"Okay." Carrie's voice shook.

Ellie looked at Aden. He looked into her eyes, a silent message passing between them.

This was all for her.

Carrie shifted to drop to the floor.

"No," Aden said as he moved to sit on the coffee table in front of the sofa. "Stay on the couch."

She obeyed him, her hand trembling in Ellie's. With her other hand, Ellie reached up and brushed Carrie's long blonde hair over her shoulder, baring her throat to Aden.

"He doesn't like to be touched, so don't move, okay?"

Carrie's eyes flashed with confusion and questions, but she nodded.

Aden leaned forward and bit Carrie's neck, right over Vincent's largest scar. Frozen, Carrie stared into Ellie's eyes, her teeth clenched tight. Hot tears streamed down her face, each one a burning testament to her pain, her eyes pleading with Ellie for the impossible—oblivion. Ellie reached up and brushed them away, offering the only comfort she could.

With a sudden jerk, Carrie's body regained movement, but she remained in place, shaking, while Aden pumped his venom into her bloodstream.

Ellie's gaze found Aden's. His eyes blazed with a love so intense, so full of adoration, it took her breath away.

As she watched him make Carrie his, Ellie made a mental note to call Mina to have a transfusion IV delivered to their room.

She was going to need it.

Aden

Aden stood motionless on the eastern ridge, overlooking the training field, which lay nestled in a valley, surrounded by a dense forest of towering white pine trees. Their snow-covered branches created a natural barrier, obscuring the area from any prying eyes, whether from the ground or the air. Jagged mountain peaks to the north cut into the dark sky, their icy surfaces gleaming under the pale moonlight illuminating the field below.

From his vantage point, he had an unobstructed view of the massive training ground, a nearly four-square-mile stretch of cleared terrain, chosen for its remote location and natural defenses. Located one hundred fifty miles into the northern wilderness, the training site was ten times larger than the one outside the city and allowed the troops to train without scrutiny.

Aden tracked the movements of the over sixty thousand soldiers gathered from his own forces and those of Rashidi, Banjora, Katsumi, and Indira. Beside him, Kane remained as still and quiet as the late spring snow falling on them. It snowed almost constantly at this elevation in this part of the region.

When Matthais' face appeared in a hologram next to him, Aden pivoted, taking several large steps backward. He positioned himself so only he and the snow-covered trees at the ridgeline were visible within the hologram's limited field of view, then answered the call. The stakes were too high for even a glimpse of the training below to reach Matthais' eyes.

"Aden," he said, his voice devoid of emotion as always.

Fuck! What did he want now?

"Matthais, I'm a bit busy at the moment."

"As always. I won't keep you then," he said, the condescending smile a mask barely concealing the contempt in his eyes. He clearly still resented Aden for challenging Vincent. "But I need you to meet Andrei in Erebu tomorrow night."

Aden shot a quick glance at Kane, noting the subtle twitch of his jaw, a giveaway that he was listening, despite his eyes remaining fixed on the field.

"Why?"

"Dietrich's western villages are in open revolt. He and Gregor have requested our assistance."

"Isn't that on Yuri's border? Can't he send Anatoly to assist?"

"I would like you and Andrei to take the point. Is that a problem? Are you too busy to do your job?"

Aden crossed his arms, feeling the leather of his jacket pull tight, much like his fraying patience. "I'm always busy."

Matthais' eyes narrowed at Aden's flippant response.

"I hope I don't need to remind you of your debt."

"What debt?" Aden snarled.

"The one you racked up when you challenged Vincent."

Was he fucking serious?

"Matthais," Aden said with a sharp edge to his voice. "Allowing my challenge to Vincent was not a favor. I invoked the right every vampire possesses. You merely let me use the arena at a time it was unoccupied. To suggest I owe you a debt for that is a stretch, at best. I already repaid the debt for Ellie, so we're square, but if Dietrich, Gregor, and Andrei need my assistance, of course, I'll be there."

"Hmm..." Matthais steered the conversation in a new direction, pointedly avoiding Aden's comment. "How is your new thrall, by the way? I hope she's been worth all the trouble she caused."

"She wasn't the problem."

"Well, I'm sure you made Elliana very happy by acquiring her friend. Ensuring your pets' happiness never seemed to be a priority of yours until now."

Matthais was never one for subtlety, but Aden ignored his pointed jab about Ellie.

"Where am I meeting Andrei?" he asked. "Should I bring any of my own troops?"

"No need. Andrei will take all he needs from here. Meet him in Capamar tomorrow night."

"I'll be there." Aden shut the hologram with a swipe and rejoined Kane.

"What was that about?" Kane asked, without taking his eyes off the field.

"Don't act like you didn't hear it."

"It's funny, and I don't mean in the 'ha ha' kind of way, that there are more insurgencies in the last year than the past one hundred," Kane said. "It's almost as if it's deliberate."

Aden's sharp look at Kane was his only response, letting his silence convey his unspoken thoughts.

They were both thinking the same thing.

Aden saw the fire in the distance as the SUV approached Capamar, its orange glow painting the black horizon. This was no ordinary fire. It was an inferno, its flames licking into the air, reaching for the sky in a terrifying spectacle of heat and light against the moonless night.

"What the fuck?!"

Kane met his shocked gaze from the seat beside him.

The stone walls surrounding the village were in ruins, riddled with gaps and piles of rubble. Dead soldiers and civilians lay piled on the ground on both sides of the gate. As the vehicle passed through, an even more horrifying sight came into view.

Gallows lined the main road into the village. From each one hung a blackened, burning corpse, swaying in the breeze, the smell of smoke and charred flesh heavy in the air. Not even the closed windows could block out the acrid smell.

"Stop the fucking car," Aden snarled, and his driver slammed on the brakes.

He surged out the door, calling Andrei's name. Kane followed close on his heels. The wall of heat from the hundreds of fires hit Aden, a suffocating humid wave, thick and oppressive.

"What the actual fuck is this?" Aden's bellow echoed into the dark night, his eyes darting around in search of Andrei.

Flanked by soldiers, he emerged from behind a burning pyre in the village square, where more bodies lay piled high.

"You're late," Andrei said with a hint of annoyance. "I expected you hours ago."

Aden strode up to him, eyes blazing hotter than the flames surrounding them. "What the fuck are you doing?"

"Exactly what my Chancellor instructed me to do," Andrei replied as if it was obvious. "I'm quelling a rebellion and restoring order."

"You call this restoring order? This is a fucking massacre."

"If you'd been here earlier, you would've seen a much different picture."

"Yeah. One that wasn't a fucking firestorm."

Aden spun around, taking in more of the village now. More bodies, their throats savagely torn and limbs grotesquely twisted, were scattered across the dirt streets. Doors hung from broken hinges, windows shattered, signs of desperate attempts to flee. Andrei and his soldiers had been thorough in their brutality.

"We gave them every opportunity to give up, lay down their arms, which, by the way, included Helios."

Surprised by Andrei's words, Aden turned back to him. "Where the fuck did they get guns that fire UV light-infused bullets?"

First armor? Now Helios? What the fuck was going on?

"The rogues they partnered with," Andrei replied. "I offered them the chance to surrender, but they refused. This is the price for their defiance."

"I thought Anatoly went off the rails." The overwhelming stench of death made Aden's stomach churn, and he fought back a gag. "Andrei, what the fuck were you thinking? There is no way this was proportionate to the crime."

Andrei sighed. "Aden, take it up with Matthais. I followed my orders."

With his boot, Aden nudged the nearest corpse on a shallow pile of bodies lying by the street.

"He told you to torture and burn this village? I thought there were twelve villages rebelling."

"There were. Between my and Gregor's troops, we hit them all simultaneously."

Aden's gaze swept over the village square, once more taking in the gruesome scene.

Soldiers pushed wheelbarrows full of corpses toward the funeral pyre. Out of the corner of his eye, he glimpsed Kane's furious expression, his body rigid with rage.

"Did you even try to get them to surrender? Or did you just kill and torch them?

Eyes blazing with fury, Andrei advanced on Aden, getting right up in his face. "Don't you fucking dare question my methods. I ordered them to surrender, and they refused. If you wanted a different outcome, you should have gotten here on time."

Unflinching, Aden stood his ground. Andrei didn't fucking scare him.

"I was never informed this was a possible outcome. You should have told me you were planning this. I've talked to you three times since Matthais called me yesterday."

"I don't run my plans by you, Aden. I think you're forgetting I outrank you."

Aden raised his hand, ready to grab Andrei by the throat and tell him just what he thought of his rank, when Kane's voice, dark and low, came from beside him.

"Aden."

Kane pointed toward the northern horizon.

Far off, at least several miles away, another inferno raged in the distance. Then another popped up just to the east of it.

Then another. And another.

Until the distant roar of flames surrounded them, making Aden feel like he was engulfed in a ring of fire.

"Those should be the last villages now," Andrei said before directing the soldiers flanking him to help with the bodies.

Aden looked at the vampire he'd considered a friend for centuries as if he was seeing him for the first time. Had he always been this callous about human life? He was brutal—so was Aden—but had he always been this vicious?

Andrei had been with Matthais since the Great Vampire Wars. Matthais was his sire, and Andrei was loyal to him. But Aden had never seen him, in all the times they worked together, obey such reprehensible orders.

"Why did you bring me here?"

Andrei shrugged. "Matthais insisted."

"You obviously don't need my help. I'm leaving," Aden said with another snarl, stalking away, unable to look at Andrei any longer. Kane followed, falling into step beside him.

"What are we going to do?" Kane asked under his breath, his eyes flashing with as much horrified anger as Aden felt coursing through his body.

"What are we supposed to do? It's already done. Fuck! I have to call Aurick."

As they neared the SUV, Aden heard a low gurgle, ominous and unsettling. His head snapped toward the sound, his sharp senses pinpointing its source.

He strode over to a pile of rubble, the remnants of what must have been a house, dust and debris crunching under his boots. Crouching, he flipped several planks of splintered wood, uncovering a small girl clinging to life. A trickle of blood ran from the corner of her mouth, her eyes wide with fear and pain.

The sight hit him hard, stealing his breath.

Five years old at most, she had brown hair and eyes the color of dark chocolate. As she looked up at him with pleading, desperate eyes, he heard the frantic, wet rhythm of her hemorrhaging, her attempts to speak producing only ragged breaths.

Dual images flashed in his mind—his mother the night of her attack when she was eight, her face pale with the terror of imminent death. And Ellie, as she must have looked at that age, with a similar expression of fear as Matthais dragged her away.

He lifted the girl's broken body from the ground, her soft cry barely audible as he shoved her at Kane.

"Put her in the fucking car."

Kane took her, her small body swallowed by his massive arms, his face a mask of shock.

"Aden, she'll be dead in minutes. We should help her along. It's the humane thing to do."

"No," Aden snarled as they reached the SUV. He yanked open the door and gestured for Kane to place her on the seat. "She's not dying tonight."

The moment their eyes met, Kane knew his intentions.

"Aden, it's treason."

"I don't give a fuck. You sit in the front with Brady."

Though Kane nodded in agreement, his eyes betrayed his doubts about Aden's sanity.

Aden slid across the back seat as he climbed in. "Brady, get us to the fucking plane fast."

"Yes, Sir," he replied as the SUV sped away.

The girl's eyes fluttered, and her breaths grew shallower.

"What's your name?" Aden asked her as he removed his jacket and draped it over her.

"Mila." Her voice, a faint tremor, grew weaker, her heart slowing with each second.

Bracing himself for what he was about to do, Aden closed his eyes and took a deep breath. He opened them again and looked down at her. Her dark hair and delicate features were so similar to Ellie's, and her innocent, trusting gaze sealed her fate.

He lifted her and laid her across his lap. The contact made him flinch, but he pushed aside the discomfort.

His fangs throbbed, and venom seeped from them as he stared down at her. The law was absolute. Creating half-breeds was strictly forbidden without

Matthais' approval. The penalty was death, but with Mila's life fading in his arms, none of that mattered to Aden.

Fuck Matthais and his laws.

"Am I going to die?" Mila asked, her eyes meeting his.

"Not tonight," he replied before he lowered his mouth to her neck, sinking his fangs into her jugular, saving and likely condemning her in the same moment.

Aden

Aden approached his and Ellie's suite. For the first time since she entered his life, he didn't want to see her. He didn't want to look into her beautiful, kind, loving eyes and tell her what he'd seen.

What he'd done.

She would cry, and he couldn't bear to see her cry.

He'd just left Aurick in his parents' suite. Sophie fled the room after learning about Mila, rushing to meet Mina in the infirmary. Andrei and his troops' brutality horrified his parents. Aden's actions with Mila shocked them almost as much, but neither one condemned him. Sophie had never hugged him so hard in his life. Aurick's eyes reflected his worry over Aden's decision, but he was more concerned about the massacre that Andrei and Gregor perpetrated at Matthais' instruction.

Aurick intended to confront him about it. Not that it would do any fucking good now. But it just reinforced their commitment to removing him as Chancellor as soon as possible. And Aden was looking forward to doing it with his bare fucking hands.

He paused outside the door. After several deep breaths, he entered, walking straight to the bar. Ellie wasn't in the living room, but he heard her soft voice talking to Vlad in their bedroom. It couldn't be normal how much she talked to an animal that couldn't talk back. Could it?

Aden gulped down two glasses of Jamison before she wandered out of the bedroom.

"Oh, Aden," she said, her delight at seeing him reflected in her voice. "I didn't hear you come in."

"You were talking to that mangy furball."

He still called the cat that, even though they made peace with each other. Ellie usually scoffed when he did it, and the way she scoffed amused him, so he did things often to get that reaction from her.

Aden turned to her, and whatever she saw on his face or in his posture made her frown. She could always read him so well.

Of course, the lingering smell and sight of soot and ash on his clothes and hair could have been the reason. Kane warned him to clean up before he saw Ellie, but for the first time in his life, Aden felt defeated.

"Aden, what happened to you?" Ellie stepped closer, her nose wrinkled and eyes worried. "What's that smell? Have you been near a fire?"

And that was all it took to push him over the edge.

"Ellie, I can't fucking do this right now." His voice was sharp and angry as he pushed past her.

He wanted her comfort. Needed it. He needed her warmth and goodness, the caress of her gentle touch, to soothe his troubled mind. But he feared he'd lose it if he had to tell the story again.

Her quiet footsteps followed him into the bathroom. Staring into his reflection in the mirror over the sink, Aden pressed his fingers against the cool marble, the pressure building until it cracked, the sharp sound breaking the silence. Fracturing bathroom counters had become a habit of his.

He felt her worried eyes on him, though she didn't speak. She let the silence he asked for hang heavy in the air as she walked to the shower and turned on the hot water.

Ellie slipped out of her pajamas and padded over to him. He watched her in the mirror, his eyes meeting hers the moment she touched his arm. Without a word, he faced her. She unbuttoned his shirt, pushing it off his shoulders, then moved on to his belt. His body obeyed all her silent commands as she undressed him.

With every inch of exposed skin and every gentle touch, Aden relaxed.

She stood naked before him, but he felt no desire. He longed for her hands on him, a yearning for simple intimacy that wasn't sexual. The ache for it was so deep inside him it buried any lust that would have been there.

When he was as naked as she was, Ellie took his hand in hers, leading him to the wet room and pulling him under the cascading water falling from the ceiling. Her honeysuckle-scented body wash lathered easily in her hands before she scrubbed the soot from his skin, the scent filling the small bathroom. Any other time, he'd refuse to let her use anything floral on him, but it matched her natural scent, and he wanted it all over him. He wanted her all over him. Urging him to lower his head, she washed his hair, the soothing touch of her hands eliciting a deep, rumbling growl from his chest.

Aden couldn't resist touching her. His hands clasped her hips, the warmth of her soft skin anchoring him. When she tried to step away, he tightened his grip, pulling her back to him.

"I'm just getting a towel," she whispered, her fingers brushing against his, and he reluctantly released her.

He stood there, water dripping onto the tile floor. Each drop echoed the hollowness in his chest, feeling lost and bereft without her. She returned, her gentle hands soothing his body and calming his racing mind as she dried him before drying herself.

She bypassed her pajamas on the floor, taking his hand and leading him into the bedroom. Shooing Vlad away from her pillow, she climbed into bed before reaching out to Aden, encouraging him to join her.

He crawled in after her, sinking into the softness of her body, the warmth of her skin against his own. He rested his head on her breasts as she wrapped her arms around him. With gentle strokes, she threaded her fingers through his hair, scratching above his ear, sending shivers of pleasure down his spine.

He clung to her, closing his eyes, finding in her everything he needed.

"I'm sorry I yelled at you," he murmured, his lips brushing over the raised, pale scar on her left breast, left by his fangs.

"Shh," she said, pressing a tender kiss to the top of his head. "Just sleep, sweetheart."

The gentle murmur of his favorite term of endearment brought him the first peace he felt since he drove into Capamar.

He pulled her naked body closer and let the steady rhythmic beat of her heart lull him to sleep.

Ellie

T he infirmary was quiet when Ellie walked in, except for Sophie's soft voice talking to the little girl in one of the beds.

The scene before her made Ellie pause. A large, brightly colored blanket swallowed the girl's small body, its bold patterns a stark contrast to the sterile white linens when she and Carrie were patients. She sat cross-legged, surrounded by a menagerie of stuffed animals. Vlad was curled up at the foot of the bed, sleeping, as Sophie sat beside her. Long, dark curls tumbled over her shoulders, and she looked far healthier than someone who had nearly died less than twenty-four hours ago. Mila's transformation into a half-breed, while traumatic, happened relatively quickly. According to Hannah, the time it took for a person to turn depended on the age at the time of the change. The younger they were, the shorter the time.

Ellie had been startled by Aden's condition when he arrived home last night. She'd never seen him so distraught, even with all they'd been through. She could still see his anguished face when she found him in the living room. Accustomed to his yelling and outbursts when he was angry or upset, his subdued, almost broken, state was far more heartbreaking.

And broken was the only way she could think of to describe him, wondering if that was how he'd been after killing Aly.

When he woke this evening, after making love to her, he told her what happened in Erebu. Ellie wanted to weep for those poor humans, but before she could give in to her grief, he told her something even more shocking. He discovered a five-year-old girl who was hemorrhaging, on the brink of death, and instead of letting her die, he saved her, turning her into a half-breed like Aurick did to Sophie when she was a child.

His actions surprised Ellie, especially considering the girl was near death. It might have been a mercy to let her die. But now, seeing her with her own eyes, Ellie knew why he did it. And like so many unexpected things her fierce vampire did, it made her fall in love with him all over again.

But she also feared for him because what he did was treason, punishable by death. If Matthais ever discovered Aden's actions, the consequences would be deadly, even though he was Aurick's son.

Ellie paused just inside the door, taking a deep breath. She didn't want to interrupt but was eager to meet the little girl.

"Oh, Ellie," Sophie said with a smile, waving her over. "I'm so glad you came. Come meet Mila."

Ellie approached the bed, her throat tight with emotion. This girl had almost died in Aden's arms as he carried her from the smoking ruins of her village. But he made the impossible choice—to save her life and turn her into a half-breed like his mother.

Mila looked up at her. Her chocolate brown eyes held a look of innocent trust. Looking at her, sitting beside Sophie, vibrant and alive, any doubts Ellie might have had about his decision melted away. How could saving this child's life ever be wrong?

"Hi Mila," Ellie said, standing next to the bed. "I'm Ellie. How are you?"

Mila looked at Sophie for guidance, and Aden's mother nodded with encouragement. The little girl tilted her head, considering the question with childlike seriousness. "I'm good. Mistress Sophie says I'm special now, like her."

"Mistress Sophie is special. You're very lucky to be like her."

"Mila," Sophie said. "Ellie is Master Aden's wife."

Ellie looked at Aden's mother, taken aback by her words, but didn't contradict her. Mila was likely too young to understand the difference between a wife and a girlfriend.

Mila hesitated, then said in a smaller voice, "Master Aden saved me."

Ellie reached out and squeezed Mila's hand. She felt neither warm like a human nor cool like a vampire, but a strangely comforting in-between temperature, reminding her of Sophie and her dad.

"Yes," Ellie said. "And I'm so glad he did."

"Mistress Sophie said I'm gonna live here now because my momma and daddy went to heaven. She said she'd take care of me forever."

Fighting back tears, Ellie reached over to pet Vlad to conceal her trembling hand. "Yes, she will. And I think you'll like it here."

The weight of what that meant bore down on Ellie. Forever had a different meaning for half-breeds than it did for humans. Mila would age more slowly and live longer than a human. She could even live forever now, thanks to AEON. And there was no one better to guide Mila through her journey than Sophie, a woman who'd walked the same path.

"Can I see Master Aden?" She asked Sophie. "My momma always said to say thank you when people help you."

Ellie looked at Sophie, curious to hear her response.

"Master Aden is a very busy man, but I'll be sure to tell him you said thank you."

Mila's face fell. "Okay."

As if sensing her distress, Vlad stretched and yawned before crawling over Mila's legs to settle on her lap, making her laugh as she rubbed his belly.

Ellie thought of Aden as she watched Mila smile and play with Vlad. She was sure he was still brooding over his choice.

But later, she'd tell him about this moment and how much joy and light remained in the little brown-haired girl he saved.

Ellie

Rubbing her eyes, Ellie stifled a yawn and swiped the hologram closed. She wasn't absorbing anything she read.

Since Aden's return from Erebu a month earlier, he'd been distracted and on edge. He and Aurick huddled in his father's office, meeting with Gerents from other regions or their commanding officers.

Aden was evasive, offering her few details. Even Kane was tight-lipped about what they were doing, warning her it was better that she didn't know. Aden told her he and his father were making plans to ensure nothing like what happened in Erebu would ever happen again, but he kept her in the dark about the specifics. And he had enough going on, so she decided not to pry because he didn't need her adding to his stress.

He'd also been insatiable, relentless in his desire for her, taking her body and blood for hours every day. It was the only thing that seemed to calm him.

But when she passed out at BloodStone last week, with a severe case of anemia, Mina, Sophie, and Keeley had all torn into them, telling them to pull their heads out of their asses before something happened they couldn't take back. After that, Aden didn't touch her for days, walking around like a scolded dog. Until finally this morning, they'd both lunged for each other in the shower, desperate. They didn't get any sleep all day.

It was worth being late for work, but Ellie was so exhausted everything was blurring together. When she wasn't at BloodStone or with Aden or Carrie, she spent time with Mila. With Sophie's permission, twice a week, Ellie gave the little girl reading lessons in the library. She was smart for her age, reminding Ellie of herself in many ways.

Determined to refocus on her task, she opened the hologram, drumming her fingers on the counter. The missing data in the sequence glared back at her like a missing tooth in an otherwise perfect smile. What wasn't she seeing?

She yawned again.

"What's with the yawning?" Hannah asked as she and Keeley walked into the lab. "You're not still anemic, are you?"

Keeley's eyes, sharp and assessing, scanned her, their intensity making Ellie uneasy. "She better not be, or I'm gonna kick my brother's ass."

"I didn't get much sleep last night," Ellie said as she fought back another yawn.

"That sounds like an Aden problem to me." Hannah grabbed a couple of empty vials and a needle. "Let's check, shall we?"

Ellie offered her arm, accepting the inevitable.

"So, did you see anything in those notes that we're overlooking?" Hannah asked to distract her, but she was so used to needles now, they didn't faze her.

"The only thing I can think of is..." She paused. "Have you ever thought of adding human blood to fill in the gaps?"

Keeley sat down on a stool opposite her. "My dad forbids using it in any BloodStone formulations."

Hannah walked over to the counter and smeared a few drops of Ellie's blood on a slide, viewing it under a microscope.

"But why?" Ellie asked. "If it can fill in the sequence gaps, why not use it?"

"We're trying to eliminate the need for human blood. Adding it to the formula wouldn't solve that? We'd still have to rely on humans to donate."

"Donation is better than it being taken against our will."

"You're still slightly anemic," Hannah said as she looked up. "Are you taking your iron?"

"Yes."

"Stop letting Aden drink from you. You need a complete break for at least two weeks."

"Fine," Ellie replied. "So, about adding human blood to the samples..."

"Ellie, we tried it a long time ago," Keeley said. "It didn't work. The sequence was incomplete. That missing component still left a gap."

Ellie pinched the bridge of her nose, frustrated. The door to the lab opened and Aden stepped in.

Her frustration melted away at seeing him. "Hey," she smiled.

Keeley pointed at him. "You need to stay away from her. She's still anemic."

He held up his hands. "I'm just here to take her to lunch, not have sex with her on the counter."

"We did that in the bathroom this morning," Ellie murmured, but then her eyes widened. "Did I just say that out loud?"

Hannah burst out laughing. Even Keeley's lips twitched, though she kept a straight face.

Aden didn't look the least bit remorseful and Ellie shook her head. Being overtired apparently caused her to pick up Aden's lack of filter.

"Don't look so proud of yourself," she said. "Keeley is right. We need to take a break."

She regretted they'd have to stop sharing blood for a while, but she couldn't deny her body was weakening.

He scowled. "We can still have sex. I just have to stop drinking your blood."

Leaning against the counter, Hannah crossed her arms. "Have at her all you want, Aden, but keep your fangs to yourself for at least two weeks or she's going to end up in the hospital."

"Fine," he snarled. "Now, can I take her to get some red meat for lunch?"

Ellie hopped down from the stool and walked over to him. "A burger sounds great right now."

"I miss cheeseburgers," Hannah sighed.

"I'll eat one for you," Ellie said as Aden dragged her out of the lab.

As soon as the door slid closed, he tugged her into his arms, leaning down to kiss her.

She hummed against his lips, laughing when he finally let her come up for air.

"I missed you, too."

An hour later, Ellie and Aden walked back into the lab. Hannah was again bent over a microscope, and Keeley was sorting some molecular formulas on a hologram above the counter.

"How was my cheeseburger?" Hannah asked without looking up.

"Delicious. I had two. And a spinach salad for the extra iron."

"Where the hell do you put it? If I had eaten like that when I was human, I would've been huge."

"I help her work it off," Aden smirked, and Ellie grabbed his arm, tugging him toward the door.

"You should go. You're already getting me in trouble with my bosses."

"Technically, I'm one of your bosses. I guess that means you're sleeping with the boss."

"If she wanted to sleep her way to the top, she should sleep with Keeley," Hannah remarked with a smirk, still focused on her task. "She's the real boss."

"Fuck you, Hannah," he snarled, his eyes flashing.

"Hannah, you're going to give him an aneurysm," Keeley said as she snorted. "Go away, Aden. We're busy."

"Fine," he snarled again, a little less vehemently, and Ellie chuckled. Although she knew she shouldn't encourage him, she couldn't help laughing at his snarling when he was being ridiculous.

He looked down at her, his eyes softening. "I'll see you at home later."

She tilted her face up for a kiss, which he obliged before heading toward the door. But Hannah's loud gasp made all of them turn and look at her.

"Why are you gasping?" Keeley asked.

"Keel, get your ass over here and look at this."

"What's wrong?" Ellie asked. "What are you looking at?"

"Your blood still," Hannah replied, and Aden halted in the doorway.

"What about her blood?" He turned back with a dark look crossing his face.

"Tell me what you see." Hannah stepped back and Keeley bent over the microscope.

"What am I looking at?"

"Look at the protein structures. Notice anything unusual?"

Ellie exchanged a quick glance with Aden before looking back at Hannah and Keeley.

"The molecular formations... I've never seen anything like it. The way they're binding to the hemoglobin..."

"Exactly."

Keeley looked at her. "I don't understand. How's Ellie's blood doing that?"

"I don't know. But look at this," she said, pulling up what Ellie now knew was a helical shape of hemoglobin on a hologram. "Look at the way it interacts with vampire blood affected by PEU deficiency."

"What's PEU deficiency?" Ellie asked but didn't expect an answer. When the two women were wrapped up in something, they didn't hear a thing.

"It's an energy deficit caused by not getting enough macronutrients, particularly protein," Aden replied, eliciting a shocked look from Ellie.

"What?" He shrugged. "Just because I find science mind-numbingly boring doesn't mean I don't possess knowledge of the subject."

With a grin on her face, Ellie moved closer to him. Though puzzled about the fuss over her blood, she couldn't help but smile because he was always full of surprises.

"It's repairing the damaged cells," Keeley said as she straightened up. "Not just binding to them, but actually restructuring them."

"I ran the test sixteen times while they were at lunch," Hannah said, running a hand through her hair. "Different samples, different conditions. The results are consistent. Whatever's in Ellie's blood, it's not just feeding the damaged vampire cells. It's healing them."

"Why would you run that test?" Keeley asked.

"I was just curious. I saw something odd in her blood earlier when I was testing for the anemia."

"What the fuck are you doing, Hannah? You have no right to play with her blood like that," Aden snarled, but Ellie shushed him.

"Can someone please tell me what's going on? What are you saying, Hannah? What's wrong with my blood?"

"There's nothing wrong. But there is something in it that's different. I've never seen it before. It's a protein, and it's probably what drives Aden so freaking crazy. Why he can't get enough of your blood." Hannah looked at him. "How much are you feeding from your other thralls?"

"I don't feed from Ellie."

"Her anemia says you do."

"He only drinks from me when we're intimate," Ellie said. "I'm not a food source for him."

"Yeah, you are. It's just that neither of you realizes it. And if he only drinks from you during sex, considering how anemic you are... Jesus, the two of you are nymphos."

Keeley snorted. "Every time I go looking for either of them, they're getting naked or were just naked."

"Nobody fucking asked you, Keeley."

"Well, I'm asking you again," Hannah said. "How often do you feed from your other thralls?"

Aden paused, meeting Ellie's eyes before he answered. "Not as much as I used to."

"Are you less hungry than you used to be? Less hungry in general?"

He frowned, a deep crease etching itself between his brows, and crossed his arms over his chest. "I haven't really thought about it. Why the fuck does that matter, Hannah?"

"Are you?" She pressed as Keeley continued to study the test results.

"I guess. If I think about it... sure."

"Whatever this protein is, and again, I've never seen it in my almost six hundred years, is meeting most of your nutritional needs. That's why you aren't as hungry, and it's why you crave her blood like a drug. It's like she's feeding heroin into your veins every time you drink from her."

"What's heroin?" Ellie asked.

"It was a human drug back in the day. One of the most addictive drugs ever created."

"Hannah, this could be the breakthrough we've been looking for," Keeley said, tearing her eyes away from the hologram.

"But only if we can synthesize it. We need to isolate it and study it. If we can break it down in a controlled environment and duplicate it, I think we can use it to fill in the ICHOR genome."

"Wait a minute," Ellie said, glancing at Aden before looking back at Hannah. "Are you saying my blood might be the key to making ICHOR work?"

"I think it might." She nodded. "But it's only *your* blood. I've never seen this protein in any other human's blood. Fuck, when Sophie told me you were special, she had no freaking idea how right she was."

"We've got to tell my dad," Keeley said. "If we can convince him to let us use Ellie's blood, we'll solve the genome problem. I know we will."

"Ellie isn't a fucking lab rat!" Aden's voice echoed through the lab. "Her blood is mine. And don't look at me like that," he snarled, pointing at Ellie when she shot him an angry glare.

"See," Hannah said. "That's exactly how a drug addict would've reacted if you tried to take away his supply."

Ellie

Ellie followed Keeley and Aden through the door to Aurick and Sophie's suite, failing to announce themselves. She and Keeley's excitement bubbled over, unlike Aden, who was still angry and sulky.

Rounding the corner, they came to an abrupt halt.

Naked and in the middle of fulfilling the compulsion, Aurick and Sophie looked up from the sofa in surprise.

"Oh, shit!" Keeley spun around so fast she almost tripped.

"What the fuck!" Aden's face twisted in horror as a slight blush warmed Ellie's cheeks.

"Oops!" She averted her gaze, giving Aden's parents their privacy as Sophie leaned forward to conceal her breasts and Aurick grabbed a blanket from the back of the couch to cover them.

"What the hell! What are you doing here?" Sophie exclaimed as Aurick's roar drowned her out.

"Get out!"

Ellie tugged on Aden's arm and pulled him back into the hall as Keeley followed, darting quickly behind the wall.

"How dare you come in here without knocking?" Sophie scolded.

"We're changing the permissions on that door today!"

"It's really important," Keeley said. "We need to talk to you."

Silence hung in the air for a moment.

"Just give us a minute," Sophie said with a sigh, followed by the distinct sound of scrambling and fabric rustling.

"Three centuries of existence, and somehow my eyes still weren't prepared to see that," Keeley said, rubbing her eyes.

"I've seen rogue battles that were less traumatic." Aden pinched the bridge of his nose.

"You've never walked in on your parents having sex before?" Ellie asked.

"No!" Aden and Keeley spoke at once.

"Really?"

"Why is that so surprising?" Keeley asked.

"I don't know." Ellie shrugged. "It just is. You're both over three hundred years old. Figured it would've happened by now."

"Why did it have to be the sofa? We sit on that sofa."

"I'm never fucking sitting on any of their furniture again."

"You two are ridiculous." Ellie snorted as she shook her head. "Are you even listening to yourselves? You're acting like teenagers. What's the big deal? Your parents were just—"

"Don't," Aden interrupted, pointing at her. "Don't fucking finish that sentence." He tugged her back against his chest, resting his chin on her head. "Some traumas can't be overcome."

This time, Keeley laughed along with her, clearly not as traumatized as Aden. Though embarrassed, more for Sophie and Aurick, Ellie appreciated the absurdity of the situation. And it gave Aden something else to focus on. He complained about Hannah and Keeley wanting to use her blood for ICHOR the whole way here, but maybe now he would calm down.

"This fucking proves doing this is a mistake," he said, the tension returning to his jaw.

Okay, maybe not.

Ellie sighed, unable to hide her frustration. "Aden, you need to let it go. If my blood can help supply the missing piece, I'm doing this if your dad says yes."

"Over my dead body," he snarled under his breath.

"What was that, darling?" She asked, knowing full well what he said.

"You can come back in now," Sophie called out, her voice carrying a hint of amusement.

Aden and Keeley peeked around the wall before Ellie pushed them both forward.

"Have a seat." Sophie gestured to the sofa with a casual wave of her hand.

"Fuck no." Aden moved to stand behind the chair Ellie sat in.

"Yeah, I'm good here." Keeley leaned against the bar.

Sophie arched an eyebrow at their chosen spots. "Really? How old are you two again?"

"Age is just a number, Mom. Trauma is forever," Keeley said with a smirk.

"Can we just—" Aden started, then shook his head. "No, actually, I need another minute to repress that memory."

Ellie laughed under her breath again. He was such a drama queen sometimes.

Aurick walked out of the bedroom with a scowl on his face.

"So, what's this about? What's so urgent that you barge into our private chambers so rudely?"

"Chambers?" Sophie chuckled. "Sweetheart, your age is showing."

"We have news about ICHOR," Keeley dove right in. "Hannah took a sample of Ellie's blood to test if she was still anemic."

"Why is she anemic?" Aurick asked with a quick glance at Ellie.

"Because your son is voracious," Sophie said with a pointed look at Aden.

"Okay." Aurick's eyes widened slightly as understanding washed over him.

"We have news about that, too," Keeley said.

"What does this have to do with ICHOR?"

"Well, when she was looking at Ellie's blood, she noticed something strange. A protein not normally present in human blood."

"What kind of protein?"

"We don't know. Hannah said she'd never seen it present in human blood before. Ever."

Aurick sat forward. "So where does she think it came from?"

"Based on the markers, it seems to be hereditary, but we'd need to study it to see if it's genetic or triggered by environmental factors. Maybe something in the village where she was born, or the mineral content in their water supply, their diet... We don't know, but we'd like your approval to study it."

He leaned back, stroking his chin. "I don't know if I like the idea of using Ellie as a test subject."

"I fucking don't either," Aden said, and Ellie reached back and pinched his thigh.

"Aden, butt out."

A grunt was his only reply.

"And Hannah thinks that if you can synthesize it, it'll solve the ICHOR genome problem?" Sophie asked.

Keeley nodded, pushing herself away from the bar.

"You know I'm opposed to using human blood in any BloodStone formulations," Aurick said.

Keeley walked closer and placed her hands on the back of the chair beside Ellie. "I know. But this is huge, Dad. We wouldn't be using her blood in ICHOR, but studying it to see if we can create a synthetic equivalent. This could be our breakthrough."

Aurick turned to Ellie. "How do you feel about this, Ellie?"

"I'm okay with it."

Aden growled from behind her.

"And as you can hear, Aden isn't. But it's my body and my blood. If studying it can lead to something that stops vampires from feeding on humans, I'm in."

"That brings me to the topic of Aden making her anemic," Keeley said.

"How is that connected?" Sophie asked.

"The protein in her blood is satisfying all of Aden's nutritional needs, and he's addicted to it."

"Vampires don't suffer from addiction," Aurick said.

"Well, your son does. Hannah equated it to a heroin addiction. She says that's what's making him crave her blood so strongly that he's practically drinking her dry."

"I'm not fucking practically drinking her dry."

"How many transfusions has she had?" Keeley shot back, and Ellie heard Aden's teeth clenching. "Anyway, this could be the answer, Dad."

Aurick's gaze flicked to Aden. His tension vibrated in the air behind Ellie, a low hum that prickled her skin and made the hairs on the back of her neck stand on end. She reached back, grabbing his hand, and he relaxed. A small smile curved her lips as she reveled in her ability to soothe him with just a touch.

"Are you sure about this, Ellie?" Aurick asked her again.

"Yes."

"Alright," he said at last, "I'll allow it."

"Yes!" Keeley whooped, and Aden growled behind Ellie again, lower this time.

"This needs to remain confidential," Aurick said. "I don't want anyone outside this room aside from Hannah and Nickolas to know whose blood you're testing. Not even the lab techs on the team. I know they're all trustworthy, but this is for Ellie's safety. Can you imagine if Matthais got wind of this?"

"And that's why this shouldn't fucking happen!" Aden roared, his fingers digging into the back of the chair, tearing the fabric. Ellie couldn't help but sigh.

Why the heck would Aurick say that in front of him?

"Aurick," Sophie warned, her gaze sharp, before turning her heated glare on Aden. "And you, if you want to destroy furniture, go to your own suite."

Aurick glanced at his wife, then offered Ellie an apologetic look.

"No one on the team would say anything, Dad," Keeley replied. "But we're all in complete agreement about who should and shouldn't know."

"I won't allow this," Aden said, his jaw clenched.

Ellie rose, circled the chair, and grasped his wrists, gently pulling his hands away. He stared down at her, his expression more worried than furious.

"Aden, it'll be fine. You need to trust Keeley, and you need to trust me."

She wrapped her arms around him, resting her head on his chest, listening to his heart, which was always strange because of how slowly it beat.

He held back for a full minute before crushing her in a hug that felt both wonderful and a bit too tight, causing a slight ache in her ribs.

But he didn't argue with her, accepting her decision without further protest, so she kept it to herself, returning his embrace and placing a kiss over his heart.

Ellie

E llie spun away from Drake's strike, her ponytail whipping through the air as she dropped low and swept his legs out from under him.

He hit the training mat with a grunt, and before Kane could move in, she'd already rolled to her feet.

"Getting slow in your old age?" she teased.

He circled to her left, a look of proud amusement in his eyes. "Don't get cocky now, Ellie Bellie."

She narrowed her eyes and growled. "I told you not to call me that."

He lunged, trying to provoke and distract her, but she was ready, turning his aggressive move against him, using a maneuver he spent the last two months drilling into her. He stumbled forward as she danced away.

"Cocky?" Ellie laughed, dodging Drake while keeping Kane in her peripheral vision. "I prefer appropriately confident."

"She's got you there, man," Drake chuckled. "Let's see how you take on both of us at once."

They moved in at the same time.

She dodged Kane's punch, but Drake rushed her from behind, locking her in a suffocating bear hug. It was his go-to move and one that always made her freeze up, forgetting her training. But this time, she snapped her head, slamming the back of it into his face. He recoiled as he released her.

"Fuck!"

She whipped around, her eyes wide with horror. He was clutching his nose, blood flowing through his fingers.

"Oh, shit, Drake. I thought you'd dodge me."

Kane reached for her throat, capturing her in a chokehold.

"Stay focused," he rasped in her ear. "Drake's fine. He's broken his nose more times than he can count. Now use your weight against me."

Ellie took a deep breath and nodded.

"Chin down," she murmured to herself, tucking her chin to protect her neck. With a single, smooth movement, she curved into herself before turning into his body. Her hands found his forearm, one at his wrist and one near his elbow. Using her momentum, she stepped wider with her left foot and pulled downward on his arm while rotating her shoulders. His hold loosened immediately.

"That's it, Ellie," Drake said as she slipped free.

She looked over at him again, and he was wiping the blood from his face, his nose already back in place.

"I'm so sorry."

"Don't sweat it. It was a nice move."

"Fuck yeah it was," Kane agreed, and Ellie laughed.

"Let's go again," Drake said as he tossed the bloody rag aside.

Together, they rushed her from the front, using their enhanced half-breed senses to their advantage, but she had learned to read their tells. Kane's shoulders tensed before he struck, and Drake shifted his weight before kicking.

She blocked Kane's punch with her forearm, but damn, it resonated through her bones, then dodged Drake's kick with a quick spin. She ducked and rolled away, then sprang to her feet.

A slow clap echoed through Aden's workout room, and Ellie turned to see Aurick smiling at her from the doorway.

"Well done, Ellie," he said, pushing off the door frame.

"Thank you." Ellie blushed under his praise. She knew she was getting better, but hearing it from him was incredibly meaningful. "I still have a lot to learn."

"We all do, no matter our expertise. Speaking of learning, I know you declined my offer to spar in the past, but would you indulge me today?"

"I don't know if I'm ready for that," she said, unsure.

"I'll be right back," Aurick said and entered the warp port in the corner of Aden's office.

"This is a very bad idea." Ellie grabbed a towel, wiping the sweat from her forehead and the back of her neck.

"It's a very good idea," Kane said. "You're stronger and faster, more balanced than you were only a few weeks ago. You're ready to try whatever he brings back here."

Aurick stepped out of the warp port, carrying two swords.

"A sword?" She squeaked when he walked back into the workout room. "I thought you'd bring a saber?"

"These are very lightweight. Similar to sabers, but more hearty to use. I've noticed the muscle mass you've built recently."

"Aden's had me lifting weights."

He handed her a sword. "This one will be easy for you, then."

It felt wrong in her hand at first, awkward and heavy. The handle was smooth against her palm, but her fingers didn't seem to know where to grip.

Aurick wrapped his hand around hers, and Ellie looked up at him. The only other time he touched her was when he shielded her from Aden's outburst. The feeling was just as strange as it had been then.

"Adjust your grip," he said. "Relax your hand and let the hilt settle."

She shifted her fingers and rotated her hand, trying to adjust to the unfamiliar weight. The blade caught the overhead light, and something flickered in her mind. She froze as the room around her shimmered, and she saw Aly in the salle with Aurick and Aden, teaching her how to use the same sword. Aurick stood behind her, steadying her arm as her sword clashed against Aden's.

With a gasp, she returned to the present.

"Are you okay?" Aurick's worried eyes met hers.

A small laugh escaped her lips. "Yeah, I just remember this sword now. And you and Aden teaching me."

She looked at Kane and Drake, realizing what she said. They were unfazed by her words. Who she was in the past wasn't a secret in the Westcott's inner circle, but it was still strange knowing they knew.

Her fingers shifted, finding their place on the handle, distributing the weight evenly. She understood now. Sword fighting wasn't about strength. It was about balance and a connection with the blade.

"You ready to give this a try?" Aurick asked, stepping back and extending his sword.

Ellie mirrored his stance.

"Remember," he instructed, beginning a slow series of attacks that she deflected. "The sword isn't just a weapon. It's an extension of yourself. Feel its movement as if it's your own."

Ellie nodded, getting her bearings. Aurick increased his speed, each exchange teaching as much as it tested.

"Your footwork is good," he commented, launching a more complex sequence of attacks that she defended against with growing confidence. "But you're thinking too much. Let the blade lead you."

Ellie took a deep breath, stepping back from her conscious thoughts, the tension leaving her body. Her sword movements became more fluid, matching Aurick's style and seeing openings she missed before.

When she landed a light tap on his shoulder, the pride in his eyes filled her with warmth.

"Now that's the girl I remember," Aurick said, a nostalgic smile playing on his lips as he bowed to her.

"I hoped you'd be here tonight."

Ellie turned from the orchid-covered workbench when she heard Sophie's voice from the greenhouse doorway. She smiled as Aden's mother walked in.

"Keeley and Hannah insisted I take a couple of days off. There isn't much I can do at the lab while they're running their tests. I'm not qualified to conduct experiments."

Stepping beside Ellie, Sophie rubbed her arm. She'd been more openly affectionate ever since Ellie threw herself at her for a hug after taking the job at BloodStone. Aden hadn't been exaggerating when he said Sophie Westcott was a toucher.

"I think it has more to do with them wanting you to rest a little. Anemia can really sap your energy."

"My red blood cells are back to normal."

Sophie donned her gardening gloves and selected a pair of pruning shears as Ellie resumed trimming her orchid.

"Still, the fatigue can linger. I know. It happened to me a lot after Aurick and I started sharing blood."

"Aden and I are figuring it out."

"It takes time. Compulsion is daunting when it's new."

"I remember you telling me that. But I had no idea how it would feel."

A plaintive meow echoed from the doorway as Vlad appeared, the door granting him automatic entry.

"You just ate, Vlad, so don't try to trick Ellie into thinking you're starving."

Ellie laughed as the black cat jumped onto the work table. Orchids weren't poisonous to cats, so she let him settle between her and Sophie's plants to take a bath.

"There's no stronger pull for lovers than compulsion," Sophie said, resuming their conversation after Vlad's interruption. "It's agony and ecstasy all rolled into one. A raw, primal force that defies all attempts to tame it. From what Hannah discovered in your blood, what you and Aden are experiencing is more potent. It must be overwhelming for you."

Ellie swallowed, feeling both embarrassed and grateful to Sophie for bringing it up. She needed a confidant, but Carrie wasn't an option. And she felt uncomfortable talking to Keeley and Hannah about it.

"I feel a little awkward talking to you about this."

Setting the pruned orchid on a nearby cart, Sophie reached for another. "Why? Because I'm Aden's mother?"

"Yes and no. You were the one to explain compulsion to me, so I don't feel weird talking to you about it. In general. But in specifics, I'm talking about your son."

"Who's a grown man in an intimate relationship with the woman he loves." Sophie tapped Vlad on the nose when he tried to grab her pruning shears. "I think it's hard to understand the nuances of compulsion for someone who's never experienced it. There's nothing more intimate than sharing your blood with the person you love. Humans fed vampires for millennia, and although it's always a pleasurable experience after you get past the bite, that isn't compulsion. As I explained the first time, it doesn't need love. It only needs blood and sex. But when love comes into the equation... it's transcendent."

Ellie switched out her orchid with a new one. "I love sharing my blood with him. More than I ever thought I would, but—"

"Sometimes it can be a little much," Sophie finished for her. "I know. It's hard not to lose yourself to it. It feels like the frightening pressure of drowning, followed by the desperate relief of that first, gasping breath of air."

"Exactly," Ellie said, relieved that Sophie understood. "I don't know what it's like to drown, but embracing it feels like staring into an abyss. Or a terrifying plunge into the unknown. But the thought of losing it is a different kind of terror. A slow, agonizing unraveling. Does that make any sense?"

"Perfectly. Embrace and enjoy your closeness to Aden, but don't lose yourself in it. I know that's easier said than done. It takes years to level out. But it will."

"Years?"

Tired of being ignored, Vlad head-butted Ellie's arm before jumping down and sauntering toward the back of the greenhouse.

"It took Aurick and me almost a decade. But I was already a half-breed then. Your human body is more fragile."

Ellie released a shaky sigh. "A decade? Oh, god, I don't know if my body will hold out that long."

"Aden will follow your lead. He'll take it if you let him. All vampires are greedy, but if you set boundaries, he'll respect them. He'll sulk, but he'll do it."

That made Ellie laugh. No truer words had ever been said of Aden.

"Mina told me the same thing."

"She would know."

Ellie stopped pruning, her eyes widening as she looked at Sophie. "Wait a minute? Are you saying Mina had sex with her sire? I thought Aden said he just sired her as a favor to you and Aurick."

"He did. But that doesn't mean they weren't intimate."

"Go, Mina!" Ellie selected another orchid to prune. "Thank you, Sophie," she said after a pause. "This helped me wrap my head around it."

"You're welcome, sweetheart. I miss spending time with you like this."

"Me, too. I can relax and clear my head when I come in here. I need to do it more often."

"I feel the same. Life has a way of getting in the way."

A companionable silence settled over them as they each pruned several more orchids. Until it was broken by the sound of a splash, followed by a hiss, then a howl, from the back of the greenhouse before Vlad zoomed past, a blur of drenched fur, leaving a trail of wet paw prints on the concrete floor.

Ellie and Sophie both chuckled.

"He must have fallen in again. He'll never learn."

"I'm sorry we barged in on you and Aurick the other day," Ellie said once they stopped laughing.

"Scarred my children for life, I'm sure."

"They probably deserve it."

"I have no doubt."

"How's Mila?" Ellie asked, and the smile that spread across Sophie's lips lit up her entire face.

"She's adjusting well. Better than I did."

"Well, she has you to help her."

"She loves her reading lessons with you."

"She's learning quickly. And she's so inquisitive. She reminds me of me at that age, which is kind of scary because I drove my dad crazy with all my questions."

"Yeah, she's going to be a handful," Sophie agreed, though her continued smile suggested she didn't mind at all.

"How about Carrie? How is she working out?"

"She's doing well, too. She's almost as quick as you are at catching on to things. She's also showing nice improvement in her reading and writing skills. I hardly have to help her anymore."

Ellie let out the breath she'd been holding. She'd been hoping Carrie would be a good fit as Sophie's assistant, giving her a purpose and a much-needed distraction from her painful memories.

"How is she other than that?"

Ellie didn't need to clarify what she was asking.

"She's getting a little better every day," Sophie assured her. "What she went through stays with a person. She'll always carry it, but someday there will be light in her eyes again."

And for that, Ellie was truly hopeful.

Ellie

"So, your mother cornered me in the greenhouse tonight."

Aden peered up from between Ellie's thighs as she lay sprawled across the desk in his office, his hands sliding her pants down her hips. He'd already removed her shirt, but left her in her panties and bra.

"Why?"

"She wanted to talk to me about compulsion again." Ellie lifted her hips, shimmying a little further back so he could tug them off her legs, before leaning back on her elbows, letting out a soft squeal as her bare back met the cold wood.

He wasn't in their suite when she finished in the greenhouse, so Ellie sought him out in his office. He'd been so delighted by her visit, he had her on his desk, nearly naked in less than five minutes.

"Why did you leave my panties and bra on?"

Aden's gaze, warm and intense, traced the curves of her body, a slow, appreciative sweep that made her stomach clench with anticipation.

"Because you're like a present. I want to unwrap you slowly."

How could just one look and a handful of words make her so incredibly wet?

"Do I get to unwrap you?"

He held out his arms. "By all means. Unwrap away."

A sultry smile curved Ellie's lips as she sat up, sliding to the edge of the desk. She tucked her fingertips into his waistband, tugging him closer.

"Where to begin?"

With slow, deliberate movements, she unbuttoned his shirt, one button at a time, the scent of him filling her senses as her hands lingered on his warm skin.

His fingers trailed over her bare thighs, each feather-light touch sending a delicious shiver of heat through her.

Sliding her hands beneath the fabric, she pushed his shirt open and down his arms, leaning forward to press a kiss over his heart.

"Ellie," he growled her name, releasing a shaky breath as he shrugged out of the shirt.

She responded by wrapping her lips around his nipple, teasing it with her teeth and the tip of her tongue. Aden's fingers slid into her hair, grasping the long, silken strands.

"She wanted to know how we were adjusting to it," she murmured against his skin as she traced the contours of his abdomen, a smile playing on her lips as she felt him tremble.

"Who? What?" Aden stammered, and Ellie laughed. The sound was rich and throaty as she reveled in how her touch could erase everything from his mind but her. She lifted her head, letting her gaze rest on his face before she spoke.

"Your mom. Cornering me in the greenhouse. Wanting to talk about compulsion."

He shook his head, a few strands of his hair falling across his forehead as he scowled. Ellie reached up and brushed them back from his face, her fingers lingering for a moment.

"Are you really bringing up my mother when we're about to fuck?"

Ellie chuckled as she moved on to removing his pants.

"She didn't want to talk about us walking in on her and Aurick, did she? I'm going to have nightmares. I know I am."

Ellie unbuckled his belt, the leather cool against her fingers as she slid it free from the loops.

"Stop being so dramatic. And while that came up briefly, what she really wanted to know was how we're adjusting and how my anemia is."

She tugged on the snap, releasing it, before sliding his zipper down, a mischievous smile playing on her lips as she discovered he was going commando.

"What did you tell her?" he asked as his fingers slipped beneath her bra straps, pulling them down her arms.

"That we're figuring it out and I'm feeling better."

Aden tilted her face up to his, looking into her eyes. "Are you really? Don't fucking lie to me, either."

"I don't lie to you." Ellie pushed his pants over his hips, then wrapped her hand around him, his cock hard and thick against her palm. A shudder wracked his body, a groan escaping his lips as his head fell forward.

"Fuck, Ellie."

"I'm still a little tired, but that's it," she continued, talking and teasing him, stealing glances down at her hand. Her fingers barely encircled his thick girth. Only the tips of her middle finger and thumb touched.

Aden bucked his hips and pulled on the strap of her bra so hard that it snapped.

"You're ruining all my underwear," she murmured, exploring his length, stroking him with a firm grip. He was heavy and hot in her hand, hard and twitching as she swept the pad of her thumb over the smooth head, gathering the moisture, a droplet clinging to her skin as she lifted it to her lips.

The sharp, salty flavor of his arousal hit her taste buds, and a low hum vibrated in her throat.

"I'll fucking buy you more."

With one arm around her, Aden pulled her closer, pushing the remnants of her bra below her breasts, his lips finding her nipple. The sensation of his warm, wet mouth was pure bliss, and Ellie's head fell back as she let out a long, low moan.

Her fingers tangled in his hair, tugging as he teased her nipple with his tongue and teeth. A thin sheen of sweat slicked her skin, goosebumps prickling and raising the hairs on her arms.

"No blood tonight?" He murmured the question around her flesh.

Though it was probably unwise, she craved the quick sting of his fangs and the intoxicating rush of his venom in her veins.

"A little. Just not too much."

He nodded his agreement, then switched breasts, teasing her other nipple to a taut, aching peak before releasing it with a pop.

"Turn around and bend over the desk," he said as he stepped back, gripping her hips and pulling her off it.

She turned without a word, his hands joining hers as she slipped her panties down her legs, letting them fall to the floor and pool at her feet. He unhooked her damaged bra and tossed it aside. Bracing herself, she leaned forward, the cool wood a shock as she rested her upper body on his desk.

"Shit, that's cold," she hissed, shivering softly, but the coolness felt strangely comforting against her heated skin, her body finally relaxing after a few seconds.

Only the rustle of Aden's pants as he removed them and the sound of her own breathless anticipation filled the room.

"You look so fucking sexy bent over my desk. I'll never be able to work at it again without picturing you sprawled over it just like this."

Ellie trembled as his hands slid over the curve of her ass and up her back, his fingertips tracing the jagged lines of her scars, leaving burning trails in his wake. Soft mewls escaped her lips, only to morph into a moan as he pressed his body against her, pushing his cock between her thighs. With just a few glides of his crown along her lips and clit, she'd soaked him with her arousal.

Ellie arched her back, spreading her legs wider as he gripped her hips, his head nudging her entrance.

"Please," she whimpered as she clutched the edge of the desk in front of her, desperate for the feel of him inside her.

She didn't want soft.

She didn't want slow.

She wanted him to thrust and plunge, hard and fast, until every inch of him filled every inch of her.

He leaned over, pressing his chest to her back, his fingers tightening on her hips, his warm breath ghosting across her ear. "I want to be gentle," he said through gritted teeth. "But I don't think I can."

"Don't," she moaned, pressing back so the tip of his cock slipped inside her. "Let the compulsion take you, sweetheart."

She felt his lips curve against her skin. "Brace yourself for the ride, baby. We'll do gentle next."

"Yes!" Ellie hissed as Aden stood, withdrawing slightly before plunging into her with one powerful, unrelenting thrust, tearing a groan from deep within her. His matching one, a low, guttural sound, reverberated through the room, almost drowning hers out.

Her body clenched against the intrusion, her back arching deeper. It brought tears to her eyes, but he felt so good, his cock stretching and filling her, that she wanted to weep. The room filled with their combined grunts and the rhythmic, wet slapping of skin. It echoed in her ears as he moved inside her with swift strokes, stealing her breath.

He set a brisk pace, thrusting so hard her teeth rattled. Her body jerked against the edge of the desk, and she could feel the bruises blooming on the front of her thighs. The slight hint of pain heightened her pleasure, triggering a surge of arousal that soaked them both, leaving her thighs slick.

Sliding over the smooth wood, Ellie's nipples burned and throbbed from the friction. Aden's fingertips bit into the soft skin of her hips, bracing her against his vigorous thrusts, even though the desk prevented her from escaping.

But no matter how hard he thrust, she knew it wasn't as brutal as he was capable of. Each movement sent tremors through her body, a bone-jarring rhythm that threatened to shatter her.

How could something hurt and feel so good at the same time?

This was the compulsion taking hold of them, the agony and the ecstasy that Sophie described. And the slow, agonizing unraveling that Ellie feared losing. She craved his fangs, his bite, and she needed to give him her blood as desperately as she needed to breathe.

"Aden, please... bite me," she begged, the sensation of fire rushing through her veins, her body clenching and trembling beneath him.

"Not yet," he growled. "Not yet."

"Please," she pleaded, the word catching in her throat, a raw, desperate plea.

He leaned over her again, his lips brushing the side of her neck. She tilted her head, offering it to him, but he only kissed her skin again.

"Not yet," he murmured again through clenched teeth before his voice softened. "Come for me, my beauty."

A sob escaped Ellie's throat as her body obeyed him, helpless against his soft command, and her orgasm tore through her. Bright flashes of light exploded behind her eyelids as she convulsed, muscles spasming, the pleasure surging through her, settling deep within her core. Aden roared against her neck as he came inside her, his cock twitching, his entire frame shuddering over her.

A hoarse groan rasped from his throat as his weight settled on top of her. "Jesus, fuck, Ellie."

Ellie pressed her forehead to the cool wood as she panted. He didn't bite her, but she came so hard that the raw intensity of her orgasm left her feeling like her body might just dissolve into the desk.

Their breathing synced as they caught their breath, their chests moving in unison, the sound a quiet rhythm in the stillness.

"Why didn't you bite me?"

"I was too frenzied. Too lost in you. I was afraid I'd take too much," he said, his lips a warm, soft whisper against her shoulder. "Did I hurt you?"

She turned her face and rested her cheek on the wood as she smiled. She ached all over, but it felt glorious, the best kind of ache.

"I'll be a little bruised, but I'm okay."

"Ellie," he growled as he pushed up, slipping out of her as he stepped back.

"Don't growl at me right now. I'm too blissed out."

His fingers traced soothing circles over her hips and ass, his silent apology evident in his touch.

"You might have to carry me back to our rooms, though. My legs feel like jelly."

He let out a low murmur of agreement as he helped her to stand, turning her around as he sat down in his chair. His body jolted as his bare ass came in contact with the cold leather.

"Fuck!"

Ellie laughed softly. "That's how I felt on the desk."

"Come here," he murmured, pulling her toward him gently with a frown. "The fronts of your thighs are bruised, too."

"Completely worth it," she said as she straddled his legs, climbing on top of him, resting her knees on either side of his thighs as she dropped her forehead to his shoulder. He pulled her against his chest, his arms gentle around her.

"Are you sure I didn't hurt you?"

She could hear the worry in his voice, and she pressed a kiss to his skin.

"Yes. I told you to let the compulsion take you. I wanted it exactly like that. I just wish you bit me."

"Now, who's the addict?" He teased, and she lifted her head.

His eyes held a trace of uncertainty, that perhaps he'd been too rough.

She pulled his face to hers. "Kiss me," she breathed into his mouth, moving over him, wrapping his cock in her hand, and guiding it to her entrance.

"Already?" He chuckled, then his breath hitched as she slowly sank down on him, taking him inside her, inch by glorious inch. She gasped as a sharp, stinging ache pulsed through her, settling low in her belly, but she welcomed the burn, swallowing his low, guttural groan, barely suppressing one of her own as her body stretched around him.

"You're going to be the fucking death of me, woman."

"I don't want your death," she breathed as her eyes met his. "I want your life."

"You have it. All of it."

Lips touching, their gazes locked. The look of utter devotion in his eyes, the deep blue shining with love and awe, stole her breath. Ellie wrapped her arms around him, pressing her breasts to his chest, the feel of the light dusting of hair tickling her aching nipples, the sensation making her tremble.

Her clit throbbed, sending waves of pleasure pulsing through her body.

"Aden." His name was a breathless whisper on her lips. "This isn't compulsion," she murmured. "This is love."

"This isn't your fucking blood, either," he snarled in only the way he could when he was buried inside her. "Hannah's probably right. I am an addict, but this isn't about that. This is about how you are so deeply a part of me I don't know where I end and you begin."

Ellie's body trembled, clenching around him, making them both groan.

"I don't know how I lived without you," he growled, thrusting his hips in a slow, gentle rhythm beneath her, exactly what they both needed after their frantic fucking. "Everything before you is a void of darkness, and you are only light."

His heartfelt words penetrated her soul, traveling straight to her heart, jolting her, as if bringing her to life. No one but her knew this man's capacity for love or the depth with which he worshiped her. It was almost unfathomable for her to believe.

Did he know she lived and breathed just as desperately for him?

Her body moved in tandem with his, a synchronized dance of push and pull, their breaths mingling, their skin slick with sweat.

"I loved you before we had sex," she breathed against his lips. "I loved you before you drank from me." She needed him to know her love for him was deeper than their blood sharing. "If the compulsion ever went away, it would change nothing."

He gripped her hips hard again, halting her movements, keeping her pressed down on him, buried as deep inside her as he could reach. The ache was again a mixture of pleasure and pain, a throbbing pulse that resonated deep within. Something in the flash of his eyes, the red around the blue of his irises, made her throat tighten.

He held her gaze, his eyes unwavering and intense.

"The last three hundred years are gone, and I can never live without you again. I won't survive it. If anything ever happened to you, I'd burn the world to the ground."

"Aden—"

"No, Ellie. Don't tell me not to say that," he snarled, and she felt it resonate inside her. "And don't tell me I don't mean it. I mean every fucking word. I'll reduce this world to ashes, leaving only smoke and ruin behind."

She cradled his face in her hands, caressing his cheeks, rubbing her nose against his. The words were a promise she knew he'd never break. The ferocity of them should frighten her, but instead, they ignited a deeper love within her.

"I know you will."

His eyes softened, and he released her from his tight grip, encouraging her to move again as she kissed him softly.

"Hey, Aden, have you seen El—"

Ellie froze at the sound of Keeley's voice from the doorway, but Aden didn't even flinch, his steady gaze holding hers.

"Well, shit. I guess you have," she sighed. "My eyes can't take any more of this..." Her voice trailed off as the door slid closed again.

Ellie laughed gently as she resumed her movements over him, Aden's familiar, playful smirk curving his lips.

"That'll fucking teach her to walk in unannounced again."

Ellie

"**D**o you want to have kids?"

Ellie's eyebrows shot up, surprised by his unexpected question.

Aden looked up from his perusal of the bite mark he left on her inner thigh less than an hour ago. He'd been inside her for hours, first in his office, then here in their bedroom. A BloodStone IV had amped up her blood and soothed her battered flesh, allowing him to take a little more from her than they both should have let him.

But when her body was unable to take anymore, she begged him for a break. She was starving, convinced she was going to pass out from both hunger and blood loss. Aden called the kitchen for the dinner she skipped earlier and the infirmary for a second BloodStone drip laced with his blood and ferrous sulfate.

She was now sitting against the headboard, a plate with a cheeseburger and french fries on her lap, and an IV buried in her arm.

"First, you can't get me pregnant unless you take LIBER."

"I can't get you pregnant unless you're a half-breed. Well, I can, but you wouldn't survive the pregnancy."

A moan escaped Ellie's lips as she bit into her cheeseburger.

"Second," she said after swallowing. "I think it's a little premature to be talking about us having kids together."

"There's no one else you'll fucking have kids with."

His snarl was both immediate and vicious, his fingers pressing into her thigh.

"Okay, retract your fangs." She pulled his hand away, the hint of a bruise already forming. "That's not what I meant. It's just that you've never even hinted that you'd want children. And after the way you've acted about Iain, I just thought it wasn't something you wanted."

Aden touched her blossoming bruise, his regret evident in the gentle caress.

"I despise kids. They're annoying and loud. Dirty and constantly demanding attention. They're worse than my mother's fucking cat."

Ellie almost said that he was always demanding attention, at least hers, but she bit her tongue at the last minute. She didn't mind his constant demands—most of the time—and he was opening up about something she never thought he would.

"What about Mila?"

His head turned, and his dark eyes connected with her curious ones. "What about her?"

"You don't despise her. You saved her."

"I made a split-second decision in the moment. There was nothing more to it than that. That doesn't mean I ever want to see her again."

"So you haven't been to see her?" Ellie asked though she knew the answer.

"No."

"Why not?"

"Because I don't like kids," he said slowly, like he thought she had trouble understanding him. "She's Sophie's responsibility now."

Ellie knew him well enough to know he was not being truthful with her. She reached up and caressed his face but didn't press him on the topic. Both of them knew the real reason he saved Mila. Ellie only had to see her once to know.

"So, you never want them?"

"Do you want me to lie, or do you want the truth?" Aden shifted so he could look at her, swapping out her plate for another with a second cheeseburger with a side of sliced apples.

"Always the truth," she said as she tossed an apple slice into her mouth.

"Do you want them?" he asked.

"That isn't an answer."

"I'll answer you when you answer me."

"That's not how this works," Ellie said as she set her plate aside, not willing to let him off the hook.

"Sure it does." He held her gaze.

Realizing she wouldn't get a response out of him until she gave him one, she answered, "Not right now. Or anytime soon. But, someday, I think I do. Your turn."

He watched her, his expression cycling through a myriad of emotions.

"If you want them, I'll give them to you, but it will be a long time before I'm ready to share you with anyone."

Ellie studied him, a small smile playing on her lips. "I'm not ready to share you either. But how are we going to do this? I know I have to become a half-breed. Do you think Matthais will ever grant you permission to make me one?"

"It doesn't fucking matter. I'll make you a half-breed if I fucking want to make you a half-breed. Matthais can go fuck himself."

When he got worked up, the "fucks" just poured out of him.

Aden tilted her face up, forcing her to meet his gaze.

"Ellie, when the time comes, I'll make you a half-breed, and I'll knock you up if that's what you really want. But you need to remember who you'd be having kids with. I'm selfish and self-centered. I'm demanding and needy, and I'm not willing to come second to a cat or a kid."

His words should have given her pause, but they didn't.

"Aden, children bring people closer."

"And they demand a lot of attention. I don't share well with others."

His fingers trailed down her thigh, sending shivers through Ellie. She understood his gentle touch was Aden's way of keeping connected to her, so she didn't take his words the wrong way. She grasped his hand in hers and squeezed gently.

"What made you bring this up tonight?"

"Sophie said something to me a while back that just had me thinking."

"Oh, yeah? What's that?"

"She said that technically, you were already my wife."

Ellie swallowed, her throat suddenly dry as she remembered Sophie's words to Mila.

"No, I'm not. Aly was your wife. I'm not Aly."

"I know that. But you're the same soul."

She moved her plate from beside her to the bedside table, then took both his hands in hers, brushing her fingers over his palms.

"Aden, when I visited those graves, I said goodbye to that life. Those memories will always be a part of me. They've merged with who I am. But I'm Ellie," she said. "If you're trying to tell me you want to marry me someday, know that my answer will be yes. It will always be yes. But Aly and Aden's life is over. This is Ellie and Aden's life."

His eyes blazed with an adoration that made her heart pound like a drum against her ribs.

"I love you to the depths of my soul."

"Look at me." She took his face in her hands. "I love you to the depths of my soul, too. Now, how about we stop talking about me being your wife and our hypothetical children so you can focus on me, your girlfriend?" Leaning in, she softly nipped at his collarbone, then soothed the bite with her tongue. When he didn't respond as she expected, she pulled back and looked at him. "When I usually kiss that spot, I end up flat on my back with your fangs sunk deep in my jugular."

"I can't take any more tonight, Ellie." He gestured to the IV in her arm. "So behave yourself, or I'll call Mina back here. I thought she was going to strangle me when we called for that IV after we promised not to share blood for a few weeks."

"Mina's not the boss of us."

"Everyone always blames me for your anemia. Like I'm the only one who's greedy and ravenous. Little do they know that you're the one dragging me down the path of temptation."

"Yeah, kicking and screaming, that's you." Ellie let out a soft laugh. "Now, why don't you put your mouth to better use?"

She slid down on the bed, and he moved over her, the weight of his body pinning her to the mattress, his breath hot on her neck.

"I can't fucking say no to you."

A shaky chuckle escaped her lips, almost inaudible above the rumble of his voice. He pushed inside her and she wrapped her arms and legs around him, her warmth surrounding him completely.

"And that's why someday I'm going to fucking end up with a bunch of bratty rug rats."

Four hours later, when Mina slid the needle into her vein, a transfusion laced with Aden's blood, Ellie knew, to the depths of her soul, that she would one day be the mother of his children.

Aden

Aden strode down the hallway on a mission. He returned to their rooms early, but Ellie wasn't fucking there. She told him she planned to read in their suite while he finished his meeting with Aurick. He just got back from Afara, having spent several days working with Rashidi and his generals, going over the latest operating plans, so he needed to brief his father.

He rushed through their meeting, wanting to see her, but all he found was an empty suite, except for the black, furry bane of his existence.

"Find Ellie," he growled, and she popped up in a hologram. She was in one of the kitchens with Chelsea.

Why the fuck was she talking to Chelsea? She should have been sent to Bíonn súil le muir.

"Georgina," he barked, and the thralls' supervisor appeared in a different hologram.

"Yes, Master Aden."

"Why is Chelsea back? I thought I told you to send her away."

"She's been experiencing severe compulsion withdrawal. I spoke to Mistress Sophie, and she said to bring her back and keep her isolated until you called for her."

Fucking hell!

"Georgina, you call me about my thralls, not Sophie. Is that understood?"

"Yes, Sir. I've always just reported this kind of thing to her, but I'll report it to you from now on. Shall I send Chelsea back?"

Aden never cared when his feeders started with compulsion withdrawal. He always had others to turn to, but that usually meant they were reaching the end of their ability to feed him. They would become clingy and desperate, and he would be finished with them. Sophie always handled their departure from his roster.

"No," he sighed. "How long can she withstand the withdrawal?"

"When it becomes this severe, only a few months."

Fuck! This was why he left this shit to his mother.

"Add her back to the rotation every couple of days."

"Yes, Sir. Should I have her sent to you tonight?"

"I know where she is. I'll find her."

Aden swiped the hologram closed and stepped into a warp port leading to the lower levels, where the thralls' kitchens were located. Which fucking one were they in? As he approached the first one, he heard raised voices coming from inside.

"Until you got here, I was his favorite. Now he never calls for me. Do you know how much pain I'm in?"

Ellie responded in a softer, yet firm, tone. "Chelsea, I'm sorry you're hurting, but I don't control who he feeds from and who he doesn't."

"If you didn't give him so much of your blood, he'd want it from me. I was his favorite."

"Yes, you've said that several times." Ellie's voice became sharper. "I don't tell him who to feed from. You should speak to Mistress Sophie or Georgina. And I don't appreciate you attacking me like this. Aden wouldn't either."

"Everything was fine until you showed up. I wish he'd just drained you in the capital."

Blind with rage, Aden burst into the room, the sound of Ellie's gasp barely audible over the roaring in his ears.

"Shut your fucking mouth, Chelsea, before I permanently shut it for you."

He grabbed Chelsea's arm and shoved her. Although he exerted minimal effort, she slid across the room, falling into a chair beside the table. She quickly regained her balance and lowered her head.

Ellie's fingers dug into his forearm, tugging as he started forward, her voice an urgent whisper. "Aden, no."

He looked at her. "What else did she say to you?"

Her worried gaze met his. "Nothing, Aden. It was nothing."

"It wasn't nothing," he roared. "What she said to you wasn't fucking nothing!"

Ellie stepped closer and placed her hands on his chest. The fiery red in his eyes was reflected in the refrigerator's metallic surface behind her. He closed them, taking a slow, calming breath, focusing on the gentle pressure of her fingers. His ragged breaths slowed, and he opened his eyes again.

"Ellie, go back to our rooms."

"Why?"

She usually wouldn't question him with thralls present, but her anxiety was obvious in her worried eyes.

"Because I need to feed. I'll see you back there in a little while."

"Aden?" Repeating his name, her tone urged him to stay calm.

"It'll be fine, Ellie."

Her eyes scanned his face, and what she saw there must have satisfied her because she nodded.

"I'm going to see Mila for a few minutes."

"I'll be less than a half hour. Don't make me come find you. I'm not in the mood to hunt you down again tonight."

She pushed up on her toes and kissed the corner of his mouth. Then she cast a lingering glance at Chelsea and left.

Aden watched her go, then turned to Chelsea. In three strides, he stood in front of her. She shook before him.

"If you ever speak to her that way again, I will drain you. Do you understand me?"

"Yes, Sir."

"Good! Now get on your fucking knees!"

"This better be important, Aurick. I was conducting virtual drills with Banjora's troops when you dragged me away," Aden said as he walked into Aurick's office.

"As you can see, Indira, Aden has arrived," Aurick said to the hologram hovering over his desk.

"Hi, Aden," she said with a shake of her head.

"Indira," he replied, unapologetic for interrupting their conversation.

"I'm going to call Katsumi and bring her up to speed. We'll chat tomorrow." Aurick said goodbye and swiped the hologram closed.

"What was that about?" Aden asked.

"She wanted to let me know that she's sending ten thousand more troops here for training next week. Can you accommodate them?"

"Yes. That's not what this is about, is it? You could have asked me that over a hologram."

He was still irritated about Ellie's encounter with Chelsea the previous evening, and taking it out on Aurick felt oddly satisfying.

His father stood and walked around his desk, settling on the sofa. "No, that isn't what this is about."

"Then, what is it?" Aden went to the bar and poured himself a drink.

"Have you told Ellie what we're doing?"

"No," he replied as he held up the glass in silent question. His father shook his head, declining the offer.

"Why not?"

"I don't want to worry her."

"She's stronger than you give her credit for. She's your wife, Aden."

Aden moved to the nearby chair and sat down.

"She's not my wife, not technically, regardless of what Sophie says. But she is in every way that matters and will be once this is over."

"Have you asked her?"

"Why do I need to ask her?"

"Because women like to be asked."

Taking a sip of his drink, Aden shrugged. "We've talked about it. We both know it's a given. Why can't we just get married?"

Aurick sighed. "I'm going to let you navigate that minefield yourself. But take my advice. Ask her. You asked Aly."

"Ellie's made it clear she's put Aly in the past, and she needs to be left there."

"All the more reason to propose to Ellie. And tell her what we're doing. Don't piss her off now. She's the last wife you're going to have, and eternity is a long time to sleep on the sofa."

"Don't be so melodramatic."

But Aden knew Aurick was right. At least about telling Ellie of their plans. But every time he meant to mention it, she distracted him with sex.

And he knew his priorities.

Sex with Ellie first. Always.

"So, what's up?"

"When do you think the armies will be ready?"

"In a perfect world, three months. Two if I push the generals hard. I thought we were planning for the summer games. Everyone will be in the capital. Limited terrain. Limited casualties."

"That is the plan, but upon further reflection, giving Matthais the advantage of his home turf may not be the right choice."

"Why not?"

"He'll have access to all his weapons. If he responds the way I suspect, he could wipe out entire regions with the push of a button."

Aden put his empty glass down, leaned back, and crossed his legs. "Weapons with the power to wipe out entire regions no longer exist."

"That's not entirely true."

"Come again?"

"All nuclear and chemical weapons were destroyed after the Great Vampire Wars. That was an absolute agreement among all the Gerents and Matthais. After surviving what we did, we couldn't take a chance of them being used in a future conflict. Many of them were detonated or buried on the sea floor when the comet hit and the plates shifted. But the rest were disarmed and neutralized. Most of them, anyway."

"What do you mean most? Does Matthais have any?"

"Yes. Nuclear, not chemical. At least as far as I know."

Seething, Aden stood up. "And you're just fucking telling me this now? How many does he have?"

"Five as far as I know, but there's no guarantee he hasn't manufactured more. I wouldn't put it past him."

Aden's mind raced as he paced the room. "Where are they located?"

"Terra dell'Ombra Eterna."

"All of them?"

"The last I heard, yes."

"Why did the Gerents let him keep a stash like that?"

"They didn't. But no one could stop him. As the Chancellor, he made the decision. He said he wanted to have a few just in case, and he'd make them available to any region that needed them."

Aden stopped pacing and spun around to face Aurick. "Do you think he's placed any of them in Erebu or Sevir Seb-Ir?"

"I don't know, but I wouldn't be surprised if he did."

"Fuck, Aurick! Now I need to rethink this. We have to lure him somewhere else. Although he could launch them from anywhere. But if he's not anticipating being overthrown, why would he have anyone standing by to press the button?"

"There's something else you need to know."

"Now you're just pissing me off. You know I hate it when you fucking throw shit at me like this."

"I know. That's why I'm telling you this now. So you take it into consideration when revising the plan."

Aden shoved his hands roughly through his hair. "What?"

"We also have four nuclear weapons."

That was the last thing Aden expected Aurick to say. Mr. Peaceful harboring weapons of mass destruction? Though he knew his father hadn't always been the peaceable man he was now, this knowledge was still surprising.

"Here in Réimse Shíochánta?"

"Yes. One here in the capital, one on the east coast, one on the west coast, and one on Oileán Cladaigh Sophie."

"That's also the east coast."

"Yes, but it's your mother's favorite place in the world, so it has its own protection."

Sighing, Aden rubbed the back of his neck. "Does anyone else know about these?"

"No."

"None of the other Gerents?"

"No."

"Matthais?"

"No one. Well, your mother, obviously. And now you."

Aden eyed Goujian hanging on the wall behind his father's desk. The over-three-thousand-year-old sword, named after one of the last kings of the Yue, had been a gift from Katsumi for Aurick's thirteen-hundred-fifty-first birthday.

"We have to get him out of power, Aurick. We can't wait any longer. We need to do this now."

"If the armies aren't ready, we can't rush in half-cocked, Aden. We have to exercise caution and patience. Otherwise, the consequences will be disastrous."

"Patience has never been one of my virtues."

"Do you have any at all?" Aurick smirked at Aden's failure to rise to the bait. "Either way, Aden, I think maybe you should make a trip to the capital. Stop in and see Andrei. See if you can get any info out of him."

"After what happened in Capamar, I might lose my shit if I see him again."

"Politics, Aden. It's all about keeping your head."

"I'm not a politician, Aurick. I'm a military leader. I'm all about action."

"But if anything ever happens to me, you'll have to be."

Aden frowned. "Don't say shit like that."

"It's true. This region is yours if I die. You inherit it."

"Matthais doesn't get to choose a new Gerent if one dies?"

"No. That was also the agreement when the war ended. Our regions are ours to pass on to whoever we want, but they must swear loyalty to the VWC."

"Vampire World Council. What a fucking joke." Aden scoffed, leaning against Aurick's desk.

Roderick appeared in a hologram in front of Aden. "Oh, good, you're both there."

"What's wrong?" Aden asked as he leaned forward.

"I just got word from the team we have stationed on the northern border. A group of rogues came over the ice and slipped in just east of Tullastone."

Fuck! Could he never get a fucking break?

"How many?" he asked.

"Uncertain at this point, but at least one hundred. We're wheels up in twenty to go assist. Do you want to meet us there?"

Annoyed, Aden pushed away from Aurick's desk. "Fuck, no, I don't. But I will. Get there and get me a report of a head count and get those villages evacuated. Move them south to Wickhan."

"My team is limited in size up there at the moment. We only had scouts on patrol, but I'm bringing a large enough contingent with me so half can evacuate while the others take down the rogues."

"Leave a couple alive so I can interrogate them when I get there. I want confirmation this is Yuri again."

"Could it be anyone else coming from that direction?" Roderick asked.

"No," Aden replied. "But I still want verbal confirmation. And we may keep these ones alive to present to Yuri when I tear his fucking head off."

"Will do. See you there."

Roderick swiped the hologram closed.

"One more fucking thing we don't need."

Aurick stood from the sofa and headed to his desk. "I'll alert the others of this latest development."

"I need to see Ellie before I leave."

"You need to tell her, Aden."

"I need to figure out what the fuck is going on at the northern border and then come up with a new plan because you neglected to mention Matthais' nuclear weapons. That's what I need to do. This fucking changes everything, Aurick."

"Are you finished venting?" Aurick asked, his irritation at Aden's reprimand apparent.

"For now."

"I have to talk to your mother. She's leaving tomorrow for the beach house. She's taking Mila with her. I should send more guards with her just to be safe."

"Why don't you tell her not to go?"

Aurick laughed. "You try telling your mother not to do something. Better yet, tell Ellie. See how well that works out for you. You still have a lot to learn about women, son. Keep me posted."

Aden grunted and left Aurick's office.

Ellie

"**M**y God, are you trying to kill me?" Ellie gasped through a breathy laugh, letting her arms fall above her head, too weak to move otherwise.

"Never," he murmured against her neck. Other than a small nick at her nipple, he refrained from biting her. She turned her face and pressed a kiss to the side of his head.

"You didn't bite me."

He lifted his head and looked down at her.

"Yes, I did."

"That wasn't a bite. That was a tease." She reached up to brush her fingers over his lips. "You don't have to be afraid to drink from me. It doesn't matter that Hannah said we have to refrain. We just have to be a little more careful."

He took her index finger into his mouth and closed his front teeth around it, biting gently to make his point. She looked up at him with a smile.

"We can't let the compulsion rule us. I don't need your blood, Ellie. Yes, I fucking want it, but I don't need it to enjoy fucking you. We fucked for months before I bit you."

"I know. I don't need it to enjoy making love with you, either, but I crave it as much as you do."

He made a face at her words, always making that face when she used the term, and she laughed softly at his reaction.

"Why do you make that face when I say making love?"

"Because it's girly."

"Well, I'm a girl."

"Yes, you are," he growled as he pumped his hips, still deep inside her, eliciting a gasp as the sensation zinged through her body. Her eyes fluttered closed as she bucked her hips in response.

He lowered his head and swirled his tongue over her nipple, soothing the tiny bite, which had already stopped bleeding.

"Thank you," Ellie said as she smiled, still not opening her eyes.

Aden pulled out of her. Their combined orgasms spilled from her, and she squirmed as he slid down the bed, settling on his stomach, and hiking her thighs over his shoulder.

She lifted her head and looked down at him. "What are you doing?"

"I can tell you're tender, so I'm going to use my venom to soothe you." He swiped his tongue over the length of her, and she moaned, her hips jerking.

"No, Aden." She reached down and grabbed his hair, pulling his head away. "I need a break. I'm only human."

He scowled but lifted his head away from her. "Did I hurt you?" He asked, always aware that it was a possibility, and she smiled at his concern.

"No. I just need time to recover. We've been pretty insatiable the last couple of days."

He rested his chin on her pelvic bone and looked at her. She cupped his cheek. "I'm okay, really."

He looked unsure.

"Come here," she urged.

He climbed back over her, lowering himself on top of her, kissing her as she wrapped her arms around him. The head of his cock pressed against her.

"Oh, no you don't. Keep that thing away from me," she said as she wiggled, laughing.

"I'll be gentle, I promise," he murmured against her lips, hiking her thigh up beside his hip.

"Don't you dare try to push into me. I know what you're up to."

"Was that too much?" He frowned and lifted his head to look down at her.

"No. It's just that my human body can only take so much. It needs a break sometimes."

He rolled off her, pulling her into his arms. She lifted her thigh over his this time, pressing closer.

"Aden," she said softly as she smiled.

"Yes, mo ghrá?" He asked, his eyes closed now.

"I want you to turn me into a half-breed."

Aden's eyes snapped open, meeting hers. "You wanna say that again?"

"I want you to turn me into a half-breed." At the panicked look in his eyes, she chuckled. "Not tonight, but I've made my decision. I want to be a half-breed when it's safe for you to change me."

"What made you decide this all of a sudden?"

Pushing onto her elbow, she trailed her fingers across his abdomen. "It isn't all of a sudden. I've been thinking about it. And we both know it's inevitable if you want me with you forever."

"You know I want you forever."

"Well, what's the problem, then?"

"There isn't a problem, but it seems a bit suspect."

"Suspect?"

Aden's fingers traced down her back and over the curve of her ass. "Yes, right after I fuck you until your brain is practically rattling, you tell me you want to be a half-breed. Are those two things related?"

She caught her lip between her teeth, and he gently pulled it out.

"Ellie?"

"What?" Pushing herself up, she sat cross-legged beside him, her hand resting on his stomach. "It would make things easier, wouldn't it? You wouldn't have to worry so much about hurting me by mistake. And my half-breed physiology would allow my blood to replenish more quickly, so anemia wouldn't be an issue."

"How do you know that?"

"I've been reading about half-breed physiology. Hannah gave me a book."

"Of course, she fucking did. I swear that woman just tries to piss me the fuck off."

"Why would my reading about half-breeds upset you?"

"It doesn't." He sat up, a look of frustration on his face. "You wanting to become one so you can keep up with me sexually does. You fucking promised me you'd tell me if it was too much."

"I do. I say stop when I need you to. And you always do." She cupped his cheek. "Hey, what is this really about?"

He shook his head. "Nothing. If that's what you want, I'll do it, but you have plenty of time. You're still young."

"Our age difference kind of makes you a pervert," she teased. "And even though I want to become a half-breed sooner, I want to wait to drink your blood until I'm at least twenty-six."

"Why?"

"Because you stopped aging when you turned twenty-five, and I want to be the elder in this relationship."

He snorted out a laugh. "You'll never be the elder, sweetheart. No matter how you try to manipulate that math, it'll never happen."

"Biologically, you're twenty-five. If I'm twenty-six, then I'm biologically older than you. Trust me, I'm super-intelligent. I know these things."

"I knew Sophie telling you that was going to come back and bite me in the ass someday."

"But you can't argue with me."

"Yes, I can," he said as he grabbed her around the waist, pushing her onto her back, his eyes going dark, a low growl rumbling in his chest.

He rolled on top of her, and she arched her back, spreading her thighs to let him settle in.

"You're a fucking little tease."

"Why is that?" she asked, her voice a breathy moan.

"Because you forbid me access to this glorious body and then spread your thighs so eagerly for me."

Ellie wrapped her arms around him as he rocked against her.

"How much time do we have?" She asked as her eyes fluttered. "How long until Kane comes looking for you?"

He looked over at the clock and scowled. "Too fucking soon."

"Do you have time to make me come all over you again?"

"I always have time for that," he growled against her throat. "But I thought you said no more."

"That one swipe of your tongue helped. Just go easy on me."

Aden pressed a kiss on the scar on her neck, and she shivered.

"Yes, goddess, but no biting at all." He lowered his mouth to her breast and kissed the puncture scars just above her right nipple.

Ellie inhaled a shaky breath, threading her fingers through his hair.

"No blood," he murmured against her skin, but she trembled when she felt him slide his hand between their bodies, brushing his fingers over the scar on her thigh, above where her femoral artery lay.

She pulled his face up, pulling his lips to hers.

"Just a little," she breathed as he pushed into her slowly, gently, groaning her name into her mouth.

Ellie walked out of the bathroom just as Aden exited the closet, fully dressed. They managed to get in a quick shared shower, but only after Kane pounded on the door.

Aden told him to fuck off, but she dragged him out of bed and into the shower, telling him they needed to be responsible.

"How long do you think you'll be gone?" She asked, pulling her sweater over her head.

"I don't know. Roderick went ahead with a contingent and will get the situation under control." Aden pulled on his boots and laced them up. "I just go in after and torture answers out of the rogues once his team subdues them."

Ellie wrinkled her nose, remaining silent about his comment. She sat on the sofa and tucked her feet beneath her. Vlad, who had wandered in while they were in the shower, jumped up into her lap.

"Why are so many rogues showing up everywhere now?"

"Ellie, I don't have time to get into this with you tonight. I'll tell you when I get back."

"You always say that. What aren't you telling me, Aden? I know you're keeping things from me. And I try not to pry because your work is really none of my business, but something serious is going on. I can see it with all the Gerents and other generals coming and going. What are you not telling me?"

"Ellie, it's nothing."

"Aden, you promised to be honest with me."

"You don't have to keep reminding me. I know what I promised," he snarled as he pushed to his feet.

"Then why don't you just tell me?"

"Because you don't need to worry about it."

"Well, when you say that, it makes me think I do need to worry."

"Ellie, I don't have time for this."

He walked into the closet and came out with his coat. She crossed her arms over her chest, fed up with his evasiveness.

"Fine. But when you get back, we're talking about it. And we're also going to talk about my tracking chip. I want it removed."

"Are you out of your fucking mind?"

"No. I'm tired of being tracked. And I want to be able to initiate a hologram."

"You know what? I don't need this from you tonight. Your tracking chip stays in, and that's final."

Ellie set Vlad aside and stood, approaching him. "Why?"

"Because it is!" His voice grew louder with every word. "There are things happening that make it too fucking dangerous for me not to be able to find you instantly."

"I wouldn't know that, though, would I?" She yelled back. "Because you don't tell me anything."

She'd never yelled at him before, but she'd reached her breaking point. He seemed as surprised as she was by her outburst.

"Why do you always have to push and push, Ellie?" He asked with a heavy sigh.

"I don't," she said, more calmly but still upset. "I just let it go because I know you're preoccupied with something important. Well, I'm done letting it go."

"For fuck's sake, Ellie. Fine, you want to initiate holograms; I'll tell Sophie to activate them. But your tracking chip fucking stays in."

"Why? Why do I need to be tracked? I always have someone with me. If it's not you, it's Drake or Keeley and Hannah. Do you have any idea how invasive it is to be tracked? I can't even use the bathroom in private."

He pinched the bridge of his nose.

"We're supposed to be equals in this relationship."

"You're a human, Ellie. You're not my equal!" His roar made her flinch as if he'd struck her.

The words were barely out of his mouth when he moved forward.

"Ellie, I didn't mean—"

Tears welled in her eyes as she stumbled backward, hand outstretched.

"Don't!" Her voice, sharp and strong, cut through the air. "Don't you dare touch me right now."

"Mo ghrá."

"No. You have no right to call me that. You know, Aden, I forgive you a lot of things. Because I know you've lived centuries being a jackass with no one to call you on it. Your parents and Keeley and everyone else around you enable your bad behavior. Allowing you to speak and act any way you please because you were wounded and broken from killing me."

Aden flinched at her words. She knew they were harsh, especially since she told him she forgave him for it. She did. Her forgiveness came almost instantly after the initial shock of her memories subsided.

But like he said, she was human, goddamn it. And like she once told him, lashing out at the people we love is a very human trait. He didn't own the patent on lashing out when hurt and angry.

"It doesn't give you the right to hurt me."

"Ellie, I'm sor—"

"No. Saying you're sorry won't fix this. I know I'm not your physical equal, and I never will be until—or, more importantly, if—I become a vampire, but I thought…" A shaky sigh escaped her lips, her lower lip quivering as tears threatened to spill, despite her attempts to blink them back. "I believed you considered us equal in every other way."

"I do. Please don't cry. And don't fucking back away from me."

"I told you not to touch me right now." She swiped at the tears that slipped free. "I love you, Aden. But I can't do this anymore."

She tried to push past him, but he grabbed her arm.

"Don't you fucking walk away from me." His command sounded more like a desperate, panicked plea, and she wanted nothing more than to go back to before she asked him what was going on. But this blow-up was a long time coming.

"Ellie, you don't get to walk away from me right now. I've let you run before, but not this time." Aden's voice grew dark, hinting at a threat. "I'll never let you walk away from me."

She yanked her arm out of his grasp, her eyes flashing angrily as she blinked away more tears.

"Don't you think I know that? Don't you think I know I'll never be truly free? Vampires call us thralls because it sounds less sinister, less demeaning, but the fact is, I'm a slave, Aden. And I always will be."

She rushed by him, choking on the last words. His stunned silence and the shock in his eyes bought her the few crucial seconds she needed to slip past him.

The door slid open, revealing Kane and Drake standing in the hallway. Anger sparked in Drake's eyes. A blend of anger and sympathy shone in Kane's. Of course, they heard everything.

Stupid goddamned half-breed hearing.

"Are you going to stop me from leaving?" She asked, her wet eyes flashing with defiance.

Without a word, they both moved aside to let her pass.

Aden's fingers, surprisingly gentle, closed around her arm. "Ellie." Unspoken but very real pain roughened his voice.

"Let me go, Aden," she said, and his grip tightened. While firmer, it didn't hurt.

"No," he growled, the sound low and rumbling in his chest.

"Stop!"

Their agreed-upon safe word, meant to be used only during sex, was her only hope of stopping him. His sharp intake of breath, a gasp through gritted teeth, showed he understood.

He let go of her, and she broke into a run, her feet pounding on the tile, echoing in the hallway.

"Ellie!" Aden shouted after her. The sheer pain in his voice made her falter, but she couldn't bring herself to halt.

"Let her go, Aden." There was a warning in Kane's dark voice. "You've done enough. And we have to leave."

"We'll leave when I fucking say we'll leave," he roared, his voice booming down the hall.

She heard sounds of a struggle, and the walls shook behind her. So she ran faster, through the courtyard and into the greenhouse, where she turned on the daylight bulbs.

The absence of his familiar footsteps confirmed he hadn't followed. Her vision blurred with more tears, and her head fell forward as the weight of her grief bore down on her, her heart shattering like fragile glass.

A minute later, the greenhouse door behind her slid open, and footsteps approached, heavy and measured. They were Drake's. To her relief, he was quiet, simply moving closer, his presence offering the comfort she needed at that moment.

"Ellie, he's an asshole, but he didn't mean what he said."

She swiped at her tears again. "Yes, he did. Aden always means what he says, especially when he's angry. It's when he lets his inside voice out."

"I wasn't alive when he killed his wife... you. I was born only two hundred years ago. But he never seemed capable of feeling anything more than cold, hard rage and indifference. It was like his heart was encased in ice, incapable of love or empathy. But then you showed up. And he's different. Yeah, he's still a dick most of the time, but there's a hidden sense of humanity within him that you set free. And I may want to tear his throat out right now, but I have no doubt, for one second, he respects you more than anyone. You're the love of his life."

So many people said that to her—that she was the love of Aden's life. And deep down, no matter how hurt and angry she was with him, she knew it was true. But his words, like daggers to her heart, still sliced her open.

Another sob hit Ellie, a deep shudder that made her shoulders tremble, her breath catching in her throat. The gentle pressure of Drake's hand on her shoulder was an unexpected comfort, and she leaned into it.

She turned toward him, collapsing into his strong embrace, her body shaking with more silent tears.

Aden

"Yuri is sending the rogues to test our defenses. It took a bit of persuasion, but several of them gave him up."

Aurick stared at him through the hologram, his expression betraying no surprise at Aden's words.

"I expected this. How many villagers did we lose this time?"

Swirling snow surrounded Aden as he strode toward the plane, the bobbing hologram at his side.

"A few hundred. Having the team on watch to warn us of activity helped reduce the numbers."

"This means Matthais knows something's coming."

Aden walked past Kane, who surveyed the pyre where the last of the rogues were burning, the heat intense and the air thick with smoke. He'd barely spoken to Aden since they left, other than to hand him his ass after they got on the plane. Not that Aden blamed him. He'd broken Kane's arm in their struggle after Ellie ran from him.

And Kane was right. He was a complete asshole.

What he said to Ellie was unintentional. He yelled it in a fit of rage, but he didn't mean it. Not in the way it sounded. While factually correct, it came out wrong.

Physicality aside, Ellie wasn't his equal. She was his superior in every way that mattered. She was smarter, kinder, and more considerate than he was, and she possessed a more loving heart. She gave her love and her forgiveness freely, and there was no equal to her in Aden's mind.

But as usual, his fucking mouth worked faster than his fucking brain. And he'd hurt her, wounded her more deeply than he ever had in the past. And he wouldn't blame her if she never forgave him.

It would fucking kill him if she didn't, and he could only hope her gentle, forgiving heart would give him another chance after everything was over.

"So, we move up the timeline," Aden said. "Fuck training. We'll make it work."

"I still haven't approached Cecilia. It can't wait any longer. Can you be ready within the month?"

"I'm ready now, if I have to be."

"Aden, don't get cocky. We only have one shot at taking Matthais out. If we miss, it will be an all-out war."

"When have you known me to miss?"

Aurick glanced sideways, a subtle twitch betraying his attention, just out of his direct line of sight. "Are you heading back now?"

"Yes, we'll be there in a few hours."

He climbed the stairs, brushing the clinging snow from his coat as he stepped into the warm cabin of the plane.

"Good. Let's meet in my office. I'll call Cecilia now and ask if we can see her tomorrow. Plan to fly to San Allena with me."

Fuck! That barely gave him enough time to find Ellie and apologize.

"Fine. I have to see Ellie for a few hours first. I really fucked up."

"Of course. Your mother left for the beach house a little while ago, and she left Carrie behind to help Keeley with Iain, so you might find Ellie with her."

Figures. Just what he needed—Ellie's friend whispering in her ear about how monstrous Aden was after their fight.

"I need to go, son. I'll see you when you get here." Aurick swiped the hologram closed.

That was unlike his father to be so rude.

Aden shrugged out of his coat and sat on the sofa as Kane entered the plane.

"We going to leave that pyre burning?" Aden asked.

"No," Kane said, his voice tight and clipped.

Great. The return trip would be as equally enjoyable as the ride out.

"Roderick is staying behind with a small team to wrap it up and make sure the remaining villagers get to safety."

"Fine," Aden said. "Let's get the fuck out of here."

Ellie

The warmth of the fire in the library did nothing to ease Ellie's troubled mind. She sat in her favorite chair, stroking Vlad as he kneaded her thigh.

She'd been trying to read for hours. But her thoughts kept circling back to her fight with Aden. It gnawed at her, a constant ache, leaving her restless and unable to concentrate. Nausea and anxiety kept her awake and unable to eat. Her insomnia, which had all but vanished, had returned, and she had no appetite at all.

When she returned to their suite, she found maintenance and housekeeping crews removing pieces of broken furniture. A new sofa and dining area table were clear evidence Aden threw a fit after she left.

This was the worst fight they'd ever had. She told him to leave her alone, but his lack of contact hurt more than she wanted to admit. She hated that she couldn't reach out to him via a hologram—just one more limitation of being human in a vampire's world. And another reason to become a half-breed. Half-breeds could at least initiate a hologram when they wanted to speak to someone.

Vlad wrapped his paws around her hand and bit her thumb, annoyed with the absence of genuine pets.

"Stop it, Vlady," she scolded but increased the pressure behind his ears as she watched the falling snow outside the window.

Drake burst through the door, and his sudden entrance made her jump.

"Ellie, come with me!"

He rushed over, his breath ragged, and yanked her out of the chair.

"Drake, what the hell?"

"We're being attacked. I have to get you out of here."

"What?"

She had to have misheard him, right?

He tugged her across the room, his grip tight on her arm. "We have to get to the emergency warp port that will take us to the escape tunnels."

Ellie pulled against his grasp. "Drake, stop! Wait a minute."

He stopped and gave her a sharp look, not releasing her.

"Ellie, this is serious. I have to get you out of here, or Aden will rip my spine out with his teeth."

Ellie blanched at the disturbing image, but she needed answers.

"Please tell me what's going on. What escape tunnels?"

With a deep sigh, Drake released her arm before he strode over and stuck his head out the door, looking down the hallway.

"The compound has escape tunnels in case of an attack. They run under the entire city, all the way to the eastern exit, where an underground hangar contains supplies, vehicles, and an airplane." The library door slid closed, and he locked it, then turned to her again. "I have to get you there and get us in the air before Matthais finds you."

"What?" Ellie's stomach plummeted with the icy grip of fear. "He's here?"

"Yes. He brought an army of vampires, and they're looking for you."

"Why me?"

The look Drake gave her made her feel foolish for asking.

"I thought all armies were half-breeds."

"They are. But it seems Matthais amassed a vampire one, and it's here."

"Where are all the Westcott's guards?"

"Ellie, I don't know." He shoved his fingers through his short hair. "Aurick called me and told me to get you out, so I'm getting you out."

"We have to call Aden."

"I tried on my way here, but it won't go through. The holograms inside the compound are working, but Matthais somehow blocked the satellites that allow them to connect to the outside."

"Where is Aurick?"

He grasped her arm again. "I don't know. He was exiting his office when he called me."

"Wait, wait, wait," she said as she pulled her arm away. "Can you pull Aurick up on a hologram so we can see what's happening? Maybe Matthais isn't even here for me."

"Aurick said he is. That's good enough for me."

"But what if he isn't? Maybe it's a mistake."

Drake exhaled a long breath, clearly frustrated with her, but he should know her well enough by now that her innate curiosity always won out.

"You have no sense of self-preservation. How the hell does Aden put up with it?"

Ellie didn't take offense at what he said. He didn't mean it the way it sounded. The nearly yearlong growth of their friendship allowed her to see past his stress-induced words.

She gave him a wry smile. "I ask myself that all the time."

"Find Aurick," he said through gritted teeth, and a hologram of the courtyard appeared at eye level.

And Ellie's world tilted off its axis.

At least a dozen vampires surrounded Aurick, systematically attacking him from all sides. They were a blur of motion, her eyes unable to keep up with their movements as he fought them off, one after the other.

"Fuck!"

Ellie was too horrified by the scene unfolding in the hologram to register Drake's response.

Matthais stood off to the right with Andrei, his face a mask of contempt. They looked on, indifferent, while another group of vampires swarmed Aurick, three of them seizing his arms and neck from behind. As he fought back, two others jammed small spike-like objects into either side of his neck. Although the hologram was silent, Aurick's roar was obvious as he flung them all away, their bodies flying like rag dolls through the air.

Three different vampires attacked him from behind, taking him by surprise and knocking him to the floor.

"How are they doing this?" Ellie asked, her heart hammering in her chest. "Isn't he stronger than them?"

Drake looked as baffled as she felt. "He should be. He's at least a thousand years older than them."

"Turn on the sound," she said, and as he increased the volume, Matthais' silky voice came through, sending shivers of revulsion down Ellie's spine.

"Aurick, stop fighting. It's over." Aurick surged to his feet before stumbling and shaking his head, as if trying to clear it.

"What's wrong with him?" Ellie asked, and Drake shook his head with a frown.

"You'll never get away with this, Matthais," Aurick said, his voice strained.

"I already have." Matthais motioned to the vampires standing behind him.

They ambushed Aurick again. As he went down, five others closed in around him, forming a tight circle that blocked Ellie's view. Sudden, violent movement within the group ended with a sight that would haunt her forever—two of the vampires emerging with Aurick's arm and leg, tossing them aside like discarded trash.

"Oh my God!" She cried, the sound raw and wounded, her hand flying to her mouth as her knees buckled. Her heart ached, and tears blurred her vision, knowing Aurick's survival was impossible.

A searing image of Sophie, devastated and broken, flashed through Ellie's mind as she started to hyperventilate.

Drake crouched beside her, his voice strained but controlled. "Ellie, we have to go."

She brushed away the tears on her cheeks, focusing on her breathing. "Where's Horatio? Why wasn't he there to help Aurick?"

Drake helped her to her feet. "I don't know. I don't know anything, Ellie. But he wouldn't have been able to fight them off, anyway. There's something not natural about their strength."

He reached up to swipe the hologram closed, but she stopped him.

"Don't. We should keep it open so we know what's happening."

He nodded but turned the volume down again. With a gentler touch than before, he grasped her elbow and led her toward the back corner of the library opposite the fireplace. The hologram followed, but Ellie couldn't bear to look at it, dreading what she might see.

Drake's gaze swept across the bookshelves, selecting a large antique Bible.

"What are you—"

Ellie's question was cut off as the wall shifted, first forward and then to the right, revealing a dark hidden passageway behind it. "What the hell is that?"

"This corridor circles around the entire perimeter of the compound with exits in each of the Westcott's private wings. We can get to the hallway outside Aurick and Sophie's suite. The warp port in their living room has access to the basement, which has access to the escape tunnels. Come on, we're wasting time."

"Wait." Ellie rushed over to scoop Vlad up from the chair, hoisting him over her shoulder, before returning to stand next to Drake. He slid the Bible back in place and then guided her into the shadowy corridor, the entrance sliding shut behind them. Sconces on the rough stone walls activated as they moved forward, illuminating the narrow passage. Ellie clutched Vlad to her chest, his warmth a comfort as she followed Drake on shaky legs.

"If he's really here for me, why can't Matthais find me via hologram? He's inside the compound."

"Because he doesn't have access to your tracking chip."

"But I thought holograms could bring up anyone inside the compound. Isn't that how they work?"

"No. Only if auto-accept is activated. Or you're a thrall with a tracking chip that's registered on the Westcott's network. Otherwise, a hologram has to be answered manually."

"Isn't my tracking chip on the network?"

"Yes, but it's private. Only those with permission to access it can find you. There are only a few of us who have those permissions. So far, the privacy settings are holding, but there are dozens of vampires crawling all over this compound looking for you. I'm sure Matthais has someone trying to hack the system, so it's only a matter of time until they break through the firewall. We have to get to Sophie and Aurick's suite and the escape tunnels before that happens."

Drake led them through the twisting passageway, the hologram bobbing along with them.

"But how are we going to get in?" Ellie asked. "Their door isn't programmed to admit me."

"Yes, it is. When emergency protocols are activated, every door in this city will open for you. Aurick activated them while I was talking to him."

Movement in the hologram caught Ellie's eye, and her heart stopped at what she saw. Matthais stood in the center of the courtyard now, surrounded by dozens of vampires. A group of Aden's thralls were on their knees in front of him, including Iris, Finn, and Chelsea.

"Turn up the sound again," Ellie whispered as she halted. Drake turned to her, his brow furrowed. His questioning look vanished, and he increased the hologram's volume when he saw what was happening.

The soft sounds of sobbing filled the air.

"Now, which one of you is going to tell me where to find Elliana?" He gestured to his right. "Or do you want to end up like your friends?"

Ellie's breath hitched as she looked where he pointed. A sob crawled up her throat at the sight of Mandi and Lily's bodies lying in pools of blood. Before she could process the horror, Chelsea's voice cut through the hologram.

"If I may, Master Matthais..."

"Shut up, Chelsea," Finn snarled, his tone sharp and out of character for him, but understandable.

Matthais backhanded Finn, sending him sprawling across the courtyard. Chelsea continued as if he hadn't even spoken.

"If she isn't in her and Master Aden's suite, she'll be in the library."

The betrayal left Ellie reeling.

"That fucking bitch!"

Ellie barely noticed Drake snarling as he swiped the hologram away, trying to understand why Chelsea would turn on her so easily.

"Why would she do that? I've never been anything but nice to her. Why does she hate me so much?"

"Because Aden loves you," Drake said as he gripped her elbow again, dragging her forward. "Matthais' vampires will reach the library any minute. They'll follow your scent and find the hidden passage. We have to get to those tunnels now, Ellie."

"What about everyone else? Keeley and Ryan? Iain?"

Carrie didn't go with Sophie to the beach house yesterday, but Mila did. Thankfully, the two of them were away. But that meant Carrie was somewhere in the compound. Was she in the courtyard? Could she already be dead, like Mandi and Lily?

"Drake," Ellie said as she pulled against his grasp, to no avail. "We have to check on them."

Vlad squirmed in her arms, hissing at how tight she was holding him. She loosened her grip, kissing the top of his head. "I'm sorry, Vlady."

The cat calmed down but dug his claws into her arm.

Drake stopped at a door built into the wall. After a biometric scan, the door opened, revealing the artwork in Sophie and Aurick's hallway.

He took a moment to ensure the hall was empty and then pulled her out of the passage. She gasped as her eyes fell on Horatio's decapitated body. She nearly dropped Vlad as Drake hoisted her over the corpse, her stomach churning at the sight of the guard's head several feet away from his body.

Drake guided her towards Aurick and Sophie's door, and they slipped inside.

Turning the corner into the living room felt like moving through a nightmare. Ellie's legs gave out, and she set Vlad down before dry heaving, her body rejecting the horror she'd just seen. Her eyes prickled with tears as she mourned for the guard who had always been kind to her.

"Ellie, that was an awful sight, but we have to move." Drake's voice was both sympathetic and insistent.

She pushed to her feet. "I want to see the courtyard again. We need to find the others."

"Ellie, there's nothing you can do for them. Nothing either of us can do. But I can get you out of here safely, which is my job. It's what Aurick told me to do and what Aden would want."

"Not at the expense of the rest of his family."

"Yes, he would," Drake snapped, his frustration bubbling over. "Your safety is more important to him than anyone's."

Ellie stood her ground, her arms crossed defiantly over her chest, a stubborn set to her jaw. "I'm not going anywhere until we check on them. Call up Keeley."

"I can force you, Ellie," he sighed, rubbing the back of his neck.

"Please, Drake."

"Find Keeley," he said, and a hologram of the courtyard appeared.

Matthais stood off to one side again, still surrounded by at least a dozen vampires in a half circle. Chelsea's body lay on the ground to his right, lifeless. And Aurick lay sprawled in front of him, his body mangled and contorted at an odd angle, his left arm and right leg lying several feet away.

"How did they do that to him?" Ellie asked, her voice choking with emotion. "He should have been able to fight them off."

If Aden could defeat a dozen vampires, then Aurick, who was fifteen hundred years older and stronger than his son, should have had no trouble fighting off Matthais' vampires.

"Those aren't just normal vampires, Ellie. They're highly trained assassins with incredible strength. I've never seen anything like it. It's almost like they're enhanced. Aurick is one of the strongest vampires in the world, but even he didn't stand a chance against them."

Ellie bit her lip to keep from sobbing out loud, tasting the blood as her teeth broke the skin.

"Why is his skin turning gray?"

"Those spikes they jabbed into his neck earlier must've had UV particles in them. They're burning him from the inside out."

"No!" Her legs gave out again, and she fell to her knees in despair. "Please turn it up, Drake."

He raised the volume, and her eyes searched the courtyard through the hologram, looking for Keeley. Ellie found her and Ryan off to the right, both restrained by two vampires. Keeley struggled against her captors, her desperate screams mixing with Ryan's violent attempts to break free.

"Iain!"

Ryan escaped the vampires' grasp and charged, but they quickly overpowered him, pinning him down as he bucked and writhed.

The nightmare unfolding in front of Ellie's eyes worsened when Carrie appeared, dragged before Matthais by a vampire. She was holding Iain, grasping him to her chest, his face scrunched up and red from crying. Pushed to the ground at his feet, Carrie barely managed to keep her grip on the baby boy.

Ellie felt something inside her break, a shattering, piercing sensation, like glass splintering into a thousand tiny pieces. She rocked on her knees as the room spun around her.

"We have to help them, Drake," she said as she surged to her feet.

"I wish we could, Ellie, but we can't. We don't stand a chance against those vampires. And as much as I'd like to, my job is to protect you. Only you."

"But he'll kill them all," she said, her voice shrill and panicked, again thankful that Sophie and Mila were gone.

They, Aden, and Kane would be the only ones to survive.

She choked back a louder sob as guilt consumed her because she was grateful that Aden would live. He would, however, declare war on Matthais for this.

Standing there, watching her loved ones at Matthais' mercy, Ellie made her choice. She couldn't let Drake save her while everyone else died.

With a quick step, she entered the warp port, locking him out.

"Ellie, what the fuck are you doing?"

"I'm sorry, Drake," she whispered, knowing she was betraying his trust but unable to abandon the others to their deaths.

His horror-stricken face was the last thing she saw as she typed in the coordinates.

In an instant, Drake vanished, and Ellie stood in the back of the greenhouse beside the koi pond.

Ellie

E llie dashed to the front of the greenhouse. She had no plan of what to do, but she had to try something.

Drake was going to kill her for this. No. Aden was going to kill her for this. Unless, of course, Matthais murdered her first.

Iain's piercing cries cut through the silence of the greenhouse. Ellie's heart hammered against her ribs as she reached the doors, skidding to a stop. She crouched behind the cherry blossom tree before anyone caught sight of her, just as Drake rushed out of the warp port in the courtyard.

Everything happened in slow motion as he looked around, looking for her, his face panicked, a mask of confusion when he didn't see her.

Through the glass doors, Ellie watched her protector—her friend—forced to his knees by Matthais' vampires.

Her fingers dug into the rough bark of the tree as guilt crashed over her in waves. This was her fault. All of it. Drake had only been doing his job, trying to keep her safe, and now he was going to die because of her. The thought churned her stomach, a cold knot of dread tightening with each passing second.

"Looking for something, half-breed?" Matthais' voice dripped with contempt.

Drake struggled in the vampires' hold, his half-breed strength impressive, but they were too strong for him. Ellie grew to appreciate and admire his unwavering dedication to protecting her. But now that loyalty would be his undoing.

"If you're here, frantic like that, then she must be nearby. Elliana, where are you?" Matthais inhaled a deep breath, his eyes flashing red. "I can smell you."

Memories of Matthais' past cruelties flooded her mind, making her tremble. She pressed herself harder against the tree, hating herself for putting Drake in jeopardy.

"Elliana, I'm losing my patience."

The silence that followed Matthais' threat was deafening, broken only by her own ragged breathing. Every instinct screamed at her to run, hide, save herself. But she couldn't move.

What had she been thinking, coming here? She couldn't save anyone. She wasn't strong enough. Or brave enough. All she'd done was make everything worse.

Matthais signaled to Andrei, who walked over and grabbed Drake's head, twisting it sharply. The sound of his neck breaking, a sharp crack that made Ellie choke, echoed through the courtyard, penetrating the greenhouse's glass doors. She shoved a fist into her mouth to stop herself from screaming.

Ellie's world seemed to halt, her vision tunneling as Andrei tore Drake's head from his shoulders with a sickening rip, a spray of blood spurting into the air. His head rolled across the floor, coming to a stop next to Keeley, who bowed her head in despair for a moment, then glared at Matthais with fiery eyes.

His gaze darted around the courtyard as if he expected Ellie to materialize now that he'd killed her guard. Rage contorted his features when she didn't appear.

"Elliana, if you don't come out here right now, there will be more deaths on your hands besides his."

Iain's cries grew more insistent as Carrie tried to shush him, her body curved over him. Keeley's sobs from the corner tore at Ellie's heart—a mother unable to protect her child.

"Shut that thing up," Matthais snarled as he stalked over, his large frame looming over them, making Carrie shrink further into herself and Iain cry harder.

"Leave him alone," Keeley screeched, her voice thick with motherly desperation and rage.

"I said shut that thing up!"

Time seemed to slow as Ellie watched him raise his hand. In that moment, all her fear, all her self-doubt, and all her paralysis vanished.

Her legs moved before her mind fully registered the decision. She burst through the greenhouse doors, sprinting across the courtyard. The distance seemed endless, each step taking an eternity as his hand began its descent toward Carrie and Iain.

"No!"

The cry tore from Ellie's throat as she slid to a stop and threw herself over them, bracing for the impact she knew would come.

The pain of Matthais' nails raking across her back was immediate, resonating deep in her body as they ripped through her shirt and the flesh of her back beneath. It felt like being torn apart from the inside, worse than any whipping she received from him in the past. The agony radiated through her, stealing her breath and making her vision blur.

She bit her tongue to keep from further scaring Iain, and the taste of blood filled her mouth. Carrie's frightened eyes reflected a mixture of gratitude, sympathy, and horror. Her friend's silent plea not to sacrifice herself warred with the reality of their situation. The weight of the choice pressed down on Ellie as heavily as the pain in her back.

Time slowed again. Her heart pounding wildly, she processed her options. She really didn't have any. Holding Carrie's gaze, Ellie saw the subtle shake of her head. "Don't," her expression screamed, but the fear in her friend's face and the screams of the terrified baby pushed her to make the only decision she could.

With every movement sending fresh waves of agony through her torn flesh, Ellie urged Carrie to slide back before she pushed to her feet. She saw Drake's headless body from the corner of her eye, the pool of blood spreading slowly across the courtyard.

I'm so sorry, Drake.

Though her grief was crippling, the sight strengthened her resolve, and Ellie knew she'd made the only choice she could live with.

"Ellie," Keeley cried her name, and she looked up, her eyes meeting Aden's sister's frantic, desperate blue-green ones. "Thank you," she sobbed, her eyes reflecting both her gratitude and fear.

"You will face me, Elliana," Matthais commanded, and Ellie forced herself to turn toward him. Her back screamed in protest, warm blood flowing freely from the wounds. Every breath was a struggle against the pain. Swallowing back the blood pooling in her mouth, she kept her voice as steady as she could.

"Please don't hurt anyone else," she managed to gasp out, fixing her gaze on the ground in front of his feet. "It's me you want, Sir. Please, just don't hurt them."

"Ellie, don't do this," Keeley pleaded. "You don't know what he'll—"

"I know exactly what he'll do," Ellie cut her off, unable to look at Keeley again. "And I know what he'll do to you and everyone else here if I don't."

Her eyes caught movement nearby. Aurick's chest rose and fell in shallow, ragged breaths, the rhythm weak and uneven. Hope and despair warred in her heart at the sight.

He was still alive. But for how long?

Another sob wracked her body, the sound almost inhuman in its raw grief.

Matthais stepped closer to her, his nearness heavy and suffocating.

"I gave your father a choice once. He made the right one. I'm going to give you the same one now. You can come with me willingly or watch everyone you love die. Then I'll drain you and leave your ravaged body for Aden to find."

The choice was no choice at all, and they both knew it.

"Ellie, no!" Keeley screamed. "You can't do this."

Ellie lifted her eyes, looking into the steely gray ones of the most evil man she'd ever known. It was the first time she dared to meet his gaze. Ellie saw her future, what was left of it, written in his.

A powerful grip seized her arms from behind, immobilizing them, and fresh agony wracked her body. She didn't need to look to know it was Andrei.

"He's going to kill you," she said. Her voice, clear and sharp as glass, cut through the background noise, warning Matthais, Andrei, and every other vampire there.

"Remove her tracking chip," Matthais snarled. "If he wants to find her, he'll have to come begging me."

Ellie screamed, pain exploding as Andrei's nails dug into her neck, ripping the chip from under her skin.

The world began to fade to black, but not before Matthais' feral grin filled her vision as he leaned close.

Drifting into unconsciousness, she heard his final words whispered next to her ear.

"At last, Elliana. I knew you'd be glorious when the moment came for you to shine."

To be continued.....

Please Review

Reviews are like crack to indie authors.
WE LOVE THEM!

They help spread the word and get people excited about us and our books.
Also, books with more reviews are organically shown
to more potential readers in the Amazon algorithm.

So if you enjoyed ATONEMENT, please be so kind as to leave a review on
Amazon and Goodreads and any other platform you leave reviews.
Thank you so much!
Below are easy review links for you:
Amazon
Goodreads

Coming Soon- Redemption

ADEN AND ELLIE'S STORY CONCLUDES
IN THE DARKLY SENSUAL BOOK THREE OF
THE BLOODSTONE LEGACY SERIES
REDEMPTION
Coming January 20, 2026

Read a Preview Here: https://dl.bookfunnel.com/py9uwklj2l
Pre-Order Here: https://mybook.to/HXaLOyy

For more previews, deleted scenes and goodies, sign up for my newsletter:
Sign Up Here: https://vehuntley.com

Connect with Me:
https://www.facebook.com/v.e.huntley.author
https://www.instagram.com/vehuntley/
https://x.com/vehuntleywriter
https://www.tiktok.com/@vehuntley
https://bsky.app/profile/vehuntleyauthor.bsky.social

About the author

V.E. Huntley is a retired producer who has spent her life telling stories in one way or another. Just ask her cats. They had to endure a lifetime of her endlessly reciting entire dialogue scenes to them, even though all they desperately wanted to do was nap.

Her childhood fear of Dracula was so intense that she couldn't sleep without the lights on and her mother guarding her bedroom door. Over time, this fear evolved into a lifelong obsession with the dark and twisted world of vampires.

So, after more than two decades in the film and television industry, she ultimately chose to pursue her true passion—writing dark, steamy romance about foul-mouthed anti-heroes with anger management issues and the sweet and resilient, yet equally spirited heroines who know how to tame them.

Besides writing, her hobbies include watching movies, reading, traveling, and keeping her husband busy with an endless honey-do list. You can find out more about her on her website, www.vehuntley.com.

Made in the USA
Monee, IL
06 May 2025

16894687R00249